For Anna with love

FADE TO
GREY

Leabharlanna Poiblí Chathair Baile Átha Cliath
Dublin City Public Libraries

JOHN LINCOLN

NO EXIT PRESS

First published in 2019
by No Exit Press,
an imprint of Oldcastle Books Ltd,
Harpenden, UK
noexit.co.uk
@noexitpress

A CIP catalogue record for this book is available from the British Library.

ISBN
978-0-85730-289-2 (print)
978-0-85730-290-8 (epub)

Typeset in 11.5pt Sabon
by Avocet Typeset, Somerton, Somerset, TA11 6RT
Printed and bound by TJ International, Padstow, Cornwall

For more information about Crime Fiction go to crimetime.co.uk
@crimetimeuk

2015

One

THE SUBJECT LINE SIMPLY READ 'Ismail Mohammed'. That was enough. Gethin Grey picked up the email on his way into work and couldn't stop smiling as he parked the car and headed over the road to the Coal Exchange.

The Coal Exchange, in the heart of the old Cardiff docklands, was a grand but faded relic of the time when the city was the globe's busiest port. Apparently the first ever million-pound cheque had been written on its trading floor. For a while it had been used as a music venue – Gethin had seen both Van Morrison and Patti Smith play there – but now it was a decrepit health hazard waiting in vain for someone to come along and redevelop it. The only life in the building came from the smattering of small businesses which rented office space along its faded corridors.

Gethin's own small business was Last Resort Legals, an organisation that offered help not to mariners lost at sea but to those unhappy souls who believed they were the victims of a miscarriage of justice.

Normally, the approach to the office depressed the hell out of Gethin. The peeling paintwork, the pervasive smell of damp, the ancient lino beneath his feet, all made him feel like he was engaged in a doomed and hopeless enterprise. Today, though, he just saw the latent grandeur.

Indulging his good mood, he took a little detour, walking out into the middle of the old trading floor and looking round at the fine wood panelling that lined its walls. One

7

day all this would surely be renewed. And today Last Resort would begin their own small revival. Today their luck had changed. Not only were they being asked to take an interest in the long running saga of Ismail Mohammed's battle for justice, but the request came from none other than Amelia Laverne, the actress and celebrity activist.

Gethin felt possessed by the energy of the Victorian entrepreneurs who'd swarmed across this trading floor in its glory days. It was time to get serious. He was being offered a chance and this time he was determined to take it. A thought came to him out of left field. Perhaps he should start wearing a suit? Catriona would like that. She would say it was appropriate to his age – mid-forties. She'd say it was time he stopped dressing like a REM roadie, ditched his black jeans and plaid shirts, cut his shaggy hair short, and got with the programme. Maybe she was right. New era: new haircut. Cometh the hour, cometh the man in a suit. Maybe.

Surfing this unaccustomed wave of positivity he walked into the office. Bex, the office manager, was there already seated at her desk, having her customary Facebook session before she embraced the working day proper.

Lately, Gethin had been finding this sight irritating – Bex sitting there all complacent and happy, cooing over her friends' baby pictures or rolling her eyes at the latest miracle diet that offered to change her considerable size. Now he just thought how lucky he was to have her, this supremely unflustered young woman, without whose managerial skills Last Resort would have been out of business years ago.

'Hey,' he said, once she looked up from the screen. 'You want to guess who's just emailed us to get involved in their campaign?'

Bex shook her head. 'No idea. Just tell me, Geth.'

Before he could answer, the door opened again and in came Lee, Gethin's right-hand woman and lead investigator, carrying a tray of coffees from the Portuguese deli.

'Hey, Lee,' said Bex. 'Bossman says he's got us a new client.'

'Anyone we know?' Lee handed over the coffees.

'You could say that,' said Gethin. 'It's only Ismail Mohammed.'

'Yeah?' said Lee. 'The black Muslim guy? Sounds good.'

Gethin was expecting a bit more of a reaction.

'Not bad, eh?'

'Nah, it's sweet' said Lee. 'You know I actually read his book.'

'Really?'

'Well, most of it. Was good. Reality. And Monica liked it.' Monica was Lee's girlfriend, a dental hygienist. They were a funny looking pair – Monica all neat and blonde and Nordic-looking; Lee older than her, closer to Gethin's age, but still irredeemably boyish with her short dreadlocks and her gap-toothed grin.

'So, you know this could be a massive deal for us.'

Lee shrugged: 'Guess so.'

Gethin frowned at his workmates. 'Don't either of you read the papers? This is actually a really big deal.' Then he thought of something. 'All right, Bex, how about this then? You know who's going to be paying our wages? Amelia Laverne, that's who.'

Finally, he got the desired outburst of enthusiasm.

'Oh... My... God!' said Bex, her mouth cartoonishly wide open. 'You are not serious. I love Amelia. Absolutely fucking love her.'

Gethin and Lee both laughed at that. Bex was a laid-back, slow-moving woman who'd been a probation officer before joining Gethin's motley crew, and it took a lot to get a visible reaction out of her.

'Well, that's something. Okay, five minutes to sort ourselves out and then we can get cracking.'

Seated at his desk, sipping his coffee, Gethin allowed himself to wallow briefly in self-satisfaction. This was how far Last Resort Legals had come in the five years they'd been in operation. They'd had some real successes along the way: the Greenpeace Two was the case that had gained them the most attention, but there had been a good few others too. Of course, the last few months had been a bit quiet, but no matter. Now they were on the verge of getting involved with one of the highest profile miscarriage of justice cases for years, since all those Irish trials back in the day. Ismail Mohammed – Izma M to his fans – was the nearest thing Britain had yet produced to Malcolm X, a properly inspirational civil rights leader.

Anyone who followed politics knew his name and the basic outline of his life story, as set out in his bestselling book *Izma M – A Street Life*. He wasn't Muslim by birth, he was a black Briton called Tyrell Hanson. He had had a troubled childhood – brought up by his grandmother with stints in children's homes. He'd lived down to expectations and turned into a drug-dealing gangster type. While living in Bristol, he'd been convicted of a murder he didn't commit – or at least that's what he said. It was while he was in prison that he'd turned his life round, changed his name and embraced Islam. Not the radical anti-western Islam that most of the pissed-off youth went for, but spiritual, peaceful Sufi Islam like Malcolm X himself had come to believe in by the end of his life. Izma's politics were still pretty militant – anti-racism, anti-capitalism, all that – but his take on his new religion was all peace and love, not hate and war.

The book had caught on in a big way. Normally, when people started banging on about moderate Islam, it was just some old beardy bloke who was obviously being paid by the government to tell the kids to behave themselves, and no one paid attention. But with Izma M, because he'd actually lived the life, people were taking notice and, of course, all the left-wing media were wetting themselves in excitement. They were always asking him to write stuff in the papers. Especially after the 2011 riots. Since then he'd been popping up all over the media, even though he was still in prison.

Before long, his new supporters had started looking into his original conviction. He'd been accused of murdering a white girl back in Bristol. There wasn't much evidence against him – no murder weapon, no motive – but he had had sex with her not long beforehand, he didn't have much of an alibi, and he totally fitted the bill as far as the police were concerned.

Gethin hadn't looked into it in much detail, but the basic shape of the case sounded all too familiar. When people were killed in urban situations, and there wasn't an obvious murderer at hand, the police often just went for a local gangster who looked the part. Juries generally didn't pay too much attention to the details they just saw a guy who looked as if he might do something like that, and that was enough for them. And anyway, who was going to start campaigning for some street thug, just because the crime he'd been sent down for wasn't the one he'd actually committed?

Last Resort Legals and a few campaigning solicitors did what they could, but, for the most part, no one gave a damn. Not unless the guy wrote a bestselling book and was in the *Guardian* every other week. That's what it took for people to start paying attention, or at least start sharing the story on their timelines. And now Last Resort would be in the thick of it. Fighting for justice for Izma M. OMG, as his daughter Hattie would say.

'Right,' said Gethin, once Bex and Lee were seated at their desks, looking expectant. 'Before we get cracking with Izma, let's get this pile of crap out of the way.'

The 'pile of crap' was the stack of unsolicited letters. Every week they would receive a dozen or so letters from serving prisoners, all claiming to be victims of miscarriages of justice and all hoping that Last Resort would ride to their rescue. On top of the pile was a missive from a murderer called Warren Harker. Gethin passed copies round, then read it through himself. 'So, what do we think?'

Lee went first: 'Obviously guilty.'

'You think so?'

She rolled her eyes in a pantomime of cynicism.

'So... are you going to enlighten us as to why you're inclined to disbelieve this heartfelt cry for help?'

'Yeah,' said Lee, 'it's all typed in capitals. I hate that.'

'Ah,' said Gethin, 'I see. Just because this poor benighted individual currently serving a life sentence for murder in the inhuman brutal surroundings of...' he peered at the address, '... HMP Belmarsh... happened to have accidentally leaned on the Caps Lock key we should consign to the dustbin of history his despairing plea for justice?'

'That and the fact that it's just a whole heap of whiny bullshit.' Lee's phone beeped and she picked it up immediately, obviously considering the subject closed.

Gethin was buzzing. God it was good to have something serious on the go again. Now he could face all these tawdry begging letters with a smile on his face. 'You sure about that?'

Lee reluctantly looked up from her phone: 'Okay, for one thing he's not actually denying he did it.'

'No. He does indeed admit causing the death of...' Gethin looked down at the paper again, '... Ryan Hedges. He does, however, claim that...'

'It wasn't his fault.' Lee rolled her eyes again.

She picked up her copy of Warren Harker's letter from prison and started reading. 'I know it was wrong what I did to Ryan, but it was an honest mistake. I had been told by a trusted friend, open brackets Chloe close brackets, that Ryan had had relations with Tasha and that is why I went to see him and then he come at me with the knife which is what led to the tragic event for which I am very sorry but it's not my fault because it was a case of mistaken identity and it is Chloe what is responsible.'

Lee tossed the letter down: 'Dickhead.'

Gethin started to smile but then the sorry reality behind the letter struck him: the pointless loss of life and the stupidity of it all – the number of grown-up children running around this world with the tempers of babies and the weapons of adults.

He sighed and turned his chair round so he could see his office manager at her desk in the adjoining office. 'Bex,' he called out. 'Did you check him out? Warren Harker.'

'Absolute no-hoper,' said Bex without looking up. 'Family washed their hands of him and didn't have a pot to piss in anyway.'

'Cheers,' said Gethin. 'So, we agreed then? Category Five for Warren Harker?'

Lee nodded and made a thumbs down gesture. Gethin picked up the copies of Harker's letter from the table and deposited them in the Category Five holding pen, a large stainless steel bin on the floor.

'Right, let's see what our next lucky contestant has to offer.' Gethin reached for another photocopied letter and winced immediately. Another bloody rapist. Gethin hated the rape cases. Mostly because of the crime itself, of course, but also because they were timewasters. The evidence was almost always so nebulous, so based on one person's word against another, that proving a miscarriage of justice was enormously difficult and even if you did get a result – and Last Resort had on a couple of occasions – nobody thanked you.

Odd really, Gethin thought: you get some gangster acquitted of a murder charge and all the *Guardian* types are going on about what a fighter for liberty you are, but you get a rapist acquitted and everyone looks at you funny, like you're just a gang of misogynists who've found a loophole. They did their best to take each case on its merits, Gethin and his team at the Tuesday morning client trawl, but no one had much enthusiasm for the rape cases, just wanting to move them on to Category Five as fast as possible.

The incoming mail was divided into five categories: The no-hopers were Category Five. Category One were those rare birds, the convicted criminals who seemed to have both a good case to be made for their innocence and the resources available to pay Last Resort's fees. Category Two were the troubling cases where there seemed a fair chance that the correspondent was innocent but very little chance that he – or occasionally she – would be able to raise the money. Category Three were the even more troubling cases where the potential client looked guilty as sin but did appear to have the funds available. Category Four, finally, were the all too common ones where the initial letter was so confusing that making any judgment on likely innocence or guilt would have called for the services of a psychic. And hiring a psychic would have been a step too far even for an organisation as unorthodox as Last Resort Legals.

It didn't take long to dispatch the rapist to Category Five, nor the three more letters that came after that. Gethin sometimes wondered why they bothered, these obviously guilty men writing to Last Resort Legals in the hope that there might be some sort of loophole that could see their conviction overturned. Then again, there wasn't that much to do in prison.

There were plenty of weeks, like this one, when there was nothing at all of any merit in the Tuesday meeting. Lee had suggested a while ago that they should scrap it, stop taking submissions straight from prisoners and only take referrals from solicitors who genuinely thought their clients had had a bad deal. But Gethin was stubborn and the fact was that several of his best cases, the ones that had made Last Resort's name, had come from letters arriving out of the blue. And, at worst, there were usually a few laughs to be had, reading out these tissues of self-serving lies. Not this week, though. This week Last Resort Legals were stepping up a level.

Two

GETHIN WAS ON A HIGH all afternoon. When it came to their regular quitting time, six o'clock, he didn't want to leave, suggesting they all go over to the pub to discuss things some more and have a celebratory drink-up. Lee had to pick up Monica's kids from the after-school club, though, so it was just Gethin and Bex who headed over to Mischief's in the September sunshine.

Mischief's Café Bar was one of the few ungentrified hangouts left in Cardiff Bay. For donkey's years it had been called the Ship & Pilot. Shirley Bassey used to sing in the back room when she was fourteen. Gethin used to play pool in that same back room in his teens, mostly before going to the Casablanca Club around the corner for a night of reggae or punk as seen through a fog of herbal cigarettes. The Casablanca was a car park now, though, and the Ship & Pilot had been made over as Mischief's, essentially an eighties disco bar thirty years too late. But the beer was cold on a hot afternoon and you didn't need to queue and there was always a chance you might pick up some new business. There weren't many of Mischief's clientele who hadn't had dealings with the law at some point.

Bex was rummaging through her bag when Gethin brought the drinks outside – beer for him, glass of prosecco for her. After a bit she gave a small grunt of relief and produced a shoulder length blonde wig.

'Who are you being tonight then?' asked Gethin. Bex

supplemented her earnings from Last Resort by singing in a bewildering variety of tribute bands.

'Claire from Steps. Doing a big hen night in Newport.'

Bex stuck the wig on haphazardly over her own short bob – ever changing in hue but currently a sort of lilac – and mimed a quick formation dance move.

'Which one was she then?'

'The blonde one, der!' Bex poked her tongue out. Then she stuffed the wig back in her bag and they got down to talking about the case.

Bex was in a state of uncharacteristic excitement about it, mostly because it was Amelia Laverne who had initiated the contact. It turned out that Bex really did love Amelia. Her eighties debut, *Mary's Prayer*, was Bex's favourite film. Gethin let her chat on, while mentally running through all the stuff he'd read about Izma on the internet that afternoon, wondering what the best way into the case would be, where to find the loose thread that they could tug away at till the case against him disintegrated.

The drive home hardly registered, not that there was much to it. From the Coal Exchange it was just twenty minutes driving from ring road to motorway to dual carriageway and then up the lane that wound through the village he'd been calling home for the last couple of years.

Gwaelod-Y-Garth sat high up on the side of the great wide valley that leads north of Cardiff. Once upon a time, it had been home to the better-off people who made their livings from the coal mines that used to line the valley floor. Now, though, it was the haunt of fashionable professionals – lawyers or media folk looking for somewhere a little bit special to bring up their kids.

All the houses in the village were built on a slope, but Gethin's place had a particularly precarious setting. You had to put the car into first gear to be in with a chance of getting up the lane that led to it. Then you had to park on a quarried out ledge before climbing up a steep flight of steps to the house itself. The house was spread over four storeys, but with only enough space for a couple of rooms on each floor as the building clung to the mountainside. The bedrooms were on the bottom two floors and the living areas on the upper storeys, so everyone called it the upside-down house. Once you reached the third-floor level, there was another small plateau off to one side that had been landscaped as a garden and was accessible from the main living room through the French windows. The views from this and every other room were spectacular, as was the level of strain on your calf muscles any time you approached the house on foot.

Catriona, Gethin's wife, loved it and so did their daughter, Hattie. Gethin wasn't so sure, though he kept his doubts to himself. He liked the house itself all right. It was an amazing place to live, no question. He was less sure about the village with its upwardly mobile vibe. He didn't fit in, but that was nothing new. He'd always been an instinctive outsider.

He stretched as he left the car, feeling looser then he had done for ages, and realised that, right now, he didn't give a damn about the neighbours. He had the case he wanted, a family he loved and an upside-down house. Tonight, he just wanted to enjoy it all. He pressed-down on the key fob and locked the car, an eight-year-old Nissan Primera he'd bought because he wasn't remotely interested in cars and the man at the garage said it would run for ever given a rudimentary level of care, which was all Gethin was likely to provide. Then he climbed the steep steps to the front door, followed by two floors' worth of internal stairs before arriving in the garden, lured outside by the sound of Hattie's laughter.

'Hey, babe,' he said, as he saw Cat on the patio with a book, one of those 'what if your husband was really a murderer?' type psychological thrillers. She looked relaxed for once, fresh from a shower, reading in the evening sunshine, one eye on Hattie and her friend Lauren doing acrobatics on their compact lawn.

'Hi,' said Cat, smiling at him. 'What happened? I was about to call you and see if I needed to slow down the dinner.'

'Ah, nothing, well no, not nothing – good news! Really good news.'

'What's happened?'

'I'll tell you now,' he said, 'but why don't we have a glass of wine? I feel like celebrating.'

Cat raised her eyebrows: 'On a school night? Must be quite something.'

Gethin went inside and found a bottle of New Zealand Sauvignon Blanc hidden behind a huge bag of salad at the back of the fridge. He picked up a couple of glasses and brought them out to the patio.

Pouring himself a generous glass, he started to fill Cat's, but she stuck her hand out almost immediately to stop him giving her any more than the merest taste. Then she carefully screwed the top back on to the bottle. Gethin couldn't help feeling a flicker of annoyance. He appreciated the way Cat acted as a brake on his wilder impulses, but it was a bit of a buzz kill. What was wrong with celebrating once in a while?

He managed to keep his irritation to himself, though, and, as the sun gradually disappeared behind the Garth, he told Cat all about his new case. He could see the relief flooding into her face as she took in that this was something serious and not just another of his pipe dreams.

When he finished, Cat hugged him and told him how happy she was, and how much he deserved this shot at a big-time case. He liked the way she said shot so it sounded like 'shoat', a little trace of the Glasgow accent she'd mostly lost over her twenty years in South Wales. But even as she hugged him he felt a trace of impatience. Her enthusiasm was genuine, yet somehow she made him feel like a kid being over-praised by his mum for producing a perfectly ordinary painting

He knew he was lucky to have Catriona in his life. She was a great mum to Hattie; she had a good and responsible job working in the NHS as a psychiatrist; she was still an attractive woman for all that her blonde hair was shot through with grey and the crow's feet around her eyes bore witness to the strains of her job and her marriage. And if she wasn't as much fun as she had been when they were young, well he knew he was largely to blame for that. She'd stuck with him through thick and thin, put up with his bad behaviour with her Scottish Presbyterian resolve, but it had all taken its toll. He had no right to resent the way she looked after him; the way she sometimes seemed more like a mother than a lover. But he did. From time to time he definitely did.

He took a deep swallow of the wine, shook his head and wished away the negative thoughts. There was a ring at the doorbell and Hattie's friend had to head off home. Gethin was free to hug Hattie and breathe in the pure scent of her shampoo and to be grateful that there was one relationship at least in his life that felt completely straightforward.

After dinner – a chicken salad followed by a scoop of homemade ice cream – all three members of the family had work to do. Hattie disappeared downstairs to her bedroom to do her homework and no doubt ignore the strict instructions to stay off all social media till she was finished. Cat went to her study to write up a couple of case files. She was working on a new drug rehab project in collaboration with several different agencies doing their best to cope with the disastrous reliance on self-medication common amongst the disenfranchised of the Valleys. Gethin took the opportunity to discreetly remove the bottle of wine from the fridge and head into the living room where he fired up the desktop to do a little more research into his potential new client.

He was focusing on the case against Ismail Mohammed, going back to the original newspaper reports of the trial. They were fairly sketchy. The trial hadn't attracted a huge amount of publicity at the time, which seemed surprising till you remembered that Ismail wasn't famous back then, he wasn't even Ismail. He was Tyrell Hanson, just another young black man who'd got himself into a world of trouble. There was a certain amount of interest, given that the victim was a pretty young white girl. The right-wing papers had played up that angle, while the *Guardian* had hardly covered the case at all, probably for fear of stoking up racial hatred. Anyway, once you allowed for the prejudices of the different newspapers, the basic facts seemed clear enough.

The victim, Hannah Gold, had been found floating face down in Bristol's River Avon on 8 June 2005. At first, she'd been taken for a suicide, but then the post-mortem revealed that she'd suffered a severe blow to the head before going into the water. The post-mortem further revealed that Gold had had sex not long before her death. Whether it was consensual or not was unclear, but semen was present and a DNA test had produced a match with Tyrell Hanson, a man known to the Bristol police as a player in the local drug dealing scene.

Gethin made a note to check out this thoroughly – DNA evidence wasn't always as clear cut as it sounded. A few minutes later he crossed out the note. It turned out that Tyrell had admitted he had indeed had sex with the dead girl. To make matters worse, there was CCTV footage of him with the victim in a Bristol bar, just hours before her presumed time of death. According to his version of events, he had simply met Ms Gold in the bar on a first date. They had hit it off and gone to have sex on the Downs, not far from the river. Afterwards they had gone their separate ways and he had no idea how she had ended up dead in the water.

Gethin winced as he read it. It wasn't hard to see how Tyrell had ended up with a murder conviction, Worst of all, at the time of his arrest he'd been in possession of an unlicensed gun. The photos of the trial suggested he hadn't done himself any favours there. He looked the same in all the pictures: a bearded light-skinned guy with his mouth set in a permanent scowl and a baseball cap jammed low over his eyes like he knew he was guilty, and was trying to hide his face from the world.

Now, though, surely it would all be different. Izma M was a changed man – the appeal judges would see that at once and then they'd look at the evidence against him properly, see how flimsy it was. Gethin could feel the buzz building, the conviction that he, Gethin Grey, would be able to overturn Izma M's conviction. In six months or so, Izma M would be a free man and Gethin would be famous as the man responsible. Last Resort Legals would be swamped with important work, and all the struggles, the ups and calamitous downs, of the past few years would be done with. He would be the man he'd always hoped to be, the man Cat always believed he could be. Cat! God, he neglected her, took her for granted. How long was it since they last... a week? Two weeks? He saved his work, drained his glass – lord, he'd finished the whole bottle – got up from his desk and went to find her in her study. As he started massaging her shoulders, she turned to him, smiled and closed her eyes and leaned back against him.

In bed, it was intense the way it sometimes can be but mostly isn't when you've been married for nearly two decades. Each one of them was as hungry as the other, their kisses meeting ready mouths, their fingers finding hardness and wetness without need for coaxing. Afterwards, she pulled him to her, buried her face in his neck and started crying.

'Oh, Gethin,' she said, 'I've missed you so much.'

Gethin started to protest but stopped himself just in time. She was right. The past year he'd been present in body but not in mind. He'd made it through, he hadn't relapsed into the old bad habits, but he'd done it by going into himself, by shutting her out of his thinking. Now, in the afterglow, he resolved to do better.

A little later, when Cat came back from the bathroom, she lay in his arms, the way she always used to, and he told her about his latest case, the way he always used to.

'The good news is that all the evidence is basically circumstantial.'

'Really?'

'Yes, at least as far as I can tell. He definitely had sex with this girl, and he seems to have been the last person anyone saw her with before her death, but no one saw him attack her or dump her in the river or anything like that. And there was no murder weapon and no obvious motive that I can see.'

Cat scowled. 'Bloody typical. I'll bet if he'd been a nice middle-class white boy the case would never have got to court.'

'No,' said Gethin, 'probably not. People would have suspected and whispered, and the girl's family would have been begging for a trial, but I doubt the CPS would have fancied it.'

Gethin stared up at the ceiling and wondered if it had been as simple as that. Had Tyrell been convicted just because he was a black gangster with a gun and a bad attitude? He nodded to himself: quite likely it was that simple. That was how things went, how the world turned. Bad luck and prejudice could easily be enough to see an innocent man convicted. If the case were to come to trial again, Gethin suspected that, given a decent barrister, an inner-city jury and an image makeover on the defendant, there was a fair chance Tyrell would be acquitted. There was reasonable doubt all over the place.

'So, do you think there are grounds for appeal?'

'I'm not sure yet. Like I say, all the evidence looks circumstantial but that's not enough. If a jury thought that was good enough to convict, there it is. We can't just apply for a retrial on the grounds that the jury got it wrong the first time and we'd like to have another go.'

'That's so unfair.' Cat turned off her bedside light and prepared to put in her earplugs, but paused to add, 'You'll think of something, won't you?'

'Yes,' said Gethin, 'I hope so.' He kissed the back of her neck, before rolling over and turning off his own bedside light. Soon Cat was asleep but Gethin just lay there with his mind buzzing.

To have an appeal, there had to be either significant new evidence or a clear indication that there was something amiss with the original trial. The first of these options was the more exciting one but, in Gethin's experience, the second option was much more common and more likely to end up with his client walking free.

If you could prove that the police hid evidence or pressurised witnesses or bullied your client into confessing, you stood a good chance of getting a result. And that would certainly be one line of attack for Gethin. He'd talk to the original lawyers and read through all the accumulated paperwork and look for a loophole. But on the basis of what he'd read in the newspaper accounts, he wasn't too hopeful.

Perversely, the prosecution case was going to be hard to attack precisely because it was actually weak. There wasn't much evidence to have thrown out of court because there wasn't much evidence at all. Just a suspect who fitted the bill. So, if there was to be an acquittal, the likelihood was they'd need to come up with new evidence. And that was okay. That's what Last Resort Legals were good at. That's why they'd been brought into the game.

Kyrenia, Northern Cyprus
15 August 2001 20.15

Danny didn't notice the change in the music at first. He'd been doing his best to ignore the combo on the little outdoor bandstand. Like every other combo in every other Mediterranean beach bar, they'd been grinding their way through the obligatory Eagles and Bob Marley covers, these three long-haired guys with their big fake grins.

What they were playing now was a long way from 'Hotel California', though. The guitarist had swapped his Strat for a bulbous stringed instrument, and he'd started playing a winding, mournful melody that was beginning to grab Danny's attention. Danny was obsessed with music, London dance music especially, and even if this eastern-sounding stuff wasn't what he was into, anything was better than the bloody Eagles.

The drummer came in next, just tapping out an ominous pulse, like a slowed down heartbeat. The fiddle player added a stark and ghostly accompaniment that put Danny in mind of the ancient burial chambers he'd seen on the island. The tune built and built for a couple of minutes, gradually drawing the attention of the other diners; mostly Brits like him and his parents. Then, all at once, the three men stopped playing and started singing together acapella-style, a high keening harmony which had the diners staring at each other in bewilderment. Finally, the music started up again, the guitarist leading the others into an increasingly impassioned restatement of the original theme.

Danny was riveted by the end. Something old and profound had reached into this tourist restaurant. He looked round to see if his fellow diners had felt the same thing. After the tune finished there was a bemused silence. Then the diners clapped politely and the band went back to their regular instruments and started playing 'Lay Down Sally'. Danny's mum was staring off into space, which was par for the course. His dad, true to his smug philistine form, had obviously tuned out the music completely, and was busy waving for someone to take their order. Danny wondered, not for the first time, how he could have so little in common with his family.

The waiter came over and Danny's dad, Lenny, ordered the steak, just like he did every night, 'Nice and bloody, Mehmet', then laughing as if he'd said something funny.

Usually, Danny just mumbled his order, 'houmous and pitta and salad please' – there weren't a whole lot of options for a vegetarian at the Topkapi – but this time he actually looked Mehmet in the eye and asked: 'What was that music?'

Mehmet looked embarrassed. 'It was an old Turkish song. A special request.'

'It sounded terribly sad,' said Sally, Danny's mum. This wasn't an unusual observation for Sally. She was prone to finding everything sad after her third bottle of white wine of the day.

'Yes, madam,' said Mehmet. 'It's a funeral song.'

'Really?' said Lenny. 'Someone died, have they?'

'No,' said Mehmet, looking like he really didn't want to discuss this further. 'No sir, nobody died. It was just a request.'

'Oh yeah?' said Lenny. 'Who from?'

'The gentleman sitting near the bar.'

All of them turned their heads to see, but the table Mehmet was pointing at was empty.

Three

GETHIN WAS IN WORK AT half seven the next morning, He'd hardly slept. His mind just wouldn't stop racing. The alcohol hadn't helped, of course, and he'd felt the familiar longings coming over him in the dead of night. Surely, he'd earned the right to let off steam a little? He'd had to wrestle with the temptation to dress quietly and slip out of the house, drive back into town and land in trouble. He'd fought it, though, had run through the mental exercises he'd learned to use whenever he had difficulty sleeping. He'd concentrated on his breathing, then made himself try to remember the exact line-ups of the Liverpool football teams of his youth, anything to assist his mind to calm down, to help him sleep instead of urging him to rise from his bed and let a little danger back into his life. Around half four, it had finally worked. Or maybe it was just the knowledge that it was finally too late for trouble. Anyway, he'd managed a few hours of fitful rest before rising early and leaving the house just as Cat and Hattie were waking.

The Portuguese bakery wasn't open yet, so Gethin headed straight inside the Coal Exchange, said 'Hiya' to Al the doorman and took the stairs up to the office. Inside, he made himself a cup of tea and fired up his computer. He still felt anxious and jittery, but excited at the same time. Stage fright. It was okay to be a bit edgy: that's what he had to keep telling himself.

He obviously wasn't the only one who was excited about

the new case. Bex was in at half eight, checking her emails to see if there was any further communication from Amelia Laverne, and Lee was at her desk by half nine, which was absolutely unheard of. She was carrying a copy of Ismail Mohammed's book.

A few minutes later, Bex called out in excitement. An email had come in from Amelia Laverne's PA. Amelia was delighted that Last Resort Legals were to be involved. Ismail's lawyers would be sending over all the trial papers by courier later that day and Amelia would be in touch personally, either by Skype or, if possible, on a visit to Cardiff.

'Nice,' said Lee.

'And the money,' said Gethin. 'Did dear, dear Amelia say anything about our fees?'

Bex gave him a look, like how dare he joke about the goddess Amelia. 'She says the fees are absolutely no problem. There'll be an upfront advance and, thereafter, we just need to invoice at the end of each week.'

'Excellent.'

'Yes,' said Bex, 'the bank will be pleased.'

Last Resort's finances were not a subject Gethin liked to dwell on. The last year had been difficult, well paid work had been thin on the ground. It shouldn't have been too much of a problem, a quiet patch, as there should have been a surplus in the bank from the year before but that had mysteriously disappeared, syphoned off by Gethin for 'investment in special projects', everyone had known what that meant, he supposed, and he knew no one was happy about it, but it was water under the bridge now. The last year he'd been good and at the end of the day it was his business and, as long as he kept paying their wages, he could do what he liked with his money. It had been stressful, though, bumping along just below their overdraft limit.

This case, however, should have them back in the black in no time. Last Resort's services did not come cheap. Some people were surprised and horrified by that – like they felt Gethin and the team should be working for free, out of the goodness of their hearts. Same went for all sorts of charitable activities he supposed, but the fact was that wages across that whole sector had gone up in leaps and bounds over the past decade or so. All the big charities paid wages that compared with most commercial employers so why Last Resort – which didn't even claim to be a charity – should be an exception, Gethin couldn't imagine. And at least they didn't spend a fortune on marketing or glossy brochures. So there you go, he had nothing to apologise for. He provided a necessary service for a fair price. End of.

The only problem with such a juicy case falling into their laps was that now no one wanted to proceed with the stuff they already had on their books. Still, the paperwork wasn't arriving till later on, so Gethin figured they could spend the morning clearing the decks.

He was just writing a quick email to a Manchester law lecturer, politely declining an offer to speak at some conference, when the lanky figure of Deano Wilson, Last Resort's part-time investigator, sloped into the office. Deano had been Gethin's first success. His life had turned round after he'd been released on appeal, a year after being convicted of a whole raft of crimes, up to and including attempted murder, in relation to a major series of car thefts in the 'M4 Five' case.

These days Deano was hardly recognisable as the wannabe gangster of yesteryear. Instead he looked like a typical modern-day dandy with his beard and tattoos and stupid hat. Though there was something in his eyes that let you know you might want to think twice before telling him it was a stupid hat.

'S'up, boss?' Deano slid into a chair opposite Gethin and pulled the brim of his hat down low over his eyes.

'Same old,' said Gethin, then he corrected himself and told Deano about the Izma M case.

'Sweet,' said Deano. 'Seriously. Anything you need from me, you know? Got a few contacts in Bristol like, so...'

'I'll bet,' said Gethin. 'And definitely we'll need you; there's going to be a lot of work for all of us. Now, how about the Newport business?'

Deano was working on the case of two kids who'd been caught up in rioting in Newport a couple of years earlier. They'd only had a few weeks in prison each, but they were nice middle-class student types and their parents were desperate to have their convictions overturned so they'd be able to work as lawyers or politicians or whatever in due course. It all boiled down to exactly who it was that had lobbed a paving stone through the front windows of the new university building by the river. As far as Deano had been able to discover, the two boys were absolutely bang to rights. However, he told Gethin he suspected he might be able to find a couple of other boys, already inside for more serious crimes, who'd suddenly remember it was them who did it in exchange for 'a little favour or two on the outside'.

'Oh yeah?' said Gethin. 'How much do they want?'

Deano shrugged. 'Ten grand each is what they're asking for. Reckon they'd be looking at another three months on their current sentences, though it could be six, or even a year if the judge decides he has to make an example.'

Gethin thought about it. 'Fine,' he said. 'I'll ask the families. Tell you what – knock them down to nine each and I'll tell the parents it's just the same as an extra year's university fees. And only half the money up front. The other half is strictly payment by results. Once our little student boys have their convictions quashed, your two mates receive the rest of the money.'

'I'll get on it,' said Deano.

Deano was a natural at this kind of criminal realpolitik. He saw the justice system as essentially a game – a game rigged in favour of the police but a game nonetheless. And why wouldn't he think that, Deano, whose whole experience had confirmed it? When he was young he'd done six months for a burglary he hadn't committed. When it came to the M4 Five case, though, he was bang to rights, but he'd got out on appeal.

It was Gethin who had found the grounds for Deano's appeal – on the proverbial technicality – while he was doing a few shifts as a paralegal for his mate's law firm. Deano had found himself back on the streets after serving just over a year. Meanwhile, Gethin had had the idea to start Last Resort. He'd needed an investigator from time to time, someone with good connections on the criminal side of the street, and Deano had jumped at the chance to put his underworld contacts to a better use.

Despite their very different backgrounds, there was a natural empathy between them. Both of them had found a second chance in life. Gethin was always meant to be a lawyer. His father was one, had ended his career as a judge. Gethin had started along that path before managing to take himself out of the game by being sent to prison when he was twenty-two. And, unlike Deano, the first time he went down, Gethin was definitely guilty. Even then he might have got away with it if he'd let his father pull some strings, but he'd refused all that, had opted to take the same medicine as any other stupid young man.

Part of him had been thrilled that his career path had been ripped up. He'd been free to find out what he really wanted to do. Ironically, after a lot of misadventures, it turned out that the law was, after all, the thing that fascinated him. Unable to become an actual lawyer thanks to his criminal record, he'd worked as a paralegal for a while before seeing the gap in the legal market that he'd started Last Resort to fill. As for what he went to prison for, he didn't like to talk about it.

After Deano left, Gethin sat back in his chair and stared at the ceiling, wondering why he didn't feel more outraged by the kind of transaction he was about to facilitate. He was sure they'd go for it, the concerned parents, as long as he dressed it up a bit and let them delude themselves into believing that justice was being done and not simply bought. The thoroughly depressing thing was that there were plenty of guys sitting in jails up and down the land who'd be happy to do the same deal – take nine grand in exchange for some more time inside. Christ but people's lives were cheap.

He sighed and made the first parental call – to the offices of a discount furniture factory in Caerphilly – and set up an appointment to see the boss, Jim Cooke, the next day. This was not going to be a conversation you wanted to have over the phone. Then he left a message for the other concerned parent, the dentist from Whitchurch, and put the phone down. He waited to see if a wave of self-disgust followed. It was hard to predict when it would strike, but right now there was nothing, just another incremental increase to his burden of world-weariness. Thank God the liberal press and all the bleeding hearts who supported his work didn't see this side of the justice game. And thank God for the Ismail Mohammed case and the chance to do some actual good.

He called Lee into the office next. She was mostly working on a long-running case, a guy called Karl Fletcher who'd been inside for fifteen years for murdering his entire family. He was a deeply unsympathetic character and the evidence against him looked pretty damning. It wasn't one of those cases that had any public support, but there were a few inconsistencies, and, most importantly, there was someone prepared to pay Last Resort's fees, a rich widow who had taken an interest in the case – and was apparently now engaged to Mr Fletcher.

Gethin didn't realistically see it coming to anything: so far, trying to find convincing new witnesses to the events of fifteen years ago had got them nowhere. But, for the time being, they were taking the money and Lee was knocking on doors, tracking down old neighbours who might have heard something. 'Wasting my fucking time, boss', as Lee herself summed it up.

'Put it on the back burner for a bit, shall we?' asked Gethin.

'Fucking right,' said Lee. 'I'm sick of it. And Karl blatantly did it. You seen those videos of him, right after it happened, when he was pretending to be all upset and appealing for witnesses to come forward? Makes your flesh crawl looking at him. Hundred to one on: he did it.'

'Yeah,' said Gethin, 'I know.'

'Only thing is he'll go mental if we dump him. You know last time I went up to Long Lartin he threatened me, said he'd hire a hitman to kill me if I didn't get him an appeal soon.'

'Christ, why didn't you say so? I'd have cut him loose right away. Are you worried about him?'

Lee laughed. 'Not worried about him. He's banged up 23 hours a day. Bit wary of her though, the next Mrs Karl Fletcher. Fucking mental serial killer groupie that she is.'

'Seriously?'

'Nah, let's just knock it on the head. We can afford to do without her money now, can't we?'

'Yeah, we can,' said Gethin, thanking God once again for the intervention of Izma M and the chance to be back on the side of the angels, but also making a mental note to monitor the Mrs Karl Fletcher situation.

He worried about Lee at times like this. She had such a big presence it was easy to overlook the fact that she was ultimately a small, physically vulnerable woman. Lee had arrived in Gethin's orbit three years earlier, when she approached him about attaining justice for an old girlfriend, Maria, who had been crudely fitted up by the police on brothel keeping charges. Gethin had persuaded a couple of witnesses to come forward to testify that they'd heard a couple of local coppers threaten Maria with being busted unless she paid them protection money. It had looked like another victory for Last Resort, but somehow word of their case had leaked out.

The two witnesses had had the fear of God put into them by the rogue cops and didn't show to testify at the appeal. Lee herself had been badly beaten up but she had shown up in court anyway. It wasn't enough, though. Maria had ended up serving eighteen months. Meanwhile Gethin had been impressed and charmed by Lee's mix of humour and steely determination. And, like Deano, she knew a lot of the sort of people who had trouble with the law, so she'd been a natural choice when Gethin decided he could afford an assistant.

* * *

The paperwork started to arrive that afternoon: boxes and boxes of it. There were three boxes that contained the documents actually used at trial – the witness statements, forensic reports and so forth – and another eighteen boxes containing unused material, probably mostly irrelevant witness statements. The early stages of a murder investigation tended to generate loads of these.

Hopefully, they wouldn't need to go through all of the extra boxes. Looking for a needle in a haystack, when you weren't at all sure there was a needle there in the first place, was not a rewarding activity. They would begin with the trial material. Bex cleared the conference table. Gethin and Lee sat down.

They started from the top of the first box. Gethin read each item first and made notes on his iPad, then passed it on to Lee, who wrote in a notebook and passed it on to Bex, who entered all the key details into her desktop.

It was a slow and painstaking process: effectively, the three of them were reliving the seven days of the trial itself, as the papers were laid out more or less in the same order they were submitted to the jurors.

Lee and Bex both begged off around six, but Gethin couldn't tear himself away. He called home at half past and told Catriona he would be late. She didn't complain, just sounded pleased that he was caught up in a case again. And she was right to be pleased, he thought. He did feel a new surge of energy. It struck him how sometimes you don't notice when things are going badly, you just keep on keeping on, deal with the work you have and try not to think that most of it is pointless and depressing. It's only when things are better, when you have a job that fully engages you, that you can acknowledge it. Same way you get through winter, not dwelling on how much you hate it till the first day of spring comes.

Four

Next morning, Gethin decided to run through his own summary of the trial, based on the notes he'd taken. Lee, Bex and Deano sat around the table listening, ready to jump in with their thoughts, looking for the possible flaws in the prosecution case.

'Okay,' he began. 'Let's start with the victim. Hannah Gold. Twenty-five years old from Highgate in North London. Degree in English from Oxford. Spent a couple of years in Tibet, teaching in a school. She was working in Bristol in a women's bike cooperative. Lots of friends but no serious boyfriend at the time of her death. That's according to a workmate called Molly Farrow. Impeccable character as far as anyone knows: no drugs, no dodgy exes, perfect bloody victim, unfortunately. At least on the face of it. You going to want to take a closer look, Lee?'

'Fine. I'll start with the Bike Co-op, bound to be full of dykes.'

'Cheers. Okay, on the day in question, and again according to the testimony of Molly Farrow, Hannah left work around six. She declined the offer of meeting Molly to see a film at the Arnolfini arts centre later on; said she had something on but refused to say exactly what. Molly says she suspected Hannah was going on a date but couldn't say for sure. After work, Hannah probably returned to her flat in St Vincent's Road, Hotwells. She was sharing the flat with another woman...'

He looked down at his notes. 'Laura Vellacott, a college friend, now working for the BBC. She says she saw Hannah that evening. Hannah was obviously preparing to go out on a date, but she didn't tell Laura who with.'

'Next time she was seen for definite was at eight thirty, when she's on CCTV entering a pub called The Beer Barge, not far from her flat.' He looked up again: 'Anyone know it? Sounds as if it's on a boat.'

'Yeah,' said Bex, 'I've been there. Did a show on it once.'

'Yeah?'

'The Inhuman League, I think it was that night. I was one of the backing singers.' She broke into song – 'I was working as a waitress in a cocktail bar...'

Gethin laughed. 'Not your most challenging gig, then. So, what's it like?'

Bex shrugged: 'Like a bar on a boat.'

'Great, very helpful,' said Gethin. 'What sort of clientele? Young? Old? Fashionable?'

'I dunno Geth, I was quite pissed that night. Youngish I suppose but trendy. Bristol, you know what it's like.'

'Lot of black guys go there?'

'Wouldn't have said so – more of a white student sort of place I think, though like I say...'

'Okay, well our black guy did go there. CCTV again – not on The Beer Barge itself but on the road. You can see him approaching and entering the Barge. Apparently, the picture's not all that good but our boy admits being there, so no point in getting obsessed with that.'

'Any footage on the Barge place itself?' asked Deano.

'No,' said Gethin. 'If they had any cameras, they didn't pick up Izma. Next thing we see is Hannah Gold and our man leaving the Barge together about an hour later. There's a couple of sightings on the CCTV of the two of them walking towards the Avon Gorge – the footage is pretty indistinct but again there's no dispute. The last sighting of either of them that evening sees them approaching a footpath that leads up the side of the gorge towards Clifton Downs. According to Izma, they were heading up there in order to have sex. There is DNA evidence that supports this.'

'That's how the police got on to him, yeah?' Deano again.

'Yes.'

'No other reason? No known association between them?'

'Nothing at all. If it hadn't been for the DNA hit, no one would ever have connected them. Anyway, point is the connection was made. Izma – let's call him that, all the time from now on, yeah, to avoid confusion – admits having sex with her. But, obviously, he says it was consensual and the CCTV backs that up, as much as it can do. It doesn't look like he's dragging her off towards the woods. At one point they appear to stop and kiss.'

'But then she turns up dead.' Lee, this time.

'Yeah,' said Gethin. 'That's the next undisputed fact. The following morning some guy with a boat on the river sees her body floating there. As to how she got there, there's no direct evidence. The local cameras don't pick anything up. There's only one in the area and apparently you could easily keep out of sight of it if you'd clocked it. So, there we are – we have a dead girl in the water and the last person to be seen with her was Izma.'

'And there's no way it could possibly have been a suicide?' Lee again.

'No, the coroner's very clear on that. Her neck was broken before she went in the water. She was definitely murdered.'

'And no other suspects?'

'No, at least none the police appears to have seriously entertained, or that the defence could come up with.

Doesn't mean they're not out there, of course. But there's nothing raised at trial and nothing I can see in the police interviews. The guy who found the body has a solid alibi for the night before, and the time of death was definitely the night before. Her only significant ex-boyfriend was living in Mexico City so that ruled him out. So, no obvious suspects. Except our Izma.'

Deano nodded: 'You think he should have talked in court?'

Gethin paused. This was the difficult question about the trial. Izma had declined to give evidence in court. Gethin could understand what the defence thinking must have been: that if Izma was cross examined, there was every chance the prosecution would have been able to at least hint at his criminal record, which would definitely have played badly. On the other hand, not saying anything played badly too. And Izma was a good speaker. He wasn't some tongue-tied thug. Surely it would have been worth the risk, putting him on the stand. 'Yeah,' he said finally, 'suppose I do. But his record, you know?'

'It's not that bad though, is it?' said Deano. 'Nothing seriously heavy?'

'Except for the possession of a firearm.'

'But that was only after he was arrested for the murder, wasn't it? They found him with a gun when they arrested him, didn't they? Up till then it's mostly bullshit stuff – possession, affray, possession with intent...'

'The gun, though, that was unfortunate.'

'Yeah, bad news.'

'Course he didn't actually shoot her. I mean, the girl wasn't shot,' said Bex after a bit.

'No,' said Gethin. 'But obviously it doesn't look good. Police go to interview a man on suspicion of murder and he has got an illegal gun in his possession. You can see how they might think they'd got their man.'

'Yeah,' said Lee, suddenly animated. 'Or you might think they've gone all out to pin it on this guy, cause he's a black man who's involved in crime, so the jury will convict him on what he looks like, not on the evidence. Cause really there ain't any.'

Deano grunted his agreement. Bex looked a little surprised. It wasn't often that Lee became angry on racial matters. A Docks girl with a typically mixed background – her four grandparents were variously Trinidadian, Irish, Greek and Somali – she was as cynical as the rest of them about career crims crying racism every time they were nicked. So when she did speak up, it was best to listen.

'That's what everyone's saying about this case,' said Gethin. 'That it's blatant racism – and it looks like everyone's right, for a change. At the same time our man is no angel, we know that. But the evidence against him, like we've said all along, is purely circumstantial. No witnesses, no forensics, no confession. That's the good news. On the other hand, I dunno about the rest of you, but I can't see any obvious flaws in the way the trial was carried out, at least not on the prosecution side. We could maybe look at the decision not to let Izma speak, but I've never seen that kind of thing admitted as grounds for appeal, not on its own. So what's our strategy?' Gethin looked at his colleagues. 'Lee, any thoughts?'

'Got to look at the girl a bit harder, I reckon. Far as I can see, soon as they got the DNA match they didn't bother. I don't buy the only one ex-boyfriend line. Pretty girl like that, there's bound to have been fellers sniffing around. Maybe a stalker even.'

'Good thought,' said Gethin. 'If there's even the

suggestion of something like that it would be very good for us. So yeah, great, you get digging around her friends, see if they can remember anything. The Bike Co-op is still going, I checked, so starting there sounds good. And the BBC woman, the flatmate, try her too. How about you, Deano?'

'Dunno yet, boss. Might look around in Izma's life, see if I can do something about the gun business, try and defuse it a bit. See if I can find any of his known associates; there's a mate called Shaun Lindo, mentioned a few times. It doesn't quite sit right for me, him having a gun when he was arrested. Apart from that I mean the obvious thing is to go and talk to the man himself. He doesn't say anything in the transcript, does he? He must have a lot more to say, but I suppose you'll be doing that?'

'Yeah,' said Gethin. 'I think I'll have first crack at Izma. Bex, can you ask the solicitor to sort me out with a VO?'

'Already on it, Geth, they say they'll get you a visiting order for next week. Don't sound delighted about our involvement, though. I have the feeling they're pretty pissed off that we've been parachuted in. But they're under orders to cooperate, so you will have the VO. You want me to check out the trains?'

Gethin frowned: 'Gartree's in the middle of nowhere. I'll drive.'

He picked up the copy of Izma's book and started to read. First time he'd ever been able to prepare for a meeting with a new client by reading their autobiography. He was a couple of chapters in, immersed in Izma's story of growing up as a mixed-race kid in Bristol and London, when Bex popped her head back in, looking thoroughly excited.

'Hey, Geth,' she said, 'I've got Amelia Laverne on the phone for you. And she's in Cardiff!'

Kyrenia, Northern Cyprus
15 August 2001 20.30

It was just a few minutes after the band had played the funeral song that Danny saw the boxer. He was gliding across the restaurant terrace, all eyes drawn to his rippling muscles, sharp cheekbones and shaven head. He looked thrillingly out of place amongst the Topkapi's middle-aged clientele.

The man behind him, older and shorter and wider, was another matter. He fitted in all too well. Places like this were a home away from home for a certain kind of North London gent. Guys like Danny's dad, all ordering their steaks nice and bloody.

You couldn't go anywhere with Danny's parents without running into one of these guys and sure enough, even here at the arse end of the Mediterranean, this one made a beeline for their table. The old guy was all smiles. His companion the boxer, this built young black guy, was expressionless, like in his mind he was somewhere else altogether. Danny didn't blame him. He wished he was somewhere else too. He'd come on holiday with his folks for the one reason that he needed a sizeable loan to get his record label up and running.

The old guy's name was Martin. The boxer was Calvin Diallo, an up-and-coming super-middleweight prospect. The Martin feller was droning on to Lenny about what a great fighter he was, how he was out here for the summer, training in his gym along the coast. Calvin didn't say a word.

Lenny grunted politely at all this, right up until Martin got to the point. He was pitching for investors to come in on this gym he had, and maybe also a piece of the Diallo action. Danny wasn't paying attention; he was just staring at the boxer, wondering how he felt about being treated like a racehorse or something, taken out for inspection by a possible investor. He didn't look too bothered, actually appeared to be scanning the bar for available women.

His attention was drawn back to the conversation when Martin stood up straight, in an obvious huff. Danny must've missed his dad giving him the brush off: 'You should remember who your friends are, Len. Don't think you don't need them out here.'

'You what?'

'Nothing, Len, well not much. Just I saw a couple of Vincent's lads out at the airport yesterday.'

'You sure, Martin? You're not fucking me about?'

'No, just passing it along, helping an old mate out. How the world works, Len, friends doing each other favours.'

'Fuck off. I'll think about it, all right?'

'Len, you're a mensch.'

After that Martin and his protégé headed back out of the restaurant, and Danny's dad sat back in his chair, looking thoroughly preoccupied. Danny thought about pitching his record label plan but decided it was not the right moment. Martin's visit had obviously disturbed him. Especially now it was clear that this was no accidental meeting. Martin and the boxer hadn't been there to eat.

They'd been there to deliver a message.

Five

GETHIN DROVE INTO THE UNDERGROUND car park at the Mercure Hotel just before quarter to seven that evening. It was an identikit business class place just to the east of the city centre. Once he'd parked, he sat in the car, preparing himself for the meeting to come. Christ he was nervous. Ridiculous really, he'd met convicted murderers in maximum security prisons without a hint of anxiety, but a woman who'd been in a few films once upon a time and he was actually shaking. He was sure he was going to make an idiot of himself. He felt like he was sixteen again, back in the eighties, watching the film that made her famous, *Mary's Prayer*. Amelia Laverne as the eponymous Mary, the tart with a heart.

She wasn't just your regular sex kitten, though, she had this obvious intelligence and class. The press used to go on about how she was the new Audrey Hepburn, or sometimes Julie Christie. Men fancied her all right, but women liked her too. All the girls Gethin had known back then had wanted to be her. He'd called home to tell Cat he was going to be late and when she'd heard why she was practically beside herself with excitement.

He tried to recall what else she'd been in after *Mary's Prayer*, but couldn't come up with much. He remembered endless colour magazine profiles, all with pictures of Amelia looking fabulous, but the names of the films she'd been promoting escaped him. She'd gone to Hollywood, of

course. He remembered seeing her in some piece of fluff –
Beverly Hills Cop 5 or something – playing the love interest,
and thinking she was wasted in it. There'd been a romantic
comedy with her and Kevin Costner he'd seen with Cat ages
ago that was a bit better, but he had no idea what it was
called.

And then he supposed the parts had dried up a bit. She'd
come back to Britain to make another film with the director
who'd made *Mary's Prayer* but Gethin hadn't seen it and
suspected it was probably a disappointment: those sorts of
reunion things generally were. But, despite the lack of hit
films, her name had stayed current. She'd written a book
at some point and then she'd been in this British TV show,
a glossy thing about a group of spies. She was in the older-
but-still-sexy role wearing glasses and having to play second
fiddle to some shiny young blonde. There'd been a bit of a
furore then about some interview she'd given, complaining
about the lack of roles for middle-aged actresses. And she
was well known for being outspoken about political stuff
as well – the Palestinians and so forth – which probably
explained why she was taking such an interest in Izma M.

Gethin took a deep breath, then got out of the car. As
he waited for the lift up to reception, his phone rang; his
daughter's picture on the screen.

'Hi, sweetheart.'

'Hi, Daddy. Mum says you're going to meet a film star.
Is that true?'

'Yes, love, funnily enough it is. In fact, I'm just at her
hotel now.'

'Oh, wow. Anyway make sure you take a selfie with her.
Mum said I didn't need to tell you that, but I know you'd
never think of it, would you?'

Gethin laughed and started walking up the stairs rather

than risk the signal cutting out in the lift. 'You know me so well! I'll see what I can do, though it might be a bit embarrassing. I mean she's a client. It's a professional relationship, sweetie...'

'Oh, Dad!'

'Okay,' said Gethin, 'I'll see. Now I need to get off the phone. You do your homework and maybe I'll see you later if I'm back in time.'

'Cool. Bye. Love you.'

'Love you too. Bye.' Gethin put his phone back in his pocket and looked around the foyer for any sign of a bar.

A passing bellboy directed him to the first floor. Once again, he took the stairs focusing on keeping his breathing regular and his limbs relaxed. He wondered if he would recognise her – he should have googled some recent photos but some idiot part of him just assumed she'd look exactly as she did in *Mary's Prayer* – the sleek black bob and the pedal pushers, or maybe that gold dress. The bar was the regulation posh hotel variety – low lighting, soft music, uncomfortable-looking furniture, beige and brown everything and a faint air of soulless desperation. The only good thing about it was that it was empty. He scanned the room for waiting film stars.

None of the handful of people there looked even vaguely film-starry, though, so he wandered round the corner in case there was a part of the bar he'd missed. Nothing there but a completely deserted restaurant, so he turned back towards the bar and, as he did so, a woman stood up at a table near the window. She started walking towards him, a small, skinny woman, wearing a grey skirt and a big brown sweater that looked warm and comfy but a long way from elegant, while her grey hair was piled up on top of her head underneath a baker's boy cap.

'Gethin Grey?' The woman smiled and stuck her hand out to shake.

Gethin stared in confusion. Surely this couldn't be Amelia Laverne: she was too small, too ordinary. He'd barely registered her when he'd first scanned the room. And when it came down to it, surely she was just too old. Maybe this was her assistant or something. He stuck his hand out to shake and looked into her eyes, her unmistakeable green eyes:

'Amelia, how lovely to meet you.'

'And you.' She let go of his hand, giving him a surprisingly frank up and down look. 'Can I get you a drink, Mr Grey?'

'Gethin, please.' He paused. He could definitely use a drink, but it was important to give a professional first impression, '… a mineral water, please?'

She tilted her head: 'You don't look like a mineral water man to me, Gethin. Have a real drink.'

'No,' he said, 'thanks, mineral water is fine,' and then, after a pause, 'I'm driving.'

'Oh, of course,' said this bird-like middle-aged woman whom he was still struggling to believe was Amelia Laverne.

They sat down at the table and Amelia ordered a mineral water for Gethin and a green tea for herself, which made her earlier enthusiasm that Gethin should take a drink seem all the odder.

'So,' said Amelia, 'I very much admire your work.'

'Oh,' said Gethin and 'Thanks' and 'I must say I admire yours too, I…'

She waved the compliment away. 'There's no need for flattery and I have no interest in talking about all that showbiz nonsense. Films never change anything. It's what people like you do, Gethin…' she leaned over and touched his arm. 'That's what changes things, that's what alters

48

people's lives, not films. So, please, can we not mention all that from now on? Just call me Amelia and see me as an activist who's lucky enough to have a bit of money to spend on good causes.'

'Sure,' said Gethin, while wondering how he'd manage to stop Bex from giving her the third degree on her film career the second they met. But maybe they didn't have to meet. He had no idea what Amelia Laverne's intentions were.

It took him a little while to winkle them out. First, the actress ran through some of Gethin's greatest hits – the Bradford Bomber, the Greenpeace Two, et al – while Gethin did his best to look selfless and saintly and not like a man who was very much hoping that his new client would just get on and transfer her money into his bank asap.

It always made him feel like a fraud when people started going on about how great he was. If those same people had seen him in his younger days, they'd have crossed the road to avoid him. Back then he was a waster and scrounger, a black sheep boy with a string of failed business ventures behind him. Only Cat between him and complete disaster.

Finally, he took advantage of a break in Amelia's paean of praise to ask what she might like to see while she was in Cardiff.

'Oh,' she said, pulling her legs up in front of her and hugging her knees like a teenager in her living room, 'I just wanted to meet you. I like to get a feel of the people I work with. I thought we might go to Bristol tomorrow, have a look at the scene of the crime as it were. I've read all the press clippings and so forth, but I haven't been in Bristol in aeons and I thought it might be helpful to have a look.'

Gethin did his best to keep a poker face as he took this in. Normally, clients did not invite themselves along with Last Resort Legals as they did their work. Neither did they breeze into town and expect everyone to change their schedules at the drop of a hat. But then, normally Last Resort's clients were not household name film stars. So what Ms Laverne wanted, Gethin figured, Ms Laverne had better get. For now at least.

'Excellent idea.' He stood up and offered her his hand. 'I'll pick you up from the front desk in the morning. What time would you like to leave?'

Six

GETHIN WAS STANDING AT THE reception desk of the Mercure, bang on ten o'clock. He'd made it to the car park ten minutes earlier and spent the time removing old coffee cups, sandwich wrappers and copies of the *Metro* from the interior, and then giving the seats a quick going over with the almost completely ineffective hand-vac he kept in the boot for special occasions like this. He was still standing there 45 minutes later, increasingly aware that, while the woman he'd met the night before might not have looked like a film star, she could certainly behave like one.

The clock was inching towards eleven when the lift opened and Amelia Laverne emerged, dragging an enormous suitcase behind her. She looked, if anything, even more anonymous than the day before. Everything she was wearing – long skirt, jumper, shawl, woolly cap – was grey. It was like she was pining for an invisibility cloak. As she approached him, Gethin wondered whether she was going to act like she was on time or be super apologetic. He reckoned the latter was more likely and he was right.

She was so sorry, she'd been completely ready, but her phone had not stopped ringing. Mostly her agent asking her, no begging her, to take a part in some new French movie – 'Oh, I said, Kristin is too busy, is she?' – and darling – she really did call him darling – it was all so stressful she'd had to meditate for a bit to get herself grounded. She was so sorry. It honestly wasn't like her at all. He had to forgive her. He did forgive her, didn't he?

'Of course.' Gethin tried to focus on the fact that she hadn't yet, as far as he knew, deposited the promised funds in their bank account. He'd emailed Bex already to see if the money had arrived but he hadn't heard back, so, for the moment, he was just going to have to suck up the celebrity self-regard.

He took her case and led the way back into the lift and down to the parking garage, asking if there was any particular school of meditation she followed.

'Oh,' she said. 'Well, I've tried a few over the years, but I'm currently following a Buddhist programme – it's called mindfulness stress reduction and it was developed by an amazing guy in Boston.' She paused and smiled at Gethin, 'I know it's a terrible cliché – pampered stars practising meditation and all that – but it does work for me. Do you meditate, Gethin?'

'No,' said Gethin. 'Not these days...' he paused, aware that Amelia Laverne was waiting for him to explain, but first he took her proffered shawl and placed it carefully on the back seat of his car. The shawl may have been plain and grey but it was made of the softest cashmere he'd ever touched and doubtless cost a fortune. Next, he loaded her case into the boot. As he did so, he wondered why he didn't ask her what her plans were, where she and her case were ultimately planning on going. Would she expect him to drive her back to London? What was it about her that made you just fall into her plans without demur? Fame, he supposed.

'So,' she said, once Gethin had the car out of the garage and on to Newport Road, heading east towards the motorway. 'You were telling me you used to meditate?'

'Try anything once,' he said, hoping to close off the conversation right there.

He could sense her turning round to look at him. 'Come on, Gethin. Tell me the truth. Are you a secret Buddhist?'

Gethin laughed. 'Not exactly.' And then – he wasn't sure why, probably some idiotic desire to gain the attention of the famous film star – he started to tell her the truth. 'If you must know, I started meditating because I was trying to stop myself from completely fucking up my life.'

'Oh, my,' she said. Gethin could feel her gaze on him now, but did his best to keep his eyes on the road. 'Let me guess, what's your vice, Gethin? Drink, drugs, women? All of them? Yeah, that's what I'll guess. You look like a man who wants it all.'

Gethin couldn't help smiling at that. 'Gambling.'

Amelia leant back in her seat. 'Maybe that's the same as going to court with these cases, that's a sort of gambling, isn't it?'

'I suppose,' said Gethin noncommittally. 'It is and it isn't.' It wasn't the first time he'd heard that theory and he at least half believed it. He liked risk – that much was true. On the other hand, he'd read in a book a long time ago that deep down what all gamblers really wanted was to lose. And that had stuck with him because it was an awful truth. When he prepared a case for court, he wanted to win all right – maybe because it wasn't his own life he was gambling with in those situations – but when it was just him alone in a casino in the dead of night, betting more than he could afford to lose, he had to own up to it, the self-destruction of it.

'I guess they're sort of flipsides,' he said finally. 'The work I do, that's gambling in a good way, the other stuff…'

'That sounds like a good way of thinking about it. Did

you come to that understanding through meditation?'

'Maybe partly. I knew I had to do something if I wanted to get my life back on track, keep my marriage going...'

'Oh,' said Amelia, 'you're married. Tell me about her.'

'She's called Catriona, she's Scottish, and she's er... the same age as me. We've been together forever. We have a twelve-year-old daughter called Hattie. Cat's a psychiatrist...'

'That must be... interesting, having a professional in the family. Does she give you good advice?'

Gethin eased off the gas, seeing the traffic slowing up ahead. Did she help him with her problems, Cat? Mostly she just tolerated them, like it was par for the course to have a husband with addiction issues. And for her, it sort of was. Her father had been a chronic drinker and now the people she dealt with in her work tended to have terrible problems – chronic drug addiction, raging paranoia, psychotic episodes, you name it. He always felt that asking her for help with his own, less dramatic, disorders would be like asking a brain surgeon to cure your cold. And, anyway, he kind of liked it that way. He wasn't the sort of person who wanted to share his problems with his partner. He preferred to cover up and keep things to himself. Typical man, he supposed.

'Kind of...' he said in the end.

They fell silent as they passed Newport, heading towards the Severn Bridge, and Gethin turned on the CD player with the Jackson Browne still there from earlier in the week.

'I love this record,' she said, as the title track, 'Late for the Sky', started up, 'really love it.' She turned to look at him. 'You didn't know that, did you?'

Gethin took his eyes off the road and looked round at her, puzzled. Why on earth would he have known that Amelia loved Jackson Browne? And then he got it – because she was famous, because she'd probably chosen a Jackson Browne tune when she was on *Desert Island Discs* or something. How weird it must be to go through life knowing that all kinds of random people knew stuff about you: what records you liked, what your favourite books were, who you went out with for six weeks back in the eighties. 'No,' he said, 'I had no idea.'

They lapsed back into silence, as the next song began, listening to Jackson sing about finding some photographs in a drawer, photographs of his girlfriend, presumably, and staring at one in particular, one in which she was caught by surprise and 'there was just a trace of sorrow' in her eyes. He looked round at his passenger again, changing lanes as they crossed the bridge into England, and he was sure there was more than a trace of sorrow in her eyes. He wondered what or who was on her mind.

Twenty minutes later, they were driving along the Avon Gorge into Bristol, Brunel's great Suspension Bridge looming above them. It was just along this road that Hannah Gold had been seen on camera for the last time as a living person.

Seven

ONCE THEY WERE OUT OF the car, Gethin looked around him and found his bearings. He brought out a photocopied map from his shoulder bag. The key sites were marked on it – the bar where Izma and Hannah had met, the place at which they disappeared off into the woods, and finally the stretch of waterfront where her body had been discovered. They were right in the middle of the route the lovers – if that's what they were – had taken from the bar to the woods.

The boat, which had been called The Beer Barge ten years earlier, was still in business as a bar, but now it was named The Ale Craft. Gethin led the way over the gangplank and into the bowels of what must once have been an old grain barge. At half twelve, it was near deserted. Gethin supposed it was more of an evening stop off for hipsters than an all-day boozer for career drinkers. The only obvious member of staff on view was the barman and even the inevitable beard couldn't disguise the fact that he was twenty-five at the absolute maximum. There was no way he was going to have been working there ten years ago. Still, for the sake of showing Amelia he was working every angle, he went up and asked if the manager was about.

'I'm the manager,' said the bearded boy. 'What can I do for you?'

'Probably nothing,' said Gethin. 'I was just wondering if any of your staff would have been working here ten years ago?'

The guy looked bemused: 'Ten years ago? Christ, I wouldn't have thought so. It was under different management back then. Are you looking for someone in particular? One of our regulars might know what happened to them.'

'No,' said Gethin, 'I'm a legal investigator looking into an old case. And it sort of involves this place...'

'Izma M, you mean? He came here the night of that murder, didn't he?'

'That's right,' said Gethin. 'I'm working on the case trying to reinvestigate exactly what happened...'

'You're working for Izma M! That's really, really cool. Listen, do you want a beer or a coffee or something? On the house. I'm Dan, by the way.'

'No, thanks.' He turned and looked at Amelia to see if she was eager for a coffee. She was just standing there looking as determinedly unobtrusive as ever, wrapped in grey cashmere, a hat pulled down over her hair. She didn't say anything just shook her head.

'Right, right.' Dan was nodding his head to show how aware he was of the importance of Gethin's time. 'But I'm sure there are people around who might be able to help. I know I've heard people talking about that night – some of our older regulars, you know?' He paused and scratched his beard. 'There's a guy called Niall, comes in on Mondays for the pub quiz – one of those guys who knows the lengths of every river in the world. He was there that night, I know, because he was having an argument about it with another of the guys in the quiz team while they were at the bar – you know, was he innocent or not? – and then Niall says he thinks Izma M was guilty because he was there that night and he saw them together. Oh...' his face drooped a little, '... I suppose that's not very helpful for you, though?'

'I dunno,' said Gethin honestly. 'The thing is my client,

Izma, never denied being there that night. What I'm wondering is if the actual killer was here too.'

'What?' Dan was becoming excited again. 'You think he might have followed Izma and that girl – I'm sorry I can't remember her name which is sort of disrespectful I know...'

'Hannah,' said Gethin, 'Hannah Gold. Well, obviously it's a long shot, but we're checking out everything at this stage. I'd love to talk to this guy Niall. I don't suppose you have a number for him?'

'No,' said Dan the barman, 'but if you give me a card or something I can give it to him when he comes in next.'

Back out on the road, Gethin turned to Amelia: 'That was more useful than I'd been expecting.'

She beamed back at him. 'That was such a brilliant theory – that someone could have followed them from the bar. Why didn't the police investigate that? I'm so pleased we've got you on the case now.'

'Hmm,' said Gethin, placing rather less faith than his client in the likelihood that this Niall guy might turn up and say 'Oh yeah, I remember someone leaving the pub right after Izma and Hannah. He was a sinister-looking murderer type with a distinctive tattoo, and what's more he left a piece of paper with his name and address on it which I just happened to have kept for all this time.'

He led the way back over the dual carriageway, heading for the main road along the gorge: 'You need a coat or anything?' He waved towards the lowering sky above them. The Indian summer seemed to have vanished for the moment.

Amelia didn't reply, just pulled her shawl a little tighter around her shoulders. As they tramped along the pavement, Gethin reflected that either Izma or Hannah must have known where they were going as otherwise it would have seemed a decidedly unromantic direction to have headed off in. Even in the daytime it was pretty depressing, especially on a day like this with summer giving way at last to autumn. The river was to their left but it was grey and unappealing, while on their right there was just a sheer cliff face. After a hundred yards or so, though, the rock face gave way to a steeply sloping wooded bank. Gethin and Amelia crossed over the road and turned right onto a flight of steps marked as a footpath.

The path zigzagged up the side of the gorge. It was hard going and Gethin was out of breath before the top. He had to stop and make a show of looking back over the gorge.

So,' he said to Amelia, who didn't seem to be out of breath in the slightest – no doubt she had a legion of personal trainers keeping her fit – 'can you see anyone getting it on on this path?'

Amelia raised her eyebrows and Gethin wondered if he'd been horribly over familiar and crossed some sort of line but then, much to his relief, she laughed not a big belly laugh but a surprisingly dirty cackle: 'Gethin, if you're seriously having to ask that, I feel sorry for your wife.'

'Fair enough.' Gethin grinned back at her and then turned and led the way up the final stretch of the path. It reminded him how much he liked walking and what a good way it was to get to know someone, the way you could just trudge along together, only talking when you wanted to. He used to walk a lot with Cat but he couldn't remember the last time. It was ridiculous, given that they lived on the side of a mountain with great walks in all directions. Maybe that was just marriage for you; if you weren't careful you'd let all the fun things go and be left with the drudgery.

As they approached the top, the tree cover became dense and claustrophobic, the wind howling through the branches.

Gethin wondered how dark it must've been, walking up there at night. Maybe it was a full moon, or maybe one of them would have had a torch on their phone. Oh, wait, it was ten years ago, wasn't it? Did phones work as torches back then? He wasn't sure, made a mental note to check it out. Actually, he was glad he was making this visit to Bristol. It would definitely be helpful when he went to see Izma in prison, being able to visualise what happened that night.

The path finally came out at a clearing. There was a row of Georgian terraced houses in front of them and a whole lot of parkland to the left. Gethin instinctively headed off in that direction. He led the way over a couple of small roads, feeders for the Suspension Bridge, making his way towards a wooded area, trying to imagine which path he would have taken if he was looking for somewhere to lie down with a woman.

'What do you think?' He waved his hand towards the copse ahead of them.

She cocked her head slightly and smiled at him: 'I think that's more like it.'

Gethin found himself flushing and turned his head away quickly. Was Amelia Laverne flirting with him?

'Well,' he said, 'I guess they could have gone anywhere around here.'

'Didn't he say exactly where they went in his statement?'

'I don't think so, just somewhere on the Downs. It was dark, remember and he probably didn't know where he was.'

'I suppose not,' said Amelia, looking around her. 'Do you remember what he says happened next?'

Gethin thought back over the statement. 'He just said that he walked back into town and didn't see her again.'

'Oh, yes, that's right. You know, when I read that it didn't make much of an impression on me, but now don't you think it seems a bit strange?'

Gethin considered it. Izma's statement said that he'd gone off towards town, which would have meant heading towards Clifton Village, with its rows of well-lit houses, pubs and shops just a hundred yards or so away across the Downs. Meanwhile, Hannah would presumably have had to walk back down the steep footpath on her own. It did seem odd, or maybe Izma M was just the sort of bloke who completely lost interest once he copped off with someone.

So either his client was – or had been back then – a selfish prick, or there was something wrong with this picture. And, unfortunately, what that pointed to was Izma was lying about parting with Hannah on the Downs, and that he had, in fact, gone back down the path with her, back down to the river where she'd met her death.

'Yeah,' he said to Amelia finally, 'it doesn't feel right, does it? Can you imagine walking back down that path on your own at night after... you know...'

'I suppose if I'd had a huge row or something... then maybe...' she looked pensive, obviously troubled that her cause, her noble Izma, was not showing up in the best of lights. Then she brightened: 'Of course, we don't know what sort of girl this Hannah was. We're not all the same. Didn't she work in a bike shop? She was probably one of those fearless types.'

'Yeah, maybe.' Gethin led the way down the steps and back to the car. At one point they stopped to peer over the wall at the river, around the spot where Hannah's body had been discovered, but there was nothing to see.

'Okay,' he said, once they were seated in the front seats of the Nissan, 'is there anywhere else you'd like to visit?'

'I'm not sure, maybe the house Izma was living in? Do you remember the address?'

Gethin flicked through his papers. '15 Somerset Street.' He pulled out his phone and started to fire up Google Maps.

'I know where it is,' said Amelia. 'It's in Kingsdown, up the hill from the BRI. The hospital. Just head for Broadmead.'

Gethin looked round at her in surprise. 'I didn't know you knew Bristol.'

'Sort of,' she said. 'I was at the Old Vic for a couple of years, when I was just starting out. I had a flat in Cotham which is just nearby.'

'You were in the theatre?'

'In lots of ways I wish I'd stayed there, but it was while I was at the Old Vic that the casting director for *Mary's Prayer* saw me...'

Gethin started the car and eased into the traffic.

'I was Rosalind in *As You Like It*.'

'And that's how you got your big break?'

'Yes,' she said, 'that's how I got my big break.' There was something doleful about the way she said it, and she turned away from him and stared out of the window as they headed for the town centre.

Gethin let the silence build for a while. 'Did you know right away that *Mary's Prayer* was going to be such a success?'

Amelia gave him a long look. 'I didn't have a fucking clue. I have never been so unhappy in my life as when I was making that film. The film everyone loves cos I looked so fucking cute when I was twenty-two.'

Gethin parked up and they climbed out and walked along till they were outside number 15. It was a smarter neighbourhood than Gethin had been expecting. He'd sort of assumed that Izma would have been living in one of the ghetto areas, St Paul's or thereabouts, down the hill from this nice, if hardly fancy, Georgian terrace. It was the sort of neighbourhood in which you expected most of the houses to be occupied by smart young families, with the odd shared student house mixed in.

Number 15 was one of the more nondescript houses in the street, painted a cream colour with a tiled-over front garden and a UPVC front door. So this was where Izma M had lived in his gangster years. It seemed a bit incongruous, but maybe that was how Izma had operated, keeping a low profile, not living where you'd expect him to. He was obviously a smart guy. And St Paul's and all that was only just down the road. Gethin nodded to himself, hoping he was starting to gain a feel for who his client had been at the time of the murder.

'So, are you going to ring the bell?' Amelia's voice roused him from his thoughts.

'I dunno.' Gethin couldn't see much point. Whoever lived there now, almost by definition, would not have been living there at the same time as Izma. Still, what the hell?

He rang. Nothing happened. Gethin thought perhaps he heard sounds of movement from inside and rang again. Still no reply. If there was anyone home, they didn't care to open the door to cold callers.

'You seen enough?'

She was looking preoccupied again and seemed to take a second to register what he'd said. 'No, I mean yes, let's go. I was just thinking how strange it was that I used to walk down this road every day when I lived near here, and later on Izma was living right in this house. It makes me feel as if our lives are connected in some weird way.'

'Hmm.' Gethin preferred not to elaborate on the profound connection between a famous actress and an imprisoned drug dealer. They went back into the car and once again Gethin asked Amelia if there was anything else she wanted to see, or did she just want to go to the station?

It took a little while to answer. 'Yes, there is one place I'd like to go before I leave. Nothing to do with this case, though, just old time's sake, I suppose. I mean, if that's okay with you?'

'Sure, if it's not too far.' He tried to maintain a tone that was friendly and amenable, but not that of a complete sap who was happy to spend the rest of the day driving Amelia around her old haunts.

'It's not far at all,' she said. Then she guided Gethin back down the hill and on to Stokes Croft, the area's main drag. Stokes Croft was the epicentre of alternative Bristol, half the buildings covered in more or less artistic graffiti and street art, and there were more artfully distressed bars and vegan cafés than you could shake a stick at, interspersed with the odd dodgy massage parlour left over from the street's recent past as a red-light district.

Before long, they took a left into St Paul's proper. As Gethin made the turn, he looked to his side and was struck by a change in his passenger. She looked younger somehow, her eyes bright, her skin taut against her amazing bone structure. For the first time since he'd met her, Gethin felt the awe that comes from being in the presence of beauty.

* * *

It was a long while since Gethin had been to St Paul's. In his youth he'd gone to reggae clubs there, from time to time, and its blackness had been very striking to a boy from Cardiff, where even the most multicultural areas weren't anywhere near all black. He was expecting it to be gentrified out of all recognition, but actually it still looked much as he remembered, storefront churches and old West Indian ladies carting bags of shopping.

Amelia was peering out of the front window, obviously trying to find some half-remembered address. She called out lefts and rights, cursed and asked him to turn round a couple of times when they ended up on one of the main roads that encircled the area. Finally, they came to a halt, halfway down yet another street of early Victorian terraced houses, quite a bit smaller than the Georgian ones up the hill in Kingsdown. Several of them were painted in different bright colours. The house she was interested in, however, was more modern, part of a run of half a dozen that looked to have been built in the fifties or sixties, presumably filling in a gap left by wartime bombing.

Amelia asked Gethin to stay in the car, so he watched her emerge and walk up to a house with a blue door. She rang the bell. Nothing happened. Then she knocked. He was just about to start the car again when Amelia bent down and yelled something through the letterbox.

She must have heard a response as she stepped back, looking expectant. A few seconds later the door opened and a black woman in an old-fashioned wig came out. Gethin was too far away to guess her age. She wasn't young, that was all he could say, while the styling of the wig suggested she was in her sixties at least.

Her first reaction to seeing Amelia at her door was exaggerated surprise. She made no effort to invite her in, rather the reverse, standing there blocking the doorway. The two women talked and, whatever Amelia was saying, it was evidently angering the older woman. She started jabbing her finger at Amelia. Gethin rolled his window down to try and hear but caught only an angry West Indian voice. Then Amelia stepped back as if she'd been struck – though Gethin was pretty sure she hadn't – and when she turned her face towards him, he could see she was crying.

Wig woman must have seen it too. She stopped shouting and wrapped her arms around Amelia instead. Gethin looked away, embarrassed to be spying on private grief. What made him turn back was the unmistakable sound of a hard slap. He swivelled round expecting to see Amelia collapsing on the floor, but he saw at once that he'd got it wrong. The black woman staggered back into her house, slammed the door behind her. Amelia shouted something, turned on her heel and walked back to the car with a strange small smile on her face. But when she got close Gethin could see that there were tears rolling down her cheeks.

'You okay?' he asked, as she climbed back into the car.

'Yes. Well, no. I don't know. I'm sorry to have dragged you along, that was something I should have done on my own...' she paused, 'and a long time ago.'

Gethin wondered whether to follow that up but decided against it. It was three o'clock, he hadn't eaten anything since breakfast and right now he just wanted to grab a sandwich and return to Cardiff.

After waiting for what felt like an appropriate beat, he asked Amelia if she'd like to go to the station.

'No,' said Amelia with vehemence. 'No, I can't bear the idea of home. Do you mind taking me to a hotel? Somewhere nice and impersonal. Do you know anywhere?'

He bit back his irritation and had a quick think. 'There's a big old hotel by the cathedral, it's a Marriott I think.'

'I remember it. That's fine. Thanks so much.'

They drove in silence past Broadmead and the giant roundabout in front of the Hippodrome. Finally, and with a sense of considerable relief, Gethin pulled up in front of the

Marriott. He walked round to remove Amelia's case from the boot, and as he did so, a gent in a top hat approached and asked if he could help with sir's luggage.

Before he could say anything, Amelia took charge. She let the porter take her bag and told Gethin she'd be in touch soon. She thanked him again and dismissed him from her presence with the same impersonal courtesy she'd shown the porter. Gethin managed to restrain the impulse to tell her to fuck off and find another chauffeur in future. Instead, he smiled and drove off, leaving her standing by the kerb, wrapped in her grey cloak of anonymity, looking impossibly tiny in her woolly hat, a star hiding in plain sight.

Eight

MONDAY LUNCHTIME AND GETHIN WAS driving back to Bristol again. He suspected he was going to be heartily sick of the journey by the time this case was done with. The crawl past Newport, the boring featureless bit till you reached the Severn Bridge, the endless greyness of the Severn itself as you drove over it. Once upon a time these might have provoked a bit of a thrill, but familiarity had long since bred contempt.

Sitting next to him this time was Lee, vaping away in the passenger seat, nodding her head in time to the Earth Wind & Fire CD which was the only thing in the glove-box collection that she deemed acceptable listening.

'How was your weekend?' Gethin asked her as they entered the motorway.

'Shit,' said Lee. 'I had a massive row with Monica Saturday morning and she's had a face on ever since. Kids were a nightmare all day Saturday because they were stuck indoors. Thank God it was sunny yesterday, little bastards could go out to the park, otherwise I swear I'd have killed them both. How about yours?'

'Oh fine, you know, quiet.' Gethin thought back over his weekend, wondering why there seemed so little to say about it. Well... it had been nice, family-ish... what was that thing someone famous wrote – all happy families are the same, something like that? Not much to say about things going good. Saturday morning they'd all cleaned and tidied according to Cat's carefully worked out system. In the afternoon, they'd gone to Waitrose and done the weekly shop while Hattie was round at her friend Lucy's house. Gethin couldn't see why they didn't do the shopping online but Cat was adamant she had to feel the vegetables, look at the meat. Saturday night, Cat had cooked and they'd watched a couple of episodes of the latest depressing British crime thriller, Gethin doing his best to keep his irritation under control. Yet another bloody serial killer for Christ's sake. Sunday the weather had been glorious and they'd had an idyllic morning pottering around in the garden – Cat directing, Gethin pruning and weeding – till she'd had a phone call. One of her clients was in some sort of crisis so she'd had to dash, leaving the roast in the oven and promising to be back soon.

In the end she hadn't made it till late afternoon and, by then, the bloom had gone out of the day and the dinner was overcooked and Hattie was upset about some row she had had with one of her friends on Instagram or something and Cat was preoccupied with the work situation and afterwards they all retreated to their separate dens, their separate worlds. Family life in the modern world, Gethin supposed, not perfect but not to be sniffed at either. He knew how lucky he was, how easy he had it compared to Lee. Being a lesbian parent had to be hard enough at the best of times and, from what he'd seen of them, she wasn't joking when she called Monica's kids a nightmare.

Now they were on their way to the St Werburgh's Bike Co-op, Hannah Gold's last place of employment. Lee had been on the phone to them on Friday and discovered that there was no one there who'd known Hannah at all well, but she'd managed to persuade the office manager to see if she could track down Molly Farrow, the ex-employee who'd testified at the trial. She'd called back first thing that morning to say that she'd found Molly, who was extremely keen to talk to them. They'd fixed up a meeting for that afternoon at the Bike Co-op and then dithered a bit as to whether Lee should go on her own, play the sister card. In the end, Gethin wanted to be there too, in case this was going to be a significant interview.

Was Amelia still in Bristol, he wondered? He hadn't heard from her directly since he last saw her, but her PA had been in touch with Bex and the initial fee had been paid into their bank account. Gethin figured he'd just wait to hear from her. For all her show of modesty, she didn't seem to have trouble asking people to do stuff when she wanted something done. If she wanted him to jump to it, she'd surely let him know.

He wasn't sure what to make of her behaviour. The strange confrontation in St Paul's – what was that all about? He had no idea, just a firm sense that Amelia Laverne was not going to be an easy client. He gave Lee the edited highlights as they drove, to obtain her opinion.

She stayed silent for a while after he'd finished the story, then turned round to him, a sly grin on her face.

'Did you fancy her then?'

'What's that to do with anything?'

'Just asking! She is a film star, Geth. She got a partner?'

'I'm not sure. She hasn't mentioned anyone.' He thought about the way she just decided, on a whim, to check into a hotel. 'I doubt it. Unless he's away somewhere.'

'Or she.'

'Christ's sake, Lee, you think everyone's gay.'

'Just saying you shouldn't jump to conclusions. Specially with actresses.'

'Actors, you're meant to say "actors" these days, even if they're women.'

'Bollocks,' said Lee. 'So she's single and I reckon you fancy her...'

'So?'

'So, that's interesting,' said Lee, smirking. 'And so when am I going to meet her?'

'Never,' said Gethin, 'if that's the way you're going to carry on. She's sort of edgy – what's that word for animals that are scared of humans? Anyway, she's a bit like that. You'd freak her out completely.'

'I can be sensitive, Geth, when I wants to be.'

'Hmm,' said Gethin, concentrating hard as he moved over to the left-hand lane to turn off on to the M32. 'You talk to Deano this morning?'

'Briefly.'

'Is he getting anywhere tracking down Izma's mate? What's his name? Shaun?'

'Shaun Lindo. I think he's starting to get somewhere, seemed quite excited for Deano. It's a bit weird the whole Shaun business. He was meant to be Izma's best mate before he went inside but now, according to the lawyers, Izma says he has no idea where to find him or what he's up to.'

'So has Deano turned up anything? Do we know if he's still in Bristol? Guys like that don't usually travel far.'

'That's right,' said Lee. 'Deano has a few contacts in business over there and he seems to think he's got a line as to where to find Shaun,' – she waved in the direction of Bristol, starting to appear in front of them – 'said he was probably going to head over later today.'

'Don't know why he didn't mention it to me,' said Gethin. 'Could have given him a lift.'

'I don't think most of Deano's contacts are about at this time of day. Strictly after dark business.'

Gethin turned off the motorway at the Ikea interchange,

let the satnav on his phone direct them through Bristolian suburbia till they arrived outside the St Werburgh's Bike Co-op, just round the corner from a pub. It was housed in what looked like a converted stable block and had a brightly painted sign hanging over an arch.

'Hippies.' Lee looked up at the sign and rolled her eyes. Then, distracted by a noise behind her, she spun round. 'Bloody hell.'

Gethin turned to see what had startled her. 'Christ, is that a goat?'

Right across the road, behind a low fence, was a little paddock area full of grazing farm animals. He stared at them in befuddlement before remembering something. 'Must be the City Farm.'

'Too right,' said Lee, 'bloody hippies.'

The Co-op turned out to be more a place to get a bike repaired than to buy a shiny new one. There was a workshop off to their right with a young Asian woman working on one of those weird bikes that people rode while almost lying on their backs. She looked preoccupied, so they kept on going towards an office with a sign saying 'Reception'. Inside, a ginger boy in full cycling gear was chatting to a short-haired sporty-looking woman. Neither of them showed much interest in ending their conversation so, after a few seconds, Lee stepped forward and said, 'Excuse me'.

There was no response so Lee said 'Excuse me' again, this time with a definite edge, and the short-haired woman reluctantly turned to face her.

'Can I help you?'

'I'm looking for Molly.'

'Oh right,' said the woman, animated now. 'You're the lawyer?' She paused, taking in Lee's appearance for the first time.

'Yes,' said Lee, not hiding her exasperation. 'I'm from Last Resort Legals, that's right. I'm Lee and this is Gethin.'

'Ah right, okay,' said the short-haired woman, no doubt reminding herself that she wasn't supposed to think someone didn't look like a lawyer just because they were a black woman with dreadlocks and a Cardiff accent. 'Follow me.'

She led the way out of the office and further along the stable block to another workshop, full of accessories, baskets, locks and posters advertising bike maintenance workshop sessions for girls. In the corner was a kitchen area and a table, at which a woman was seated reading a copy of the *Guardian*.

She looked up as they entered, a big woman with dyed red hair in a rockabilly style, a fifties dress and plenty of tattoos. She was wearing glasses to read the paper, but took them off as soon as she'd clocked them as being the people she was waiting for.

'Hey,' she said to Lee. 'You're the woman who called, yeah?'

'Yeah,' said Lee. 'I'm Lee and this is Gethin who I work with.'

'Cool, I'm Molly.' She motioned to them to sit down. The short-haired woman headed back to the office and Molly put the kettle on, while starting up an easy line of chitchat.

Teas made, she sat back down at the table and turned to Lee: 'So, what do you want to know?'

'Well...' said Lee, then looked at Gethin.

Gethin shook his head. Lee had made the initial contact and he suspected it wouldn't sit well in this environment if he started asserting his masculine authority.

Lee carried on. 'I'd like to know a bit more about Hannah obviously – what sort of person she was – but mostly, yeah, I want to know as much as possible about the day she died.

Anything at all you can remember about that, love. We're just trying to make some sense of what happened there.'

'I'm glad. It's about time.' Molly looked down, lost in thought, then raised her head and stared at Lee: 'You are working for Izma M, right?'

'Yeah,' said Lee.

'Okay, I read his book, you know? I didn't want to at first. Obviously, I had this image of him, as this evil gangster who killed my friend and then pretended he was innocent. You know what I'm saying?'

'Of course. Anyone would.'

'Yeah, so for ages I didn't want to read it and people kept telling me about it and I'd just tell them to fuck off, but, eventually, I was staying at a mate's house in London and there it was in the bedroom and I started reading it and you know it really got to me, his story. I was surprised, the whole journey he'd been on – I know it's a bit of a cliché – but the story he told, how honest he was about the kind of life he lived and how he turned it all round – well it impressed me. And the fact that he says he didn't kill Hannah... well it made me rethink the whole thing. I mean, I feel sort of guilty that I just went along with the police line. You know, here's this evil black man...' she paused and looked at Lee, her face scarlet with embarrassment at having revealed herself to be a closet racist.

Lee smiled back at her. 'Don't worry, darling, I knows a few evil black men. Not like there's no such person. And it seemed like he was the logical suspect, right?'

'That's right. But after I read the book I started looking back at that time. Trying to figure if there'd been anything weird going on. Any blokes around. I started to think differently about what had happened that night. I'd never properly understood it before. It just seemed out of character for Hannah to be going off with some gangster type guy. I'd always wondered whether he'd drugged her or something but then, like I say, I read Izma's book and you can tell he's a sensitive person.' She paused again. 'I suppose you've met him?'

'No,' said Lee, 'not yet.' And then she kept quiet, not wanting to put Molly off her flow.

'Oh right, anyway you can just tell that he's quite a special person and I could totally understand why Hannah might have fallen for him. I mean I'm not sure, but I wonder whether she might have been seeing him for a bit, and not saying anything about it because she thought we – her friends, you know – might have disapproved of him or something.'

'Hmm.'

'But like I say, I was trying to look back and see if there was anything I'd missed. Whether there'd been any weird guys hanging around Han or whatever. You know someone who might have been stalking her or something, and then when they'd seen her with Izma they might have freaked out. You see what I'm saying – or does that sound crazy?'

'No,' said Lee, 'not at all. In fact that's just the sort of theory we've been wondering about so if there's anything you remember that could be a massive help.'

'Right,' said Molly, 'Well, like I say, I was thinking about it for ages and it was only just a week or two ago that I remembered something she told me. It was a conversation we'd had in a pub one night, and it must have gone completely out of my mind but the other day I was back in that same bar, the Highbury Vaults, you know, in Cotham?'

Lee nodded encouragingly.

'And it just all came back to me, how she'd been telling me about this guy she'd seen in Bristol a few days before – I think this was maybe a week before she died – she said he was an old boyfriend from home. She grew up somewhere in North London, I think. Anyway she'd seen this guy and she was saying he was still really into her, but she wasn't sure whether she wanted to see him again.'

'Did you think she was going to?'

'I don't know,' said Molly. 'She asked me what I thought, and I think I said maybe she should stay away from him.' She paused and frowned: 'I was pretty disapproving. I was like a serious baby feminist back then, badly down on macho type guys, and I'd got the impression that was what this guy was like. And...' she tailed off.

'And?'

'And if I'm honest, I was really into her, you know? I was hoping something might happen even though I knew she was basically straight. But it wouldn't have been the first time...' She broke off and looked Lee straight in the eye. 'You know what I mean.'

'Yeah,' said Lee, 'I knows what you mean.' Then she laughed and leaned forward and clashed fists with Molly. 'I knows exactly what you mean, girl.'

'Right,' said Molly, 'right.'

'So did you get the impression she might have been a bit scared of this guy, then?'

'Yeah,' said Molly, 'I think she was a bit.'

'Well, that's interesting. You don't happen to remember his name, do you?'

'I've been trying. I'm pretty sure she didn't say what his surname was, but I think she said his first name was Daniel. I know that's not much help; about half the guys our age are called Daniel, it seems like, but it's something, isn't it?'

'Definitely,' said Gethin, feeling like it was about time he reminded everyone he was there. 'We can see if any of her London friends or family remember a boyfriend called Daniel, or even just any old boyfriend of hers who might have moved to Bristol. That's a big help. Thanks.'

Gethin and Lee stayed a little longer at the Bike Co-op, but Molly didn't have anything more to add. Still, it had surely been a worthwhile trip, Gethin decided, as he drove them back to Cardiff.

'If we can put a name to this Daniel, at the very least it gives us something to work with, a decent alternate theory as to what might have happened to Hannah – that this Dan guy could have been stalking her, or just bumped into her when she came back down the hill from the Downs and gone crazy and killed her.'

'Yeah,' said Lee, 'just what I was thinking.'

'Wow,' said Gethin, banging his hand on the steering wheel. 'I just thought of something. The barman on that boat bar place, he was called Daniel.'

'Really?'

'Yeah.' Gethin thought about it some more, tried to bring the bearded boy's face back to mind. 'But no, he couldn't possibly have been old enough to have been at school with her.'

'Okay then, if you're sure. You want me to check out her family and friends, see if anyone's got a definite name for this Daniel?'

'Good,' said Gethin. 'You get on it tomorrow. Meanwhile, I'm going up to Gartree.'

'Fuck,' said Lee, 'you're going to see Izma? Why didn't you say?'

'Just had the text from Bex while we were doing the interview there. Izma says he'll see me tomorrow afternoon.'

Nine

WHEN GETHIN REACHED HOME, HE found Hattie lying on the sofa in the living room, reading a copy of Izma M's book. When she saw him she put it down and, all excited, told him what an amazing book it was and how proud she was that her dad was going to be fighting for justice for him.

Gethin lapped it all up at first, then found himself attacked by a twinge of worry. It was early days for the case and he didn't want to lead Hattie down the primrose path. He hoped he wasn't teaching her to believe in fairy tales, where everything works out for the best in the end. After all, that was not what life, or Last Resort Legals, had taught him.

But then again, surely idealism was to be encouraged in the young. Plenty of time for life to do its worst. So at dinner they all chatted happily about the case. If it wasn't Hattie romanticising Izma M, it was Cat asking for more details about Amelia Laverne –what she was really like, and what she was wearing, and did she have a partner, and why are you such a typical man that you can't give decent answers to any of these questions? He felt happy and alive, ready for the adventure.

In bed they had sex, and it was good again. But afterwards, he didn't drop off to sleep along with Cat. Instead he lay there, staring at the ceiling, his mind full of ideas and plans, trying to figure out the angles. That was okay for a while, but then he started to wish he could just turn the thoughts off and have some sleep. It was at that point that the old craving started to work its way back into his head. The disguise it wore was of concern. If you can't sleep it's because you need to relax. You can't relax if you're thinking about work all the time. You need something to take your mind off it. And what better to distract you than a little flutter? After all, it had been the best part of a year now. He knew he could take it or leave it really...

He fought it, this siren song. And managed to beat it in the end, succeeded in wrestling his mind back towards the old standbys. He had named nine of the Liverpool team who beat Arsenal in the 2001 Cup Final when he finally dropped off to sleep.

When he woke again, the bedside clock showed 2.45. Christ. The craving was back redoubled. What else was he going to do now, wide awake as he was? Didn't they say the best thing was to get dressed and do something else for a while if you really can't sleep?

It only took fifteen minutes to make it to the casino, driving fast on the empty roads. The casino he favoured, Les Croupiers, used to be in the city centre and had something raffish and exotic about it. Now it was housed in a retail park on the edge of town, close to the Cardiff City football ground, nestling between a sports shop and a branch of Next, and was about as glamorous as its location suggested.

There were a dozen or so cars parked outside in the quiet hours of the night. Gethin pulled up next to a Range Rover that belonged, he thought, to a farmer called Mervyn, from out Cowbridge way. He wasn't certain about it, as it'd been over a year, fourteen months of white knuckle gambling sobriety, but he was pretty sure that was Mervyn's car. He was a roulette man, Mervyn, a steady loser rather than a reckless one. He brought cash, never reloaded, left his debit card at home. He would lose what he could afford night after night after night. Gethin used to despise that kind of gambling. He'd always believed that, if you were going to take a risk, you should take a man-sized one. Tonight, though, was going to be different. Tonight he wasn't gambling out of desperation but as a spot of well-earned relaxation. What was that slogan all the betting companies were forced to put at the bottom of their TV ads? Stop when the fun stops – something like that. So that's what he was going to do – stop when the fun stopped. And to make sure he was going to take a leaf out of the farmer's book, he walked over to the cash machine outside the 24-hour Asda and took £200 out. Putting the cash in his front pocket, he stashed his wallet underneath the driver's seat, then locked the car. As soon as he'd lost the whole £200 or had won £200 more he would stop. Simple as that.

When Gethin walked in the front door of the Casino he almost collided with two guys coming in the other direction.

'Hey,' said one of the guys.

Gethin tried to ignore him, stepped to one side and started towards the door leading through to the gaming floor, but the guy was having none of it. He managed a drunken sidestep of his own and clapped an arm on Gethin's shoulder.

'Geth man, what's up?'

Reluctantly Gethin turned and looked at the guy. Nils Hofberg – Christ, the last decade had treated him rough. Nils had been the boy to succeed out of Gethin's generation of Cardiff cool kids. An actor mostly, though he'd been the singer in a couple of bands as well. He'd gone up to London after his first proper film part. He was ridiculously good-looking back then. Now, he was balding and fat with a beard that looked more unkempt than hipster. He was sweaty and drunk and had a crazy light in his eyes. The guy with him was way younger, sort of Middle Eastern looking and wearing horrible casual clothes that were probably incredibly expensive.

'I'm good.' He paused, suddenly aware of what he was doing, walking into a casino in the middle of the night in flagrant breach of the solemn promises he'd made to Cat, to Bex and, of course, to himself. But this was different, definitely different. He had changed, wasn't the same old Gethin, so the old promises no longer applied. So, yeah, he was good… 'You doing okay?'

'Yeah,' said Nils, 'I'm good too.'

Jesus, thought Gethin. He might be dealing in half-truths, but Nils was definitely lying through his teeth. He looked terrible. 'This is my friend Mario.'

'Marco,' said the younger guy, sounding pissed off. 'I told you ten times my name is Marco.'

'Yeah, yeah, sorry,' said Nils. 'Listen, we're just going for a drink back at Mario's place. Going to call up some girls. Bad girls. You want to come?'

'No, thanks.' Gethin wondered if he was making a mistake. Would it actually be the lesser evil to go to this Marco's place and do whatever, rather than enter the casino? No, it didn't have to be. Sure, he'd made mistakes in the past and now he had to be careful, but who didn't, really? And what was life anyway, without the occasional risk?

'Nah,' he said to Nils, slapping him on the back with forced bonhomie, 'I'm good. Just stopping by to see a client. Catch up soon, yeah? Heard you were back in town.'

'Oh, yeah?' said Nils.

There was something odd about the way he said it, Gethin thought, like he wanted to know who had told him he was back. But that was Nils, for you, self-obsessed to the max. So he just shrugged and waved him goodbye as he headed into where the action was.

On the gaming floor he stood there, breathing in the atmosphere; the faint smell of Chinese food from the restaurant upstairs and the top-note of anxious sweat. An Australian croupier he half recognised came over and said hello and offered him a drink and some chicken wings. He rejected the wings and took a mineral water. He wasn't going to let alcohol muddy his thinking. He was going to gamble responsibly, stop when the fun stopped, all of that good stuff.

It was a quiet night. There were some Chinese folks round a table playing Mah Jong, a few lads playing roulette at one of the wheels, a group of middle-aged couples who looked as if they'd been out for dinner somewhere and didn't want the fun to stop, standing round the next one. Gethin wandered over to the cashiers and changed his two hundred pounds for ten-pound gambling chips.

He climbed the stairs to the poker room, but it was completely dead. Just as well. He was out of practice and poker was not a game for the rusty. It was not a game for him at all really: the fact that it was a test of skill and character and not simply blind luck always pulled him in and inevitably spat him out once he ran up against someone with more skill and character. No, this wasn't a poker night, this was a gambling responsibly night, and that meant roulette or blackjack or both. Those were the games where the house advantage wasn't too swingeing.

Blackjack was the best if you could remember the basic strategy. Then the house advantage was only around two per cent, even less if you could card count, which Gethin couldn't. With roulette, it was more like three per cent, but that's what Gethin decided to try first. He'd loved the theatre of the ball swinging around the wheel ever since he was a child and his grandfather had given them a mini roulette set. Gethin laughed at the memory – what would people say these days if you gave a child a roulette wheel?

He put a chip down on red. Watched the ball come to rest on the zero. Neither red nor green but the extra slot that gave the house its edge. Some casinos gave you back half your stake when the ball landed in the zero. Not this one. Gethin put two more chips down on the red. Ball came down on the black. Lost again. Stuck four chips down. Won. Let the chips ride. Won again. Fine, he was ahead, time to move on.

He sat down at one of the blackjack tables opposite a croupier with blue hair, looked like an art student moonlighting. For all the hair dye and the inevitable nose ring she appeared impossibly healthy and fresh-faced. Gethin wondered if she was hit on a lot. Nils would have tried, that was for sure. Once upon a time, maybe Gethin would too. Not now, though, not just because he was married, but because of the thing that happened these days, now he was well past forty. He supposed it was the same for everyone: you'd see a girl, a young woman, and you'd fancy her just the way you would when you were her age, because really inside you feel like you're the same person you always were, but then, when she looked at you, you'd have the awful realisation that while you might still be twenty-two on the inside that's not what she saw. She saw some bloke old enough to be her dad with his tongue hanging out. And that was something to be avoided.

Anyway, sexual transgression had never been Gethin's vice. He'd been faithful to Cat since forever. New flesh wasn't the addiction that had landed him into trouble over the years.

He smiled at the young woman, Polly her name was, according to the badge on her blouse.

Polly smiled back: 'You want to play?'

Gethin sat down on the stool opposite her. It was a simple enough game, blackjack. You and the dealer took turns to draw cards, you added the numbers on the cards together as you went along. Jack, queen and king all scored ten. Ace scored either one or eleven as you chose. The aim was to reach as close as you could to twenty-one without going over it. If your cumulative total went over twenty-one then you lost. Simple. You could complicate things a little, if you were feeling flash, and started splitting your hands in two. But most of the time Gethin kept it simple. Gambling for him wasn't really about skill so much as placing your faith in the gods, just waiting to see what fate had in store for you. He liked the powerlessness of it, the fact that there was absolutely nothing you could do to determine whether the next card that was drawn was a three or a king, you just had to wait and see.

Gethin laid down two ten-pound chips. Polly dealt the cards. A seven and an eight for Gethin, a jack showing for her. Advantage Polly. Probably. Fifteen was neither one thing nor the other. Gethin signalled for another card. A king. Damn, he was busted. He laid down another twenty pounds' worth and they did it again. This time he won. The next two times Polly won. Then Gethin did. And so on. After a while luck seemed to turn Gethin's way. He won six or seven hands, checked his stash and realised he was a hundred quid up. He looked around for a clock to check what time it was, then shook his head at his own stupidity. Casinos don't do clocks. He dug his phone out of his pocket to check the time. It was almost five and, oh shit, there was a missed call from Cat. Bollocks. She never woke up in the night. Except when she did, obviously. There was only one thing for it, he'd have to go. He was half off his seat, smiling apologetically at Polly, when he thought one last hand couldn't hurt. Double or quits: stick the whole pile of chips on one last game. There was two hundred pounds there. If he won, he'd be three hundred pounds up for the evening. If he lost he'd be a hundred down. Which was nothing really.

He pushed the pile of chips on to the gaming surface. Polly smiled: 'You're sure?'

'Yeah,' said Gethin, 'I'm sure.'

Polly dealt the cards. Gethin had an ace and a five making six or sixteen as he pleased. Polly had a ten. Gethin nodded for one more card. His turn to get a ten. He stared at it: this wasn't ideal. He had to call the ace as a one now which made for a total of sixteen. The general rule of thumb was to ask for another card when you were on sixteen, but Gethin had a sense there were still a lot of high-value cards left in the deck. He hadn't been counting as such, but he had a sense.

'I'll stick,' he said.

Polly turned over her second card. It was a three. Now the odds were overwhelmingly with her. She took another card. Nine. Which made twenty-two.

'Your lucky night,' she said, as she shovelled chips over to Gethin.

'Looks like it.' He thanked her for the game, tipped her a couple of chips, and cashed out. Walking back to the car, five hundred pounds in his pocket, he felt well pleased with himself till his phone buzzed again – a text message from Cat – 'WHERE R U'. What to do?

His first thought was to say nothing and drive home as fast as he could. Cat didn't need to know where he'd been exactly. She'd just freak out and there was no need. After all, he hadn't lost money, far from it.

He was just passing Culverhouse Cross when he felt his phone vibrating in his pocket. He sighed and pulled it out, then called out 'yes' to answer it.

'Hi, darling.'

'Gethin, where are you?'

'Just out for a drive. I couldn't sleep. Thought I'd take the car out and clear my head, think about the case, you know?'

'Oh thank God for that. I was really worried. I thought maybe you were, you know... you're not are you? You're not going to...'

'No,' said Gethin. 'Course not, love. That's all ancient history. Just driving around. I'll be back soon. You go back to sleep.'

'You're joking. I'll be waiting.'

Ten

GETHIN STOPPED IN AT THE office in the morning, suffering from having barely slept the night before. In the cold light of day, he knew he'd taken a hell of risk going to the casino. Yes, he'd got away with it, on all levels, but he'd been lucky. And as he knew all too well, you couldn't keep relying on luck. What he had to do now was focus on the important matter at hand, getting a result in the Izma M case. On his way in, he bumped into Deano. Deano had a cap jammed down low over his eyes and a pained expression on his face.

'Christ,' said Gethin, 'hard night, was it?'

'Don't ask boss, don't ask.'

'Alex's place again?' Alex was Deano's cousin. He was the manager of a new bar in town, The Palace of Gin, specialising in 'botanical and artisanal gins' apparently. Deano helped out behind the bar from time to time. Gethin suspected that this was what lay behind the new beard, hoping to increase his chances of attracting the attention of the hipster girls who frequented the place.

Deano grunted something that might have been confirmation and followed Gethin inside. While they waited for the kettle to boil, Gethin asked if he was getting anywhere in the hunt for the elusive Shaun.

'Kind of. Went over there yesterday. Word is he's a pretty serious operator. Dealing yeah, but wholesale rather than street level. And nobody seems to know where he actually lives – he's like super secretive. But a girl I know gave me the address of this café bar where he hangs out a lot.'

'Any use?'

'Nah, well, he wasn't there anyway. The waitress said she didn't know him. She was obviously lying, I have the impression that's par for the course when it comes to this guy, no one wants to land in his bad books. Anyway, I just told her straight what it was about, and said if she did happen to see him, maybe she could give him my number. If he wanted to help his mate out of prison, like.'

'So is that it? You just going to wait and see or have you some other leads?'

'No, this is the thing boss, had a text from him last night.'

'From Shaun?'

'Says he'll meet me today. One o'clock, in the Spoons, by the station.'

'Nice one. Give us a bell soon as you've seen him. I'll be visiting his mate inside.'

'Oh right, yeah that's today. Well, give my regards to all the boys up there.'

It was half past one by the time Gethin made it to the corner of Leicestershire that housed Gartree Prison. There was a canal-side pub nearby, a place he'd used before when visiting guests of Her Majesty. It was a big characterless place, all conservatories and two main courses for £7.99, throwing away the advantages of a great location. Fortunately, the weather was just about good enough to sit outside, so he ordered fish and chips, the safest looking option on the menu, and a cup of coffee, and sat and watched the canal barges pass by for a while, letting the accumulated stresses of the late night and the morning's three-hour drive slough off him.

Five minutes of this and he felt his phone buzz. Bex with a list of messages for him. Some routine stuff plus an email from Izma's lawyers checking he'd received the VO and, oh yes, a message from Amelia Laverne – which was no doubt the real reason for Bex phoning up.

'She's nice, isn't she?'

'Hmm,' said Gethin.

'And she really likes you. She wants to invite you to an event in London. Some sort of gala dinner for human rights activists. Apparently, there'll be an invitation for you in the post. Amazing innit?'

'I guess,' said Gethin, wondering once again what Amelia Laverne's agenda was, what she wanted from him. 'And what's Lee on today?'

'Lee's here doing stuff on the internet. Mostly checking her Facebook I think...' she broke off as a voice shouted something in the background and then started laughing. 'She says she's working very hard and totally deserves a pay rise.'

'Just as soon as she's proved our boy's innocence. How about Deano, over his hangover yet?'

'More or less, he's just taken the train over to Bristol.'

'Fine,' said Gethin, seeing his lunch approaching, 'let me know if anything else comes up.'

Gartree Prison was a low, ugly building, appropriately sited in the midst of some flat ,featureless countryside. He left his phone and laptop in the car, as he didn't have any legal status as far as this visit went. At such short notice, Izma's lawyers had only been able to obtain Gethin a standard VO granted to friends and relations. So no recording equipment. Instead, he took a notebook and a pencil and headed into the visitors' centre, waited to have his name checked off the list, and then, a thorough pat-down before being ushered into the visitors' centre, a big drab hall with basic tables and chairs and a snackbar in one corner.

There were a few tables already occupied: tearful husband and wife reunions, gloomy parent and wayward son encounters. There was no sign of Izma yet, so Gethin took a seat at a table as far as possible from anyone else. A steady stream of prisoners entered; the familiar mix of bad boys and career villains. Gethin was finding it hard to concentrate on the job in hand, kept replaying the events of the night before in his mind. Gambling again. What on earth had possessed him? It was always the same: an obsessive desire as great as any sexual passion. He'd survived this time, sure. But next time?

There must be something lying behind it, some psychological malformation. He needed therapy. He promised himself that he would do something about it, just as soon as he'd seen Izma M.

Sitting back in his chair, Gethin sought to clear his mind, to focus. He closed his eyes, then opened them again as he sensed a significant flurry of excitement in the room. Looking over to the prisoners' entrance, he saw a wiry looking guy with a big afro and even bigger beard coming through. The man was bantering with the guard leading the way and then, as he entered the hall, calling out greetings in a broad London accent to fellow prisoners and screws alike – all bruv this and blood that. It was Izma M, without a doubt.

Gethin stood up to greet him.

'Hi, I'm Gethin Grey.'

Izma M looked him up and down and Gethin took the opportunity to do likewise. He wasn't that tall, probably no more than 5'10", but his hair gave him an extra couple of inches. He was lighter skinned, more Arab-looking than Gethin expected, probably the prison pallor that affected everyone, made all inmates fade to grey, but his black eyes were extraordinarily compelling. Gethin felt as though Izma M was staring right into his soul. Not a comfortable feeling when you had a soul as tarnished as his.

Izma nodded to himself, said 'Whassup Bruv', and pulled Gethin to him for a hug, taking the opportunity to whisper in his ear: 'You got anything for me?'

Gethin waited till the hug was over before giving the slightest shake of his head. Izma responded by rolling his eyes in a show of disappointment.

Gethin knew well enough that it was pretty much normal practice for friends and relations to pass over a little bag of weed, or whatever, when they came to greet their loved ones, but the risks for him of doing such a thing made it out of the question. Surely, Izma must have known that.

'Just messing with you, mate,' said Izma, obviously reading Gethin's discomfort and sitting back in his chair, a big grin on his face.

Gethin grinned back, feeling slightly aggrieved but also happy that this Izma wasn't just some humourless ideologue. 'Bastard.'

'You got to have a laugh when you can, locked up in this place. Tell you what though, bruv, there is one thing you could do for me.'

'What's that?' said Gethin, his eyes narrowing.

'Cup of tea and three Twixes.'

'Fair enough,' said Gethin and he headed over to the snack bar. Prisoners weren't allowed to go up themselves.

He dropped the chocolate bars in front of his client. 'Thought you were more of a body is my temple sort of guy.'

'Not for me,' said Izma. 'Old boy in the cell next door. Has a sweet tooth like you wouldn't believe. And no one ever comes to see him so…'

Gethin found himself oddly touched by this small

act of kindness. Most people he visited in prison were, understandably enough, totally self-obsessed. Already he was feeling at ease with Izma, could see why people were so ready to rally to his cause. 'Okay,' he said, 'let's get down to business.'

The visiting time went by fast. Izma was funny and smart and interesting when it came to talking about politics – which is what he loved to do. He spent a lot of the time quizzing Gethin about his opinions on this and that issue – racism, Islamophobia, police surveillance, etc, etc – and seemed interested in what Gethin had to say before coming out with opinions of his own that were invariably provocative but basically sensible. There had been suggestions in the press that Izma was too good to be true, that his articles were written by some *Guardian* journalist, but it was quite evident to Gethin that this was bollocks – racist bollocks at that. Izma was a seriously smart fella and no mistaking.

The only difficult parts of the conversation came when they had to get down to the nitty-gritty of Izma's case. Then, for someone who was generally so articulate, he became strangely tongue-tied. Mostly, he just wanted to refer Gethin to the court records – 'It's all there, bruv, just read the papers. Not proud of how I acted, but I was a different boy back then, you know what I'm saying?'

Gethin tried his best to persuade him to focus. 'Yes, I get that, of course, and obviously I've read what's in the court records and all, but look, me and my associate went over to Bristol the other day and we walked up the side of the gorge to the Downs, to where we figured out you and her must've gone. And what I don't really understand, right, is why you walked off to Clifton and she went back down the gorge? Can you just talk me through that? I know you don't want to, but it's important if I'm going to prise you out of here.'

Izma looked down at his cup of tea, biting on his lower lip. 'Look boss, it's all in the report. What can I tell you? I'm not proud of what happened. How many times do I have to say it – I just walked off and left and then…'

Gethin had considerable experience of sitting in prison visiting rooms opposite men who were telling him lies. Some of them were confident and well practised, others mumbled and stroked their beards the way Izma did. Not that anything Izma said sounded like an outright lie, more like it was only half the story. There were things he was leaving out, Gethin was sure of it.

'Come on, man,' he said, 'you're telling me you and this girl, Hannah, you've been on the Downs together doing your thing and afterwards you don't go for a little drink or something, you don't even walk back to town together. Instead, you go one way and she goes the other, even though – am I right? – she didn't live in that direction?'

'Her bike was back there.'

'Okay,' said Gethin. That was news. 'So you just let her go back to her bike by herself. Not much of a gent, were you?'

Izma jerked his head up and, for the first time, Gethin glimpsed the old Izma, the gangster called Tyrell.

But the anger went as quickly as it came and Izma leaned towards him: 'Listen, you want to know why we didn't walk off together? Let's just say things didn't go too good in the woods there. It was a bit… quick, let's say, and afterwards she was sort of pissed off and I was just embarrassed, you know…' he sat back and folded his arms, looking Gethin in the eye. 'Now you get it?'

'Yeah,' said Gethin, surprised and touched that Izma should have confided something so personal. 'Yeah, I get it.

And thanks. If I'm going to help you I need to understand exactly what happened.'

Five minutes later Gethin was back at his car. He got in and checked his phone. There were half a dozen messages from Bex. All of them said the same thing – call her urgently. He hit the return call button.

'Bex, what's happening?'

'It's Deano, Gethin, he's in the hospital, intensive care, over in Bristol.'

Kyrenia, Northern Cyprus
15 August 2001 23.00

Later that night, Danny was out by the pool listening to music when his dad appeared. Closing the patio doors behind him, he motioned for Danny to take off his headphones. Normally, Danny would have made a fuss about this, but something in his dad's face told him not to.

With the music off, he was struck by just how silent it was out here at his parents' villa on the edge of Kyrenia, and how dark the night with the new moon hidden behind a cloud. His dad, Lenny, sat down on the sun lounger opposite, his face in ghostly silhouette as the moon emerged from its hiding place.

Just as Lenny was about to say something, the silence was interrupted by a godawful screeching sound. It took Danny a couple of seconds to realise that it was just a couple of stray cats fighting – Cyprus was full of the mangy animals. But, in that couple of seconds, he saw something that looked unpleasantly like terror cross his dad's face.

'Hey,' said Lenny, 'are you all right? You're enjoying the holiday, yeah?'

Danny nodded, trying to wish away what he'd just seen.

'And the studying? That's going okay? World can't have too many lawyers.' He laughed weakly at his own joke and Danny decided that his dad's unaccustomed vulnerability might actually make this the perfect time to strike.

'Listen, Dad, obviously I'm still planning on being a lawyer and everything, but meanwhile I've also got this idea for a business.'

'A business? What kind of a business?'

'A record label. I know I don't have much experience, but I do know music and what's going on out there, and I've been making a lot of connections. I really believe there's money to be made…'

95

Lenny put his hand up. 'Okay, stop it there. That's good you want to start a business, we'll talk about it tomorrow. When we're out on the boat.'

Danny sighed. He'd been planning on begging off the boat trip, but now he was going to have to go. 'Okay, sure.'

He was expecting his dad to be heading off to bed but, instead, Lenny leaned in towards him, his face entirely grim and serious now. 'You remember one time I took you to a place in St John's Wood. I had to pick up something from a safety deposit box?'

Danny thought about it. Christ, it was ages ago, he couldn't have been more than twelve, but actually he did remember. It's not every day you go to some super fortified private vault. 'Yeah,' he said.

'Good,' said Lenny, 'very good. Now, you still have a good memory for numbers?'

'Yeah, dad, I still have a good memory for numbers.'

'Right, well, concentrate hard, cos this is important.'

Lenny reeled off an eight-figure number. Danny repeated it back to him. Then Lenny changed the subject for a little while before asking him to repeat the number again. Danny got it straight off. If he was told a number he would see it in his mind, as if written down, and then he would take a mental photograph of it, which he could summon up whenever he needed to. After a few more tests. Lenny seemed happy. 'You want to know what the number is for?'

'I'm presuming something to do with the safety deposit box?'

'Yeah, that's exactly what it is. Something happens to me – I have a heart attack, too much Steak Diane, whatever – you go there and give them a number and everything you need will be right there. I'd tell your mother but, you know, she's delicate…'

'Yeah,' said Danny, 'I know.' And he watched his dad go back through the patio doors as the new moon disappeared behind another cloud.

Eleven

IT WAS GOING TO TAKE Gethin two and a half hours to reach the Bristol Royal Infirmary according to the satnav. As he drove, Bex filled him in on what she knew.

'It was awful, Geth, he was on the phone to me when it happened.'

'When what happened?'

'A car hit him. Sounds like it was deliberate.'

'What? How on earth could you tell?'

'Well, I couldn't tell at the time, he was just talking to me and then there was this awful noise and the phone must've fallen on the ground or something and I could hear people shouting and the sound of this car driving off really fast, tyres squealing and everything.'

'Jesus,' said Gethin. 'So what happened then?'

'Well, nothing for a moment and then someone else picked up the phone, a woman, and she was sort of hysterical and saying that a car had, like, driven on to the pavement deliberately to hit someone. And I just told her to call 999.'

'Christ.'

'Yeah.' Bex was obviously making a big effort to try and keep herself together. 'So then – oh, Geth, it was really awful – then I had to just wait for more news. I didn't know if he was dead or alive or what. I just kept calling his phone and finally someone answered and it was a paramedic and they said they had Deano in the ambulance and they were taking him to the ICU at the Infirmary.'

'Did they say how bad he was?'

'Not exactly, but it's obviously really bad cos they asked if I knew his family, could I tell them where he was? Oh fuck, Geth.'

Gethin cut in: 'How long ago was this?'

'I don't know, wait, it was about ten past two, I think, when he called. I remember it was just after the news finished on the radio. I can check on my phone if you like.'

'No, no, that's fine. Why don't you call the hospital again, see if there's any update? And call me back as soon as you hear anything.'

In the end, it was another hour before Bex called back, by which time Gethin was caught up in heavy traffic approaching some roadworks on the M5 and starting to lose it himself. What the fuck had Deano landed himself in? Had the guy he'd gone to see something to do with it? Why would a friend of Izma's try to kill Deano?

Finally, Bex called back. Good news up to a point. She hadn't made any headway on the phone but Lee had taken the train over and was at the hospital and she'd grabbed a doctor who told her Deano had multiple injuries but he was not likely to die of them.

'Thank Christ,' said Gethin.

'Yeah, though it sounds like he's pretty bad, his legs are completely mashed. Oh God, Geth, he's only a kid really...'

'I know.' Gethin drummed on the steering wheel as the traffic crawled past the roadworks.

'I feel like it was my fault, Geth.'

'You what?'

'Well, I was talking to him on the phone when it happened. If he'd been paying attention, he might have been able to move out of the way.'

'Christ's sake, Bex, it was him who phoned you. Hardly your fault. Look, I'll get off this phone, though, before I crash into something. Call me when there's more news.'

It took ten more minutes to clear the congestion; but thereafter the road seemed magically empty. As Gethin drove, he wondered if he was actually to blame. Had he sent Deano off to put his head in the lion's mouth without even realising it? He just needed to know what had happened, who Deano had been talking to, just Shaun or somebody else? Maybe it wasn't even to do with the Izma case. Deano was a naughty boy; plenty of people probably had a grudge against him.

After a tense, sweaty crawl along the approach road to the city centre, Gethin parked in a reserved space in the hospital car park and hustled inside, feeling hot and nauseous. He was still wondering if he'd sent Deano into some sort of trap. Once inside the hospital, he found his way, eventually, to the waiting room for friends and family outside the Intensive Care Unit. Lee was sitting there, drinking coffee and looking several shades paler than usual. Her face lit up when he arrived and she hugged him hard before starting to fill in more details.

'He's going to be all right, Geth. Well, unless he's really unlucky or something. His legs are totally busted up and he has broken ribs and concussion and has lost a lot of blood, but they reckon his heart and lungs and everything are okay. So that's good, yeah?'

'I suppose,' said Gethin. 'I mean, yeah, thank God, but what the fuck's happened? Bex said he was run down deliberately.'

'Sounds like it,' said Lee. 'There's been coppers going in and out of the ward, so they must think something's up.'

'Have you spoken to any of them? They said anything?'

'No, tried to but they weren't having any. It's on Twitter, though. Some kid says they saw the whole thing – tweet was like "it's fucking mad just saw a car drive up on the pavement straight at some random guy". I can show you it on my phone, if you like.'

'I'll take your word for it,' said Gethin. 'They didn't film it, did they?'

'Nah,' said Lee. 'Sounds like it happened too quickly for that.'

'You any idea exactly where he was or what he was doing?'

'Not exactly. He was out Fishponds way, apparently. But I did speak to him earlier, before it happened.'

'What did he say?'

'Said he'd been to see Shaun, you know, Izma's old spar, and it went okay and he was following up a lead.'

'He didn't say what?'

''Fraid not, said he'd tell me about it later. Sounded like he was just arriving at wherever it was.'

'And that was when?'

'Around one, I checked on my phone.'

'And the car hit him when?'

'Just after two.'

'So, it looks like he went to see this lead, whoever it was, and just after he left someone tried to run him down.'

'Seems that way.'

'Did he sound scared at all, when you spoke to him?'

'Nah, just normal Deano, you know?'

'Christ, what a fuck-up. Do you think we'll be able to talk to him today?'

Lee shrugged. 'Dunno. I asked one of the doctors, but they were too busy and I'm not a relative or anything. You could try asking his mum, though.'

'What? Deano's mum's here?' Gethin looked round the waiting room trying and failing to see any sign of her. Lynn, her name was. He'd only met her once or twice but there was no one in remotely the right gender and age bracket to be seen.

'She's just gone to the lav. In a right state, as you might imagine.'

They fell quiet and, sure enough, a minute or two later the waiting room door opened and in came Lynn. Gethin remembered her as a lively woman with dyed blonde hair, cut in that slightly spiky short style much favoured by her generation of Cardiffians. She still looked the same, but the liveliness was dialled right down to zero by shock. Lee promptly took her arm and seated her on a peeling red sofa.

'Thanks, love.' Lynn took a deep breath: 'I spoke to the doc.'

'Yeah?'

'He says they're operating now. He's two broken legs and some broken ribs and they think he's punctured a lung, but what they're doing now is removing his spleen.' She started to cry then forced herself to stop. 'How bad is that, do you know? Is it important? Does it mean he's going to have to have a bag or something? He couldn't bear that.' Her voice was going high and hysterical. Lee stroked her arm and tried to calm her down while Gethin did what you do in these situations in the modern world and started frantically googling 'spleen removal'.

'Hey,' he said, having speed read the NHS summary, 'it's not too bad. Looks like you can carry on as normal without it.'

'Oh, thank God,' said Lynn.

'In fact, you're less likely to have certain cancers if you don't have it, it says here, but you are more likely to have infections and stuff, so you may have to take regular antibiotics.' He carried on scrolling down. 'But it is definitely a good job they're removing it if it's damaged, cos otherwise...' he tailed off.

'Otherwise what?'

'Well, you know, it could have been bad news.'

'Oh, dear God.'

'Well, the good news is it sounds like a pretty routine operation, I'm sure he'll be all right.' Gethin stopped himself there. What on earth was he talking about? He'd googled spleen removal two minutes earlier and now he was some sort of expert surgeon. Time to shut up.

Queueing up in Costa for three lattes, Gethin tried to make sense of what had happened. It certainly looked like Deano blundered right into the middle of something. Hopefully, when he came round from the operation, he'd be able to tell them who he'd been to see that lunchtime, what this lead was that Shaun had put him on to.

The business with Deano made him think how lucky he'd been the night before, how easily it could have ended in disaster – losing his money then stumbling back out to the car to fetch his bank card to lose a lot more money – he knew how that went, all right. Sure, better to lose money than your spleen, but even so. How could he have been such an idiot? It was weird – immediately after a gambling binge it all just seemed so obviously stupid and unappealing. And yet he knew that sometime in the future – maybe a few weeks, likely a few months, if he was really lucky a year or two – it would come creeping back. There'd be that inner voice telling him to take the risk, telling him he had to do it to feel alive.

He dismissed the train of thought. As of now, things were simple, he had transgressed but there was no harm done. Deano would be okay, and he would hand Gethin the evidence he needed to launch Izma's appeal and then everything would be fine.

Back upstairs, he distributed the coffees. There was still not much news from the ward. Lee had gone in to ask and they'd told her Deano was in the operating theatre and he'd be back up in due course, but probably not for a couple of hours as it took a while to come round from the general anaesthetic. They all went quiet again after that. Lynn looked like she was mouthing prayers to herself, Lee was doing the quick crossword in an old copy of the *Times* and Gethin was staring blankly at some property show on the telly when the door to the waiting room opened and in walked Amelia Laverne.

As ever, she was swathed in expensively drab knitwear and, while she wasn't wearing a hat, she had her hair up in a sort of old-fashioned schoolteacher-type bun. But where she was normally – in Gethin's limited experience – quite deliberately low-key, this afternoon she was obviously buzzing with excitement.

'Hi Gethin,' she said. 'I'm so sorry about all this. I came as soon as I could.'

'Right,' said Gethin. How the hell had Amelia found out about Deano? And how had she reached the hospital so fast? 'Were you in the area or something?'

'I'm still at the Marriott,' said Amelia, 'I wanted to reconnect with Bristol, I suppose. Anyway, please, this isn't about me.' She turned towards Lee. 'Are you a relative?'

Gethin stepped in. 'This is my colleague, Lee Ranger; she's working on the case with me. And this is Deano's mother, Lynn. Lee, Lynn, this is Amelia Laverne.'

Lee was cool enough, just stuck out her hand to shake and said, 'pleased to meet you.'

Lynn, though, was a mess. She just stood there for a moment, looking stunned. 'Oh my God,' she said finally. 'You've come to see Deano. Thank you so much.' Like Amelia was the Queen doing her hospital rounds or something.

Amelia didn't seem too phased, though. She was doubtless used to this sort of thing. She stepped forward and put her hand on Lynn's arm. 'I'm so sorry to hear about Dean. Is there any news?'

'He's in surgery,' said Gethin. 'We should hear more soon. Thanks for coming, Amelia, but how did you know...'

'Oh, your lovely Rebecca told me. I called your office to see how the visit to Izma had gone and Rebecca told me what had happened, so of course I had to come. I mean, I feel somewhat responsible, having brought you into this investigation. It is something to do with the investigation, what's happened to Dean, isn't it?'

'That's the hypothesis we're working on for the moment,' said Gethin, horribly aware that he was talking like a TV copper.

'I talked to him just before it happened,' said Lee, thankfully sounding like herself. 'He was off to follow up a lead, then an hour later he is run down. Seems pretty clear to me.'

'Oh my God,' said Lynn. 'Do you think he might still be in danger if they find out that... you know...'

Before Gethin could come up with a reassuring answer, the door opened and a doctor came in.

'Mrs Wright,' he said to Lynn, 'do you want to step out here?' He waved towards the corridor. 'I have some news for you.'

'Oh, Christ.' Lynn followed the doctor outside.

Gethin, Lee and Amelia stared at each other, then at the floor, for an interminable couple of minutes before Lynn

104

came back.

'Thank God,' she said. 'The operation's been a success. They've taken out his spleen before it could do any damage and they set his ribs back and fixed his legs, I dunno, pinned the femurs or something, but he's okay. He's going to be okay. Oh God, I'm sorry.' She slumped down on to the sofa and started crying, her head in her hands.

Lee sat next to her and put her arm around her shoulders.

'That's great news,' said Amelia.

'Yeah,' said Gethin, doing his best to fight a feeling of dizziness. What on earth did Amelia think she was doing, turning up like this? It was a difficult enough situation without everyone having to work out how to relate to the film star in the room. He would have asked her to leave if it wasn't for the fact that she was effectively his boss, the person paying his wages.

He turned to Lynn, who had stopped crying. 'Did the doctor say when Deano would be back on the ward or whatever?'

Lynn made a visible effort to pull herself together, gently removed Lee's consoling arm from her shoulder and straightened her glasses. 'Well, he said Dean should come round from the anaesthetic pretty soon, but he'd still be quite woozy for a bit and they'll have him on morphine for the pain. He should be back on the ward in a couple of hours and they said it was okay for me to sit with him, but I don't know about you all...'

'Course not.' Lee stood up. 'Tell you what, I'll go and have another word with reception there, but I shouldn't think there's much chance of the rest of us seeing Deano till tomorrow morning.'

Lee headed down the corridor and, somewhat to Gethin's horror, Lynn took the chance to thank Amelia profusely for coming to the hospital and then started telling her what a wonderful actress she was and how much she loved *Mary's Prayer* when she was a teenager. Gethin could see Amelia wince slightly at this, not least at the realisation that she was older than Deano's mum. Thankfully, Lee was back quickly and reported that the receptionist had said there was absolutely no way anyone would be visiting Deano that night, apart from immediate family.

'So,' she said to Gethin, 'why don't you go home and come back in the morning? I'll stay here with Lynn till her sister arrives.' She turned to Amelia then. 'Thanks for coming, love. I'm sure everyone appreciated it.'

Once they'd made it through the gauntlet of the inevitable mini shopping mall that every hospital has these days, and were breathing the marginally fresher air of Upper Maudlin Street, Gethin found himself feeling honour bound to ask Amelia if she'd like a lift to her hotel.

Little to his surprise, she agreed and, after he'd spent fifteen minutes accomplishing a journey that could have been walked in substantially less time, she insisted that he park in the extortionately expensive car park and join her for an early supper.

He called home. Catriona wasn't back yet but Hattie was there, and he told her he'd be late because he was having dinner with Amelia. Hattie was excited and said it wasn't fair that she hadn't met her yet, and Gethin laughed and then Hattie said, 'Mum will be sooo jealous' and Gethin felt momentarily paranoid, before realising all she meant was Catriona was another big Amelia fan. He called Cat's mobile next. It went straight to voicemail, so he left a garbled message explaining that something bad had happened to Deano and he was just having dinner with Amelia Laverne. After he hung up, he thought again how weird it was that having dinner with a star seemed like a more important and remarkable piece of news than someone being deliberately run down by a car.

Over dinner – salad for her, pasta for him, mineral water for both of them, which at least meant the bill wouldn't be too bad – they discussed the case. Gethin explained that the one positive side of what had happened to Deano was that he had clearly flushed out a bad guy which did, on the face of it, tend to back up the theory that Izma had not murdered Hannah, that the actual killer was still out there somewhere. Amelia looked properly excited by this development, but the thing she really seemed keen to talk about was Gethin's prison visit. She was eager for every detail Gethin could recall with regard to Izma. How long was his hair? What was he wearing? Was he very thin? Did he have an aura about him? In particular, she wanted to know if he'd said anything about his childhood. Gethin had to disappoint her on that question. He hadn't been there to conduct a general interview, he'd been focusing on the matter in hand, appealing against the murder conviction. Anyway, surely if she wanted to know about Izma's childhood, all she had to do was read his book.

'Do you think I could come with you next time?' Amelia asked, once she'd exhausted Gethin's stock of memories of Izma.

Gethin had been half expecting this and did his best to kick the problem down the road. 'Depends,' he said. 'If we can obtain enough VOs, no problem, but if it's like the last time I could only have the one, so I can't promise anything...'

Amelia reached across the table and took his hand. 'Please try,' she said, 'it would really mean a lot to me.'

'Of course.' Gethin gently extricated his hand, the

thought occurring to him that Amelia was obsessed with Izma M in a kind of mirror image of the way people were obsessed with her.

The meal over, Amelia insisted on ordering a coffee for Gethin to perk him up for the drive back. While they waited for it to arrive, she sat back in her chair and looked down at her hands before raising her head and asking Gethin: 'Have you ever made a really, really terrible mistake?'

For a moment, Gethin thought she must somehow have found out about his gambling relapse, but there was something darker, sadder in her tone than that. He thought about telling her about it anyway – 'help me, I'm a degenerate gambler' – but decided against it. Instead, he thought back quickly over his life. What were the really bad mistakes? Probably being arrested when he was young and screwing up his chance of being a lawyer. But he felt he had found his own way in life thanks to his youthful recklessness, had avoided living his life permanently in the shadow of his dad. Finally, he shook his head.

'No,' he said, waiting for his nose to go the full Pinocchio, 'I don't think I have. Lots of small mistakes, but no big ones that I haven't learned something from.'

Amelia sighed. 'Good for you. But I'm not talking about work, I'm talking about something more important than that, much more important...' she tailed off, looking on the verge of tears; real tears, not actress tears.

Gethin waited a while, then said gently. 'Do you want to talk about it?'

Amelia Laverne stared at him, then lowered her eyes. 'No,' she said, 'not yet. Maybe soon. Maybe I'll have to tell you soon.'

Twelve

GETHIN DECIDED TO MAKE A detour on his way out of Bristol. There was a jewellery shop in Clifton village that he knew Cat liked. And when he spotted a parking place right outside, he figured this was a plan that was meant to be. So he went in and looked around and eventually settled on a pair of silver and jade earrings that he thought she'd really like. The jade wasn't bright green and industrial-looking but pale and delicate and the silver work was intricate and just very Cat. A hundred and fifty quid was a lot of money to spend on an impulse buy but what better way of using his winnings, gaining some lasting benefit from what he could now see was a moment of madness. And much better that the money should go on Cat than on himself. There was no way he should be rewarding himself for such utter foolishness.

He was a little nervous when he handed the earrings over after dinner. Jewellery was never the easiest thing to get right but Cat's eyes lit up as soon as she saw them. She put them on and Hattie agreed that they looked lovely on her. It was only later, as they were preparing for bed, that Gethin caught her staring at him, her mouth a thin, worried line. And when they went to bed there was no gratitude-inspired sex, just a murmured 'Sorry love, I'm exhausted'. Not that Gethin minded too much: he was shattered too, and the next day was going to have another early start.

He made it back to the hospital just after nine, following a gruelling rush hour drive. He was, as predicted, thoroughly sick of the Cardiff-Bristol commute, though he'd lessened the suffering by listening to a new album from a Scottish sort-of folksinger called James Yorkston, which he was enjoying despite the bleakness of some of the subject matter. Funny thing with sad songs: sometimes, as you'd expect, they made you sad; other times, and this was one of them, they provided comfort. One of the songs was about visiting a friend in hospital, which seemed oddly prescient as Gethin pulled into the BRI car park.

Lee was waiting for him at the Costa, as agreed. She'd ended up staying over in Bristol the night before, providing support for Lynn and her sister Mags. She'd called Gethin around ten to let him know that Deano was recovering well after the op.

Gethin grabbed a coffee and a croissant and came over to join her.

'How's the patient?'

'Good, apparently.'

'Have you spoken to him?'

'Not yet. Lynn's been in a couple of times really quickly, but they're not letting visitors in till after the ward round. Probably be about ten. But yeah, he seems to be doing fine.'

'Thank God for that.'

'Could have been, well, could have been a lot worse...' she leaned forward then: 'Have a bit of news for you, Geth, forgot to tell you with everything kicking off last night.'

'Oh, yeah?'

'I have a name for the mysterious Danny. I spoke to Molly, you know from the bike café, the other night.'

'What, you went over to Bristol?'

'On the phone, she called me up.'

'Oh, yeah?' Gethin raised his eyebrows.

Lee kicked him under the table. 'Nothing like that. She just wants to help with the investigation. She feels really guilty about what happened.'

'So she called you?'

'I'm the friendly face of Last Resort Legals, aren't I? Sensitive young woman like that, she's not going to want to talk to a grumpy old git like you.'

'Yeah, yeah. So, do tell, what did this attractive lesbian have to say for herself?'

Lee kicked him again but couldn't stop a smile from spreading across her face. 'She said she'd been thinking hard about what Hannah had said to her about this ex-boyfriend, and she'd woken up a couple of days ago and suddenly remembered his name. It's Bliss. Danny Bliss.'

'Great. It's quite an unusual name too. Have you checked him out yet?'

'I was just about to when all this happened.' She waved her hand in the general direction of the ward. 'I told Deano as well. I'd just heard from Molly, so I suggested he asked Shaun if he knew anything about this Danny Bliss. Then Deano called me back a little bit later to say that Shaun blanked on the name but he was going off on this other lead.'

'I'll give Bex a bell now, put her on the case looking for Danny Bliss. What do we know about him?'

'North London like Hannah, that's what Molly thought. And probably about the same age, so mid-30s now.'

When they finally went in to see Deano, he was an awful grey colour, covered in bandages and attached to God knows how many drips. Gethin found himself choking back tears when he saw him. Deano wasn't quite young enough to be his son, but he wasn't far off and Gethin felt a wave of something powerful wash over him, a mix of guilt, responsibility and care.

Deano managed a wave and a feeble approximation of a grin as they approached the bed. Lee reached there first, leaned in and kissed him on the cheek.

'Fucking hell, Deano, I wouldn't like to see the state of the other guy.'

The smallest of smiles: 'The other guy was a car.'

As Lee turned towards Gethin, he could see the tears in her eyes.

Gethin walked forward, awkwardly tapped Deano on the shoulder, which looked to be the least damaged bit of him on show.

'Arright, boss?'

'Christ, Deano, what the fuck happened?'

'Can't talk here, boss. Not safe.'

Gethin stared at him. Was this some kind of brain injury going on? No one had mentioned anything like that but... 'Sorry, mate, what d'you mean?'

Deano grimaced and said something in an inaudible whisper. Gethin leaned in close.

'He was here, boss, right here in the ward. I saw him.'

'Sorry Dean, who're you talking about?'

'The cop, ex-cop, the one I went to see, Malcom Haynes. He was here, mate, I saw him.'

'Is this the guy you went to see after Shaun?'

Deano's eyes widened with panic. 'Shh,' he said.

Gethin leaned back in and whispered. 'Are you saying you went to see an ex-cop called Malcolm Haynes? You had some sort of lead?'

Deano nodded.

'And you saw this Haynes in the hospital this morning?'

'Yeah,' said Deano, talking with obvious difficulty now. 'He came in with the cops.'

'You sure?'

Deano nodded. His eyes were closing now, probably the morphine kicking in.

'Was it him who ran you down?'

'Dunno boss, sorry. It was so fast. But...'

'Yeah?'

'Be careful.'

'Course,' said Gethin. 'Don't worry, Deano, you're safe here.'

Deano didn't answer. He had drifted all the way into sleep.

* * *

Back down at ground level, having yet another coffee in a café over the road from the hospital, Gethin and Lee discussed what Deano had told them. Lee started googling 'Malcolm Haynes Bristol' and Gethin peered over her shoulder as she scrolled through the results, before clicking on a link to a private security company. Lee clicked through to the 'About us' page and found a picture of the boss. This particular Malcolm Haynes was a middle-aged bloke in a blazer with thinning blonde curly hair and a reddish face – looked like a career boozer keeping it more or less under control. His biography referred to his fifteen years' service with the Avon and Somerset Constabulary.

'Bingo,' said Gethin.

'Yeah,' said Lee. 'Looks like a right cunt, pardon my French.'

'So what do we reckon? That Haynes knew something about the original case. Do you remember seeing his name in the court papers?'

'Don't think so. Didn't testify at the trial, anyway.'

'I don't remember him either. Do you think Deano really saw him in the hospital?'

'Could be,' said Lee. 'Fucking coppers, you know what they're like.'

'But what would the purpose be? It could only attract suspicion if he was the one who ran Deano over.'

'Maybe a warning. Just letting him know he can reach him any time.'

Gethin pondered that. It was an ugly thought, but ugly the way life was.

His phone rang. Bex.

'What's up?'

'Is Lee with you?'

'Yeah.'

'Her phone's going straight to voicemail. I'm going nowhere with this Danny Bliss and I just wanted to check I had the name right?'

Gethin waved at Lee to attract her attention: 'Hannah's old boyfriend – the name is Danny Bliss right? B-L-I-S-S, yeah? Bex is having trouble finding him.'

'Far as I know, boss. How else are you going to spell Bliss?'

Gethin put his phone back to his ear. 'You hear that?'

'Yeah,' said Bex. 'I tried a few different spellings anyway but had no luck. It's weird, Geth, the only Danny Blisses I can find are either children or over 50. Or else they're either American or Nigerian. He's not a Nigerian, is he, the guy we're looking for?'

'Meant to be North London Jewish, I think.'

'That's what Lee said, and I've looked all over and there's no sign. Not on the electoral register anywhere in Britain, not paying bills, nothing on Facebook, not even on bastard LinkedIn.'

'Weird. You think he might have emigrated or something?'

'Possibly, though people who do that are likely to be on Facebook. Unless they're hiding.'

Gethin felt a flicker of excitement. Maybe Danny Bliss's invisibility was a good sign. If the guy had gone off grid it could be because he had something to hide. Like murdering his ex-girlfriend.

'Bex, have you checked birth records for the relevant period?' He paused, did some sums: 'say, 1975 to 1985, just to be on the safe side.'

Lee started signalling to him to come off the phone so he ended the call and turned to her.

'Have to go over to the hospital, boss. Police are talking to Lynn and she wants us there.'

They found Lynn in the visitors' room on Deano's ward. She was on a sofa facing two coppers, a man and a woman, seated on chairs. She did not look happy.

'Thanks for coming,' she said. 'These two are trying to tell me that this is all some drugs thing. They're saying Deano was a drug dealer. I tried to explain but they won't listen.'

The male copper stood up and looked Gethin and Lee up and down. 'Who are you then?'

'I'm Gethin Grey from Last Resort Legals and this is my associate, Lee Ranger. Dean is an investigator working for us on a case.'

The copper stared at them, making no effort to suggest he felt they deserved even the slightest degree of respect.

'If you say so,' he said. 'Well, as Mrs Wright says, we're looking into the incident. And given Dean's own record and the history of the person he claims to have been visiting, Shaun Lindo, I have to say that we are indeed investigating the possibility that it might be drug related.'

'Oh for God's sake, I just told you that Dean is working on a case. He went to see Shaun because he's a key witness.'

The cops looked at each other, exchanging knowing smiles. 'Oh, of course, Izma M. You're digging into that old bollocks. Bloke's as guilty as they come. Though I don't expect you'd mind about that. You're probably gaining a decent whack to dig through all that ancient horseshit and find there's nothing there, just like everyone else has.'

'Ker-ching.'

That was the female half of the double act. Gethin took a breath and willed himself not to rise to it.

'Okay,' he said. 'Let's set aside what you think Dean's motivation might have been, and stick to the known facts. We are in agreement that he was deliberately run over, yes?'

The male cop grunted some sort of agreement.

'Right, so do you have the number of the car that hit him? You must have CCTV all over the area.'

'Yes we have the number.'

'So who does it belong to?' said Lee, once it became clear that the copper had no interest in saying any more.

'Stolen,' said the female copper, like she didn't want to be left out. 'It was taken from a second-hand car lot yesterday morning.'

'Okay,' said Gethin, 'and do you have any idea who stole it? Second hand car lot, there's bound to be some security footage.'

'Unfortunately not, the car was parked in a camera blind spot, apparently.'

Another long pause and then the copper decided she'd had enough fun and carried on. 'We've found the car, though, last night. It was abandoned in Fishponds. There are signs of the collision, but whoever stole it had wiped it down so there are no fingerprints, far as we can see.'

'And you think this is just some sort of drug dealing vendetta?'

Male copper took up the baton. 'No sir, we just suggested that this was a possibility given the police records of the parties involved. However, bearing in mind what you've now told us, we will, of course, consider the possibility that this attack was in some way related to your investigation. Though I must say I find it hard to see why it would be in anyone's interest to attack someone working on a ten-year-old crime investigation. Especially one in which the identity of the murderer had already been established beyond reasonable doubt.'

Gethin had had about enough of this. Without thinking, he took a step closer to the male copper. 'Really pleased to be in the presence of the great detective, the all-seeing eye. You're like bloody Santa Claus – you know who's been naughty and who's been nice, don't you, DC...? You didn't say your name, did you?'

The copper just smirked at this, obviously pleased with himself for winding Gethin up to this extent. 'DS actually, DS Khan, and likewise, it's always a pleasure to meet another ambulance chaser.'

Gethin was right on the point of losing it, all the frustrations of the last few days – the gambling debacle, Deano in the hospital – about to boil over, when Lee stepped in.

'Hey, darlin,' she said to the female copper. 'Why don't you and me have a nice sensible chat before these boys have to find a room so they can explore their unresolved tensions?'

The copper couldn't restrain a bit of a smirk at this. Lee carried on: 'We don't want to take up any more of your time, but we would just like to know one thing. Have you interviewed Malcolm Haynes about this?'

The female copper looked quickly at DS Khan, received no response. 'Who's that?'

'The feller Dean had been to see immediately before he was run over. Runs a security company out there in Fishponds. You probably know him.'

The cops looked at each other again. 'Doesn't ring a bell,' said DS Khan.

'It ought to,' said Lee. 'He used to be one of yours.'

Khan made a show of thinking hard and then looking surprised. 'Oh yeah, Mal Haynes. Don't know him but I've heard the name.'

'Yeah well, maybe it's time you put a face to the name, cause we may not be highly trained police investigators but it seems pretty strange that Dean should have gone to ask this gent some questions, then ten minutes later...'

'Fine,' said the copper. 'We'll look into it.'

Half an hour later, Gethin and Lee were climbing up the hill from the Infirmary towards Kingsdown, in search of Shaun Lindo. They'd discussed going to see Malcolm Haynes first, but decided that without knowing what Shaun had told Deano there wouldn't be much point. On the other hand, if this Shaun had been behind the attack on Deano, they were taking a bit of a risk going to see him at all. As they walked, they debated strategy.

'Probably best if I go in on my own,' said Gethin. 'Just in case, you know?'

'My hero. Appreciate it, Geth, but I reckon it's probably best the other way round. You going to see a guy like this, he isn't going to give you anything. Middle-class white bloke comes round his yard, he's going to keep schtum at best, chase you out with a shotgun at worst. Ghetto girl like me, though. I knows how to talk to the natives, like.'

Gethin wasn't happy at the idea. Partly he worried about

Lee. Partly he felt like putting himself in danger as penance for his stupidity the other night, but he had to admit she had a point. They came up with a plan: Gethin would call Lee's phone before she went in and she'd keep the phone on in her pocket so he could hear everything that went on. If it sounded like she was in trouble, he could pile in there or call the police.

It was only when they arrived at Shaun's address, the one Deano had left with Bex the other morning, that Gethin realised he'd been there before.

'This is Izma's old place. Shaun must've been living here the whole time.'

They carried on walking past the house till they came to a little corner pub with a couple of tables outside. Gethin went in and bought an orange juice and then sat down outside, with a clear view of the house. He called Lee's phone and she answered and put it carefully in the inside pocket of her jacket, before heading over the road.

Gethin watched as Lee knocked on the door. He wasn't expecting her to have any more luck then he'd had when he came by with Amelia. But he was wrong. Seconds after she knocked the door opened and Lee went straight in. Gethin put his phone to his ear, trying to look casual, as if he was having a conversation, not eavesdropping.

'Wasn't expecting you for another half an hour,' said a voice: male, black, Bristolian.

'No worries,' said Lee.

'Yeah, it's cool, I needed to go anyway. Little bastard's up here.'

Gethin heard footsteps climbing the stairs.

'Cheers for this. Connor's in there doing some drawing. Only be out for a couple of hours. Appreciate it, yeah?'

'Scuse me,' Lee's voice now. 'Who do you think I am?'

'You're the childminder, Aimee's friend. I just called you to look after Connor for a bit.'

'I ain't no babysitter.'

'What? Who the fuck are you then?'

The voice was aggressive now and Gethin felt himself tensing.

'My turn first, bra.' Lee sounded completely unruffled. 'You're Shaun Lindo yeah?' A pause. 'Don't bother pretending you're not.'

'Fine. Who the fuck are you?'

'I'm Lee and I'm here to find out what you said to my colleague yesterday?'

'Who's that then?' The voice now mixing hostile with baffled.

'Deano. He was probably wearing a stupid hat, asking about Izma M.'

'Oh right, so you're a legal investigator as well? You don't look like one.'

'Yeah, I understand, you think I look like a childminder. Have to say you're not much of a judge of character. You ever see that show where you have to guess what someone does for a living? You would have been shit at it, mate.'

'You come in my yard and insult me, some fucking nerve.'

'You invited me in and if you want to be rid of me, fine, just tell me what you told Deano. You sent him to see an ex-copper called Malcolm Haynes, is that right?'

'That's right,' said Shaun, 'so what's the problem? Something happen to your mate?'

Gethin was straining to hear whether Shaun sounded like he was playing the innocent but without seeing his face, and hearing his voice distorted by the lining of Lee's jacket, he didn't have a clue. He'd ask Lee afterwards, see what she reckoned.

'You could say that. He's in the hospital, bra. Someone ran him over. Just after he went to see your mate Mal.'

'He's not my mate, just a dirty fucking copper, that's what I told your guy, the cat in the hat.'

'So what's he have to do with Izma?'

'What d'you think, sistah? He's the cop fitted Izma up for the murder.'

'You know that for sure?'

'Can't prove it. But I have one question for you, one question you can ask Malcolm Haynes if you've the bottle, cause he is not a very nice man. Ask him where Izma bought that gun.'

Gethin was so focused on listening to the conversation that he didn't notice the woman approaching Shaun's front door till she was right there, giving it a knock. It was disorientating to simultaneously hear it through the phone.

'Okay, sistah,' said Shaun. 'That'll be the real childminder, so if you don't mind this man has things to do. Give my regards to big Mal.'

When Lee came out, she carried on walking straight past Gethin and into the pub, giving no indication they knew each other. Gethin waited for a bit, drank some of his orange juice, then headed inside, joining Lee at a table by the window with a good view back down the street.

'So what d'you reckon to brer Shaun?'

'Dunno, couldn't get a handle on him. Did you hear how his accent kept changing? Like he's not sure who he is or who he's meant to be. That's what I felt. And his house, it's not like what you'd expect at all. It's all super neat and tidy, with a fancy kitchen, new white leather sofas and stuff. Christ, Geth, there was a coffee table with a copy of the *Daily Mail* on it.'

'Weird,' said Gethin, trying and failing to make much

sense of this information. He'd met quite a few villains in his line of work, but not too many house proud ones. 'And the stuff about the copper, Haynes?'

'Dunno, could be kosher or could be sending us on a wild goose chase. Only one way to find out, though. Oh hang on, here comes Shaun now. You have a look, Geth.'

Lee drew back from the window, allowing Gethin to lean forward and gain a decent view of the street. A tall, light-skinned black guy was walking towards him; looked a bit like the ex-footballer Stan Collymore. As he approached the pub, Gethin jerked his head back. It looked as if Shaun might be heading in, but he only stopped to say a quick hello to somebody outside before strolling on down the road, then stopping next to a silver Mercedes.

'Nice motor,' said Lee.

'Looks like he's doing well for himself.'

'Doesn't it? You think we should follow him, boss?'

'Might be a bit tricky on foot. The car's in the car park, remember?'

'Oh yeah, bollocks.'

Thirteen

IT WAS FOUR O'CLOCK BY the time Gethin and Lee made it back to the office. They'd driven out to Fishponds to have an initial recce of Malcolm Haynes' office, which turned out to be a unit on a little trading estate off Lodge Causeway but appeared to be firmly closed for the afternoon. A final visit to the hospital – Deano was asleep but doing well, by all accounts – before the drive back through snarled up traffic around Newport.

Bex made both a cup of tea and quizzed them about Deano's health, before giving them her own news.

'You know you suggested I had a check through the birth records?'

'Yeah.'

'Well, guess what I found? A North London Jewish boy called Daniel Bliss born in 1980 – have a look at this.'

Bex handed Gethin a printout of a birth certificate. It was in the name of Daniel Leonard Bliss. The year was indeed 1980. The birthplace was the Whittington Hospital in London. Gethin knew it. He'd been there once, to the A& E department, half a lifetime ago and in somewhat traumatic circumstances. The parents were named as Leonard and Sarah Bliss and the mother's maiden name was Fineberg. It didn't explicitly say that Daniel Bliss was Jewish, but it looked likely.

'Great,' said Gethin, handing it back to Bex. 'Any joy tracking him down?'

'Well, yes and no,' said Bex, grinning. 'I found him eventually, but you have a look at this and you'll see what the problem was.'

Bex handed them copies of another printout, a newspaper story by the look of it. The story came from the *Daily Mail* and bore the headline 'North London family killed in boating disaster'. Gethin scanned it quickly. Apparently, three members of the same family had all perished at sea, just off the coast of Northern Cyprus. The three were 58-year-old businessman Leonard Bliss, his 49-year-old wife Sally, and his 21-year-old son Daniel. There had been an explosion on the boat, a yacht called *Just a Gigolo*. Initial reports from the local investigators suggested a faulty stove may have been to blame. Foul play was apparently not suspected.

'What's the date on that?' Lee asked, once she had got the gist.

'18th August 2001,' said Gethin.

'But that's four years before Hannah was murdered...'

'Weird, isn't it?' said Bex. 'I went back through all the birth records, five years in each direction just in case, but this is the only Daniel Bliss born in North London during this time frame.'

Gethin frowned: 'Was Molly sure about the name?' he asked Lee.

'Pretty sure.'

'Well, how about you return to her and double check? And find out everything she can remember about what Hannah said. Try and make sure it wasn't someone who just looked like her old boyfriend.'

'Okay boss, I'll give her a call now.' Lee slid out of the office.

'Make any sense to you, Bex, this business?'

'None at all. I wondered for a bit if he could have faked it all, but I read a few more stories and it seemed pretty clear. The boat really did blow up, there were witnesses and – this is gross – some bits and pieces of the bodies showed up.'

'Bits of bodies?'

'Like a thigh and a foot still in a shoe and a wallet and bits of clothing.'

'Jesus!'

'Told you. And there's witnesses saw all three of them go on the boat so...'

'But it's weird that there's this sighting four years later. You'd have thought she knew what he looked like.'

'Exactly.' Bex paused, as she thought of something. 'Unless maybe he was born abroad, or something?'

'Maybe. Is there a photo?'

'Not that I saw. Just the mum and dad in all the stories I've read, but I could dig around.'

'That'll be great, Bex. If we could show it to Hannah's friends in Bristol we could definitely rule out the possibility that this Danny Bliss had somehow come back from the dead. The old flatmate would be good, if she's around.'

'Fine, Geth, I'll look into it. But, to be honest, it seems like it would be more useful looking into the copper, the cunt who ran over Deano.'

'We don't know he did.'

'Fair enough. But looks likely, doesn't it?'

Gethin grunted his agreement, then checked his emails. Two of them immediately attracted his attention. One from Amelia Laverne and another from her PA. Gethin checked that one first and gave a sigh of relief when he saw it was just confirming that a payment of £3000 had been made into the Last Resort account to cover the first week's fees. The email from Amelia herself was less satisfactory. She was pushing hard for a trip to Gartree to see Izma M. She'd been in touch with the lawyers and, apparently, they'd said she could use a visit they already had booked for that Friday. Oh joy, thought Gethin, a Friday spent on the motorways of the Midlands with Amelia Laverne. Still, in the circs, it was best to keep her sweet.

* * *

Hattie had a face like thunder when she climbed into the car, clutching her school bag and flute case. She slammed the door and only put her seatbelt on when Gethin made it clear, via the medium of mime, that it was a precondition for making the car move. She refused to laugh at his mugging and waited till they were halfway home before deigning to speak at all.

'I want to drop the flute.'

'Why's that, love?'

'Because it's a stupid instrument.'

Privately, Gethin had to agree. The only reason they'd picked the flute for Hattie to play years earlier was that the ever-practical Cat had favoured its extreme portability. Still, he knew that he should at least try to stick to the approved parental script.

'It's not stupid. It's just an instrument. It's only the music that can be stupid or not stupid. And besides, you're good at it.'

This was half true. Sometimes Hattie was good at it; lately, though, she seemed to be getting worse to an extent that Gethin figured had to be deliberate.

'No, I am not. I'm still only on grade two and my teacher said she was not going to put me up for grade three after all. So face it. I'm no good at it and I want to quit and do something that's actually interesting with my time.'

'I don't think your mum is going to be very pleased about that.'

'Oh, sad! Why do you always have to agree with mum about everything? Can't you have an opinion of your own for once? You know the flute's a stupid instrument.'

'I dunno,' said Gethin. 'You've seen *Anchorman*...'

'Exactly. It's a joke instrument. It's funny when some middle-aged bloke plays jazz flute in a comedy film. It isn't funny when a twelve-year-old girl plays it. It's embarrassing.'

'What d'you mean embarrassing?'

Hattie didn't say anything and when Gethin turned to look at her she'd gone bright red.

'Nothing,' she said. 'It's just stupid and I want to give it up.'

'Okay, love, I'll have a word with your mum later on.'

They were almost home now. On arrival Hattie headed for her room to do her homework and message her friends and Gethin took a bottle of Brewdog's so-called Punk IPA from the fridge. He found the company's marketing fantastically irritating. In what sense is a bottle of beer punk? Because it's made by an aggressively expansionist Scottish brewery apparently. On the other hand, it was far and away the best tasting bottle of beer available from his local mini supermarket, so he just had to suck up the PR. He pretty much sucked up the beer too and was just thinking about opening another one when he heard Cat's car pulling into the garage. He dropped the empty bottle into the recycling and repressed an urge to wash his mouth out so Cat wouldn't smell anything.

Cat seemed preoccupied when she came in. Gave him a quick peck on the cheek and didn't say anything about the beer. She asked a couple of form questions about Deano but, once she'd established he wasn't at death's door, she soon lost interest and headed off to her study, saying she had some files to go through before dinner.

'Fine,' said Gethin. 'I'll have a beer and do a bit of research.'

No flicker from Cat. Work was obviously piling up on her. Gethin took his drink and his laptop out on to the terrace, the late September sun still hanging in there. He spent half an hour googling Malcolm Haynes without finding any fresh revelations. He was a typical ex-copper running a security company. Someone on yelp.com claimed they had been overcharged by him, but no big deal. There was nothing to suggest that Haynes was actively dirty.

Gethin sat back in his chair, tried to think it through. Shaun had suggested Malcolm Haynes supplied the gun that Izma had been arrested with, the crucial piece of evidence that had surely swung the jury against him. What Shaun hadn't specified was why. Gethin could guess, though. If Haynes had been a dirty copper at the time, he could easily have been involved in whatever drug dealing Izma and Shaun were up to. One thing was for sure he would have to be very careful indeed when it came to approaching Haynes. With a bit of luck Deano would have a bit more info to add when he came to properly.

Dinner was pasta pesto cheered up by a salad that mostly came from the garden. Conversation revolved around Hattie's schoolwork. She was doing a project on the Industrial Revolution and Gethin dredged up a few, possibly shaky, facts about the iron industry in the South Wales Valleys, pointing out of the window to their right, explaining that there had been an iron mine there back in the eighteenth century. In fact, you could still go inside the tunnels and see the remains of the mines.

'Really,' said Hattie, 'wouldn't that be dangerous?'

'Yeah,' said Gethin, feeling that occasional flicker of sadness that he didn't have a boy child who might be excited at the possibility of hidden tunnels into a mountain, rather than worried about the dangers. Though, of course, he knew that not all boys liked that sort of thing, blah, blah, blah...

Anyway, Hattie didn't really want to talk about the Industrial Revolution. What she wanted to talk about was media studies. She'd been asked to interview someone who worked in the media about their job. This might have been challenging for some schoolkids, but not those at Hattie's school, Gethin figured. Hattie went to the pick of the local comprehensives – notionally a church school but Cat had made short work of that – and there was no shortage of parents with jobs at the BBC, just up the road.

'Yeah,' said Hattie, 'so I was thinking it would be cool if I could interview Amelia Laverne. When are you seeing her again, Dad?'

He turned to Cat. 'Actually, I need to talk to you about that. Amelia is determined to go and see Izma for herself and she has it booked in for Friday, so I'll probably not be back till quite late.'

Cat frowned: 'That's a real nuisance, Gethin. I have to go to Cerys's hen night thing.'

It was Gethin's turn to look puzzled: 'Who's Cerys? You didn't mention...'

'You know Cerys. She works at the Hirwaun office, lots of blonde hair. I wasn't going to go to the hen, but then I saw her the other day and she seemed like she really wanted me to be there so... anyway, don't worry, I'll find a babysitter. Or maybe we can arrange a sleepover, love.'

'Cool,' said Hattie. 'Anyway, if I give you this' – she

129

handed Gethin a printout of some kind of questionnaire – 'can you ask Amelia to fill it out?'

Gethin submitted to the fait accompli: 'Okay love, I'll give it a go. No promises, mind.'

It was only when they were preparing for bed that Gethin broached the subject of Hattie's flute lessons: 'I really think she's had enough, you know?'

Cat just kept on removing her make-up in front of the dressing table mirror. 'Fine,' she said eventually. 'Why shouldn't she fuck up as well?'

'What do you mean?'

Cat turned to face him. 'You know, Geth. You know perfectly well.'

Gethin paused, desperately trying to decide whether this was a fishing trip which just needed a firm denial to make it go away or whether Cat somehow knew what had happened, in which case a denial would make a bad situation much, much worse.

Cat just shook her head and then bent down and picked up something from the dressing table, handing it to him.

It was the little box her earrings had come in.

'Take them back, Gethin.'

'Why?' he said, 'I thought you liked them.'

'Oh, I like them all right, Gethin, they're lovely. What's not lovely is that you paid for them with gambling money. That's what's happened, isn't it? You went out the other night and because you were feeling bad about lying to me and because, for once in your wretched life you must have won some money, you bought me these. I should have guessed straightaway. Any time your husband gives you an unexpected gift, it's because he has a guilty conscience. Basic rule of married life, that is.'

Gethin thought about denying it. Then, wisely, decided against it.

'Oh, Cat,' he said. 'I am so, so sorry.'

'You're sorry, Geth, of course you are. You're always fucking sorry. But this time, I can't believe it. I thought things were really better, you had this case, you and me the other night. I really thought, Gethin, I really thought. And then I'm doing the washing, emptying your pockets out, thinking about how close we are again, and out drops a gambling receipt...'

Gethin thought about protesting, about pointing out that he'd won and telling her he'd flushed it out of his system. But, even as the words were about to come out, he had the sickly remembrance of having said them so many times before. Better to shut up and take his medicine. He braced himself for a volley of abuse then looked up at his wife and was utterly disconcerted to see that she was crying. Cat hardly ever cried. He walked over to her, tried to put his arms around her, but she batted him away.

'You bastard,' she said. 'You useless fucking bastard.'

Kyrenia, Northern Cyprus
16 August 2001 11.05

Just after 11 o'clock next morning, Danny and his father were standing on their private dock waiting for Sally. The sun was already broiling hot and Danny was desperate to be out on the water – cool down, cold drink, all that. In the bright light of morning, the weirdness of last night seemed like a bad dream. The sea was impossibly blue and the boat was quite something – a forty-foot motor yacht called Just *A Gigolo* after Lenny's favourite song. Danny reckoned it cost his dad about four hundred grand and it was just like a big floating stretch limo with a cocktail bar on top. Sailing it or driving it or whatever was easy and fun. It didn't actually have any sails, but it did have a steering wheel and an accelerator, so driving seemed like the right word.

Ahmet, the cook-cum-gardener-cum-butler, was bustling about loading their stuff – food and booze mostly – on to the boat. And, thankfully, his dad looked tanned and relaxed, if a bit of a stereotype in his Hugo Boss yachting outfit. 'This is the life,' he said, and for once, Danny found himself hard pressed to disagree. He was doing his best to look smiley, ready to talk his dad into investing in his grand plan.

It was another fifteen minutes before Sally emerged from the villa. Danny was never sure whether she took so long fucking about with her make-up because she was too pissed to do it properly or because she enjoyed screwing his dad about. Half and half probably. His dad just stood there tapping on the steering wheel muttering about being married to Mata bleeding Hari. He often called her that. Danny wasn't exactly sure why, probably because she had a bit of an exotic look about her. She was like a proper Arab Jew, Sephardic was the word. He had a bit of that look himself, he liked to think.

Anyway, Mata bleeding Hari finally condescended to climb

aboard the boat and Ahmet helped them cast off and Lenny took the wheel and drove them out into the Med. When they were a quarter of a mile or so offshore, he let Danny take the wheel and they headed west. They were making for a particularly pretty bay about twenty miles away. It didn't take long and the gentle wind, the views and the sun seemed to brighten up everyone's mood. Lenny manoeuvred the boat into position for a particularly good view of the bay, then they dropped anchor and Sally started laying out the lunch.

Danny was pleased to see there was plenty of veggie stuff, cheese pies and houmous and salad. His mum poured out glasses of white wine and, for once, Danny joined in. He waited till they'd finished the food before launching into it. 'You know, Dad, I was talking last night about my idea...'

Lenny nodded and said, 'Yeah, tell me about it.'

His dad seemed to understand, just nodded to himself as Danny was talking, and then asked one simple question: 'So what do you need to make it happen?'

Danny told him: 'Ten grand, Dad, that would do it. For that, I can put out the first eight records – record them, press them and promote them. And that would be the first year taken care of and, by then, I'm certain I'd have made the money back, several times over, in fact.'

Lenny smiled. 'You reckon? Well, what do I know about this grime? I don't know anything, but I can see you do and if you want to give me a breakdown of the figures, the cost per record, the wholesale prices you'll be selling them at, all of that, then I think we might have a business, you and me. Fifty-fifty split okay with you?'

Danny blinked. It hadn't occurred to him that his dad would be a business partner not an investor. But, to his surprise, the notion didn't bother him. He smiled back and said, 'Yeah, that's fantastic, yeah.'

'Great,' said Lenny. 'Always good business putting out records by schwarzers. My cousin Morris did pretty well with that in the seventies, you know, the reggae music. None of them know how to read a contract. If they have a hit just buy them a car and they'll love you forever.'

'Schwarzers! Come on, Dad, it's 2001.'

'Oh, pardon me, politically correct, aren't we? Don't like to call a nigger a nigger.'

'For fuck's sake.' All Danny's good feeling was gone. 'It's not funny, Dad.' Feeling too angry to say anything else, he took his T-shirt off, walked over to the edge of the deck and dived off into the sea.

He was a good swimmer, Danny, and he dived under the waves, then let himself float up gently. He powered forward for another fifty yards before diving down again, waiting for his anger to subside. Maybe it didn't matter what his dad thought. He didn't mean anything by it anyway; it was just like him to say stuff like that to show what a hard man he was. Just showing off.

Danny kicked hard towards the light and resurfaced just in time to see his world change forever.

Fourteen

GETHIN WAS DRIVING TO SULLY, his back hurting from the sagging mattress in the spare room. In the course of a largely sleepless night, he had come up with the name of the one person he knew with connections in the upper echelons of the Bristol police force. Seeing the man in question was something he still never looked forward to, even after all these years, but he needed him to find out more about Malcolm Haynes, needed to talk to someone who could find out what kind of copper Haynes had been and exactly why he'd left the force prematurely.

So now he was driving down to Sully to see the Judge. His dad. His Honour Anthony Grey, the Judge. His old man, the bastard judge. The old bastard. It was months since he'd been down this way. Six months probably: he had brought Hattie down here at Easter. Cat had refused to go and Gethin couldn't blame her. All those Scottish jokes he liked to tell when she was around... Jesus. But Hattie had wanted to see her grandfather, so he'd given in and gone down there for tea one Sunday afternoon. And it had been okay. No shouting, no insults, the old man was actually quite fond of Hattie and he kept his temper for once.

To reach the Judge's place, Gethin drove round the edge of Penarth, the seaside town across the bay from Cardiff, then carried on past the weird mediaeval country park at Cosmeston Lakes and turned off the main road once he saw the sign to the caravan park on the left. He carried on past the park itself, remembering that Bex was always banging on about the car boot sale they had there on a Sunday. He followed the road round to the right as it became little more than a track, well used by walkers and less so by cars. There were only a handful of houses along the lane: posh, secluded places.

The Judge's house was the most secluded of the lot. It was surrounded by a ten-foot-high fence to make sure no walker had a sight of it. Rather than go through the rigmarole involved in parking his car within the compound, Gethin found a space in a small clearing one hundred yards further down the lane and walked back to the house, doing his best to prepare himself for what was to come.

Next to the big wooden gates that guarded the house was an intercom. Gethin pressed on the buzzer and waited. He waited some more, then pressed on the buzzer again, this time for a good ten seconds. Finally, there was a click at the other end of the system and a voice rasped out the one word: 'What?'

'It's me.'

The gates started to open.

Gethin stepped inside and looked around. Christ, it was becoming overgrown. The garden was always intended to be lush but now it was overwhelming. You could barely see the house for the trees and bamboo glades and rampaging shrubs. You could just about follow the path to the front door, but really only just. He made his way forward carefully, finding it difficult to banish the notion that he should watch his footsteps for fear of treading on a snake.

The house itself was modern, built in the nineties by his parents as their retirement dream home. How they'd gained planning permission to build in the midst of a beauty spot Gethin didn't know, but he suspected the answer might lie in his father's job title. What was Judge Dredd's catchphrase? I am the law. That was about right for Gethin's dad and all.

The tragedy of it was that Gethin's mum had never lived there. The completion date for the house had been delayed and delayed and they weren't finally set to move in until a year after the Judge had retired. A month beforehand, Margaret, Gethin's mum, had come back from a cruise with food poisoning, been taken to hospital, contracted MRSA and died within the week.

The Judge had spent the next five years suing everyone concerned to hell and back, with some success, but the dream home had become little more than a retirement bunker, a constant reminder of his loss. When Gethin thought about the house, he always saw it in semi-darkness, the curtains drawn, his father surrounded by papers, raging against the world, marooned in his miniature jungle on the outer reaches of suburbia.

Even once you made it through the surrounding vegetation, the house gave nothing away at first sight. All you could view was an imposing blank wall with only a single heavy wooden door for variation. It looked like the doorway into a forbidden city. Before Gethin could knock, however, the door opened and there was his father, the Judge, large as life. He was wearing a suit, just as he had done every day of his career. The only concession to retirement was the absence of a tie.

He wasn't a big man, the Judge, but he had an extraordinary head, too big for his body, and topped by a shock of white hair. Leonine was the word Gethin always found coming into his mind when he thought about his dad. There was definitely something of the lion about him, and not the cuddly sort.

Father and son stared at each other. It was hard to

know, Gethin suspected, which of them looked the more disappointed in the other.

'Coffee?' The Judge turned his back on Gethin and led the way into the house.

'Thanks.'

Gethin followed him inside. The door opened straight into the house's central space, a huge living area two storeys high. To the left was the kitchen, to the right the bedrooms. Straight ahead was a huge glass wall. The curtains were drawn so there was some light in the room, but what should have been an epic view of the Bristol Channel, looking back eastwards towards the Severn Bridge, was entirely obscured by foliage, a green oppressive canopy.

The house was spotless, as it always was every time Gethin visited. There was help, he supposed. He imagined a silent Filipina scrubbing and hoovering, but he'd never seen any sign of such. He'd never seen anyone in this house apart from his father. Maybe he had poker nights with a bunch of retired lawyers every Thursday. Again, Gethin didn't know, but he doubted it. He was pretty sure his father still went to the club every Friday lunchtime, though. That was the Glamorgan Club where the city's lawyers and business leaders went to eat the roast beef of old England, washed down with plenty of claret. Gethin imagined the taxi, showing up like clockwork to take the Judge there every week, and then picking him up, half pissed, a few hours later. His father would know the driver's name; Trevor or Faisal.

The big central room – Gethin didn't really know what to call it, it was part atrium, part living room, he supposed – was dominated by a series of trestle tables, the sort you'd see in an architect's office, all covered with papers. Gethin was pretty sure that each would be related to a different legal case – some hospital trust he was suing, or some piece of work he was advising a crony on. The Judge didn't have interests outside the law, so far as Gethin was aware. One table, though, did catch his eye. It featured, amongst the piles of papers, a series of what looked like police mugshots. He was tempted to ask what they were to do with, but long experience had taught him that direct questions rarely elicited a useful response from the Judge.

He followed his father into the kitchen, where he started fiddling with his fancy Italian coffee making machine. Neither of them said a word. Gethin quite enjoyed the sport of this, seeing which one of them would give in first and come out with some attempt at standard social intercourse. Much to his satisfaction, it was his father who cracked.

'What are you here for? Want some help letting criminals out of prison?'

Gethin smiled. 'Nice to see you too, Dad. And yes, as you so sensitively deduced, I do want some advice.'

'Must be a big case if you've come all this way.'

'I suppose,' said Gethin, 'you've heard of Izma M.'

'I do read the papers,' said the Judge. 'Even at my advanced age. He's some half-educated West Indian drug dealer who's gone to prison for murder and turned into a Muslim terrorist. Then he wrote a book and now all the bleeding-heart liberals think he's some kind of saint.' He shook his head in disgust. 'And now they've brought you in?'

'Yes, I'm the last resort.'

'I imagine you are.'

Once the coffees were made – a cappuccino for Gethin and a double espresso for the Judge – they headed back into the big room, the war room, as Gethin found himself thinking of it.

'Tell you what, Dad, it's sunny out, why don't we sit on the deck?'

'Fine,' said the Judge, and he led the way up the staircase to the gallery that overlooked the big room. Follow the gallery in one direction and it led to more bedrooms. The Judge turned the other way and pulled open the screen doors that led to the deck. The sun was shining right at them, so that Gethin had to shield his eyes.

There was a hot tub over to the left that, as far as Gethin was aware, had never been used. He was assailed by a momentary vision of his father seated in the jacuzzi, surrounded by nubile interns, but managed to bat it away quickly. If his father had had any liaisons since his mother died, Gethin didn't know and hoped very much to continue not knowing. They sat down at a fancy wooden table, doubtless fashioned from some endangered South American hardwood, and Gethin took a minute to savour the wraparound view. On a clear day like this, you could see all the way up to the Severn Bridge, some thirty miles or so to the east, or down towards Ilfracombe on the Exmoor coast, thirty nautical miles to the south-west.

'Did you come to ask me something specific? Because if all you want to do is look at the view, I have work to be getting on with.'

Gethin was tempted to ask what kind of work a retired judge was doing but decided to leave well alone. He dragged his eyes away from the view and turned to face his father.

'There's something I think, I hope, you might be able to help with.'

'To do with this Ismail Mohammed person?'

'More or less.'

'Remind me, who was the judge?'

'Drayford,' said Gethin. 'Laurence Drayford. Lord something or other these days.'

'I know,' said the Judge. 'He always was a terrible social climber. But a good judge, knew how to control a courtroom. High-class summaries too.'

'I agree. I have no problems with the way he handled the case at all. It's the defence I have issues with. And the jury, of course. But the judge was fine.'

'So what's your angle?'

'I'm not sure. I'm working on a few different theories. But there's one name that's come up that I could use some help with.'

'Hmm.'

'It's an ex-copper called Malcolm Haynes.'

'Force? Rank?'

'Bristol and Avon and I'm not sure, but a DC I think.'

'Have you really come here to ask if I know some retired Bristolian Detective Constable? Do you have absolutely no resources of your own?' The Judge stared out over the Channel.

'Yes, Dad, I have plenty of resources, as you put it.' Gethin could hear his voice becoming shrill, like a little kid who's just been told off. He made a conscious effort to slow down and give it some basso profundo, but it was no good. He was doomed always to be a little kid when he talked to the Judge. 'I just thought with your... connections, you might be able to dig around for me.' Gethin mimed an elaborate handshake. He couldn't be absolutely one hundred per cent certain that his father was a Freemason – he'd never found any robes or what have you – but he would have been prepared to bet his house on it.

The Judge said nothing, acted as if he hadn't heard.

'If you're too busy I'll use my own... resources, no problem at all.'

Gethin figured he could see two warring desires at play in the Judge. Half of him simply wanted to put down Gethin. He had, of course, been livid when Gethin had gone to prison all those years ago, screwing up his glorious legal future once and for all. But he was in some ways even more angry now that Gethin had found his own way into the legal business. As if he was cheating the system somehow.

On the other hand, he could sense his father's need, his desire, to be back in the thick of the action. In the past, Gethin wouldn't have had the patience to deal with the situation. He would have stormed out and left the Judge to it. But this time he didn't, wearied perhaps by the row with Catriona. So, he simply stood there and waited for his father's curiosity to get the better of him.

'One question,' said the Judge. 'What's the relevance of former DC Haynes to your investigations?'

'He was still on the force at the time of the murder, and he was one of the cops who arrested Izma three months later. You may recall from the reports at the time that Izma was in possession of a firearm when he was arrested. Intelligence we've received suggests that Haynes may have either planted the weapon or been responsible for supplying it to Izma in the first place.' Even as he was talking, Gethin was struck by the way in which it was impossible to address his father without deploying the language of the courtroom.

'And when did he leave the force?'

'He rather suddenly took early retirement shortly after Izma's conviction. He runs a little security outfit in Fishponds these days.'

'Ah,' said the Judge.

'Yes, doesn't exactly inspire you with confidence. The thing is one of my team – Dean, I don't think you've met him – received the initial tip off. He went over to have a word with Mr Haynes and half an hour later someone drives a car straight at him, almost kills him.'

'And you think that was Haynes' doing?'

'I don't know. Obviously it's a possibility, but then again, the feller who gave us the tip off may be playing some sort of double game. Either way, before I go and wander into Haynes' path, I'd like to find out a little bit more about him, figure out how careful I need to be.'

The Judge went silent for a bit. 'All right, if you really have no other way of finding information, I'll make a call. You sit outside here and check your Facebook page or whatever it is you do with your time.'

He was gone for a surprisingly long time, twenty minutes or so. Gethin amused himself by pacing around the deck trying to find a spot where the mobile signal would stay strong enough for him to attend to his emails.

When the Judge came back out on the deck he looked, Gethin thought, a little worried.

'I've spoken to a couple of people,' he said. 'The former Chief Constable and a senior serving officer, and neither of them is exactly enthusiastic about your Mr Haynes.'

'They remember him, do they?'

'Oh yes, both of them knew immediately who I was talking about. The former chief – Brian, a decent golfer but promoted a little way above his capabilities, if you ask me – referred to him as "the original bad apple". The serving officer simply said that it was a miracle he wasn't in prison and suspected that he may have links to other serving officers who are, shall we say, protecting him.'

'Oh.'

'Yes,' said his father. 'You had better tread carefully. The serving officer told me, and this is a direct quote, "there is absolutely nothing I would put past that man".'

'That,' said Gethin, 'does not sound good. Did you ask them specifically about the Izma M case?'

'Yes I did, and I would say that neither of them was aware Haynes had any material involvement in the case, beyond what's already on the record. But then again, neither of them seemed surprised by the suggestion that he might have had some more sinister involvement. Indeed, I would characterise the reaction of the serving officer to the suggestion as alarmed, rattled even.'

Gethin nodded. It was more or less what he'd expected but he was definitely going to have to think through the implications.

'Gethin.'

He looked up, startled, as his father almost never called him by his name.

'You need to be careful.'

'Don't worry, Dad, I'll make sure to carry my trusty AK-47 to any meetings we have.'

'It's not funny,' said his father, his voice suddenly angry. 'This is a serious man and you need to respect that. And now, if you don't mind, I have things to be getting on with.'

As they walked back through the living room, Gethin had his eye caught once again by the table with the pile of mugshots on it.

'Who are they?'

'Graduates of assorted courts I've presided over.'

'People you've sentenced?'

'Yes, that's right.'

'Can I ask why you've got their photos out?'

'No.'

As they reached the door, the Judge paused and gave Gethin another searching up and down look. 'Everything all right at home?'

'Yes,' said Gethin, giving the Judge a taste of his own medicine.

'Have you been gambling again?'

'No.'

The Judge closed his eyes, as if the sight of his son was too much to have to put up with: 'You're not even a decent liar.'

Kyrenia, Northern Cyprus
16 August 2001 13.30

It must have been the flash of the explosion on the sea that Danny saw first, before he heard the noise of it and felt the shock of it. Then a further half second for his brain to make sense of it. The boat, his parents' boat, the boat called *Just a Gigolo*, had exploded in front of him. There was debris flying everywhere and, oh fuck, something had hit him hard on the head and then he was underwater, his mouth full of sea water, fighting his way back to the surface. He emerged coughing and spluttering and almost immediately collided with a jagged piece of fibreglass which cut his forearm as he tried to bat it away.

The debris was still falling: he saw something that looked like it might be a piece of flesh and, without warning, found himself vomiting – houmous and salad exploding out of his mouth in some weird echo of the eruption he'd just witnessed. A wave hit him, and he went under again. He stayed down as long as he could, terrified that when he came up again he would be surrounded by fragments of his parents.

He held his breath until he couldn't stand it any longer, all the while trying to persuade himself that what he'd just seen was a hallucination, the result of banging his head on a rock. But then he came back up to the surface and had to accept that this was no illusion. Someone had blown his parents up. Someone would have blown him up too if he hadn't chanced to be in the water. Another piece of debris, a metal strut of some sort, came towards him on a wave so he ducked under the water again and, as he did so, he had a dreadful thought – maybe whoever had blown up the boat was somewhere nearby.

When he came up again he looked around wildly, but there was nobody to be seen. Already the sea was starting to calm down. Apart from the husk of *Just a Gigolo* bobbing about in the water, and the remnants floating around it, there was nothing to suggest an unimaginably awful event had taken place. No one was screaming, there were no sirens blaring or passers-by asking what had happened, just the odd sea bird and a terrible buzzing inside Danny's head. Somewhere in the midst of the buzzing he could have sworn he heard an echo of the funeral music of the night before. He looked around wildly as if expecting the band to be there playing on a nearby boat. Then he shook his head and tried to focus.

He felt for the place at the back of his skull where the first unidentified flying object had hit him, expecting to come upon a bloody gash, but there was nothing, maybe the beginnings of a bump. He'd always had a hard head. The cut on his arm was bleeding a little and already stinging like a bastard, but it didn't look serious. Was there any chance his mum or dad could have survived the blast? He forced himself to look around some more, accepting the chance that his gaze might fall on a severed arm or leg, but he couldn't see any sign of life. There was no way he could imagine anyone might have survived such a thing.

It was unbelievable, impossible to take in. He trod water, dodging the odd chunk of boat and wondering what the hell to do. Then he heard the sound of an approaching motor boat in the distance. For a second, he felt relieved: help was on its way. And then it struck him that, far from being helpers, these might be the people responsible for the explosion – maybe the 'friends of Vincent' who had been spied at the airport. There was no way he wanted to run into them.

He turned round to face the shore, took a great gulp of air and dived under the water, swimming as fast and hard as he could towards dry land. He came up now and again for more air and, once he'd got a couple of hundred yards away from the wreck, gave in to the impulse to look back. He ducked back under as fast as possible. The motor boat he'd heard was indeed close to the wreck of his parents' yacht. Maybe, just maybe, they were good Samaritans come to try and lend a hand, but Danny sure as hell didn't want to find out. Diving back under he prayed to a God he didn't believe in that no one had seen him.

And once more this faithless God let him down. When Danny risked taking another look back, he saw that the motor boat was heading towards him. Christ, he was still fifty yards from the shore. Furiously, desperately, he started kicking for dry land and at least the chance of escape. But even with his head beneath the water he could hear the motor boat coming closer.

Fifteen

IT WAS STILL ONLY MID-MORNING, just after eleven, when Gethin made it into the office. He was doing his best to wrestle his thoughts away from resentment towards his father and on to the matter at hand – how to proceed with the case. Malcolm Haynes certainly had to be investigated, but would walking straight into his lair and asking him difficult questions be likely to bear fruit? For one thing, what was Haynes going to say? Oh yes, I'm bang to rights, I fitted Izma M up, sorry about that? For a second thing, it seemed entirely feasible that annoying Malcolm Haynes could land you in hospital – if you were lucky.

All he could think of was to go back to Shaun, try and find out more about Haynes – how he was connected to Izma, what the gun business was all about – and then start to build a case carefully and discreetly.

Bex waved him over as soon as he came through the door.

'Geth, come and look at this!'

Her voice sounded hoarse.

'You getting a cold, Bex?'

'Nah, it's just from last night. I was doing the Bonnie Tyler Experience in Port Talbot. Wrecks my throat every time, singing like that.'

'Christ, lucky you.' It always made Gethin a little sad to think of Bex, who had a beautiful voice, spending her time pretending to be other people. On the other hand, though, she seemed to thoroughly enjoy it. He pulled up a chair next to her and Bex passed over a sheaf of papers, another printout from the web.

'What is it?'

'More stuff about Danny Bliss. I found a long piece about it all in the archives. It didn't show up in my original search because it was behind the *Times* paywall, but I decided to fork out for a subscription and see what they had and I'm glad I did. One of their Insight reporters went out to Cyprus a couple of years after the boat blew up to find out what really happened. Apparently, it started with a tip off that Danny's father wasn't exactly the respectable businessman he seemed to be. You just have a read of that and see what you think.'

Gethin took the printout and sat down at his desk. The story was spread out over four pages of the newspaper under the headline 'Who Killed The Kingpin?' According to the article, Danny Bliss's father Leonard had been some sort of criminal mastermind, the man responsible for bankrolling all manner of criminal activity across London, but specialising in high-end bank robberies. The journalist had indeed been tipped off that the boating explosion might not have been all that it seemed. He had started off with a suspicion that the whole thing was a put-up job, that the Bliss family had faked their own deaths. Eventually, following extensive interviews with Cypriot police and forensics people, he had accepted that there was definite proof that both Leonard and Sally Bliss really had perished in the explosion. However – and this bit Bex had circled and placed an exclamation mark next to – there was no absolute proof that young Daniel Bliss was dead. There was some clothing that was probably his but no conclusively identified body parts, no teeth or whatever. Gethin grimaced at the thought of some poor bloody forensic lab tech trying to identify a person from a collection of exploded fragments.

The question the writer was posing was whether Danny Bliss had been responsible for the explosion – whether he had blown up his own parents to steal his father's money. Leonard Bliss was rumoured to have had a considerable fortune stashed away somewhere and the Scotland Yard unit in charge of recovering ill-gotten gains had been unable to find any trace of it.

'Bloody hell,' said Gethin, then kept on reading.

While much of the focus was on the Danny Bliss theory, the article went on to list various other parties that might have had an interest in seeing Leonard Bliss dead. Inevitably, the Islington crime family, the Adams gang, was mentioned in dispatches as was a firm from Edmonton run by some infamous hard nut called Vince Loader. None of them – surprise, surprise – had anything to say when asked to comment on the sudden demise of their former associate.

Gethin turned to Bex: 'What d'you reckon?'

'Far out, isn't it? If he didn't die in the explosion, he could be the guy Hannah met...'

'And it might also have given him a motive to kill her,' said Gethin slowly. 'I mean, if he didn't want to be recognised. Let's say he's moved to Bristol, where he didn't know anyone, and he is living under an assumed name, and this old girlfriend clocked him one night...'

'That does sort of make sense...'

'Yeah, it sort of does. I wonder who we could talk to, see if it holds any water.'

'Might be worth showing around a photo.'

'Do you want to see if you can find a half decent picture of Danny Bliss somewhere? Ideally something better than this one.' He was pointing to the picture in the paper, a shot of an angelic early teenager in a terrible suit, probably taken at his bar mitzvah. 'Meanwhile, I'll get on with digging into the Malcolm Haynes end. You know when Lee is expected back?'

'She texted from the hospital. She was about to leave, should be back in an hour and a half.'

'Can you call her back? Tell her to wait for me there. We need to have another crack at Shaun. Tell her I'll meet her in the same pub as last time in about an hour. I'll send a couple of emails and I'll be on the road.'

He booted up his desktop, opened Outlook, and had just started to write a reply to Amelia's PA when his eyes started feeling really heavy.

The next thing he knew, Bex was shaking him awake.

'You all right, Geth?'

'Yeah, course. I just fell asleep, I suppose.'

'You okay? Cos, to be honest, you don't look it. Moment you walked in this morning I was worried about you.'

'It's nothing, just didn't sleep well.'

'Uh huh.'

'You know, this awful business with Deano…'

'You haven't been gambling again, have you?'

There was something motherly about Bex, despite her being more than a decade younger than him. It wasn't just her size, though that was definitely part of it. But there was something about her made you want to present her with your troubles and have her tell you it was okay.

'I fucked up again, Bex. I am a complete and utter wanker.'

'Casino?'

'Yeah.'

'Which one?'

'Les Croups.'

'Classy. Does Cat know? Oh, let me guess, that's why

you're tired and look like shit. She kicked you out.'

'Spare bedroom.'

'You're lucky. You were married to me and pulled a stunt like that, you'd be in A&E right next to Deano.'

'I was married to you, Bex, I wouldn't have dared.'

She looked him up and down: disappointment mixed with weary affection. 'I thought you were going to meetings to deal with this.'

'I stopped, didn't I? Thought I was over all that.'

'Well, you were wrong, weren't you? Fuck's sake, Geth, couldn't you just be a coke addict or something? It'd be a lot cheaper.'

Gethin forced out a laugh. 'Yeah, you're probably right. I'm really sorry, Bex. And the only good thing was I didn't lose any money, I actually won some. Yeah, I know, that's not the point. But it could have been worse. And I promise you, I won't do it again.'

'Easy to say, Geth, let's see you actually do it,' said Bex. 'But anyway, right now I'm going to call a cab to take you to the station. You can take a train over to Bristol, have a kip on the way, and you might actually be some use and not just cause a pile-up on the M4. I'll let Lee know you'll be late. Oh, and a bit of a development. While you were having your forty winks, I had an email from Laura Vellacott, Hannah's old flatmate. She's back from holiday and happy to talk to us. She works at the BBC in Bristol, so I'll give you her number and maybe you can fix up to meet her as well.'

'Will do,' said Gethin. 'And thanks. Don't know where I'd be without you.'

'In prison,' said Bex, and there was no sign she was joking.

* * *

Laura Vellacott turned out to be free that lunchtime so Gethin arranged to meet her first. Lee was cool with the change of plan, said she'd call a friend and see Gethin back in the pub about three.

Gethin dozed away the train journey and felt revived when he disembarked at Temple Meads. He caught a bus up to Clifton and made his way to the café on Whiteladies Road that Laura Vellacott suggested.

It was a vegan place populated mostly by anorexic girls. He must have stood out like a sore thumb as he was barely through the front door before the palest, most wan looking young woman of the lot stood up from her table and waved to him.

He made his way over.

'Laura? I'm Gethin.'

'Great. I was going to wait for you but I don't have long so I already ordered.' She pointed at a plate of avocado and alfalfa sprouts. 'You want anything?'

'Just a coffee.' Gethin turned to the counter. 'Can I buy you one?'

'Coffee?' said Laura Vellacott. 'No, I wish. I can't tolerate caffeine. Maybe a dandelion tea?'

Gethin fetched the drinks and sat down opposite Laura. She was quite a contrast to Hannah Gold's other friend, Molly. It made him wonder what Hannah herself had been like – loud and big like Molly or careful and quiet like Laura.

'I've been thinking really hard,' said Laura. 'Trying to remember. I expect everyone who knew her has been the same. We all thought we understood what had happened – she'd just copped off with this random guy who'd murdered her. It's not something I'd ever imagine doing, but Hannah had a bit of a wild side. Anyway, like I say, that's what I'd thought. And then Izma's book came out and, well, after that I didn't know what to think. I expect everyone says that.'

Gethin smiled at her. 'That's natural enough. So is there anything else?'

'Not really. I mean, I remember the night it happened. She came in from work and she was chatting to me a bit while she was getting ready to go out. She was joking about some woman at work who had a crush on her.' Laura paused, stared wide-eyed at Gethin. 'You don't think she might have something to do with it, do you? The woman from the Co-op... I'm sorry I can't remember her name.'

Gethin thought about it. Could Molly have killed Hannah out of jealousy? Could she have followed her that night and murdered her? Molly looked strong enough, but it was hard to imagine.

'It doesn't seem likely.'

'Apart from that, I don't know what to say. She was obviously excited about this date she was going on. And a bit mysterious about it. I asked who it was and she just put her fingers to her lips and said she was sworn to secrecy for the moment and, anyway, I wouldn't approve. And I've always assumed that's because it was Izma. She was right, I wouldn't have approved of her going off with a drug dealer. But that's not anything new, is it? God, I really wish I could help you but...'

'Did she ever mention someone called Danny? Maybe an old boyfriend. Second name Bliss, though he might not have been calling himself that.'

'Danny,' said Laura. 'Well there are loads of Dans around, but I'm sorry, I don't think...' She stared down at her depressing plate of alfalfa sprouts, looking almost on the point of tears. Then she pulled her head back up. 'Wait a minute, I do remember something. There was a guy she knew called Danny from back home. I don't know if he was an old boyfriend, though, I thought she said he was like a third cousin or something. He was from London and he ran this bar in town. A sort of flash, ghastly place with loud music and guys in suits. She asked me to go with her once, because we could get free drinks. I wasn't too keen as I don't drink, well I did a tiny bit back then, but anyway. I did go down there with her once but I really didn't like it, so I just left her to it. God, I wonder if that's where she met Izma. It was that sort of place, people who looked like footballers and blonde girls with lots of hair. Not exactly me.'

Gethin dug out the bar mitzvah photo of Danny Bliss. Laura couldn't positively identify it as being the same man who was running the bar.

'Do you remember what the bar was called?' asked Gethin.

'I'm sorry, I don't, but I can tell you exactly where it was. Just off Welsh Back by Queen Square. It's not there anymore, but I'm sure you could ask around or google it or something.'

'That's great, thanks. And he was definitely called Danny or Daniel?'

'Yes,' said Laura, 'I'm sure.'

* * *

Lee was right in position when Gethin arrived, seated at the pub window, her chair pitched at the perfect angle to see anyone coming or going from Shaun's flat. She wasn't alone, though. Molly from the Bike Co-op was seated next to her, laughing at something Lee must have said.

'Hey,' said Gethin, 'nice to see you again.'

'Yeah and you,' said Molly. 'I came down to give Lee a hand. She wanted to see if I recognised somebody.'

'Oh right.' Gethin was confused. He had the picture of Daniel Bliss with him, but he didn't think Lee knew about it. 'Who are you meant to be identifying?'

Molly laughed: 'I don't know. Some dude lives over the road, apparently.'

'Thought it might be helpful, boss,' said Lee.

Gethin would tease Lee later about her actual motivation for inviting Molly down to the pub. 'Actually, it's good you're here, Molly, I have a picture I'd like you to have a look at.'

He scrolled through the pictures on his phone till he found Daniel Bliss in his bar mitzvah suit.

'Does this guy look familiar? He would have been older when you'd have seen him – mid-twenties – I know it's hard to tell…'

Molly stared at the picture intently. 'Is this Hannah's old boyfriend?'

'Yeah, that's Danny Bliss. I know Hannah never introduced you, but I was thinking it's possible you might have seen him around.'

Molly stared at the picture some more then handed the phone back to Gethin, shaking her head. 'I'm sorry, it's just too hard to tell. Do you have any newer photos?'

'We're working on that. There's one really strange thing about Danny Bliss, though.'

'What's that?'

'He's officially dead.'

Gethin enjoyed watching Lee and Molly's jaws drop, before filling them in on the strange tale of Danny Bliss, presumed drowned at sea and yet possibly at large in Bristol four years later.

'Did anything Hannah said to you suggest she knew about any of this, or that Danny was maybe living under a false name or something like that?'

'Christ, I don't think so. I'm sure something like that would have stuck in my mind. She did say he'd changed, but I really can't remember anything else.'

'How about a guy called Danny who ran a bar in the city centre, some sort of old friend or possibly cousin of Hannah's?'

'Oh,' said Molly, 'you know what, that sounds familiar. Do you know where it was exactly?'

'Just off Welsh Back, apparently.'

'That's it. It was called Zenon, maybe Zeno's. I ended up drunk there once. Not my sort of place at all but I mentioned it to Hannah and she said she knew the owner. I don't think his name was Danny. She called him by some nickname; let me think.' Molly scrunched her eyes up like a little girl wishing really hard for something, then opened them up again, a delighted smile on her face. 'Dante, that's what she called him.'

'Dante,' repeated Gethin. 'Well, that's not far off. It's what you might call yourself if you didn't want to be just another Dan.'

'And you're a pretentious knob,' chipped in Lee.

'That as well,' said Gethin. 'I don't suppose you know what happened to him?'

'No,' said Molly. 'Might be worth going down there and asking.'

'I thought it had closed down?'

'It's called Fairchild and Daughter now. It's a hipster deli-cum-bar, but you know what things are like. It's probably just the same people with new beards. Or they might know what happened to the old owners. It only changed recently.'

'Cheers.' Gethin tapped the info into his phone.

'Hey,' said Lee. 'Look where I'm looking.'

Out the window. Shaun was indeed leaving his house. He was wearing jeans and a white polo shirt, and he was looking intent on something. In no time, it became obvious that what he was intent on was crossing the road and entering the pub. He actually kicked the door open.

'You,' he said, pointing at Lee and walking towards the window table. 'What the fuck are you doing back here? You spying on me? Well, you can stop it now, I ever see you in this road again you're fucking dead, you hear me?' He was right above them now, jabbing his finger in Lee's face.

Gethin felt compelled to intervene. 'Calm down,' he started to say, but before he could finish getting the words out, Shaun simply, and without any warning, punched him very hard and full in the face. Gethin crashed to the floor, knocking over drinks and chairs as he went. Molly started screaming and Lee grabbed a bottle like she was about to attack Shaun with it.

Shaun simply reached out, calm as you like, and took the bottle from her. 'Watch yourself,' he said and turned to leave the pub, stamping down on Gethin's stomach as he walked over him.

And then he was gone and Gethin was trying to sit up, winded and gasping for breath and bleeding from his nose. 'Fuck,' he said. 'Can you help me up?'

Molly and Lee took an arm each and hauled Gethin back on to a chair. He felt around his nose gingerly. Nothing obviously broken, but it hurt like a bastard. He bent over and tried to take some deep breaths, wondering if he was in shock. It was a long time since anyone had hit him and he could only remember it happening in the past in the context of a fight, when you worked up to it and were prepared to be hurt. Never like this. To be attacked so swiftly and violently without any build-up was deeply unsettling. It didn't exactly threaten his manhood – he wasn't stupid, he knew he wasn't that young anymore and there were bigger, fitter, younger blokes out there – but still it was a hard lesson in life's basics, any time you received a fist in the face.

Distantly aware that Molly was asking him if he wanted a glass of water, he willed himself back into the world and watched her walk over to the bar where Lee was talking to the barmaid, a sulky looking woman in her thirties.

'What do you mean you haven't got a phone?' Lee was saying. 'This is a pub.'

'It isn't working.'

'Fine, why don't you use your mobile to call 999 then?'

'What for?'

'To call the police, what do you think? That guy just attacked my mate.'

'I didn't see anything.'

'Look at him, look at his bloody face.'

The barmaid shrugged: 'I just saw him fall over. Must have hit his face on the way down.'

Lee looked at her in disbelief, then bowed her head. 'Oh, I get it. Told him I was in here, did you? You his bit on the side, are you? Hope he's worth it, love. Come on,' she said, 'let's get out of this shithole.'

Once settled in a vegan coffee bar in Stokes' Croft, Molly started talking: 'I have seen him before. I definitely have.'

'The guy who hit me? Shaun? He's Izma's old pal allegedly. Though he doesn't seem like it, the way he's behaving.'

'He's Izma's friend? That is weird.'

'Where did you see him before?' asked Lee.

'At the Bike Co-op. It wasn't long before Hannah passed. Maybe a week or so. I heard her having a row with someone and I came out to have a look at what was going on. And it was her and that guy shouting at each other. As soon as they saw me, they both shut up, which was weird, and he just fucked off. I remember him, though, because he looks a lot like that footballer.'

'Anyway, I asked Hannah what was going on and she said he was just kicking off about some repair work – how he'd been overcharged. And I took it at face value. I mean, people are arseholes. And the guy was on a bike and everything. But I remember thinking at the time that it was weird, because Hannah was normally so nice that people didn't kick off with her. But then, to be honest, I forgot all about it.'

Gethin tried to compute this news. 'Doesn't sound likely it was just about his bike. She'd met Izma by then, hadn't she?'

Molly thought about it. 'Yeah, I reckon so. She'd been a bit secretive, like she had something going on, for a couple of weeks, I think.'

'Stands to reason it must be something to do with Izma then. Maybe he was warning her off or something.'

'Yeah,' said Lee. 'Maybe Shaun's bike needed fixing and Izma told him that this girl he knew worked in a bike co-op. And he took it along and, being the nice friendly chap we now know him to be, had a bit of a row. Could be as simple as that.'

'Could be,' said Gethin.

'Well, there's one person should be able to tell you and that's Izma. When are you going to see him again, boss?'

'Tomorrow,' said Gethin, 'I'm going to see him tomorrow.'

After leaving the café, Gethin realised he could easily walk to the station via Welsh Back. He strolled down past the Colston Hall and across the big roundabout and down King Street with its mix of ancient and modern pubs till he came to the waterfront, with its selection of floating restaurants.

The former Zenon was easy to find. Molly had remembered the new name right. It was indeed Fairchild and Daughter. It had been painted pale green inside and out and had the obligatory selection of mismatched furniture that looked like it had been sourced from a Victorian primary school. It advertised itself as an all-day coffee house, but it didn't take Gethin long to decide that this was really still a bar by any other name. There was a Gaggia machine behind the bar and a selection of uninspiring cakes displayed on cutesy Edwardian stands, but there was an underlying smell of stale booze, and a row of lager pumps at the counter. And the person serving wasn't some kooky girl in a fifties print dress but a tattooed Pole who looked like he'd be happier working the door than practising his latte art.

'Hey,' said Gethin. 'Does Dante still own this place?'

The guy shrugged. 'Not anymore.'

'Oh right, you know where he is now?'

'Maybe.'

Gethin dug in his pocket and handed over twenty pounds. 'Okay, I'll have a skinny decaf latte. And you can keep the change. And the coffee.'

The guy nodded morosely and pocketed the money.

'He has a hotel.'

'You know where?'

'In the Cotswolds. It's called the Remington. Google it.'

'Thanks,' said Gethin. 'Will he be there now?'

'Fuck should I know?'

'Fine,' said Gethin and, feeling absolutely exhausted, he headed off to Temple Meads and slept most of the way back to Cardiff.

Sixteen

GETHIN WOKE EARLY THE NEXT morning. Waiting for the kettle to boil, he watched the sun rise above Caerphilly Mountain to the east. It was quite a view he had from the kitchen window. Look left and you could see the valleys stretching away to the north towards Merthyr. At the foot of the valley, cars were starting to file down the main road towards Cardiff. Look to the right and you could see the city itself: the castle tower, the spire of St John's Church, the massive struts of the Millennium Stadium, and beyond all that the Bay and the great grey bulk of the Barrage that had turned Cardiff's tidal estuary into a boating lake.

At least Cat had let him back into the marital bed last night, strictly for sleeping purposes only. It had been touch and go, though. When he'd returned home with his black eye starting to bloom, she'd taken one look at him and said: 'So... someone got you before I could.'

He'd done his best to laugh but she'd just stared at him and said, 'I wasn't joking' and headed off to her study to make some phone calls. Later on, though, she came to see him in the kitchen, where he was making some pasta for their tea, and she rested her head on his shoulder, the way she usually did, and asked him if it was hurting and fetched him a couple of ibuprofen. And during supper, she made a big effort to be cheerful. Hattie had been horrified and then quite excited by the black eye. The notion of her dad battling with criminals played out as heroic more than alarming. Gethin kept waiting for Cat to step in with a putdown, but not a bit of it. At one point, she even said: 'He's very brave, your dad.'

He finished making the morning tea, then headed downstairs where Cat was already in the shower. When she came out she was all business: running through Hattie's necessities for the school day and reminding him there would be a babysitter there when he returned from the prison, assuming that that was earlier than she got back from Carys's hen do. Then she was off to work while Gethin took charge of Hattie. He gave her breakfast then drove her down the hill to school. She was all excited about the Amelia Laverne project and made him promise to get Amelia to fill out her questionnaire soon.

On the way to Bristol, in the car, he listened to a collection of live material by Nic Jones, an English folk guitarist and singer whose career had been tragically cut short following a terrible car accident driving home from a gig one night in the early eighties. He'd ended up with a busted arm and no memory of his songs or even how to play the guitar. And to add insult to injury, his old records were unavailable due to a copyright dispute so all you could obtain on CD were these compilations of live recordings his friends and fans had sent him to try and help him remember his songs – and indeed who he was – when he was recuperating. There was one song of his – a dark and brooding folk ballad called 'Annan Water' – that Gethin reckoned he could listen to every day forever and never have fully plumbed its depths.

There had been a time when Gethin was a little embarrassed about his affection for folk music, begun by listening to Andy Kershaw on Radio 1 as a teenager. But these days – now everyone had a beard and a fondness for craft ales – it was easy enough to be an out and proud folkie.

To his surprise, Amelia Laverne was ready and waiting when he arrived at her hotel, in the foyer wearing jeans and a T-shirt, accessorised by sunglasses and a sky-blue baker's boy cap. Everything was as understated and expensive as ever but somehow, where she usually looked genuinely unobtrusive, today she seemed ostentatiously understated. You were rather meant, Gethin thought, to look at her and wonder.

Soon they were on the M5, heading north towards Birmingham and Amelia asked what had happened to his face. He gave her an edited, played for laughs, version of the Shaun affair, which had her all sympathetic and touching him on the arm and telling him how brave he was. Which he enjoyed even though there had been precious little bravery involved. He'd just acted as a punching bag. But still.

Next, he told her a bit about the Danny Bliss mystery, which had her thoroughly excited.

'God,' said Amelia. 'If he's the killer, do you think he might still be out there? Do you think he could be the one who attacked your detective, Mr... Mr Dean?'

'It's possible,' said Gethin 'but I should warn you that in cases like this there are always strange anomalies – witnesses who've died in mysterious circumstances or whatever – and nine times out of ten there's nothing sinister about it. Life is just weird sometimes, you know?'

'Yes,' said Amelia. 'I know that very well.'

They lapsed into silence then and, after a while, Gethin turned the Nic Jones CD back on and the two of them listened to him sing about the seven yellow gypsies who came to the rich lady's door and persuaded her to kick off her high heeled shoes of Spanish leather and run away with them. Her husband, the Lord, catches up with her eventually but she's unrepentant. 'Last night I slept in a feather bed, the sheets and the blankets around me / Tonight I slept in the cold open fields in the arms of the seven yellow gypsies.'

The gypsies are hung for their impudence at the end of the ballad. Gethin wondered momentarily whether he might have been able to get them off on appeal. And then he wondered about the woman sat next to him and why the song had made her cry.

* * *

At the prison, they received VIP service. They had clearly been given Amelia's name in advance, as the normally grim-faced security staff were on a charm offensive. A couple of them had even brought along photos for her to sign, which she did with good grace, and there was none of the intrusive body searching that mere mortals had to put up with when visiting their loved ones.

Once they were inside, Izma kept them waiting. Gethin passed the time queuing up for refreshments, exchanging the yellow and brown food and drink tokens he'd bought outside for three teas and three Twixes, on the off chance.

Ten minutes had passed and Amelia was becoming increasingly jumpy, wanting to interrogate the prison officers as to whether there was some sort of mistake, when finally Izma arrived.

At first, it looked like a reprise of last time – Izma glad – handing and bantering with the staff and fellow prisoners. But when he came to sit down with Gethin and Amelia, he looked wary and irritable. He didn't bother with the whole handshake and hug business, just sat down opposite them at the table, looking as though he'd been distracted from his busy schedule and wasn't happy about it.

'So why are you back again so soon?' he asked Gethin.

'Just have a couple of questions for you, following up some investigations we've made.'

'Don't know why you've bothered. I've told you everything I know.'

'Well,' said Gethin, trying to keep his voice reasonable, but all too aware of Amelia's jittery presence alongside him. 'Let's just see about that. I'll ask you a couple of things and you never know what might shake loose, what might help you to get out of here.'

Izma slumped back in his chair, the picture of martyred resignation. 'Sure, fine, whatever.'

Amelia clearly couldn't bear it any more. She leaned forward and said 'Hello, Izma. I'm so excited to meet you. Your book, it's just so, so real.'

Izma barely made eye contact. 'Do I know you?'

Gethin stepped in: 'Sorry, I should've introduced you. This is Amelia Laverne.'

'Ah right, you're the one paying for all this. Thanks.' He didn't sound remotely grateful.

Gethin couldn't bear to look at Amelia, didn't want to see her crushed by Izma's rudeness. Instead, he ploughed on as if she was just some intern he'd dragged along to a prison visit.

'What can you tell me about Malcolm Haynes?'

'That cunt.'

'Yes,' said Gethin, 'that cunt.'

Izma seemed to come alive for the first time since he'd sat down with them. He looked around the room carefully, noting exactly where the screws were and how bound up in conversation his fellow inmates were. Then he leaned in towards Gethin, his voice lowered: 'Ain't saying anything about him in this place. Walls have fucking ears here, you know?'

'But there are things I need to know.' Gethin kept his voice right down too. 'Shaun suggested that Haynes may have planted the gun on you.'

Izma looked genuinely surprised by this. 'Nah man, that's bullshit. Tell Shaun to keep off the weed.'

'Well, that leads me on to another thing. Shaun has not exactly been cooperative. In fact, he's been positively obstructive. You see this?' Gethin pointed at his eye.

Izma looked at Gethin's shiner and broke out a smirk: 'You have to talk to Shaun right. He come up rough, you know what I mean? He don't like people meddling in his business.'

'Except it's your business too.' Gethin was doing his best to keep his temper. 'If you want to get out of here, I'd advise you to have a word with your brethren there.'

Izma looked off to one side, made as if to spit on the floor: 'Yeah, all right. Whatever.'

'Fine. Now, back to the matter of the gun. If it wasn't planted, did Haynes supply it?'

'I dunno. I don't think so,' said Izma, definitely jumpy.

'Thing is,' Gethin went on, 'my investigator was run down by a car just after he'd been to see Malcolm Haynes.'

'Bruv,' Izma was actually whispering now. 'That's what I'm saying, you have to be careful what you say and who you say it to. Specially when cops are involved.'

Izma looked down at the table, frowning hard. Eventually, he raised his head and, his voice closer to its normal volume, announced that he wanted to go back to his cell. 'Sorry, man,' he said to Gethin, 'talking about this shit is just messing with my head. What is it they say? It's the hope that kills you. Whoever come up with that must've been in jail some time, I guarantee it.'

Izma started to stand up, but before he could rise fully

out of his plastic seat, Amelia reached over and touched his arm.

'Can I just ask you one thing?' she said. 'It's not about the case, honestly.'

Izma didn't sit back down but he didn't carry on rising either, just sort of hovered. 'You're the boss.'

'No,' said Amelia, 'I'm nothing of the kind, I just don't like to see injustice. Anyway it's just, you know, as I said I read your book and I thought it was so moving and I wanted to know if you ever found out who your birth parents were?'

'You what?' Izma looked at her with bewilderment.

'I don't want to hit a nerve or anything,' said Amelia. 'It's just that I have a good friend who was adopted and it made such a difference to her when she found her birth mother, so I was wondering if you ever found out or if you would like someone to carry out a search for you?'

Izma shook his head dismissively. 'Why should I care? Just some stupid slag got herself pregnant with a black baby and couldn't handle it. Why do I need to know someone like that?'

Amelia looked appalled. 'But you don't know. Don't you want to know?'

A small, bitter smile. 'No darling, I can't say it's exactly uppermost in my mind these days. You know what I'm saying? Got other things to worry about. So, unless you've something else, I'm going to go back to my cell, have a smoke and try to forget about all of... this.'

The moment the prison doors closed behind them, Amelia started crying. She stopped just as they arrived at the car.

'Listen,' she said. 'I have an idea.'

* * *

169

Amelia's idea was that, rather than drive straight back to Bristol and Cardiff, they should stop off at a country house hotel somewhere nearby. It had been upsetting seeing Izma in prison and she couldn't face sitting in a car for hours. Gethin did understand, didn't he?

Gethin sort of understood. Well, he understood that Amelia Laverne lived the kind of life in which you could follow your whims and, if you didn't like something, you could generally make it go away with the judicious application of that miracle cleanser known as money. He wasn't against the idea of a night in a nice hotel in principle, but he didn't relish the prospect of telling Cat he wouldn't be back, not the way things were between them. But what choice did he have?

He asked Amelia if she had somewhere particular in mind but, before she could come up with an answer, he had an idea of his own.

'Tell you what,' he said, 'do you mind if we head for the Cotswolds? It's not too far and there's a place I'd like to check out. It might possibly have some bearing on the case.'

She was happy enough to go along with this and – much to his relief – made it clear that she would be paying. All that remained was to okay it with Cat.

When he called her mobile, he expected to reach voicemail, but she picked up straightaway. Niceties were skipped.

'What is it?'

'Er, it's Amelia Laverne. She's decided she's too traumatised by the prison visit to travel and she wants us to stay over in a hotel. I'm really sorry about that. Will it be okay?'

'What? Is it okay for you to spend the night with a famous actress?'

'Oh Cat, come on, it's not like that…'

She laughed, not especially pleasantly: 'Oh, don't worry, I know that. What would a beautiful actress want with you?'

* * *

The beautiful actress appeared at dinner that evening looking every inch the part. For the first time since he'd met her, Amelia had her hair down. Also full make-up, jewellery and a simple, yet somehow shimmering, shift dress that Gethin suspected might well have cost roughly as much as his car and he couldn't help but call to mind that famous gold dress from her first film.

Somehow, he managed to repress his initial impulse to say 'wow', replacing it with a more appropriately restrained, 'You're looking nice'.

'Oh,' she replied, like she hadn't noticed what she was wearing. 'Well, it seems a shame not to dress up a little, when you're in a place like this.'

'Absolutely,' said Gethin. Then, looking down at himself, wearing the same chinos and Ralph Lauren shirt he'd had on all day: 'Sorry to be letting the side down.'

'Don't worry, you look fine. You didn't know you'd be staying over.'

'No,' said Gethin, then he fell silent, thinking Amelia had clearly packed a fancy outfit in her shoulder bag. She must have been planning to stay over all along. Or maybe that was just how people like Amelia rolled. Always ready to glam up at a moment's notice. She was incredibly hard to read. Maybe she really was the girl next door from *Mary's Prayer*, only a little older. Maybe they were just a man and woman in a lovely hotel, sitting down to dinner together with everything possible.

The Remington was quite a place, a boutique hotel set in a former Cistercian abbey just north of Chipping Camden. There were grounds to walk around in, including its own lake. There was a spa, a library, a cigar humidor. Inevitably, the rooms all had clawfoot bathtubs, handmade beds and Egyptian cotton everything. There was something a little brash about it, though. It wasn't a place to sink into comfortably, but rather somewhere that was trying very hard to impress you all the time. It was designed, Gethin supposed, to appeal to a thirty-something metropolitan clientele. You imagined that plentiful quantities of cocaine would have been consumed in its bathrooms. Gethin had asked after the owner, referring to him simply as Dante, and had discovered that, while Mr Green wasn't around that night – in London on business – he would be back in the morning, and would, of course, be delighted to meet his new guests.

The receptionist was obviously good at her job. She had immediately recognised Amelia, and from that moment on the staff were attentive to the point of obsequiousness. No sooner had they sat down for dinner than waiters were turning up with *amuse-bouches* and wine recommendations. Gethin had been prepared for Amelia to refuse wine in favour of an organic elderflower something or other, but not a bit of it. She'd ordered a fancy sounding Loire white that was doubtless listed at some eye-watering price, but no matter. Thankfully, Amelia had made it clear that this too was all her treat. If any of this showed up on his credit card bill, Cat would eviscerate him.

Through the first three courses of the tasting menu, it was all the kind of complicated *MasterChef* food that sounded more exciting than it actually tasted – plenty of foams and gels and sous-vide cooking – but was still pretty nice. Gethin happily made his way through the scallops and foie gras and the John Dory, while Amelia stuck to the lighter options – a wild garlic tart and an avocado dish – before joining him on the John Dory.

It was right after the fish course that Amelia reached over and laid her hand on top of his.

'Gethin,' she said, leaning forward over the table and looking lovely in the candlelight. 'Would you like to go to bed with me?'

He couldn't speak, couldn't even move. Just sat there with his fork suspended in mid-air trying to process the blizzard of thoughts and feelings ranging from lust to terror to that great British all-rounder, embarrassment.

Amelia leaned back a little and put her finger to her lips. 'Shh,' she said, 'don't say anything yet. I'm not suggesting we have a relationship. I know you're married and I know you love your wife and, as I'm sure you know, I'm married too.'

'I thought you were separated. It said in Wikipedia...'

'Try not to believe what you read. We don't live in the same place, but we still fuck. You know, from time to time. So, as I say, I don't want to endanger any of that and I will certainly never tell anyone. I am rather good at keeping secrets and I trust you're the same. But I do want you to take me upstairs and lay me down. Right now. So...'

She stood up from the table, picking up her shawl and her handbag: 'Are you coming with me?'

Gethin sat there transfixed, watching her extremely shapely arse walk away from him, swinging very slightly in the dress which seemed to have become magically tighter in the past minutes. Up till now, he hadn't really let himself think about whether he fancied her. She was a client for one thing; she was a famous film star for another. And she had to be a good few years older than him. Not that she looked it, at least not with her clothes on. So, did he fancy her? He let his eyes follow her arse. Lust started to make its presence felt, but it was embarrassment that really made him act. Gethin couldn't face sitting on his own with waiters bringing more fancy food and inquiring whether madam might be returning soon.

He rose from the table and took a few paces before realising he'd left his jacket on the chair and had his napkin more or less attached to his midriff. He dropped it on the table, picked up his jacket and told a bemused maître d' that that would be all, thanks. A final moment of indecision ended with him grabbing the bottle of wine from the table. There was at least a glass left and he suspected he was going to need it.

Amelia was waiting for him at the bottom of the grand staircase that led up to the bedrooms.

She took his arm in hers as they walked. Gethin slipped his free arm around her waist and, as they went down the corridor to Amelia's room, let it move an inch or two lower than was strictly respectable. He let go of her waist for her to open the door, wondering whether he was really going to do this. He felt as if he was moving through a dream. In fact, more than that – he felt he was in a very specific recurring dream. It was one in which he would be getting off with a woman – usually a rather spectral non-specific woman but occasionally, and embarrassingly, someone he knew. In the dream, just as things were becoming interesting, he would remember he was married and no longer allowed to do that kind of thing, and then he would wake up and find Cat sleeping next to him and feel a glow of relief that he was a good person, that he hadn't strayed.

But now there was no waking up option, now his

immediate future was in his own hands. It was up to him to find out whether he had been a good husband – in this respect at least – only because temptation had never really come knocking. Certainly not temptation that looked like Amelia Laverne.

He closed the door behind him and placed the wine bottle on the dressing table, still feeling weirdly disconnected from his body. He offered Amelia a drink and she nodded and said sure. He poured out two small glasses and drank most of his down in one. Amelia simply held hers in front of her, licking her lips in a cartoonish yet powerful display. When she had his full attention, she dipped her finger into the glass and traced a line down her chest. As she did so, she lifted her dress far enough away from her skin for Gethin to see her bra-less breasts and her finger circling an erect nipple.

'Would you like to lick them dry?' she asked, her voice a husky purr, again slightly stagey but undeniably effective.

Once again, Gethin was unable to talk. As if someone else was controlling his limbs he leant forward just as Amelia shook her shoulders free of the dress, letting his tongue follow the wine downwards, while his hands came up unbidden and slipped Amelia's dress over her nipples. He noted with guilty relief that her body looked no older than Cat's. Good genes and personal trainers had done their work. He could feel his cock, previously only half convinced, start to resemble a girder in his chinos. He was over the Rubicon now.

Amelia moaned and grabbed on to his head as he licked her breasts dry. Then she bent her head down and whispered in his ear. 'I want you to fuck me now and please, don't be gentle with me, I can't bear gentle.'

Gethin didn't reply, confining himself to a grunt and a firm squeeze of her perfect arse before starting to kiss her neck with reckless enthusiasm. Amelia made a sound in her throat then brought her lips down to meet his. They kissed hard and long. She broke off the kiss, pulled her dress down to the floor and slid out of her knickers, then lay back on the bed, ready and waiting for him.

Gethin pulled off his shirt and trousers as quickly as he could, but found himself half toppling as his left leg became stuck. He balanced on the dressing table and untangled himself without too much trouble, but in those few seconds the frenzy abated. He wondered if he looked ridiculous, too old, too fat and out of shape. He wasn't especially overweight, but he wasn't some studly actor with a personal trainer sculpting his abs, not by a long chalk.

Amelia didn't seem to mind. She just reached out an arm to pull him on to her. He could smell her now, her arousal. Lying on the bed next to her, their legs intertwined, he started to kiss her breasts again.

'Bite them,' she said, 'hard.'

He wasn't sure if she meant the nipples or the flesh around them, so he tried both tentatively at first, then harder as she urged him on.

Then he decided to move lower down. He started kissing and licking his way down towards her bellybutton. It was then that he was distracted by a series of livid red marks on her stomach. He raised his head slightly to see them better. They looked like burns.

'Christ,' he said, 'what happened here?'

'There?' said Amelia, something panting and frantic about her tone. 'That's where a man stabbed his cigarette out on me.'

'What?'

'He didn't want to, I had to beg him to do it. I came so fucking hard.'

Gethin reared up. 'I'm sorry, are you being serious?'

'That's what I like, Gethin, that's what I need.'

This was not remotely what Gethin had expected. Part of him wanted to pull his clothes back on as fast as possible and run back down the corridor to his own room. Another part of him, though, some awful secret part, wanted very much to stay.

It was at exactly that moment that he heard his phone emit a distinctive notification tone. It was the one he used for Hattie's calls. He started to raise himself off the bed.

'You bastard,' said Amelia. 'If you answer your phone right now, I swear to God I'll kill you.'

'I have to check. It's a text from my daughter. She's at home with a babysitter, something might be wrong.'

'Oh for fuck's sake, go on then.' Amelia lay back on the bed, her right hand slipping between her legs, rubbing herself and staring at him.

He grabbed the phone and looked at the message: 'Make sure u ask Amelia Laverne about my questionnaire xxx.'

He looked back at Amelia Laverne, lying there waiting for him, wanton and desperate in the grip of longings he barely understood, but suspected came from a place of deep unhappiness. And, phone in hand, he felt the presence of his daughter, the repository of his hopes for the future. Was he really going to jeopardise that whole relationship for this?

'I'm sorry,' he said. 'I can't.'

He couldn't bear to look at her, wasn't brave enough. Bending down, he picked up his boxers, pulled them on as quickly as he could, then found his trousers. Behind him on the bed, he could hear the sound of sobbing, not quite crying but awful writhing convulsions. He buttoned up quickly and turned around.

She was lying on the bed curled up in a ball, her whole

body rocking with each spasm of grief, her fist jammed in her mouth in an inefficient attempt to keep it quiet.

All Gethin wanted was to run away, to escape from the room and never see Amelia Laverne again and to pretend none of this had ever happened. But he knew that was a cowardly step too far. With a heavy heart he sat down on the bed next to her and reached out to stroke her back.

'I'm sorry,' he said, and then, for want of anything better to say, he repeated it. This sparked a reaction. She started drumming her fists against his back and side. It hurt a bit but Gethin welcomed the pain, needed it to assuage his own guilt.

'It's nothing to do with you,' he said, once her fury seemed to have subsided. 'It's just I have a family. I can't, I just can't jeopardise…'

'You cowardly fucking bastard, if you care so much about them, you should have stayed downstairs. It's me, though, isn't it? You've seen how I am and you despise me.'

'No,' said Gethin. 'No, it's not that.' Though it was, of course it was, at least partly that.

'Twice in one day. It's too much – twice in one fucking day.'

'What do you mean?' Christ, had there been someone in the hotel that morning? Did she have a mental health problem, sex addiction or whatever?

'First Izma, then you, you bastard. First Izma won't talk to me, then you won't fuck me. So just fuck off and leave me. I mean it.' She reached down to the floor on her side of the bed, picked up a shoe and hurled it at him, hitting him hard on the side of his head. 'Just fuck off. Leave me alone and fuck off.'

Seventeen

GETHIN ROSE EARLY, HAVING SLEPT predictably badly, woken up by an acid reflux attack almost as soon as he'd finally managed to drop off. He had no idea what to do about Amelia Laverne. He devoutly hoped that she would affect to have forgotten the whole thing come next morning and would have been more than happy to follow suit.

He'd been sorely tempted just to get up and drive home in the middle of the night – there was something particularly depressing about a luxury hotel room when you were in it alone and unhappy. However, duty had overridden his impulse. Duty being a polite word for the need to keep Amelia Laverne's money on tap.

Dear God, let Cat never find out about it. Another, perverse, thought struck him. Maybe Cat would actually be pleased to learn he'd had a sexual skirmish with Amelia; maybe it was kind of indirectly flattering. Perhaps he could spin it a bit, suggest that Amelia had come on to him and he politely turned her down. Maybe with just the briefest, most regretful of kisses so he didn't seem like a total wuss. Yes, Cat might like that and it might set fires burning. Help her find a way back to seeing him as an exciting, attractive man and not just a lying gambler.

Anyway, he was down at breakfast bright and early at eight o'clock, but there was no sign of Amelia and, when he went to ask after her at reception, he was informed that she'd called a taxi at 6.30. And no, the receptionist was sorry, but she had no idea where the cab was taking her to. Gethin felt more of an idiot than ever. As if Amelia needed him to chauffeur her about.

He asked whether Dante was likely to be around soon, hoping to rescue something at least from the debacle.

'Sure thing,' said the morning receptionist, an unnecessarily perky redhead who gave off an air of moonlighting from drama school. 'If you go in for breakfast, you'll see him there.'

'Oh,' said Gethin, 'I thought he was in London.'

'No,' said the receptionist. 'Why did you think he was in London?'

'That's what the woman who checked me in last night said.'

'Well, maybe he was then. Anyway, he's in there now if you want to say hello.'

'Fine.' He wondered whether this Dante feller had been deliberately trying to avoid them the night before. And if so, why?

The breakfast room was deserted. Gethin suspected that most people who stayed at the Remington didn't get up too early on a Saturday. His mind flashed on a vision of him and Amelia lying in bed together, surrounded by the remnants of breakfast, the air pungent with the smells of sex and coffee. He shook his head to make it go away, wondering whether what he felt was regret or relief that it hadn't happened.

The room felt all wrong for breakfast, full of heavy velvet chairs and low tables. It looked like somewhere for after-dinner whiskys and cigars, not poached eggs and smoked salmon. Gethin poured himself a glass of fresh orange juice from a selection laid out on a sideboard, then sat down at a table laid for one.

He was just studying the breakfast menu, and wondering where Dante was, when he heard the sounds of raised voices coming from behind the door at the far end of the room.

Seconds later, the door opened and a young blonde woman in a waitress's outfit came in, followed by a dark-haired man in a sharp but crumpled suit. The man was older, somewhere in his 30s, and he was clearly in the middle of giving the girl a fearful bollocking. He also looked very much like a man who had not slept all night but had ingested large quantities of what people like to call party drugs. He gave absolutely no sign of having noticed Gethin's presence, just carried on berating the girl for a series of crimes which appeared to include the failure to fold the napkins according to some arcane pattern, serving the wrong Cabernet Sauvignon to a couple the night before, and 'dressing like a refrigerated nun'.

'People come here expecting a bit of glamour, love, not some stuck-up former head girl waiting to go up to Oxford. G – L – A – M – O – U – R, you got that?'

The girl didn't say anything and just looked as though she was about to burst into tears. Gethin coughed loudly in the hope of distracting this asshole from his bullying tirade.

Finally, the asshole deigned to register Gethin's presence. He turned away from the unfortunate waitress and gave him a quite terrifying smile: 'I'm sorry you had to hear that. We'll be right with you. And do have the Eggs Benedict, they really are very good.'

He smiled again, an inappropriate reflex grin that reminded Gethin of Gordon Brown as Prime Minister, trying to look likeable and failing horribly. The asshole turned back to the girl: 'Ellie, don't just stand there, take the man's order.'

He looked back at Gethin, inviting him to join in his humiliation of the unfortunate Ellie, and made as if to head off.

Gethin made his move. 'Excuse me,' he said. 'Are you Dante?'

'I am,' said the asshole. 'I'm sorry, have we met?'

'No.' Gethin decided not to beat around the bush: 'I'm investigating the murder of Hannah Gold.'

The asshole Dante looked at him, obviously confused. 'I'm sorry, I was under the impression you were working with Amelia Laverne.' He turned to the unfortunate Ellie. 'Our guest would like the Eggs Benedict. Now fuck off.'

Ellie fucked off and the asshole turned his attention back to Gethin.

'I am working with her, but not on her acting career. Ms Laverne is funding an investigation into the Izma M case, in an attempt to prove his innocence.'

'I see.'

He tried to read Dante's reaction. The guy obviously wasn't pleased, but then he'd been in a foul mood to start off with.

'You knew Hannah Gold, didn't you?'

'We're related,' said Dante. 'Second cousins or something. Our parents are friends.'

'And you saw her in Bristol a few times before she died?'

'She used to come into my bar from time to time. Wow, you're not seriously suggesting I killed her, are you? What the fuck would I do something like that for?'

Gethin noted that he hadn't actually denied the accusation, just deflected it with another question.

'Do you remember when you last saw her?'

'A few weeks before she died, I think. I can't remember exactly.'

'Was anything going on with her, did you think? Did she mention any boyfriend trouble to you?'

Dante laughed: 'Do I look like a bloody agony aunt? Of course, she didn't. She was just a nice little save-the-world, eco-friendly student type and I was her tacky, club-running cousin. And no, before you ask, I was four thousand miles away when she died.'

'Oh, yeah?'

'I was in New York, staying at the Gramercy Park. I remember it well because my mother phoned up to tell me about Hannah. And I'm sure I could prove it if I had to. But I don't. Because you're not a cop, you're just some wet behind the ears liberal who falls for any old sob story.'

Dante paused then and gave Gethin a good hard look. 'Actually,' he said, 'you don't look like a typical do-gooder. I suppose there must be some money in it for you. That right?'

Gethin shrugged.

'Of course, there is. So don't try taking the moral high ground with me, mate. And now let me tell you something I reckon you don't know. You ever wonder where my airy fairy cousin met a bad boy like Izma?'

'Your bar?'

'That's right. I was the one who introduced them and I feel bad about that. But that's all I feel bad about. So, if there's nothing else, I'll leave you to enjoy your breakfast.'

Gethin couldn't think of any follow-up to that, short of demanding to see New York hotel receipts, so he just nodded and said thanks and waited for his Eggs Benedict to show up.

Once he'd eaten them – and, to be fair to the asshole, the eggs were really good – he started making plans for the day. He couldn't face going straight home, not after what had happened, so he called Bex and Lee and persuaded them to come in for a planning meeting.

Then he texted Cat, telling her he'd be back in the afternoon, and hit the road.

When he made it into the office, clutching a takeaway cappuccino from the Portuguese, Lee was sitting with her feet up on the desk, laptop propped on her thighs.

'Whassup?' she said, as he loomed into view. Then, after giving him a proper look over: 'Jesus, Geth, you look dreadful.'

'Probably better than I feel.' He dropped into his seat and took a major swig of coffee.

'Big night, was it?' asked Lee. 'You and Cat go somewhere?'

'I was at Gartree and ended up staying in a hotel cause Lady Amelia didn't want to drive back the same day.'

Lee gave him a seriously searching look. 'Made you sleep in the car, did she?'

'Listen, I really don't want to talk about it. Not right now. And the visit was a complete waste of time. Izma just doesn't want to know. Here we are working our socks off trying to get him out of prison but when I go up there it's like I'm distracting him from his busy schedule of playing ping pong and reading the Koran.'

'Weird.'

'Yeah, really weird.'

'But so's the whole case, boss. No one's acting like they've read the script, you know what I mean? I've just been talking to Deano.'

'How's he doing?'

'Much better. He's on the regular ward now, should be home in a day or two. Which'll cheer him up. He's still convinced this copper is out to rail him.'

'He have anything else to say?'

Lee frowned. 'Not a whole lot we didn't know already. One thing he did say was that he thinks everything changed when he mentioned the name of Danny Bliss to Mal Haynes. He says it was like Haynes wasn't bothered at all till that name came up, then he went a bit strange and basically told Deano to fuck off.'

'Interesting.' Gethin turned round to face his office manager: 'Hey Bex, you any further with the Danny Bliss thing? Know if he's alive or dead yet?'

'I've left a few messages around the internet asking for info – his old school has a website with a forum for ex-pupils, that sort of thing.'

'Cool. And I've done a bit of investigation myself.' He filled them in on Danny 'Dante' Green, hotel manager and asshole.

'At least that explains how Izma and Hannah came to meet. I couldn't ever really see that before. Do you think he could be Danny Bliss?' asked Bex.

'I suppose it's possible. Not sure it matters all that much. He's definitely another Danny who Hannah knew from back home, so he kind of fits the bill. There's just the question of the alibi.'

'I could call the Gramercy Park Hotel,' said Bex, 'and see if they've got a record of him being there.'

'Okay, keep us posted if anything comes up. Because, if he wasn't there, I'd love him to be in the frame. Meanwhile, I've been thinking about it all and I reckon my pal Shaun is definitely the person we need to talk to some more.'

'Sure,' said Lee. 'Don't see a lot of evidence he wants to talk to us, though.'

'No,' said Gethin. 'But I've asked Izma to have a word, so hopefully he'll behave himself next time.'

'Wouldn't bank on it,' said Lee. 'If you're seriously

thinking of going to see him again, may I suggest you carry one of these?'

She dug in her shoulder bag and brought out a black, cylindrical item. At first sight, he thought it was some kind of cosh.

'Shit, Lee, you can't carry one of those. If the police find it they'll crucify us.'

'It's just a torch,' said Lee. She held it out towards Gethin and he could see that it was indeed a torch, about seven or eight inches long. He supposed you could hit someone with it at a pinch, but it was hardly going to impart a great sense of security.

'Yeah, but...'

Then Lee pressed the button on the base and, suddenly, he was completely blinded by an unbelievably strong beam shining straight into his eyes. He threw himself to one side to escape from it.

'Fuck's sake, turn that off!'

Lee did as she was told, laughing all the while. 'See what I mean, Geth, it'll give you a few seconds to move away from a situation if you need to.'

'Jesus,' said Gethin, once his sight returned.

'Good innit? There's a strobe mode as well that'll really freak someone out. You want to borrow it?'

Before Gethin could say yes, please, he felt his phone ringing in his pocket. He looked to see who the call was from and was surprised that it was the Judge. He raised his eyebrows at Lee as he walked into his office and swiped up to accept the call.

'Hi, Dad.'

'Gethin, I was in the club yesterday and I had a rather odd conversation. You know Terence Donoghue?'

'Yes,' said Gethin, cautiously. Everyone knew Terence

Donoghue. He was probably the richest lawyer in Cardiff, certainly the best connected. He had his own firm, known for their lobbying skills. Lots of big corporate clients. Would probably represent the Bin Laden family if they fancied digging for oil in Wales.

'Well, as I say, I was having lunch yesterday when Terence sat down opposite me' – this was a feature of the Glamorgan club, everyone had their lunch at big communal tables so the city's movers and shakers could have casual off-the-record chats about whatever without having to set them up formally – 'and started talking about this and that, the fracking business and so forth. Then, just as I was wondering why he felt the need to tell me about all that, he started asking after you, what you're working on and so forth. I was taken by surprise, as you might imagine. I mentioned the Ismail Mohammed business, as it's a matter of public record, and he pretended to take an interest. Then, he finally got to the point.'

'Oh, yes?'

'He told me that it had come to the notice of one of his clients that you're asking after the whereabouts of someone called Daniel Bliss. Is that right?'

'Yes,' said Gethin, his brain working fast. What kind of client of Terence Donoghue's would be interested in Danny Bliss and, more to the point, how the fuck did they know Last Resort were looking for him? 'Go on...'

'Nothing more than that really. Except he said that his client would be very interested indeed in any information you came up with. He suggested you give him a call to discuss the matter. Said it might be considerably to your financial advantage.'

'Interesting,' said Gethin. 'What d'you make of it?'

The Judge took a minute to decide. 'I think you should tread carefully. If Terence is interested enough to go through that sort of rigmarole with me there must be some serious money involved.' He paused again: 'Can you tell me anything about this Daniel Bliss?'

'Not much,' said Gethin, 'except that he's meant to be dead.'

'Oh,' said the Judge. 'Now that really is curious.'

'Isn't it?'

Another pause. 'If you do find this Daniel Bliss, you might want to consult a little before calling Terence. You have my number, of course.'

After he came off the phone to the Judge, Gethin, Lee and Bex headed over the road to The Deck café, for another coffee and, in Bex's case, an elaborately decorated cupcake. They sat outside and tried to form a strategy.

Bex started by pointing out they needed to focus on the basic question – which was not who killed Hannah Gold, but how to get Izma out of jail. There'd been plenty of murder convictions overturned without the actual murderer being identified.

They considered this for a while – was there anything they'd learned so far that could be grounds for appeal?

'Mal Haynes and the gun,' said Lee. 'If he planted it, that's all we need.'

Gethin nodded: 'He just needs to type us a nice confession and our work here will be done.'

'Shaun,' said Lee. 'He'll have to give up Haynes. It's the only way that works.'

'But he doesn't fancy it, does he?' said Bex, daintily picking off a strawberry from the top of the cupcake, 'Sent poor Deano over there like a lamb to the slaughter.'

'Fair point,' said Gethin. 'Any other way we might get evidence on Mal Haynes?'

'Izma himself, surely?'

'You might have thought, but I asked him, and he denied it.'

'So, you don't think it's true?'

'I dunno, I didn't believe Izma either. That's what doesn't make sense about it. He seemed pretty definite that the gun wasn't planted, but when I asked if Haynes had supplied it, he didn't reply. His whole attitude is really strange. I'm not sure how much help he's going to be to his own cause.'

'Prison's probably done his head in,' said Lee. 'I've seen it happen. People become sort of used to it, you know? Don't exactly like it but they're scared of the outside world as well.'

'Yeah, true dat,' said Bex, while carefully using a finger to hoover up the few remaining cupcake crumbs. 'You know what, maybe I'm wrong. Maybe we do have to find the murderer. Cause I think maybe it's staring us in the face that it's Shaun. I mean he's totally acting like a guilty man, smacking you in the face like that. You should press charges, you know?'

Gethin rubbed his face. It had pretty much stopped hurting but the remains of the black eye were still visible: 'Dunno about that. The barmaid pretended she didn't see anything, so it would be tricky to prove. Anyway, I can't see how that makes sense. Why would he have killed Hannah? And, even if he did it, why on earth would Izma be protecting him? Surely he'd have to have known?'

'Not necessarily,' said Lee. 'But you're right, it doesn't seem likely. What I reckon is, he's still doing a lot of business and he doesn't want people like us turning up and getting in the way.'

'Sounds about right,' said Gethin. 'Either way we have to go talk to him again. If anyone can open this up it's him, and he just needs to realise that the quickest way to be rid of us is to tell us what he knows and stop pissing about. Meanwhile, let's back up a bit. Who else have we in the frame as murder suspects? For starters, I suppose there's the Dannys. Either the mysterious Danny Bliss – though it'd be nice if we knew that he was actually alive at the time – or dear old Dante Green the hotelier. Any news on his alibi, Bex?'

'Christ, Geth, give me a minute. I've emailed the hotel but no news yet. How about this girl from the Bike Co-op? Sounds like she had a bit of a crush on Hannah. Do you reckon she could have done it?'

'No,' said Lee. 'No way.'

'If you say so.' Bex raised her eyebrows and grinned. 'Anyone else?'

Gethin shook his head.

'Me neither.' Lee stood up, stretched. 'Anyway, some of us have things to do, homes to go to, girlfriends to take shopping. See you Monday.'

Gethin and Bex watched Lee heading north over James Street in the direction of Monica's flat.

'Right' said Bex. 'Got to go home. Doing a "Someone like Adele" show tonight at the Blackwood Miners' Institute and my gown's stinking. But… are you okay, Geth? Why aren't you at home? It's Saturday. I don't mind, you know, not like I have a family to worry about, but you never come in on a Saturday. Has Cat found out you were gambling again?'

'Yeah, she has and well… you can imagine.'

'You're such a tosser. But you know that, I guess. So come on, you're not going to fix things sitting here. Go round the corner to the flower shop, buy her something nice and go home and face the music. You'll come through it. It's not like it's the first time, is it? Cat knows what you're like. And she loves you. Everyone knows that.'

'I hope so.' Gethin wondered whether to tell Bex about

what had happened with Amelia, but decided not to.

The flowers, at least, were a good idea. Gethin saw Cat's lip tremble when he produced them. And she immediately made a fuss about how lovely they were. Hattie came out of the room and did the same and the two of them busied themselves selecting the ideal vase and deciding where to put it.

That was the high watermark of the weekend, though. Thereafter, there was an atmosphere of studied artificiality in the household. There were no rows. When Hattie was in the room they played their parts, but when they were alone together, Cat was polite and remote, and any time Gethin tried to say anything to her, to talk about what had happened with the gambling, or even just how her hen night had been, she would just shake her head and change the subject to something infuriatingly neutral – 'You think we should get new cushion covers for the sofa in the living room?' 'Have you got Hattie's dentist appointment in your diary?' and so on.

At night, she went into the pretending-to-be-instantly-asleep routine while Gethin lay there and wondered if this was a deliberate punishment tactic or just a cooling off period: Cat keeping things neutral as an alternative to losing her temper. He tried to distract himself by thinking about the case but couldn't come close to unknotting it. All he was reasonably sure about was that Shaun was the key but whether he would be willing to unlock it was another matter. Finally, he dropped off to sleep, only to be tormented by a series of bad dreams, the worst, the most nightmarish of which, involved being in bed with Amelia Laverne with his father standing at the end of the bed, judging them.

Eighteen

GETHIN HAD BEEN IN THE office on Monday morning for half an hour before Bex announced that she thought there might have been a break-in over the weekend.

'You didn't turn off the computers at the wall on Saturday, did you, Geth?'

Gethin just stared at her. He never turned anything off at the wall. He'd grown up in a household where his father went nuts if a light was left on or a television plugged in and he had made a point of wasting electricity with impunity throughout his adult life as a result.

'No, I didn't think so. But someone did.'

'Odd.'

'Yeah, and I've a feeling things have been moved around on my desk just a little bit. How about yours?'

Gethin looked at his desk. There were papers all over the place but, actually, now he looked at them, maybe they weren't disordered in quite the way he'd left them. He checked the stacks of paper relating to the Izma M case, all piled up around the conference table. It looked like they were all there – though, God knows how you'd tell if a few were missing.

'How about your PC? Mine is password protected but I know yours isn't. You want to check if anyone's been nosing around?'

Gethin stared at his PC for a few seconds, wondering how he'd find out a thing like that. Then he had an idea. He clicked on Explorer, went to his 'my documents' folder and clicked on the tab to have them ordered by how recently they'd been opened. And, sure enough, all the documents relating to the Izma case looked to have been accessed around seven pm the day before.

'Christ, looks like someone was in here yesterday evening. They've had a look at all the Izma M files. Couldn't have been Lee, could it?'

'No way,' said Bex. 'Why would she use your computer instead of hers? And she certainly wouldn't go round turning off the plugs. Who else could it be though?'

Gethin remembered something: 'I had a call from my dad on Saturday. He said Terence Donoghue had been asking about us.'

'Oh, yeah?'

'Apparently, he had a client who'd found out we were looking into Danny Bliss, and Donoghue passed down the message via the Judge to say that, if we found out anything, could we let him know?'

'How on earth did they know that?' Bex thought about it. 'Probably they saw one of the posts I put up asking for information. So it looks like they decided not to wait till we called. I wouldn't have thought Donoghue would do something like that. They're a big respectable firm.'

'But I bet they know some people who will find out stuff for them, no questions asked,' said Gethin. 'Like the newspapers, you know – "we don't phone hack, we just pay some dodgy ex-copper to do it for us."'

Even as he was talking, the image of Mal Haynes flitted through his mind. Haynes Security, what exactly did they do...?

'You know what?' he said. 'I think we may have wandered into deep waters here.'

* * *

Gethin and Lee tried to make sense of it all as they drove over to Bristol later that morning. All they could say for sure was that it looked more and more as if Danny Bliss wasn't dead after all, and that there were people out there very anxious to find him. And, of course, if Danny Bliss was still alive, it raised the possibility that he'd killed his parents and faked his own death. In which case, he might not exactly be happy to be found.

The main purpose of the Bristol trip was to collect Deano from hospital and drive him back to Cardiff. When they arrived at the BRI, though, it was clear that it was going to take a good couple of hours before he could be discharged, so Gethin left Lee and Deano talking and walked up the hill to Kingsdown to have another go at extracting information from Shaun. This time, Gethin insisted on taking the lead.

Lee handed him her trusty torch and told him to be careful.

When he rang on Shaun's doorbell, there was no response at first. On the second try a woman's voice called out, 'Who is it?'

'Gethin Grey. I'm a lawyer working for Izma M.'

'Okay, coming.' He heard steps coming towards the door and an inner door being unlocked. Stepping back a couple of paces, he put his hand on the torch, ready for action should it be opened by an enraged Shaun.

It wasn't. It was opened by a well turned out white woman in her early 30s with expensively tousled blonde hair and elaborate make-up. She looked like one of those women who work on a department store perfume counter.

'Hello,' she said, 'I'm Denise. I'm afraid Shaun isn't here

at the moment, but he'll be back shortly if you'd like to come in and wait.'

'Thanks.' Gethin followed her through the porch area and straight into the living room.

The house, as Lee had said, was spotless. The whole ground floor had been knocked into one. At one end, there was a living room with the obligatory massive TV and leather sofas. At the other, a state-of-the-art kitchen complete with range cooker, breakfast bar and acres of matching cupboards.

'Do you mind taking your shoes off?' said Denise as they entered, 'and try to be quiet, please, my little boy's asleep upstairs.'

'Sorry.' Gethin slipped out of his Timberlands and left them by the front door.

'Coffee? I make a mean cappuccino.'

'Sounds good.'

It didn't look like any drug dealer's place Gethin had ever seen, and he'd been into a few over the years, in one role or another. It was more like a showroom from a furniture shop: not IKEA, somewhere a bit glitzier than that. Everything was so new and even the baby stuff, a stash of toys and a playpen, was stacked neatly in the corner. It wasn't that drug dealers didn't have expensive stuff, but the spotlessness, the neatness and the lack of three guys sitting around watching TV, chatting about their new phones and doing lines off the coffee table, was disconcerting. Maybe Shaun was just a very disciplined dude who kept his business well away from his house. Or maybe he'd gone straight. Perhaps that's why he was so defensive, not to say violent; maybe he was just trying to protect a hard-won new life.

Denise finished making the coffee and Gethin joined her at the breakfast bar.

'Lovely place,' he said.

Denise beamed at him: 'Isn't it? You should have seen it a few years ago, though – it was such a bachelor pad. Then I came along and, well, I said to Shaun this place needs a woman's touch. At first, he was like totally resisting it, but then I started making a few little changes and you know what? These days he's really into it. We watch the makeover shows on the telly together and Shaun makes notes about things we like and on Sundays we used to go out looking for stuff. Course it's a bit different now with the baby.' She paused and looked at Gethin intently: 'Do you like antiques?'

'Not really,' said Gethin, as much to bring the conversation to an end quickly as because he had any strong opinions on the subject. Denise was delighted.

'Oh God, me neither. I can't stand them. I like new stuff. Having someone else's old stuff with all their germs. Gives me the creeps.'

'Mmm,' said Gethin, doing his best to sound sympathetic rather than faintly alarmed. 'So what's Shaun doing?'

'Oh, business, you know? He's always in and out in his line of work.'

Gethin was tempted to ask straight out what line of work that would be – but decided to let it ride. 'Oh, right.'

'Yeah, he works all hours, Shaun. You have to these days with all the immigrants and that, all working for minimum wage and overstretching the NHS. It's not fair on the rest of us. It's not like I'm a racist or anything – I mean, look at Shaun – and he agrees with me anyway, but enough is enough, don't you think?'

'Hmm,' said Gethin, in the most neutral tone he could muster. Surely she couldn't be talking about Shaun's drug dealing? That was still one area of commerce where a highly motivated local could get ahead. Or maybe the Albanians were taking over or something. Drug dealers for UKIP – that would be a thing. Before he could say anything more, they both heard the outer door open and then the sound of someone wheeling in a bike and taking off their helmet before opening the inner door. That was Bristol for you – even the drug dealers were eco-friendly cyclists.

'All right, love,' said Shaun, before looking around and clocking Gethin: 'Fuck are you doing here?'

'C'mon love. He just wants to ask some questions about your friend Izma. And keep your voice down, Connor's sleeping. Look, I know you don't like talking about all that awful stuff, but sometimes we all have to do things we don't like.'

Gethin just about managed not to burst out laughing, hearing Shaun being addressed like an errant schoolboy. He raised his hand cautiously.

'Look, Shaun, I was just passing by and I wanted to ask you one quick question we're really hoping you might be able to help us with. We think we may have identified a possible suspect for Hannah Gold's murder, but we're having a lot of trouble tracking him down. All we have at the moment is just his name…'

'Oh, yeah,' said Shaun, his tone flatly hostile, 'who's that then?' He showed no interest in hearing Gethin's reply, just pushed past him so he could plug his iPhone into a charger.

'The name's Danny Bliss – Daniel Bliss. He was an old boyfriend of Hannah's and he showed up in Bristol just before she died. You ever come across him or hear his name?'

'No,' said Shaun, before Gethin had properly finished speaking, and clearly making no effort whatsoever to search the memory banks. 'Never heard of him.'

'You sure, love? Sounds like it's really important,' said

Denise, excited at the thought of unmasking a murderer.

'I'm sure,' said Shaun. 'Now fuck off out of here, before I fucking kick you out.'

Gethin was just about to comply when the doorbell rang.

'Fuck,' said Shaun, 'you wait here.'

As Shaun walked over to the door, Gethin noticed the iPhone right next to him on the breakfast bar. Denise was busy putting something in the bin and, on an impulse, he disconnected the charging cable and slipped the phone into his pocket. If Shaun didn't want to talk, maybe his phone would give up its secrets. It was a reckless thing to do, but Gethin felt reckless.

You could hear Shaun talking to someone in the porch now. The new voice sounded angry. Then the inner door opened and Shaun came back into the room, followed by a big man with a drinker's face and the body of an athlete gone slightly to seed.

'Oh, hello Mr Haynes,' said Denise. 'Would you like a coffee?'

'No love, he's not really staying for long. How about you nip upstairs and check on Connor while the three of us have a little discussion?'

Denise looked put out but complied. As she was heading up the stairs, she waved at Gethin. 'Nice to meet you,' she said, 'and Shaun – remember, he is only trying to help.'

All three men waited till there was the sound of the door closing upstairs and a grizzly toddler waking up.

'So, you're the cunt's been asking questions about me?' said Haynes.

Gethin tried to place his accent but couldn't quite. It wasn't Bristol but not quite London either, probably somewhere along the M4 corridor. Swindon maybe.

'Am I?'

'First, some twat in a stupid hat comes round my office asking me if I sell illegal weapons. Then the fucking Chief Constable calls me up asking why he's getting enquiries about me from some retired judge over in Cardiff. Yeah, I reckon you've been asking questions. I've met the monkey and you're the fucking organ grinder. Isn't that right?'

'Look,' said Gethin. 'All I'm trying to do is help Izma M, your mate. Surely you want that too, Shaun? I really don't see where all this hostility is coming from.'

Haynes got in first: 'Well, that's very nice and public spirited of you, but haven't you heard of leaving well alone, letting sleeping dogs lie and all that? St bloody Izma is guilty as charged. Whatever bleeding heart lefty is paying your wages may not like to believe it, but that's the truth. Izma killed that girl – don't know why exactly, some sort of accident, I don't know, gave her a slap and she hit her head going down, that kind of thing – end of story. And now some clever cunt like you comes along interfering in people's legitimate business. I suggest you butt the fuck out of it. Don't want to find yourself in intensive care like your mate, do you?'

Gethin decided retreat was definitely the better part of valour at this point, seeing as he was stuck in a room with two big, dangerous blokes.

'Fine, I won't bother you again.' He started heading for the door, trying his best to project calm under pressure.

And then the phone rang. Shaun's phone rang with a distinctive and deafening ring tone. And it was quite obviously emanating from Gethin's pocket. He didn't wait to try and explain, he just ran.

It was only when he hit the pavement outside he realised he didn't have his shoes on. Christ! Immediately, inevitably, he stepped on a sharp stone that sent a bolt of pain shooting up his leg but he didn't stop moving. He could hear Shaun and Mal Haynes behind him shouting threats.

He was running down the road towards the pub, his feet were killing him; there was no way he could keep this up. He thought about running into the pub and asking for sanctuary, though after the way the barmaid had been the last time, he wasn't at all sure that would work.

He could hear his pursuers gaining on him and was about to dive into the pub anyway when he saw a bike, a trendy looking number coated entirely in luminous green paint, leaning up against the side of the pub, like someone had just left it there for a second. He grabbed it and discovered that it was unlocked. A moment later he was pedalling as hard as he could down the road. It was still hurting his feet but pedals were a definite improvement on pavement. Behind him he heard cursing and then Shaun shouting: 'You get your car, I'll get my bike.'

Gethin felt like punching the air. All he had to do was reach the end of the road and make a couple of turns and he'd surely have lost his pursuers. After fifty yards or so, he came to a T-junction and saw that he'd have to give way. He reached his fingers out to squeeze the brakes only to discover there was nothing there.

Oh for God's sake, he'd stolen a bloody fixie – one of those bikes with no gears or brakes. They were supposed to make you at one with the bike through the lack of extraneous gadgetry or some such idea. Gethin had an old mate who was obsessed with them, saw it as a kind of Zen thing. There was definitely some way of making the things brake but he was seconds away from shooting out on to the road and he couldn't remember it properly. It was something to do with pedalling backwards but, even as he tried to do that, he realised he was too late, his momentum was driving him forwards into the road and there was a blue van coming towards him at some speed. It was all he could do to swerve out of its way but in doing so he completely lost control and, before he knew it, the bike had crashed into a post box and he was flying through the air. Thankfully, he managed to roll as he hit the ground, and an oncoming car steered out of his way while hitting its horn vigorously. By the time he was back on his feet and in charge of the bike, though, he could see Shaun coming fast towards him on his own bike.

Gethin jumped back on the fixie, and headed left, downhill. It was in the direction of the city centre and potential places of safety. His feet were raw, his knees and left elbow throbbing from the fall. He pedalled down as fast as he could but sensed Shaun coming up behind him. As they came to the bottom of the hill, he could see a major junction up ahead. There was a queue of traffic waiting at the lights. His options were narrowing dramatically. If he braked – if, indeed, he could manage to make the green beast brake – and waited at the lights, Shaun would surely catch him. Instead, at the last moment, he swerved the bike hard to the right, shot across the road in front of the oncoming traffic and into a narrow laneway. As he did so, he saw Shaun in his peripheral vision hurtling past him down towards the lights. He'd gained himself a little bit of a lead.

Not for long, though. The laneway Gethin was on fed on to the main road a little further west. This time he had no choice but to brake. He just about managed it through a combination of pedalling backwards and leaning to one side, so that he skidded to a stop just in time to avoid being engulfed by two lanes of oncoming traffic.

He could see Shaun coming towards him, hammering along the pavement with complete disregard for pedestrians.

Gethin was trapped. He couldn't move into the traffic without risking death and he couldn't conjure up any momentum to cycle away from his nemesis.

'Give me my phone, you cunt.' Shaun jumped off his bike.

Gethin had momentarily forgotten he had Shaun's phone. Now, though, he realised it could be a lifeline. He grabbed it out of his pocket and under armed it towards the road.

'Fuck,' yelled Shaun, caught between the desire to pound the living daylights out of Gethin and the need to save his precious iPhone from being crushed.

In the end, he did what any modern day citizen would, and opted to save the phone, diving into the traffic to the accompaniment of squealing car brakes and much horn blowing. Gethin saw the chance to kick off on his bike, scraping his poor feet one more time as he did so, and headed to his left, downhill and directly towards the BRI, where he would surely be safe. He powered down the road, his feet killing him, but what the hell, till he came to the next set of lights. He managed to slow down a little to give them a chance to change, then saw a clear road opening up ahead of him with the hospital only another hundred yards or so away.

Just then, a car coming up the road towards him suddenly slid over into Gethin's lane, completely blocking his forward progress. As he got closer he could see that the driver was Haynes. Shit.

Somehow, Gethin managed to make a tight U-turn without tipping over. He could hear Haynes manoeuvring his car behind him. Gethin turned left into a big side road, the one that led down towards the Colston Hall, but Haynes' car was on him already, crowding him into the side of the road. He saw an opening in the building to his left, some sort of little pedestrian alleyway, and went for it.

Instantly, he knew he'd made a terrible mistake. This was no ordinary lane that he was heading into at speed but Christmas Steps. This was a near vertical cut-through from Park Row down to Lewin's Mead below. Gethin remembered walking down them sometime in the distant past. They were a sort of tourist attraction, an olde worlde enclave of antique shops arranged down a precipitous slope.

In his memory, it consisted entirely of steps and he prepared himself for an imminent total wipe-out, to be thrown down a long stretch of stone steps at high speed. But, as he hurtled towards what looked like certain doom, he realised he'd had it wrong. There was a short set of steps almost beneath him but then a stretch of regular if steep pathway. If he could just cling on to the bike he might be okay. The bike bumped once, twice, three times as he went down the first flight of steps. He thought he was about to shoot over the handlebars but managed to throw his body weight backwards and hold on. Then he was on the flat downhill stretch: there were pedestrians in front and he screamed at them to move out of the way, dodging an old couple with a swerve which almost took him into a Victorian lamp post set in the middle of the path. Then he saw more steps coming towards him, many more steps, two more flights the same length as the one he'd come down already.

Adrenaline had him well and truly in its grip now as he gunned the bike towards them, almost past caring what injury he was about to sustain. The bike sailed down the first flight: bounce, bounce, bounce. Gethin somehow managed to balance perfectly as he crashed back down. The second flight, though, was a different matter: he must've slightly shifted his weight to the right and with each bounce the bike tilted further and further over, threatening to catapult him through the window of the pub at the bottom. Somehow, he flung himself over to the left and, amazingly, the bike responded. Maybe there was something to this Zen thing after all. He lurched and bounced to the side of the pub and then, there he was on the flat, travelling much too fast towards a very busy main road but still riding, still alive and uninjured.

He managed to join the flow of traffic heading towards the Broadmead roundabout. All he needed to do, he reckoned, was reach the roundabout and take the first left and he'd be back at the hospital. He scanned the oncoming traffic for any sign of Shaun or Malcolm Haynes, couldn't see any, then risked looking over his shoulder. No sign there either, which was hardly surprising, given the route he'd had to take.

Now the adrenaline was easing off a little, he could feel his feet screaming with pain each time he pedalled. God knows what they would look like when he took off his socks. Lacerated to fuck, he suspected.

The hospital loomed up on his right. He waited for a break in the traffic, before cutting across the opposite lane and mounting the pavement. He leapt off the bike and propped it up against a handy bike rack. He would call the pub later and tell them where it was. Very sorry and all that, but sometimes needs must. As he walked alongside the big blue atrium with its Costa Coffee concession, he saw Lee sat at the window table. He knocked on the glass and gave her a wave, then kept on going towards the entrance.

He'd almost made it when a bike swooped on to the pavement out of nowhere and Shaun jumped off, eyes wild. He gave a kind of howl of inchoate rage and started after Gethin, who ran as fast as his hobbled feet would let him towards the sanctuary of the hospital. Shaun looked certain to make it to the door first when he crashed to the ground, howling in pain as his face made sudden communion with the concrete. It took Gethin a second to realise what had happened. It was Lee, she'd stepped out of the hospital just in time and was now standing over Shaun's prone body.

'Lucky you had me here to trip the cunt,' she said to Gethin, who could only grunt his agreement.

Shaun started to struggle to his feet but Lee pushed him down hard with her foot.

'Look dickhead,' she said, 'there's about a million security cameras watching us right now. If you want to go straight to jail, do not pass go, all right, have a pop at me. Or if you have any sense in your head, you could just fuck off.'

She stood back and let Shaun, still winded and now bleeding from his nose, struggle to his feet. He gave Lee the hardest stare a man with a bloodied nose could manage and said, 'You'll get yours, love, don't you worry.' Then he turned his back on the two of them and walked back up the hill towards his home.

'Fucking hell, boss,' said Lee, 'that's the last time I let you out on your own.'

Nineteen

GETHIN WAS TOO SHAKEN TO say much on the ride home. Lee was insured to drive his car so he sat in the passenger seat, gingerly inspecting his feet while she chatted away to Deano who was lying across the back.

It was only after they had crossed the bridge into Wales that he started to breathe easier. Then it struck him how absurd that was. If Shaun or Malcolm Haynes wanted to exact vengeance – or simply put the fear of God into them – they knew where to find them. The Last Resort office address wasn't displayed on the website – too many nutters out there – but if you knew where to look it couldn't be that hard to find out. And they'd already had a break-in.

By the time they'd dropped Deano off at his mum's place and arrived back at the office, Gethin was starting to become seriously worried. It was already late afternoon so he told Lee and Bex to go home with their laptops and have a think about possible alternative workspaces for the next few days.

Once the others had left, Gethin sat alone in the office, trying to centre himself. He tried to remember the meditation techniques he'd learned, tried to clear his mind of everything but his immediate physical reality, tried not to think about Shaun or Mal Haynes or Izma M or Amelia Laverne or Cat. It worked up to a point. In fact, he'd almost drifted off at his desk when he heard someone trying the outside door. He jumped out of his seat.

It was Bex.

'Geth, what are you doing here? You should be at home lying in a hot bath. Your poor feet.'

'I know, I just...'

'Cat?'

'Yeah.'

'Aren't things any better?'

'Not really. She's not shouting at me anymore but she's not speaking to me either. I don't know which is worse.'

'Go home, have a bath, show her your feet and show her you care about her...' she paused and raised her eyebrows theatrically, 'as a woman.'

'Jesus, Bex,' said Gethin, once her meaning had sunk into his addled brain. 'That's really the last thing... but yeah, I know what you're saying.'

* * *

Bex's advice was still ringing in his ears when Gethin made it back to the upside-down house. Cat was there already, feet up in front of the TV with a cup of coffee, no Hattie. Mondays after school she went off to her music lesson with Bella. So it was just the two of them.

'What happened to you?' Cat turned down the volume on the six o'clock news.

'What d'you mean?'

'You're limping.'

'It's nothing.' Gethin stared down at his feet, encased in an old pair of trainers he'd found at the office. 'No, it's not nothing. I was chased by someone and I didn't have any shoes...'

He looked over at Cat, across what seemed like an acre of living room. All he wanted was for her to take him in her arms, make it better, make the fears and the hurt go away. She wasn't having it, though.

'What do you mean, you didn't have any shoes? Did someone catch you shagging their wife?'

Gethin winced. Sometime he was going to have to tell her about Amelia, but not now. One thing at a time. He gave her the edited highlights of his chase across Bristol and, by the end of it, Cat had softened a little.

'Sit on the sofa and take off your socks. Let me have a look.'

He did as he was told. He knew he was in good hands. She was qualified as a medical doctor and, while she didn't relish being called upon to deal with every family ailment, she knew what she was about.

She didn't waste time on expressions of sympathy, just cleaned up the wounds efficiently.

'Shall I bandage them up now or do you want to have a bath first?'

There was something brittle about her tone.

'I'll have the bath now.' He made his way gingerly downstairs.

He was enjoying a good soak, starting to relax for the first time in what seemed like months, when Cat came in. She sat on the toilet seat and waited till she had his full attention.

'I've been fucking someone else,' she said.

'You what?' said Gethin, not because he hadn't heard what she'd said but because it simply did not compute.

'You heard me.' Cat's voice was high and tense but determined. 'I've been fucking someone else and you didn't even notice. You don't ever think about me, not really. You take me for granted, you treat me like shit and you think I'll always be here for you, cleaning up your mess, earning the money to pay for your fuck-ups, raising your child, bandaging your fucking feet.

'Sometimes I feel like I want to kill you because I can't bear it that I'm invisible to you. So I started fucking someone else and I waited for you to notice, for you to see. And you still didn't because everything is about you. And then, like an idiot, I thought things were going to be okay again, now you had this case, I thought you were really present again. But what do you do – you go back to the fucking casino, the first chance you have. And I went back to him, let him fuck the living daylights out of me. And you still didn't notice. Scratches all over my back and you didn't see. You don't ever fucking notice. I had to fucking tell you myself!'

Gethin lay in the bath, stunned. Absurdly, he had Bex's advice running through his mind – treat her right, make her feel like a woman. As ever Bex had been right. Bex was always right. He was just too late. The bathwater felt cold suddenly and he was all too aware of his vulnerability, lying there naked. Who was that French woman in the revolution who stabbed someone in the bath? He was struck by a visceral fear that Cat was about to pull out a knife, turn the bathwater red.

Feeling absurd, wet and naked, he clambered out of the bath, grabbed a towel and wrapped it around his waist, disbelief and understanding battling it out inside him. His wife had been fucking another man. He knew he was meant to be angry but, right now, there was only guilt. Guilt and sadness.

'Oh, Cat.' He opened his arms to her, his towel falling to the floor. 'I'm so sorry.'

'Time's past for that.' She stood up and moved quickly towards the door.

As the door closed behind her, he took her place on the

toilet seat, his head in his hands, trying to make sense of what he'd heard. His head was buzzing, as if someone was shouting inside his skull. After an unfathomable while, he realised he was dry.

He dressed and went back upstairs. Hattie had returned from her music lesson and Cat was making her a snack and chatting away as if nothing had happened. When she saw Gethin she immediately started fussing around him, bandaging his feet, while Hattie bombarded him with questions about what had happened. As she talked, he could feel the anger building inside him. Finally, she went off to her room.

The pair of them, husband and wife, waited till they heard their daughter's door close and her music started up. As one, they turned to face each other. Cat had her head held high, her jaw stuck out as though she was ready for the fight.

Part of Gethin felt like planting one firmly on that jaw, see how she liked those apples. But he restrained himself. He was not, thank God, that kind of man. But he was angry.

'You want to explain to me why I'm meant to be the one feeling guilty in this situation? You're the one who's been, as you so eloquently put it, fucking someone else and apparently it's my fault. Well, ain't that convenient? For you.'

Cat stared at him, her voice weary. 'Like I said, Geth, it isn't enough just to snore alongside someone if you want them to stay faithful. If there'd been any sign that you gave one single shit about me, I would never have done this, never. I just didn't know what else to do to make you see...'

Gethin noted that she had gone from weary to tearful in a matter of seconds. It was all a little theatrical, as if she'd been rehearsing for this moment. Well, he wasn't going to play along.

'For fuck's sake.' He rose to his feet. 'You're not going to make this my fault. You – you've broken the contract, the basic fucking trust that has to be there. You've done that, not me. I've never done that. All these years and, God knows, I've had some opportunities.'

'Like who? You wouldn't notice if a woman...'

'Shut up.' Gethin was really angry now. 'This is not about my failings, this is about you trying to wreck our marriage because of some bullshit about me not noticing you. Well, I'm noticing you now all right and I'm not fucking liking what I'm seeing. Right now I can't even bear to look at you, you cheating cunt.'

On that elegant note he headed downstairs. He put an overnight bag together and went down to the car. He didn't slam the door for fear of upsetting Hattie, though she'd be upset soon enough, he supposed. But, for the moment, he just had to leave.

Twenty

HE DIDN'T WANT TO GO anywhere he might know people. Fortunately, Cowbridge Road, in Canton, offered a range of boozers that no one he knew would be seen dead in. He left the car in a deserted shoppers' car park and surveyed his options, contemplating the King's Castle and the Admiral Napier, before accepting that times like these were precisely what Wetherspoons were invented for.

Standing at the bar of the chain's local outpost, The Ivor Davies, he drank three pints of the strongest ale on offer. He drank them fast and methodically, staring straight ahead and seeing nothing, his mind whirring. He thought about Amelia Laverne, how she'd wanted him to hurt her physically so that she'd feel something, and Cat, how she'd hurt him psychically in the hope that he'd feel something. What did he feel, really? Hurt, or like he wanted to dish out some hurt, or both? There was anger all right, but a frustrated anger, because he couldn't say whether it was himself or Cat he was angry with, or just life itself, the way it can bend you and the people you love out of shape.

He thought about going to Amelia Laverne, giving her what she wanted, taking out his anger on her skinny, scarred body and – much to his relief – was simply revolted at the idea. That wasn't him. He thought about going back to Cat, climbing into bed with her, making her his own again, taking back his property or something. Wasn't that how you were meant to feel, as a man? But he couldn't bear that either. Not even knowing who it was that she'd been with. That she could have done that to him, in such an apparently cold-blooded way, he struggled to understand.

Somewhere midway through the third pint, the alcohol started to properly work its magic. Fuck it, he decided, if she wanted to indulge herself, throw all her promises aside and fuck some fucking stranger, why on earth shouldn't he do what he liked to do? Take a little risk, have a little flutter.

Finishing his pint, he went straight back behind the wheel, fully aware of how irresponsible he was being but not giving a flying fuck, and drove to the Leckwith Retail Park, where he just left the Nissan clumsily sprawled across two parking spaces and headed inside, ready to do his worst.

He bought a large whisky from the bar and felt a sudden sense of calm, the fury that had been building up in his skull dissipating. He was amongst his people now. He had come home. He even knew just what he wanted to gamble on when the time came. He had his debit card and the company credit card in his wallet. He was ready, rocking and righteous. He kind of knew it was the drink talking but, you know what, he didn't care.

He played a couple of hands of blackjack first, just warming up, seeing who was around. In the course of twenty minutes' play, he was fifty quid up, then thirty quid down and finally twenty pounds up. More importantly, he spotted his ideal adversary, the man who he was sure would match him bet for bet in a game of Punto Banco. The guy's name was Rashid. He was a property developer mostly, but with his hands in a few other bits and bobs – an Indian restaurant in Penarth, a sandwich bar in Rumney and so on. He was extravagantly dodgy, was always trying to persuade you to buy tickets for big sporting events at ridiculous prices, but he did it all with good humour, and when he was gambling he took his wins and his losses in his stride.

A half hour and two more whiskys later, Gethin made his move. He asked Rashid if he fancied a private game of Punto Banco. Rashid looked him up and down – probably for visual clues as to Gethin's current level of drunkenness and/or prosperity, then said sure and had a word with the Australian floor manager. Soon they were seated at the Punto Banco table at the back of the room, along with a croupier called Claire, a Black Country girl.

Punto Banco is a card game with the element of skill taken out. Even more so than Blackjack. With Punto Banco, the dealer deals the cards, you turn them over and you win or you lose. No need to kid yourself you're playing a game of skill. No question of card counting, just pure dumb luck. Are you feeling lucky? You better be. There were just the two of them playing. Gethin sat on one side of the table, Rashid opposite him. At the end of the table, Claire dealt the cards. Rash was the banker; he got to set the limit for each hand.

After an initial run of luck, Gethin launched into a long losing streak and began to coast past all the different limits he'd set himself – first five hundred quid, then a thousand, at which point his overdraft was maxed out. He could have – God knows, he should have – stopped then, but he didn't. He had the Last Resort Legals credit card in his wallet. And that came with a four grand limit, all free and clear as Bex religiously paid it off every month. So he went again. And watched the losses mount up, a thousand down, then back almost to evens and then a final disastrous slide as the milestones flew by, one grand, two, then three.

It didn't take long, half an hour max, before Gethin found himself right at the end of the line. Rashid was going to call £500 as the stake for the next hand, Gethin was sure of it. He couldn't afford it. Of course not. He couldn't afford to be there in the first place. He didn't have money to lose like this: he had a family – well, a daughter at least – a house, a business.

Right now, though, it wasn't simply an abstract sense of not being able to afford it, but something more urgent. He was within a hundred pounds of the Last Resort credit card's limit and he was about to accept a wager for £500. He only had one £50 chip left, so he would have to fake a laugh and say, 'Let's just deal the cards, Rash. I'll go get the money afterwards in the unlikely event I don't win'. And Rash would laugh and say, 'Sure, it's good to get some exercise walking over to the cashpoint machine'.

That would be embarrassing, that walk, but the embarrassment was the least of it. By now, he was in a whole different world of wrongness. So he'd better win. He'd better take £500 from Rash and walk away from the table with some tattered shreds of self-respect surviving. More money would come in soon. Amelia would pay them again at the end of the week. If he still had five hundred pounds, he wouldn't need to go cap in hand to Cat and beg her for a sub – at this time of all times he didn't want to do that. He could try asking Bex to front him up whatever was left of Amelia's advance but that, in some ways, would be even worse. Things were already fucked up with Cat, but if Bex found out he'd been gambling again with the company money she'd probably quit and Last Resort would be well and truly fucked. Christ... he just had to win this hand.

'Five hundred then?' said Rash.

'Sure,' he said instead, 'five hundred is good.'

Claire the croupier shuffled. Gethin had once read an article about an American poker player who'd found a way of gaining an advantage at Punto Banco by observing the minutest differences between the bottoms and tops of cards. He would ask the croupier to turn certain cards around and gradually build up a sense of when the cards he favoured were liable to show up. It was hardly infallible but it shifted the odds very slightly in favour of the gambler and – if he or she was able to cover their losses for long enough – the winnings should eventually stack up. The guy he had read about won seven million in one night using this system, though the casino – true to form – had refused to pay out. Gethin more or less understood how it worked but also that there was no way he could do the same thing. He had neither the patience nor the eyesight.

So he just sat there, nerves fizzing, while Claire dealt a card to him and a card to Rash, another card to him and another card to Rash. Temporarily unable to breathe, Gethin picked up his cards. He let out a long sigh when he saw what he had. Thank God he wasn't playing poker; his chances of bluffing anyone while in this state were nil. He had an ace of hearts and the six of clubs for a total of seven. It wasn't great, but it was pretty decent. The odds were definitely in his favour.

The rules of Punto Banco were simple – highest score wins, with the maximum score being nine. The scoring system was a little eccentric, though – picture cards all scored ten and an ace one, but when you added the scores together only the final digit counted. Thus, a king and a three added up to thirteen, but was only counted as three, and was easily beaten by a three and a five, which would score eight. So a total of seven was more than okay. You automatically rested on a score of seven, while if your two cards gave you a score of five or less, you'd be given a third and final card.

Gethin waited for Rash to show his cards. He prayed they'd be the kind of rubbish that he'd been drawing all night. They were: Rash had a pair of jacks. Two zeroes in effect. Claire dealt the third card. Gethin knew the odds were well in his favour now. The only cards that could beat him were an eight or a nine. Rash picked up the card, looked at it and punched the air in triumph. Gethin felt as if the world was giving way beneath him, as if the room was spinning, as if the floor was coming fast to meet him.

The next thing he knew, he was lying on his back, staring up at the polystyrene roof tiles, Rash's face looming over him, shouting something that took a few seconds to process.

'I was only having a laugh, mate. It was your hand.'

'You what?'

'You won, mate. I had a useless bloody king. No need to throw a fit.'

'Bastard.' Gethin dragged himself back to his feet, righting his chair and sitting back down. Rashid passed him £500 worth of chips.

'Okay,' said Gethin, the gambling rush roaring through him again. 'Same again.'

Rashid and Claire looked at each other. Rashid raised his eyebrows and Claire shook her head microscopically, like she didn't think it was her place to say, but if she had to take a view, she didn't think it was a good idea.

'Sorry, mate,' said Rashid. 'You've had enough. I should have seen the signs earlier but, well, I was too busy winning all your money. What just happened there, well, I don't want you having a heart attack on my account. And... I know it's none of my business but...'

Gethin felt a rush of outraged pride. He was a grown-up, wasn't he? If he wanted to take the occasional risk to spice up his life a bit, who the hell was Rash to stop him?

He turned to Claire: 'Is there anyone else...'

'No sir, I'm sorry. Mr Rashid is right. I think you've gambled enough tonight. Maybe I can call you a cab? Or we can offer you a meal. On the house, of course.'

How dare they treat him like a child? 'Fine,' he said, 'fine. I'll go.' He rose with a show of outrage but part of him knew he had all the dignity of a seven-year-old who'd had his sweets confiscated.

Out in the car park, he was just struggling to operate his remote control when he felt a hand on his shoulder.

He turned round to see a very large security guard.

'Sorry, but I'm afraid I can't let you drive, the state you're in.'

Gethin wanted to argue but, out in the cold night air, he was all too aware of just how drunk he was.

'Fine, I'll find a cab.' He waved his arm towards a car idling outside the casino.

It was only when he was sitting in the front seat of the car, Melody FM on the radio, that Gethin realised he had no idea where he was going to go.

Twenty-One

'YOU'RE DRUNK,' SAID THE JUDGE, as he opened the door. He was wearing a dressing gown so old that Gethin remembered it from his childhood.

'I wish you had died and not mum,' said Gethin.

'So do I,' said the Judge. 'I'd have thought you were old enough to know that we don't always get what we wish for. Though I'm not at all sure that you've learned anything at all.'

'Oh God,' said Gethin, following his father into the kitchen, 'Oh God, Dad, Cat and...'

The Judge held up his hand. 'That's enough. I'm going to bed. I advise you to drink plenty of water and do likewise. The bed in the guest room is made up. I'll see you in the morning.'

Gethin began to protest then stopped. The Judge was right: no good was likely to come out of opening his mouth any further. Instead, he was overcome by a sense of utter exhaustion. He poured out a pint glass of water and took it up to the spare bedroom where he fell asleep without either undressing or moving under the covers.

Waking at seven from what felt more like a coma than a night's rest, Gethin knew at once that he wouldn't be getting any more sleep. He spent ten minutes staring at the ceiling, alternately cursing himself and Catriona, then forced himself to start assessing the damage he'd done.

He had lost £4,800. It was roughly the amount of money

that he might have hoped to have paid himself over the first month of the Izma M investigation. Losing it was, by any standards, a disaster. He wasn't immediately worried about Cat finding out, the £550 in his pocket would probably be enough to stop that happening, at least for a week or two. The real fuck-up was looting the Last Resort account, that could be disastrous. If Bex happened to check the balance, she would go utterly ballistic. No way she'd carry on working for him after that. Unless by then he had a result in the Izma case. Amelia had said something about a bonus payment if they were able to turn up sufficient new evidence for an appeal to be granted. Maybe he could do that before Bex discovered what he'd done. Maybe.

Unable to bear being alone with his thoughts any longer, and desperate for a cup of coffee, Gethin dragged himself out of bed.

When he arrived downstairs, the Judge was already up and dressed. 'So,' he said, handing over a coffee, 'may I assume that you've been gambling again and, as a result, Catriona has kicked you out of the family home?'

'No,' said Gethin. 'Cat's having an affair and that's why I was gambling.'

'I see. Do you imagine she might see things differently?'

Gethin raised his eyes to the ceiling. Once a judge always a judge, two sides to every story, prosecution and defence. Could he not simply take his son's side for once?

'Yes, Dad,' he said wearily, 'I imagine she would.'

The Judge nodded. 'You need to mend the fences. One affair, in my experience, can be forgiven. We all make mistakes. In the meantime, you're welcome to stay here for a few days.'

'Thanks,' said Gethin, 'appreciate it. Sorry about... you know... what I said.'

The Judge nodded his acceptance and changed the subject: 'The Ismail Mohammed case, how is that progressing?'

Gethin gave his father an edited résumé of the events of the last few days. As he reached the part about the Last Resort Office being broken into, he had an idea. If he was going to be staying at his father's anyway, why not go the whole hog?

'Do you think we might be able to work from here, just for a few days, till everyone's calmed down a bit?'

'Fine,' said the Judge. 'You can use the kitchen table.'

Lee and Bex both seemed happy enough with the idea when he called them. Bex would drive them over in an hour or so. She had some news as well, she said.

After he'd made the calls, Gethin stayed on the deck for a while, staring out at the Bristol Channel, watching an oil tanker making its ponderous way towards Avonmouth, over on the English side. Made him think of his impending doom, the credit card bill due to arrive on the Last Resort doormat at the beginning of next week. He tried to keep his mind on the case, what their next move should be, how the hell he was going to crack it in no time flat, but found himself thinking about Cat instead. And, in particular, wondering who it was that she'd been shagging.

Probably another shrink, he reckoned. She regularly went off to conferences. Christ, they used to joke about it, how her colleagues were always copping off with other people there. Had she been warning him, telling him those stories? Had there been messages, that he needed to be careful, to cherish her? She'd always seemed so devoted, the way she'd put up with his serial fuck-ups. Was she right about all that, what she'd said to him last night? Was it really his fault that his wife was fucking some shrink from Derby on the cotton sheets of a Premier Inn?

To make matters worse, his feet were killing him. He'd hardly noticed the pain from his various cuts and abrasions through the chaotic night but now a couple of the deeper cuts were starting to throb. He went back inside and asked his dad for a couple of ibuprofen. They were in the bathroom cupboard, lined up neatly alongside all the other medical supplies. It was a stark, masculine zone, everything clean and tidy and no sign of feminine frippery, no beauty products or nice little touches, just simple functionality.

Bex and Lee arrived a little before ten, Bex apologising for having become lost in the Sully backroads. The Judge was reasonably civil, showing them round the house to much appreciative oohing and aahing.

The sight of Bex gave Gethin pause. She really would kill him if she found out about the money he'd lost. Or kill the company at least – without her management skills they'd be sunk in no time. He just had to close this case, receive Amelia's bonus. He took a deep breath, closed his eyes momentarily, then exhaled.

'So,' he said to Bex. 'You said you had some news.'

'Yeah, first thing is I heard back from the hotel in New York, the Gramercy. They said they did have a record of a Mr D Green staying there on the night in question.'

'All right,' said Gethin, 'so that's that then?'

'Probably, but there was one weird thing. I called up to check it was a British D Green and not some random American. And the person I spoke to said it was a bit odd: there was no passport record at all, and there really should be if the person was British.'

'That is weird. I suppose he could have an American passport? Or maybe he knew someone who let him book in anyway – he's that sort of guy.'

'But why would he care? Why wouldn't he just give them his passport?'

'Maybe because D Green isn't his real name?'

'Cause actually it's Danny Bliss? Could be. Talking of Mr Bliss, you know I've been fishing for people who knew him? Well, I've had a really interesting reply. There's this guy who says he was big mates with Danny when they were like nineteen or twenty, but then he'd gone off travelling and ended up spending a few years in Croatia, DJing and stuff. Anyway, when he came back everything had changed. He hadn't really thought about Danny or anything except, one day, he was bored at work or whatever and decided to google his old mate and see what he was up to and instead he found out that he was meant to be dead. Then he saw my post asking for people to get in touch.'

Gethin frowned: 'But he hasn't seen him recently or anything?'

'No.'

'Sorry, Bex – but I don't see how that helps.'

'He says he has photos of Danny from right before he's meant to have died. Pictures of him out clubbing and stuff. He says he'll email them over and that's going to be a lot more use than that stupid bar mitzvah picture we've got.'

'I suppose,' said Gethin. 'If he's Dante Green, I should be able to identify him.'

Bex busied herself with the Wi-Fi network while running through some Blondie numbers. Gethin wondered whether her belting 'Heart of Glass' would annoy the Judge, then decided he really didn't care and headed up to the deck with Lee for a vape.

'Are you worried about Shaun or his mate coming after us?' asked Lee.

'Not sure. Way I see it there are two possibilities. Possibility number one – Shaun and Mal Haynes are engaged in some kind of illegal activity, nothing to do with the Izma M business but they don't appreciate us getting in the way. Possibility two – they are somehow involved in the Izma case and/or the murder of Hannah Gold and they seriously want us to stop investigating.'

Lee nodded: 'Sounds about right.'

'Yeah, I think it has to be one or the other. If it's possibility one – they're just a pair of drug dealers or whatever – I don't think they're very likely to come after us. So that would be good news for our safety but bad news for our investigation as it's completely irrelevant. On the other hand, if it's possibility two there's a real risk they might come after us – bad for our safety, but good for our investigation.'

'Nicely put, boss. And I can't see them finding us out here, that's for sure.'

Just as Lee said this, there was the sound of a car approaching. They both turned to look and saw a large black Mercedes snaking its way along the lane. They stood there not speaking as it slowed down right by the entrance to the Judge's house, then carried on down the lane.

'Fuck,' said Lee, 'I'm getting jumpy in my old age.'

She put her vaporiser back in her bag, 'C'mon, let's get to it.'

Gethin was about to follow her inside when his phone buzzed. He had a new voicemail. He'd never heard the call itself; obviously, the erratic mobile signal was going to be a major pain in the bum if they had to stay there for long. Standing at the edge of the deck where the signal was strongest, he called his mailbox, hoping to hear Cat's voice with some kind of olive branch.

'This is Amelia,' the message began. 'You seem to have

switched off your phone or something. I can't get through to you. Anyway, I thought I should let you know that I'm going to visit Shaun today. There's something I need to find out about Izma and he must know the answer. I was hoping you might come with me, but I suppose I'll just have to go it alone.'

Shit. He tried to call Amelia and her phone rang but she didn't pick up. What on earth was she playing at, going to see Shaun on her own? Surely she'd gathered that he wasn't exactly a friendly soul? And what on earth did she mean by saying there was something she needed to find out about Izma? He thought back to their prison visit. It hadn't really struck him at the time but there'd been a sense that she had her own agenda – all those questions about Izma's childhood. And now she'd gone blundering off to see Shaun, like little grey riding hood.

Gethin headed back inside and told the others the news to general bewilderment. He floated the idea of driving over to Bristol but Lee pointed out that it was too late for that. When they called Amelia's phone again, it went straight to voicemail.

'We'd better just keep trying,' said Bex. 'If she doesn't get back to us in a couple of hours, maybe someone should go over there.'

Gethin tried not to panic. Surely she'd be back in touch soon? If anything happened to Amelia, he was well and truly screwed. No goose, no golden egg.

Meanwhile, Bex was waving him over to look at something on her laptop. 'Hey,' she said, 'the Danny Bliss photos have come through.'

On screen was a big, blurry photo of three young men in a nightclub. All three sported shaved heads and sunglasses. Two of them were black and the other one looked

Mediterranean, Greek or Turkish maybe. That guy sported a little moustache and was doing his best to look tough, while the other two guys simply did look tough.

Gethin pointed at the Turkish looking one – 'That's our Danny, is it?'

'Yeah, changed a bit didn't he, from when he was the bar mitzvah boy? No wonder nobody recognised him.'

'That's what Hannah was meant to have said, wasn't it? That he'd changed a lot. Is that the best shot?'

'Yeah, probably.' Bex scrolled through a few more pictures. A couple of them had Danny in the midst of group hugs with a bunch of other tough boys, all taken from too far away to be much use, then there was one shot that just had Danny in it, which looked like the best one for an ID except it had a terrible case of red eye.

'Might be able to fix that,' said Bex. 'I'm sure there's an app that can sort it out.'

Gethin looked at the photo hard, tried to square it with Dante the asshole hotelier and couldn't. There was a vague resemblance maybe, but that was it.

'I don't think it's Dante,' he told Bex. 'Not that that necessarily means much. As I said before, there's no reason Hannah couldn't have known two different Dannys from North London. Anyway, do what you can with it and then print out some copies. Ta.'

Bex got on with some photo manipulations and Gethin went back upstairs in search of a signal. His phone started buzzing as soon as he went outside. A text from Cat reminding him that there was a parents' evening at the school the next day. Nothing else – no apology or enquiry as to how he was progressing. And there was a voicemail from Amelia.

It was very short and barely audible. 'I've just seen

Shaun and I may be away for a couple of days,' she said, before cutting off abruptly. Christ, just what he needed. He had the sense of everything slipping away from him. He was trying to focus but his head hurt from last night's whisky and his feet from the cuts and he really wasn't at all sure there was a way out of this hole he'd dug for himself.

Downstairs, Bex was printing off the photos of Danny Bliss, and emailing a scan over to Izma's lawyers so they could pass it on to their client.

The others wanted to eat so Bex sorted out a lunch of Yorkshire Provender soup drawn from the Judge's depressing selection – one for each day of the week. Gethin himself was too stressed and hungover to eat anything at all.

Instead, he found himself staring idly at the table on which the Judge had laid out the mugshots of people he'd put away. Amongst them was a picture of a man in his late twenties wearing a rugby shirt. He stood out from the rest by virtue of not looking like an obvious criminal – other than a faint resemblance to a much younger Tony Blair – with no visible tattoos, no wariness around the eyes, just a nice young man standing in a nice garden. Gethin recognised him at once. It was the former, or soon to be former, Last Resort client Karl Fletcher. The photo, if he remembered rightly, had been taken six months before Karl stabbed his parents and sister to death then burned down the house in an unsuccessful attempt to pass the whole thing off as an accident and get his hands on their money and life insurance.

'Whoah, Dad,' he called out, 'I'd forgotten you were the Judge on the Karl Fletcher case. What did you give him again?'

The Judge looked up: 'Life meaning life, or as close as

we're allowed to that. Minimum of thirty years.'

'You know he got married?'

'Yes and I believe his lady wife has been paying you to find evidence for an appeal.'

'Oh,' said Gethin, 'you know about that.' He sighed. 'Well, we have bills to pay, you know? And we're never going to find anything so...'

'Hey,' said Bex, thankfully bringing the unwelcome subject to a close. 'Got an email back from Izma's lawyers already. They sent the photo straight over to him – dunno how they managed to do that so quickly, he must have special privileges – and he says he's never seen this person in his life and he thinks we're wasting his time. And not just that but apparently he doesn't want to cooperate with us any further.'

'What?'

'Yeah, how does that make any sense?'

Gethin thought about it. 'Maybe it's because he does recognise the photo. Maybe there's some connection between him and Danny Bliss he doesn't want us to know about.'

'Or maybe he's just guilty and he's afraid we're going to prove it once and for all.'

'Could be,' said Gethin. In fact, this was a notion that had been nagging at him since the first time he'd met Izma. He just didn't behave the way most people who'd been wrongly convicted do. There was a fatalism about him that Gethin had assumed came from his religious faith, but maybe it was just from knowing he was guilty. Perhaps this whole campaign to release him from prison was just the result of a bunch of starry eyed liberals refusing to see that their hero was a murderer. Oh God, he hoped not. If Izma turned out to be guilty, there would be no bonus, no nothing.

'So, what do we do?'

'Carry on regardless, I suppose,' said Gethin, all too aware that he had no other choice. 'After all, it's not Izma who's paying our wages, it's Amelia.'

'Wherever she is.'

Twenty-Two

GETHIN WAS UP VERY EARLY the next morning. He sat at the kitchen table, typing up a summary of the case as it stood and hoping to hell he might spot something he'd missed. When the phone rang and he saw Amelia's name, he grabbed for it too quickly and succeeded only in knocking it to the floor, by the time he'd picked it up and answered, the line was dead. He tried calling back but it went straight to voicemail so he put his phone back down on the table and stared at it, waiting for her to ring again. He was shaking, sweaty with anxiety.

It was another hour, nearly eight o'clock, before the phone rang again. Gethin answered at once.

'Amelia?'

This time he could hear her voice, though just barely. It sounded as though she was whispering. 'Gethin,' she said, 'I'm sorry about this but I think I may have landed myself in some trouble. Could you possibly come to where...'

The phone cut off. Gethin called back. Voicemail. Called again. Voicemail again. He waited in case she was calling him back simultaneously. Nothing. For the next five minutes, he kept on calling but still no joy. He texted to call back as soon as she could, then called Bex and Lee and told them what had happened.

Half an hour later, he was back on the road to Bristol with Lee once more in the passenger seat. She had her torch in her lap, ready for a reunion with Shaun. Gethin was hardly relishing the prospect of seeing him again, but Amelia was clearly in trouble – and she was last heard of going to visit him – so he couldn't see any other option.

They didn't talk much on the ride. Lee had kicked off by going on about how lovely the Judge was once you got to know him, and Gethin, too stressed to think what he was saying, replied 'You're just lucky you didn't have to grow up in the same house as him.' The second the words were out of his mouth, he remembered that Lee had grown up in a children's home, so complaining about your dad being a bit strict was hardly tactful. She didn't call him on it which made it worse. By way of making up, he dug around in the CD wallet till he found something he thought she might like, an old Bill Withers album. But when it led off with 'Ain't No Sunshine', it just made him think about Cat. Christ, how had everything gone so completely to hell?

Once they'd pulled up outside the pub down the road from Shaun's place, Lee suggested she might be able to call a guy she knew in St Paul's to provide some backup.

'Sounds like a good idea.'

Lee tried the number but there was no reply. 'Actually, I'm not surprised, he's not exactly a morning person.'

Gethin checked his phone. It was still only 9.25. Not a popular time with your self-employed doorman types. Hopefully, it would give them some slight advantage with Shaun as well, if he was there.

'Better get on with it, eh?' He led the way down the street, Lee just behind him, torch in hand.

Shaun's door swung open and Gethin took an involuntary step back before registering that it was not Shaun but his girlfriend Denise standing there. She was dressed for work in a smart skirt suit and full make-up. There was a pushchair behind her with a little boy strapped in, holding a smartphone. Denise looked seriously worried.

'Are you looking for Shaun? He's not here. I don't know where he is. Have you seen him?'

'No,' said Gethin. 'But we're looking for him. When did you last see him?'

'Yesterday,' said Denise. 'There was this weird woman here when I got back from work and they were talking about something that they obviously didn't want me to know about. He just said he'd call me later and went off with this old bag lady sort of person and he didn't call and he didn't come back and I'm so worried and I don't know who's going to pick up Connor from the childminder and... oh God! You see Shaun never does this sort of thing. I know when people meet him they think they know what sort of person he is, but he's a real homebody, Shaun. He hates not sleeping in his own bed. I think it's because of his childhood. Do you think he's all right?'

Gethin just about managed not to laugh at the suggestion that Shaun might be the person in danger in this scenario and concentrated on the important question: 'This lady he was with, can you describe her at all?'

'Like I say, she was sort of like a bag lady. She was pretty old, fifty or sixty, quite small, no make-up, just looked a right state, all dressed in this awful grey thing that looked like a sack.'

That sounded like Amelia all right. 'And they didn't say anything about where they were going?'

'No.'

'How were they travelling? On foot or in a car?'

'In Shaun's car,' said Denise.

Bollocks, they could be absolutely anywhere by now.

'What do you think she wants with him? Do you think she's blackmailing him or something?'

'No, nothing like that. She's completely harmless, it'll just be something to do with Izma M.'

'I should have thought of that.' Denise looked slightly relieved. 'All sorts of weirdos are on at him about all that.'

'Do you have any idea where he might've gone? Friends or family?'

'I'm sorry, he's a very private person.'

'Well, if you do hear anything, here's my card,' said Gethin. 'Just give me a ring, yeah?'

She took the card and Gethin and Lee walked back to the car.

'Hate to say it, Geth,' said Lee, 'but maybe we should call the police?'

Gethin thought about it. On the one hand it probably did make sense, on the other he was afraid that, if the cops took over the show, that would be the end of his involvement – and his proximity to Amelia's cash.

'Not yet, I don't think. I mean, it's not like she went off unwillingly. Why would they care?'

'S'pose.' Lee didn't look convinced.

Before Gethin could say anything else, his phone rang. A Cardiff landline number.

'Hello,' he said.

'Dad!'

'Hey love, what's happening?'

'You have to come and get me, Dad. I've got a terrible migraine and I called mum and she didn't reply and I really, really need to go home...' she broke off to sob loudly into the phone.

Gethin took a deep breath. This was just what he didn't need.

'Are you sure you can't just stay there with the school nurse? I'm right in the middle of...'

'No, Dad, I can't...' another burst of sobbing.

'All right, love, try and calm yourself. I'll be there as soon as I can.'

Gethin told Lee what was going on and she said she'd stay.

Gethin made it to Hattie's school, on the northern fringes of Cardiff, in fifty-five minutes, while Lee stayed in Bristol to see if she could dig up any leads on the missing Shaun. Another five minutes of trying to find the right entrance – realising just how much of the school liaison stuff he left to Cat – and he was reunited with his daughter, who looked as though she was auditioning for the part of tragic heroine in the school play. She made a performance of rising from the sofa she was sitting on as if it took up the last of her strength, while shielding her eyes from the light with one hand and reaching out blindly for Gethin with the other.

'Oh, Daddy,' she said, 'thank God you're here. I'm feeling absolutely terrible.'

By the time they made it to Gethin's car, however, the migraine seemed to be wearing off with near miraculous speed.

'Dad,' she said, once she'd strapped herself into the passenger seat, 'what's going on with you and mum?'

Gethin took a deep breath. So much for Cat keeping everything under wraps. He thought about denying that anything was going on but discarded the notion. Hattie was obviously upset enough to have engineered this whole migraine business and she deserved some sort of explanation.

'Well,' he said carefully, 'we have had a bit of a row. Your mum thinks I don't take enough notice of her, that I'm too wrapped up in my work.'

Hattie snorted. 'What about her? She's always working.'

Gethin grinned, touched by Hattie's loyalty. 'Yeah, well,

it's the way she sees things, so I suppose we're just giving each other a little bit of space to calm down and then we'll talk things over properly and I'm sure everything will be fine.'

Hattie didn't say anything for a while, just sat there in the front seat biting her lip. Gethin started up the car, nosed out of the car park and headed for home.

Finally, Hattie spoke up: 'You know she's having an affair?'

'What?' And then, before he could help himself, 'How do you know that?'

'Mum told me all this stuff about you being away on business for a couple of days but I could tell she was lying so I asked what was going on. She gave me the same stupid nonsense about how you're working too much. So, anyway, later on I was just borrowing mum's phone for a bit because she has a better signal than me and I needed to send a message to someone and then I noticed she had a WhatsApp account and I thought, oh that's cool, and I sort of accidentally clicked on it and, before I could close it or anything, I saw these messages.'

Normally Gethin would tell off Hattie for obviously spying on her mother, but now he was too interested in what she'd found out.

'And I saw this absolutely gross message to mum from some Swedish guy.'

'Swedish guy,' thought Gethin. Probably someone she'd met on an international conference. Some fucking Scandinavian shrink who ran half marathons every weekend before having it off in the sauna while wearing a quilted fucking gilet.

'At least, I think he's Swedish,' said Hattie. 'Is Nils a Swedish name?'

'Nils? I'm not entirely sure.' Gethin somehow made his mouth say something entirely different to what he was thinking. 'I think it can be Swedish but it's more likely to be Danish.'

Or, on very rare occasions, Welsh, especially when belonging to a washed-up singer slash actor. Christ on a fucking stick, Cat was shagging Nils Hofberg. Not some boring shrink in a suit but a coked-up waster. Not someone who made Gethin feel inadequate by comparison, but the very person he would always think of when he wanted to feel better about himself – 'at least I'm not as much of a fuck-up as Nils Hofberg'.

'Dad, be careful!'

He was approaching the roundabout way too fast, his foot having been jammed on the accelerator from the moment he heard the name Nils. Braking quickly, he still came on to the roundabout before he could look to his right. Thankfully, there was no other traffic, so no harm done. 'Sorry, love, was just a bit shocked, didn't concentrate for a moment.'

'You mean you didn't know? God, mum is a bitch.'

'Don't call your mother a bitch.' Gethin turned into the lane that led up to Gwaelod-Y-Garth. 'It's not as simple as that, this grown-up stuff.'

'I'm not an idiot. Cheating on your husband is wrong. It's not complicated. I mean you've never cheated on mum, have you?'

'I'm sure I've let her down in other ways,' said Gethin. 'We're none of us perfect, sweetheart. People make mistakes and you should try not to judge them too harshly.'

'What? Are you saying it's okay for mum to cheat on you with some Danish bloke?'

'No.' Gethin parked the car. 'I'm not saying that.' But, as

he led the way indoors, he wondered what he was saying, what he was feeling. Discovering Cat's infidelity was one thing but finding out it was Nils Hofberg, now that was a real head spinner.

It made an awful sort of sense, he realised, once the news had had a moment or two to settle in. They had all known each other way back when. When Gethin was working behind the bar at the Madison on Charles Street, the in place for Cardiff schoolkids at the end of the eighties. Nils, at 21, was a bit of a local celebrity. His band had played in London a couple of times, which was more than anyone else's band had managed. And Cat was part of that year's intake of students, a serious girl with dyed blonde hair and grey green eyes and a fondness for ethnic touches in her clothing, no doubt picked up on her gap year in India. She wasn't the usual type of girl to take an interest in Gethin and Nils – generally, it was the wannabe bad girls who made a beeline for the obvious bad boys. It was Nils, he remembered, who had talked to her first because that's what Nils was like. When he was high, which he generally was, he talked to everyone, chatted up every girl in the bar indiscriminately. But it was always Gethin she'd had her eye on. At first he'd resisted it, was sure he didn't want to settle down just yet, but she'd hung in there, quietly determined, and eventually he'd given in and really... that was all she wrote.

For all his faults, Gethin had been faithful to Cat ever since. And Nils, well he'd always liked Cat too. He enjoyed having a serious person to talk to occasionally. He'd even written a song about her once: 'Elsa, She-Wolf of the Library' it was called; came out on his second album. But Cat had never taken him seriously. Until now, it would seem. Nils Hofberg! Fucking hell.

Cat arrived home just before six, looking flustered. The first thing she did was to call out to Hattie, who was sitting next to Gethin in the living room, both of them working on their laptops. 'Sweetheart, are you okay? I had a message from the school.'

'Yeah,' said Hattie. 'Where were you, mum? Dad had to come and pick me up.'

'I'm so sorry. I was in a meeting up in the Merthyr office and reception is terrible up there.'

She was lying. Gethin could see it clearly. And he started to wonder how many times in recent months she'd come in saying stuff like that. 'Oh, I'm sorry I'm late, I had an emergency call out, I have to go to a conference in Birmingham next weekend, my phone ran out of charge…' How many times had she lied to his face? And him never suspecting a thing? What was the saying: 'Fool me once, shame on you, Fool me twice, shame on me.' Or was it the other way round? Might as well be. Shame on both of them.

He stood up to go. Hattie immediately jumped up next to him. 'Don't go, Dad. Don't let her drive you out of your own house. If anyone should be going, it's her.'

Cat turned to Gethin, furious: 'What have you been telling her? I thought we agreed… oh I can't believe this, you sad bastard, trying to use Hattie against me. God, what have you told her?'

'He didn't tell me anything, mum. I found out myself. I was just borrowing your phone and…'

'Shit, no.' Cat sat down hard on the sofa and burst into tears. 'Oh Hattie no, you shouldn't have. It's not what you think, really, it's not important…'

Gethin, meanwhile, felt his phone buzzing in his pocket. He risked a quick peek, concerned that it might be Amelia.

It was a text from Bex. 'When are you back? Something you gotta see.'

Suddenly, he was impatient to get out of there, to return to his case. He loved Hattie, he still loved Cat, but he really didn't want to be stuck in the middle of some soap opera showdown, not with the stress levels he was already experiencing. 'I have to go.'

Cat and Hattie both turned to him. 'I'm going to stay at my father's again tonight. Maybe tomorrow evening we can have a proper talk about all this.'

Cat wiped away her tears and nodded. Hattie was indignant. 'Dad, no, you mustn't.'

Gethin opened his arms and she stepped forward for a hug, her turn to start crying.

'Listen, love,' said Gethin. 'It'll be all right. We all love each other. We'll work it out.'

And then he was out of there and in the car, listening to Bruce Springsteen's break-up album, *Tunnel of Love*, and hoping that his words to Hattie were more than empty platitudes. Then a fresh worry hit him. Had Bex seen the credit card balance? Was she waiting to give him what for?

In fact, Bex was nowhere to be seen when Gethin arrived at the Sully house. The Judge was busy sorting through his mugshots and making notes, and Gethin wondered whether he was wasting time when Amelia was still missing. He checked his phone to see if a message had come in while he was driving. Nothing. He picked up the blown-up photo of Danny Bliss, tried again to see if he could recognise the future Dante Green in there somewhere. There was definitely something familiar about the guy, he just couldn't quite think who he reminded him of.

Then someone came out of the bathroom. The someone

was wearing a Kate Bush wig and a witchy black dress. It took him a second to make sense of the apparition.

'Christ, Bex,' he said, 'really didn't recognise you there.'

Bex laughed and pulled off the wig. 'Not bad, eh?'

So that was what Bex wanted him to see – her latest transformation. There was something about this particular quick change act that freaked him out a little. He was used to Bex turning into assorted blonde belters – Dusty, Madonna, Claire from Steps – but seeing her as ethereal Kate Bush was genuinely weird. Could anyone turn into anyone if they wanted to?

Just as he was thinking this, something fired at the back of his mind and then came barrelling to the forefront. It was to do with the picture of Danny Bliss in the nightclub. He'd known it had reminded him of someone but he hadn't been able to think who it was, because he'd only been considering the obvious candidates – thirty something Jewish blokes who'd come up in the course of the investigation.

But suddenly – spurred on by seeing Bex's unlikely disguise – he realised that the person Danny Bliss reminded him of was not Jewish at all, but a devout Muslim.

'Bex,' he said, 'have you got a decent picture of Izma M anywhere?'

'Expect so.' Bex rooted around in the pile of papers on her makeshift desk and came up with the book jacket photo of Izma M, the famous shot of him on his way to court.

Gethin took it and put it next to the picture of Danny Bliss. He studied the photos carefully.

'Fucking hell,' he said. 'Are you seeing what I'm seeing?'

She leaned over his shoulder. 'God, yes I do.'

The resemblance between the two photos, once you noticed it, was undeniable: the mouth, the nose, the eyes, the cheekbones, the overall shape of the face. All the things that can't easily be changed. The differences were in the hair and the beard and, though not by that much really, the shade of skin colour – and all of those, of course, are easily changed. Even the skin colour could be altered with tanning lotion. And yet, and yet... it was making Gethin's head spin. Could this apparently dead Jewish kid be one and the same with the black activist? How? And, come to that, why?

'That's absolutely amazing,' said Bex. 'Come here and have a look at this, Tone.'

Gethin looked at her with astonishment. Had she really just called His Honour Judge Anthony Grey 'Tone'? The Judge didn't seem to mind, just came over to see what the fuss was about.

'Dad, what do you think?'

The Judge pursed his lips. 'I must say it looks like the same person to me, but I'm struggling to understand how that could be.'

'Me too,' said Gethin. He paused to collect his thoughts. 'Okay, let's start with what we know about Danny Bliss. He's a North London Jewish kid, quite Middle Eastern looking, loves hip-hop and grime and all that. He's gone missing, presumed dead, after his parents' yacht was blown up off northern Cyprus in 2001. That's the last time anyone heard anything about our Danny. Everything suggests he's dead, except the fact that his body was never recovered. Which isn't enormously surprising if you die in an explosion at sea. Okay so far?'

'Yes,' said the Judge, 'but I think you might want to consider the fact that, shortly after you started looking for this Danny Bliss, I was contacted by my esteemed legal colleague Terence Donoghue, who seemed to be extremely keen for any news of young Mr Bliss, whose father, it may be noted, was a prominent member of the gangster classes. Which suggests that his client may not be convinced that Mr Bliss is as dead as he is painted.'

'Good point,' said Gethin. 'And, meanwhile, there's Izma M, who comes to public notice in 2005, when he's arrested and convicted of murder in Bristol. That's four years after Danny Bliss was last seen in Cyprus. Which fits fine with this theory. There's just one small problem.'

'What's that?' asked Bex.

'The book. Izma's book. It tells his life story and that doesn't include growing up Jewish then suddenly turning black due to excessive exposure to hip-hop. Surely someone would have called him out if it wasn't true?'

'I'm thinking about that,' said Bex. 'I mean we both read it, right, and it seemed real and everything, but you know what strikes me now? When Deano started investigating, he told me he was having trouble running down any of the people mentioned. And remember at the beginning, he says he's changed a lot of the names of the people and the name of the children's home and all that stuff to avoid causing embarrassment or whatever. Hang on...'

Bex picked up the book and found the page. 'Here it is – "I've changed the names of many people and institutions who appear in this book, sometimes to protect the innocent, sometimes to avoid libel actions from the guilty, but mostly because I wanted my story to be a universal one, one that has relevance to anyone out there who knows what it is to live a street life."'

'That's rather convenient, isn't it?' said the Judge.

'It certainly is,' said Gethin. 'And Deano couldn't find anyone to back up Izma's story?'

'No. Well, what he said was he couldn't waste too long trying to find people called Briggy who live somewhere in

London but, given how famous Izma is, he was surprised more people didn't come forward or say that they knew someone who knew someone... the only people who did seem to know him were Bristol guys like your mate Shaun.'

'And when did Izma move back to Bristol? Does he say exactly when, anywhere in the book?'

'Dunno.'

'Oh, hang on,' said Gethin, 'I'm sure he mentions something about Arsenal winning their third double just after he moved there. And that was the 2001/2002 season.'

'Just after Danny Bliss goes missing.'

'Well, bloody hell,' said Gethin. 'If this is right, Christ.'

It was only a few minutes later, out on the deck checking his messages, that Gethin started to realise the repercussions of his discovery. If true, it would be a sensation all right, but not one that would necessarily help Last Resort. No one – certainly no one on the liberal left – wanted to know that this hero of the oppressed, Izma M, was actually a child of privilege engaged in some weird blackface act. And not only that but, the more he thought about it, the more it was clear that, if Izma M was hiding the secret that he was really Danny Bliss, he had a very strong motive for killing Hannah Gold. In fact, it all fell into place – the old boyfriend Hannah had run into, the one who had changed a lot... it made Danny/Izma look guiltier than sin. Gethin wondered what on earth their client, Amelia, would make of all this. He couldn't imagine she'd be pleased.

Amelia, where the hell was she? He waited as the signal bars on his phone came back to life and a series of messages popped up. No less than five of them were from Hattie, and a quick scan suggested they were all offering outraged support for him and furious anger with her mother. And then, thank God, there was a text each from Lee and Amelia Laverne.

He read Amelia's text first. 'Everything is okay. I will be in touch soon. Do not contact me, I will contact you.'

If it was meant to allay his worries, it had the opposite effect. The tone didn't sound right for Amelia. Could someone – presumably Shaun – have Amelia and her phone in their clutches and be trying to stop anyone coming after them? Or could Shaun even have killed her? Jesus. Though, why would he do that?

Amelia's phone went instantly to voicemail when he tried it.

Lee's message just said, 'Call me'.

'All right, boss?'

'Lot going on. You got any leads for Shaun?'

'Nothing solid. I spoke to a few people who know him but he's a secretive feller by the sound of it. No one even knew about the place he lives, or that he had a girlfriend. He always has plenty of money, apparently. Word is it's drugs, but wholesale end. You don't go to him for a couple of grams of Charlie.'

'Nothing at all about where he might be hanging out?'

'The only lead I've got to speak of is some old fella gave me his grandmother's name and address. Apparently, it was her who raised Shaun and they're meant to be quite close. She still lives in St Paul's but I went round there and no one was in. Probably just out at the bingo or whatever. You want me to hang around and try again later?'

'God, Lee, I dunno.' Gethin told her about the text from Amelia – or at least from Amelia's phone – and she agreed that it sounded worrying.

'Fine,' she said, 'I'll go back round there. If she's not there, I'll sit on her doorstep and wait.'

'Won't that look suspicious?'

'Would if it was you, Geth. Neighbours will be thinking all sorts. Me though, I blends in, like. Anyone asks, I'll tell them she's my auntie.'

'Tell you what, Lee. Give me the address and I'll see you there in an hour.'

'You sure? You've already been over here once.'

'Yeah, but what can you do? I'll buy a couple of cans of Relentless from the services. See you in a bit.'

* * *

Gethin was already on the outskirts of Bristol, coming in on the M32, when he realised he'd missed something completely obvious. There was one known associate of Shaun's who was more than likely to be involved in Amelia Laverne's disappearance: Malcolm bloody Haynes. Maybe they were all at Malcolm's place. Or his office, that would be perfect. Away from prying neighbours, surrounded by barbed wire.

He turned right into St Paul's, following the directions from his satnav. It was only when he entered the street on which Shaun's grandmother lived that he realised he'd been there before. This was the same street that Amelia Laverne had directed him to, the place where she'd had the confrontation with the old West Indian woman.

As he parked the car, a shape emerged from the darkness of the house's postage stamp front garden. Lee held up her hand to signal to Gethin there was no need to get out. Instead she slipped into the passenger seat.

'Still no sign of the old lady, Geth.'

245

'Do you want to hear something weird?'

'Maybe?'

'I've been here before. To this house. Amelia Laverne made me drive her here. Said it was a personal matter. You remember I told you about her having a massive barney with this old lady, for no apparent reason?'

'Yeah, I do. So this is where it happened? The woman Amelia had a row with was Shaun's grandmother?'

'Exactly. What do you make of that?'

'Christ knows. Be an interesting question to ask the old biddy when she finally makes it back from church or bingo or wherever the hell she is.'

'Right,' said Gethin. 'Meanwhile, I've realised we've overlooked an obvious connection of Shaun's.'

'Who's that then?'

'Malcolm Haynes.'

Lee burst out laughing 'You may have overlooked him, Geth, but I do actually have a brain. I've asked all over. Nobody really knows him.'

'Really?'

'Well, loads of people know who he is, ex-copper and all, and word is he's someone you don't want to mess with. But no one knew about a connection between him and Shaun. Whatever they're up to, they're keeping it close.'

'Did you go over to his yard?'

'Haven't had a chance. I've been hanging around here most of the evening.'

'Let's go and have a look now. Come back here later.'

'Suits me.'

Gethin reset the satnav and threaded his way out of St Paul's and briefly back on to the motorway before taking the Fishponds exit and driving slowly down Lodge Causeway. Rather than go all the way into the trading estate where

Haynes Security had their office and risk giving the game away, he parked on the main road.

All was eerily quiet on the trading estate. There were half a dozen industrial units, all surrounded by chain link fences. They passed a delivery outfit on their left, plenty of vans parked up in the compound, but no sign of life. Haynes Security was over to the far right. There were no vehicles outside and no lights on in the office unit. The sign on the locked gate was simple and discreet. It just said, 'Haynes Security', no phone number or web address. This didn't appear to be an outfit that was intent on attracting passing trade.

It was dark in the office but that didn't mean it was empty. Gethin had a vision, taken from some TV crime drama, no doubt, of Amelia trussed up like a chicken in the back room, alone and terrified, trying but unable to scream because of the gag in her mouth, just waiting for Mal Haynes to come back and do something awful to her.

He stepped back and surveyed the fence. It was around ten foot high with a gate, also chain-link, in the middle. He looked closely at the gate section, to see if it provided any footholds, but it had obviously been designed with that in mind.

'What d'you reckon? Any way in?'

'Not without fence cutters, Geth, and even then there's an alarm on the office.'

Gethin shook the fence in frustration. Almost immediately, there was some frantic barking and the sound of a very angry dog. It wasn't in the Haynes Security compound, thankfully, but the next one along; even so, it was a clear indicator that it was time to leave. As one, they headed back to the car.

'You reckon she's in there?'

'Doubt it,' said Lee. 'Seems like a risky place to keep someone prisoner. I mean, it's quiet now but in the day there's going to be people around. If you're worried about it we can come back in the morning.'

'Fine. Let's go see if Grandma's home.'

It was nearly eleven now and the main drag through Stokes Croft was buzzing with life as they headed back to St Paul's. Shaun's gran's street, however, was as quiet as ever. But this time, there was a light on in the hallway. Gethin parked the car in a space outside.

Lee stepped ahead of him as they approached: 'Tell you what, Geth, might be an idea if I take the lead here.'

She knocked on the door gently. No reply. She knocked again a little louder. Still no reply. Once more without a response and Lee leant down to the letter box and called, 'It's about Shaun'.

Finally, a call came from indoors. 'All right, I am coming.'

The door opened and it was indeed the woman Gethin had seen arguing with Amelia. This time, though, he was seeing her up close. She didn't have her wig on, just a hair net, and she looked old and frail.

'Who are you?'

'I'm a legal investigator,' said Lee. 'I'm trying to find Shaun. We're concerned he may be in some trouble.'

'Where is he?'

'That's what we don't know, ma'am. We were hoping you might have some idea. He left home yesterday morning and hasn't been heard of since.'

The old lady laughed. 'You investigating every time a man doesn't come home for the night? Must have a lot of work.'

Lee joined in the laughter: 'True, missis, true that for sure. No, the thing about your Shaun is he was with someone when he disappeared.'

'Who's that then? Not Denise? Oh my lord, I bet I know who it is. It's her, isn't it?'

'Who?'

'That raasclaat Amelia. She comes back here, sees we all living happily ever after thank you very much, and she has to fuck it all up. It's her, isn't it?'

'Yes,' said Lee. 'As far as we know, he was with her yesterday morning. Are you saying they have some sort of prior relationship?'

'Ain't him she's interested in. It's that red boy she's after. She just asking questions about him the whole time, refusing to leave well alone.'

'You mean Izma?'

'Of course, everybody obsess with that boy now he in prison. She bothering Shaun about it night and day. I'm not surprised if he had enough of it.'

'Are you saying he was angry with her?'

'Well, of course, nobody want some stupid bitch coming in asking questions and upsetting the applecart. Not when you got the money rolling in every month like that.'

'Sorry, what money?'

The old lady hesitated. Gethin could see a look of calculation crossing her face. 'Nuttin much. Izma just give Shaun a little allowance for helping him out on the outside, you know? Now I've had enough of this, it's time for my bed.'

'Fair play,' said Lee. 'Sorry to be bothering you like this, missis. But do you have any idea where Shaun might've gone? Does he have some special place he likes to go?'

The old lady shook her head: 'I don't know nothing about that.' And she started to shut the door in Lee's face.

Lee moved quickly to put a foot in the way: 'Just one last thing. You mind telling me why Amelia is so interested in asking about Izma?'

The old lady laughed again. 'She thinks she's his fucking mother, don't she?'

'I'm sorry?' Then Gethin finally got it. That's what Amelia's interest in the case was really about. 'Is she?'

The old lady gave him a withering look. 'Course not. It's Shaun's her child, innit?'

Twenty-Three

GIVEN THE LATENESS OF THE hour, and the sense that, wherever Shaun had taken Amelia, it was likely to be closer to Bristol than Cardiff, Gethin suggested they stay over. It was only when they had checked into the Premier Inn by the bus station, though, that he realised just how exhausted he was. They had planned to have a bit of a discussion of the case before crashing, but in the end it was all he could do to stagger up to his room and take most of his clothes off before he was sound asleep.

He woke up briefly in the night and found all the lights on. He took a piss, turned them off and went back to sleep.

He was woken again, at seven, by a whole series of texts from Hattie, basically saying how much she hated her mum and wanted him to come home. Christ. He lay there for a while staring at the ceiling, trying to pull his thoughts into focus. He texted back that he would see her at home later and tried to return to sleep, but it was no good, thoughts kept crowding in on top of each other. At half past, he texted Lee and she was awake too, so they agreed to meet in the breakfast room and try to work out what to do next.

'I think I may have figured out what's going on here,' she said, once they were seated with a full English and a pot of tea each.

'Good for you. I can hardly figure out my own name this morning.'

'Yeah, well, you have a lot going on, innit. I have a feeling that the key to all this is the same as it is to most things – if in doubt, follow the money. So you start with this kid called Danny Bliss, right? Well, I've done a bit of googling about what happened and it looks like his dad was one major criminal type. That's why he was living in Cyprus – out of the reach of the law. So he must be loaded. No one goes to the bother of blowing you up unless there's a lot of money floating around. So this Danny escapes alive, somehow or other, and comes back to Britain. Well, like as not, he knows where the money is. And he also knows there's people out to kill him, yeah?'

'With you so far,' said Gethin.

'Cool, well keep on paying attention. So, he basically goes into witness protection, not by going to the police, he does it all by himself, takes on a new identity, grows a beard, makes friends with a sunlamp, hey presto, he's a black man.'

'That's the bit I find it hard to get my head around.'

'Dunno why, boss. Not these days. All the youth talk like they're black for starters and there's so many people have a bit of black in them, you can't tell for sure. Maybe if they've blond hair and blue eyes, but I've even known one or two got a black grandad and still look like that. I mean, what you going to do – call for a DNA test every time you see someone talking black but looks a bit light-skinned? You dress black, you have some black mates, you listen to black music, who's going to call you out?'

'Okay, fair enough.'

'Yeah, so there he is hiding out in Bristol and then he runs into some girl in a club and, fucking hell, she recognises him. It's his old girlfriend. So he meets up with her a few times, takes her places no one he knows would ever go and,

I dunno, maybe he decides it's too much of a risk having her know who he really is so...'

'I hope you're not going to say he kills her?'

'Happens, boss. Anyway, he ends up in jail, as we know. But Shaun still has some of his money, I guess, so he's all right.'

Gethin thought about it. 'Makes sense.' He thought some more: 'Then Amelia blunders in.'

'Yeah, exactly, in comes Amelia who's obviously a bit fucking loop di loop and she's decided Izma's her son. Looks like she had a black baby she gave away or something – wouldn't be the first one to do that.'

Gethin nodded sympathetically. He'd always assumed that must have been Lee's own story, the reason why she grew up in a home.

'Yeah, boo hoo. Anyway, she's asking Shaun all these questions and maybe she's coming a bit too close to the truth...'

'Fuck, you reckon he's killed her?'

'Hope not, Geth. I mean maybe it's all okay, maybe they've figured out they're mother and son and they're having a nice little reunion. But let's hope we find her sooner rather than later. Might be an idea to call the police, report her missing, have the media involved.'

Gethin thought about it. 'Yeah, probably. Unless it just freaks him out and makes him do something stupid. I'll call Amelia's PA, she's been with her for years, see if she's heard anything and if she thinks we should call in the police.' He scrolled through his phone, looking for a number for the PA, and failed to find it. 'Bollocks, I'll call Bex.'

Gethin and Lee checked out of the hotel and drove back to Fishponds. As Lee had predicted, the industrial estate was very different in the morning rush hour, busy and bustling, full of traffic coming in and out. The two of them were sitting in the car listening to 5 Live, waiting for Mal Haynes to show up and wondering what to do next if he didn't, when the phone rang.

'Bex.'

'Hi Geth, I've talked to Laura and she's not too worried. Said Amelia's always going off piste. She sent Laura a text saying she was taking some time out and should be in touch when she was ready.'

'Same sort of thing we had.'

'Yeah, exactly. And Laura says it's par for the course. So, she really doesn't see any need to go to the police. Amelia really hates being in the media, apparently.'

Gethin thought about it more, trying not to be over-influenced by his overwhelming need to keep Amelia and her money onside. And there was no real probable cause, was there? 'What would we say, anyway?' he asked, more or less rhetorically. 'Amelia's gone off with some bloke and we think he might be dodgy?'

Lee leaned over and tapped on Gethin's phone, indicating that he should switch on the speaker so she could join in the conversation.

'Hey Bex, did you ask if she had any way of tracking Amelia by her phone or something?'

'Hi Lee, I did but apparently it doesn't work if the phone is switched off, and hers seems to be, so it's not much help.'

'Has she got an iPhone? Bet she has.'

'Yes,' said Gethin, 'why?'

''Cause they have a thing called Find My iPhone. It even works when the phone's turned off, apparently.'

'Brilliant idea,' said Bex. 'I'll call Laura now and find out if she had it enabled.'

They didn't have too long to wait till Haynes showed up.

They'd had time to listen to three tracks off a Joni Mitchell compilation – deemed just about acceptable by Lee – when a Lexus pulled up. Mal Haynes emerged and opened the gate.

Gethin watched as Haynes drove his car into the compound then unlocked the office. He didn't look nervous, no sign that he had a film star tied up in his storeroom, but then Mal Haynes didn't seem like a man who rattled easily.

'That him?'

Gethin nodded.

'You want me to go in there with some bullshit excuse, see if there's any sign of Amelia?'

'Might be risky, Lee, so let's give him a minute or two, see what he does.'

Turned out this was good advice as, less than a minute later, Malcolm Haynes emerged from his office, set the alarm, walked back to his car, drove out through the compound gate and locked that too. Gethin had slumped low in his seat to avoid detection, so he was relying on Lee to keep him informed.

'You think we should follow him, Geth?'

'Suppose so.' Gethin cautiously pulled himself up to see Malcolm Haynes preparing to drive off.

He waited till Haynes had gone past him then eased the Peugeot on to the road. Haynes was already turning right into the main road, Lodge Causeway. Gethin had to wait for another two cars to go past before he could follow suit. That was probably a good thing, he figured. What little he knew about following someone in a car suggested that you should always leave at least one other car between yourself and the person you were trailing. Only trouble was it made it a bit tricky to see what your target was up to and, when they came to the next junction, Gethin almost lost Haynes completely but gambled on a left turn at the amber light and caught up with the former copper again as they rolled past Eastville Park, heading for the motorway.

At the next junction, Haynes swung right on to the slip road for the M32, heading north, and Gethin followed suit. Once they were on the motorway, things were easier. Gethin kept a couple of cars behind. Before long, they were approaching the M4 interchange and Gethin braced himself for a last-minute turn-off, in case Haynes had business in Cardiff or London, but no, he just sailed on past. Where could he be going? Most likely off to some completely unrelated job. But, in the absence of any other leads, this would have to do.

They were just approaching Junction 14, the turn-off most familiar to Gethin as the gateway to Leyhill Prison, a popular address for his clients, when his phone rang. Lee picked it up and switched on the speaker.

'Hi Bex, you have anything?'

'Yeah, I have.'

'Fantastic.'

'It seems to be right in the middle of woods somewhere. I think there may be a little house or something, but I'm not really sure, as it's hard to tell from the satellite picture.'

'Whereabouts is it?'

'Warwickshire, quite near Stratford-on-Avon.'

'Great, send us the address and I'll stick it in the satnav,' said Gethin. 'I think we're heading in that direction already.'

'How come?'

'We're following Malcolm Haynes, heading north up the M5.'

'That sounds right. Hang on, I'll bring it up on my laptop now.' A short pause. 'You need to carry on to Gloucester, then take the A40.'

'And Amelia's still not picking up? Her PA hasn't heard anything?'

'Not really – one more text this morning, basically saying don't worry, but the phone must have been turned off again immediately.'

'Okay, text me the exact address and we'll be there as soon as we can.'

They sat in silence after the phone call ended, Gethin trying not to dwell too much on images of an open grave in a dark wood.

'One thing,' he said eventually, 'if someone's sending texts from her phone, even if it's not her, she can't just have been killed and left there. I mean she could be dead – we have to face that – but Shaun must still be there.'

'And it looks as though Haynes is on his way there too, which wouldn't make much sense if Shaun's killed her.'

'Good point.'

Gethin was so sure that Malcolm Haynes was heading for the same place as them that he almost overshot the exit. He'd been expecting Haynes to make the turn, and when the copper headed straight on instead, he had a moment of indecision before sliding on to the slip road at the last second, skidding slightly as he braked hard.

'Fuck's sake,' said Lee, 'would you mind going easy on the Lewis Hamilton impersonations?'

'Sorry,' said Gethin, once he had the car under control. 'D'you think I've done the right thing? Should I have stuck with Haynes?'

'Nah, the quicker we reach wherever Amelia's phone is, the better.'

* * *

In the end, it took over an hour, winding past places called Dumbleton and Sedgeberrow, taking a wrong turn in Evesham, before they turned off down a lane signposted to the village of Lawton. A mile or so down there was another smaller lane leading off to the right, simply marked 'Private Road: No Trespassing'. The satnav was adamant that this was the correct way, though, so Gethin drove the car as slowly and quietly as possible over a rickety little river bridge, then through a series of farm buildings before the lane, now nothing more than a track, started to veer off to the right. After a couple of hundred yards, they reached a point at which the satnav suggested they should follow an even tinier path into the woods. He turned to Lee.

'Walk in from here, yeah?'

Lee nodded and Gethin pulled the car as far over to one side of the lane as he could.

Outside in the fresh country air, he registered for the first time that it was an absolutely beautiful day. They were surrounded by picture postcard British countryside; rolling hills, ancient woodlands, a pretty river burbling away in the distance, even the odd hayloft to be seen. Any sensible person would be stopping for a picnic, followed by a blissful nap in that late summer sun that seemed all the more luxurious because you knew you wouldn't be seeing its like again until next year. But instead he was about to walk into the dark, dark woods armed only with... yes, armed with what exactly?

'You have your torch?'

'Course.' Lee tapped her shoulder bag meaningfully.

Gethin opened the car boot and rummaged around for anything that might double up as a weapon. All he could see was an old garden spade. It looked horribly clumsy as a weapon of either attack or defence but he decided it was probably better than nothing, so he pulled it out.

Lee burst out laughing. 'Ready for some hand-to-hand gardening are we? Or you planning on doing some gravedigging? Like that WWF wrestling fella.'

'The Undertaker.'

'That's the one. For Christ's sake, Geth, considering the company we keep, you're a bit lacking in the self-defence skills.'

'It's lucky I've got you to help out, isn't it?'

'Damn right.' Lee led the way down the track into the woods.

After a couple of hundred yards, the tree cover was complete. The autumn leaves were starting to fall but the canopy was intact still. Gethin brought the location of Amelia's phone up on his own Google Maps. It wasn't completely precise but it seemed to be somewhere in an area of maybe thirty metres diameter. They were getting very close to the edge of the green circle and, as yet, there was no sign of anything resembling human habitation.

As he peered at the map, he spotted something that he should surely have noticed earlier. The woods they were walking through were less than a mile across country from the Remington hotel. They were, in effect, approaching it from the back. He told Lee what he'd discovered.

'What does that mean?'

'Dunno, doubt it's a coincidence, though.'

'Did he strike you as dodgy then, the Dante geezer?'

'Yeah, seriously so.'

'Better walk on our tippy toes then.'

They carried on walking through the woods until the trees gave way to a clearing and, just a few yards away, there was a building. It looked like a miniature castle. It was, Gethin supposed, a folly. Probably once a part of the grounds of some old and fancy estate. It was circular and three storeys high, with a kind of cupola at the top. This, presumably, was where Amelia Laverne was either hiding out or being held captive, depending on whether you were a glass half full or glass half empty sort of person. Every instinct Gethin had was screaming be careful.

They drew back into the cover of the trees and waited to see if their approach had been noticed. Apparently not. There was almost no noise. Birds up in the tree canopy, the hum of cars on the distant road. Also a faint sound of lapping water, which was strange as they were some considerable distance from the river. Maybe it looped around or something.

They appeared to be at the back of the building. There was no sign of any door, so very carefully they edged round in a circle, keeping under cover of the trees as much as possible. At some points, though, the undergrowth was so thick that Gethin figured crashing through it was more likely to draw attention than a quick flit along the grass. Gradually, the front door came into view. There was a car parked outside it – Shaun's Mercedes.

Gethin looked round at Lee and she gave him a 'come on – what are we waiting for?' look. He took a deep breath, tightened his grip on the spade and moved out of the tree cover on to that gravelled driveway. Almost immediately, he tripped over a stray tree root and let out an involuntary cry.

At once, there was a voice from inside the folly.

'Mal,' shouted the voice, definitely Shaun's, 'is that you? Thank fucking Christ.'

The door opened and out came Shaun, looking like a man at the end of his tether, sleepless and sweaty, but with a big fake grin plastered across his face. The grin faded the second he saw who his visitors actually were.

'You again,' he said to Gethin. 'Fuck does it take to make you fuck off and stop putting your nose into my business?' He stepped forward, naked aggression in his eyes.

Gethin raised the spade in what he hoped was a defensive but threatening manner.

'Fucking hell, it's Farmer Giles,' said Shaun. 'Come to dig your own grave, have you?'

He started moving from side to side like he was looking for an opening, laughing at Gethin all the while. Gethin kept the spade up, mimicking Shaun's movements and wondering what to do next when Shaun decided he'd had enough of the playacting, reached into his back pocket and produced a gun. What sort of gun it was Gethin had no idea, as you rarely came across them in Cardiff, even in his line of work. It was a pistol, grey and utilitarian, the sort of thing you saw police officers carrying occasionally. This was the first time that anyone had pointed one at Gethin in anger, and he wasn't enjoying the experience.

'Christ,' he said. 'No need for that. I'm just here to try and...'

Before he could finish his sentence, there was a blur of action. Lee, whom Shaun had made the mistaken of ignoring up until now, raised her torch and gave Shaun full beam right in the eyes. He instinctively raised his hand to protect his vision and staggered backwards. Lee didn't hesitate to press her advantage, stepping in fast and launching an aerial judo kick which connected squarely with Shaun's balls. He went down like a howling sack of cement, dropping the gun in agony. She kicked him a couple more times while he was on the floor, hard enough that Gethin couldn't help wincing. Then she ducked down and picked up the gun.

'Fuck's sake,' she said, when Shaun had recovered enough to look up at her. 'Whatever shit you've got yourself into here, mate, you are seriously out of your league.'

Shaun stared at her balefully but didn't make any attempt to rise off the floor.

'Now, unless you want my boss here to get seriously agricultural on your ass, it's time you answered a few civil questions. All right?'

Shaun nodded. He looked, Gethin thought, as though he was close to tears. For a supposed gangster there was something weirdly soft about Shaun. He had all the front but, as Lee had demonstrated without breaking sweat, front was all he had. He was doing his best to prove the old adage that bullies can dish it out but can't take it. By and large, bitter experience had taught Gethin that this was completely wrong. Your typical bully was more than happy if their prey attempted to fight back. Shaun, though, looked to be the exception who proved the rule.

'Okay,' said Lee, Shaun's gun steady in her hand: 'Question one. What is this place?'

'I don't know. It is what it is. Mal knew about it. Said his mate owned it.'

'His mate's name is Dante Green?' asked Gethin.

'Never heard of him,' said Shaun. Then he paused: 'You mean Dante from the Zenon bar? What's he have to do with it?'

'Sounds like your boss isn't letting you in on the secrets, bruv. He's giving you the mushroom treatment,' said Lee. 'Now for question two: Where's Amelia?'

'Here,' said Shaun, his breath still ragged, 'she's here.'

'Alive?' asked Gethin.

'Yeah, yeah, she's alive all right. Just take her out of here. It's all gone to fuck, hasn't it?' He turned his head slightly to look at Gethin. 'You cunts, you don't know what you've done, stirring up shit when everything was fine. There wasn't any problem 'til then. You think Izma wants out of prison? Course he doesn't. He loves it there. You think he's innocent? He ain't fucking innocent.'

Gethin ignored this and just kept to the main deal. 'So where is she then?'

'I'll show you, if fucking superdyke here lets me get up.'

'I'd watch your mouth, mate, if you want to have any more kids.' But Lee motioned him to stand up anyway. He was still stooped over a bit from the kick in the balls, and bleeding from the mouth, where he had taken the brunt of Lee's Dr Marten.

'Come on,' he said. 'This way. Her ladyship's in the pool.'

Gethin and Lee looked at each other and shrugged, then followed Shaun around towards the back of the building. Lee kept the gun in hand, but was no longer bothering to point it directly at Shaun.

As they came round the back of the folly, Gethin could see that there was an entrance leading straight into the basement of the building. A big wooden door with a bolt guarded it. Shaun slid the bolt to one side: 'She's in there.'

Lee had the gun back up and pointing at Shaun again. 'Fine, you stand over there, out of harm's way, and Geth, you have a look inside.'

Gethin opened the door, took a step forward, then checked himself just in time. The basement room, which must have been in more or less complete darkness before he opened the door, was almost entirely filled, as far as he could see, by a swimming pool. Not a recently installed, modern pool but what looked like an old Roman bath. He stared at it, wondering if Amelia's body was going to be floating there. Then, as his eyes adjusted to the gloom, he spotted her. There was a platform to the left-hand side of the pool with some old bits of garden furniture lying around and also a mattress, which was currently housing a wriggling body.

Wishing he had brought Lee's torch, Gethin made his way cautiously around the side of the pool until he came to the mattress. The writhing figure was indeed Amelia Laverne. She had her hands cuffed behind her, her feet tied together and a scarf around her mouth as a rudimentary gag. Gethin undid the gag first and then the rope binding her ankles. It wasn't too difficult as Shaun had clearly only made it to the basic level of Boy Scout knot training. He had to help her to her feet, though, as her balance was thrown off by having her hands cuffed behind her back

Amelia didn't say anything at first, just leaned against Gethin's chest and started crying. He put his arms round her carefully and waited till the intensity of it had subsided, then led her gently towards the outside world.

She staggered backwards as she came out into the bright light and Gethin had to catch her to stop her falling into the pool. She recovered herself and walked purposefully out into the sunshine.

Gethin saw Lee gasp at the sight of her. No wonder. In the sunlight, Amelia looked a truly sorry sight. Wrapped in her grey cashmere, which seemed more sack-like than ever, no make-up and smudges of dirt all over her, her hair sort of half up, half down, she looked like a starving orphan from a Victorian melodrama until you saw her face which seemed to belong to someone very, very old who had lately seen far too much. The pitifulness of it all was horribly emphasised by the handcuffs.

'Hey,' said Gethin, 'where's the key to the cuffs?'

'Sorry, yeah, have it here.' Shaun stuck his hand in his pocket.

'Slowly,' said Lee, pointing the gun directly at him. 'Any

funny business, I'll take great pleasure in blowing your bollocks off.'

Shaun took the advice to heart and very slowly brought his hand out of his pocket, proffering a small key ring with two keys on it.

'Chuck it over,' said Gethin, and Shaun complied. Gethin fiddled about trying to insert the key properly into the lock. As he finally managed it, Lee gave Shaun a particularly withering look.

'Lovely way to treat your old mother. Must be proud of yourself, boy.'

'Whaaat?' Amelia looked electrified. 'What did you say?'

'Oh shit,' said Lee. 'Did you not know? I thought this was the whole point?'

'What, what are you saying? Are you saying he's my son? This, this... thug.'

'Yeah, I think so,' said Lee. 'That's what his nan told us...'

'No!' Amelia flew at Lee, apparently determined to shut her up before she could say any more. Lee, encumbered by the gun, couldn't fight her off properly and they both collapsed to the ground.

Shaun, seeing his opportunity, legged it towards the car. Gethin ran after him but Shaun had a decent head start and was inside the car with the door locked before Gethin could reach him. He put the car violently into reverse and Gethin stood back. Whatever was going on there, it wasn't worth being run over for.

As Shaun disappeared, he walked back round the folly and found Lee and Amelia together in a Madonna and child pose; Lee sat on the ground cradling Amelia's head in her lap as she sobbed and sobbed.

Twenty-Four

THEIR RETREAT FROM THE FOLLY was a tense affair. It was obvious that Amelia Laverne needed some looking after – and not the sort you obtain from the staff of a five-star hotel. She was dead against calling the police – in mortal dread of the publicity storm that would follow. She just wanted to be left alone to recover, she said. Gethin thought momentarily of taking her to his father's place, then discarded the idea. The Judge was not what you needed when you'd been through a trauma. Cat, the psychiatrist with all the PTSD experience, was the obvious choice. So Gethin called home and said he needed a favour and Cat had yelled down the phone at him until she heard exactly what the favour was, at which point she calmed down very quickly and started asking questions about dinner. What did Amelia like to eat and why on earth hadn't Gethin given her more notice? Gethin skated over the latter question, not wanting to freak out Cat completely before they arrived, and focused on the former, suggesting that Amelia might like a nice bowl of pasta.

Amelia relaxed a little when Gethin promised not to involve the police. She tried to sleep for a while. As they crossed the Severn Bridge, it looked as if she might even have succeeded but then she jerked awake with a start.

'Oh, God,' she said. 'Oh, dear God.'

Gethin and Lee didn't say anything, just waited for her to start talking, if that was what she wanted to do. Eventually, it was. In halting tones, punctuated with fits of sobbing, she filled in the story that Gethin had started to guess at.

In the early eighties, she had been in Bristol, acting in rep. After weekend shows she'd taken to going out dancing to funk and reggae at the Dugout Club. It was there that she'd met Sylvester, a young black guy from St Paul's – 'the most beautiful man I'd ever seen. I just wanted to lick him' – and one thing had led to another. Then one day – just after her final play, her star turn in *As You Like It*, closed – she discovered she was three months pregnant.

There had been no question she would keep the baby – how could she refuse to carry Sylvester's golden child? But things had gone terribly wrong. Sylvester was stabbed to death when she was six months pregnant. Crazy with grief, she'd gone away to Greece on her own and lain on a beach in Kefalonia until it was nearly time. When she returned to Britain, she'd had the baby and then, just a week later, there'd been a message from a casting agent who'd seen her in *As You Like It* and wanted her to audition for *Mary's Prayer*.

Amelia had had a choice – to be a twenty-one-year-old single mother with a black baby or to give the baby up and be a film star. Her dismayed parents had been adamant that she should take the latter course, that she shouldn't ruin her life, that no one had to know. The thought of giving her beautiful baby to strangers was too much to bear, though.

And then Sylvester's mother, Dorcas her name was, had stepped in. She said she'd take the baby back to Barbados to be raised with his cousins. She'd made it sound idyllic and Amelia had given in. She'd signed some papers and embraced a new life. And it was only much later, when she read Izma's book – this story of a boy, of just the right age, abandoned by his parents and brought up by his grandmother in St

Paul's – that she'd started to wonder whether her baby really was in Barbados. Only then had she started to suspect the truth: that Dorcas had simply stayed in Bristol and kept the baby to replace her own lost boy.

That was what lay behind her interest in the case. And that was what had led her to Shaun's door. She had figured that he was the one person – apart from Sylvester's intransigent mother – who might be able to tell her if Izma really was her son. Shaun had seemed flustered by her questions but had finally agreed to drive her up to Gartree, where the two of them would meet Izma and all her questions would be answered. That's what Shaun promised her but, instead, he'd taken her to the folly. At first, he'd treated her okay and claimed they just had to wait till they could obtain a VO to see Izma. But then Mal Haynes showed up – she didn't know his name but she described him well enough. Mal and Shaun had had a huge row about her. She'd tried to run away but Mal Haynes had caught her, cuffed her and locked her in the pool room. That was the night before and she'd been there until Gethin showed up and rescued her. And now everyone was telling her Shaun was her son – and not Izma – and she didn't understand anything anymore.

Just a few minutes after Amelia finished the tale of her own personal tragedy, they pulled up outside the upside-down house. Gethin rang the bell to give warning of their arrival, opened the front door and led the way upstairs.

Catriona and Hattie were waiting in the living room. Gethin had rarely seen such plainly warring emotions as Cat was displaying. She stared at him as if she wanted to wring his neck, but when Amelia Laverne followed him into the room she looked positively awestruck. Hattie, meanwhile, was simply thrilled. A couple of weeks earlier she'd never heard of Amelia but since then she had transformed herself into a fan. *Mary's Prayer* was now officially her third favourite film ever.

Amelia was wrapped up in her shawl like a butterfly doing its best to return to the safety of caterpillar mode. She'd been shaking when Gethin rescued her from the underground pool and she was still shaking now. The news that Shaun was her son seemed to have completely unhinged her.

Cat leaned forward to talk to her directly. 'Ms Laverne.' Her voice and manner moved into professional mode. 'You've obviously been through a considerable trauma. Come with me into the guest bedroom and I'll run you a bath and find you some fresh clothes to put on.'

Amelia didn't say anything to this. Instead, she just hugged her filthy clothes even tighter, but then Cat reached out a hand and, like a child, Amelia took it and followed her downstairs to the bedroom.

Gethin gave an actual sigh of relief. Cat was exactly the person one needed in this situation and, for the first time in what seemed like forever, Amelia Laverne was no longer his immediate responsibility.

'Dad,' said Hattie, 'what's going on?'

Gethin was trying to assemble a PG-rated version of recent events when his phone rang.

'Bex.' He waved apologetically to Hattie and stepped out into the garden. 'What's happening?'

'I've just had Shaun on the phone, completely freaking out at me, going on about how he's in danger of his life. And he really does sound terrible, like really, really scared.'

'What did he say?'

'He wants to have a meet with you and he wants somewhere to stay, well, somewhere to hide is what he said.'

'Did he say who he was hiding from?'

'Haynes, he said; you know, the ex-policeman?'

'Yeah, Bex, I do just about know who that is.'

'Anyway, right, he's sitting by the side of the road somewhere outside Newport waiting to hear from you, if you can help him.'

Gethin frowned. 'How did he have our number?'

'From the website, I expect, like any normal person. I've just got it patched through to my mobile while I'm out of the regular office.'

'Suppose that makes sense.' Gethin tried to think. Could it be true that Shaun was running for his life in fear of Mal Haynes? Haynes was not someone you remotely wanted to fuck around with but what on earth would the motive be? Wasn't it more likely that this was some kind of trap? That Shaun and Haynes were working together and just trying to lure Gethin, and by extension Amelia, out of their hiding place? 'Okay, Bex, text me his number and I'll call him, try and find out what's going on.'

Gethin stared out at the view of the city spread in front of him. For the first time, it struck him that there was something he had in common with his father. They both lived in places with amazing views. Lords of all they surveyed. Or something like that.

His phone beeped. Gethin opened Bex's text and called the number.

'That you, Mr Grey?'

Gethin couldn't help laughing. The bloke had tried doing him major harm several times over the last few days, but he still felt compelled to call him 'Mister'.

'Yeah, this is Gethin. You planning on coming around and sticking a gun in my face again, is that the idea?'

'No,' said Shaun, and his voice really did sound ragged. 'Nothing like that, I swear. It's him. It's always been him, pulling my fucking strings. And now he's after me and I swear, bruv, if he catches me he's going to kill me. You have to help me.'

'Why me?' said Gethin. 'You think you're in danger, go to a police station.'

'You're joking,' said Shaun, his voice high and shrill. 'He used to be one of them. In fact, you ask me, I think he still is. I go into a police station, they'll serve me up to him on a plate. No way, no fucking way. It's down to you, man, you're the only one can stop him now.'

Gethin couldn't help but be swayed by the urgency in Shaun's voice. If he was acting, he was one fucking good actor. But it still begged so many questions. He started with the basic one. 'Why is Haynes after you? He's your bud, far as I've seen.'

'Fuck,' said Shaun. 'Can't you see it? It's about the money. It's always about the money. Now, are you going to help? If you help me, I'll tell you everything, the whole fucking story.'

The sensible thing would be to hang up, leave Haynes and Shaun to battle it out. At the same time, if Haynes really was after Shaun's blood, he was unlikely to stop there. If he thought Gethin knew something about him, he'd come after him too. If they could pull Shaun on board, though, there was a chance of bringing Haynes down once and for all. He was inclined to take the risk but where should he tell Shaun to come? Not the house, that was for sure. Maybe the Judge's place. That would be better but still risky. Then he had a thought.

'There's a pub called The Fisherman's Wife,' he told Shaun. 'It's in a place called Sully, near Cardiff. Your satnav will find it. I'll see you there in the car park an hour from now.'

* * *

The Fisherman's Wife was around the corner from the Judge's place, at the southern tip of the little peninsula. It was a big rambling pub, popular with families in the daytime and much favoured as a romantic destination in the evening. Its garden looked out over Sully Island, an uninhabited little outcrop that was connected to the mainland at low tide but separated from it by a dangerous channel at high tide.

Gethin had chosen it as a rendezvous because there was only one way in by car. You could walk there easily from the Judge's place but there was no through road. The only way to the pub came from the other side of the peninsula. He could park at the house, walk down the footpath and take up a position that would give him a clear sight of any cars approaching the pub. So if Shaun wasn't alone, he could simply walk back up the path, no harm done.

He explained the plan to Lee as they drove back down from the Garth mountain towards the sea. He'd waved her out into the garden after putting the phone down on Shaun and told her she should best stay and keep an eye on everyone at the house. She'd just shaken her head and tapped her shoulder bag and asked him if he knew how to fire a gun.

'Don't need much of a plan, really. Not if you're the one with the gun,' she said in the car, once he'd laid it all out.

He turned on the radio to distract himself from thinking about the danger he was driving towards. A panel of alleged football experts was arguing the toss about the following day's premiership fixtures and Gethin was just about to change the channel when they broke for news and travel. Travel came first. There were no problems reported on the M4, so Shaun should be there on time. Then came the news bulletin and Gethin was barely listening until the third item grabbed his attention.

Ismail Mohammed, better known as the writer and activist Izma M, has issued a statement from Gartree prison, where he is currently serving a life term for murder. Mr Mohammed has announced that he is no longer attempting to clear his name. He accepts full responsibility for the murder of Hannah Gold in 2005 and wants to draw a line under the matter. He will continue to campaign on civil rights issues but strictly on behalf of others and not himself.

'What the fuck?' said Gethin.

'Dunno boss, sounds to me like someone's nobbled him.'

They drove on in silence for a little while, trying to figure it out. Gethin got there just a half second before Lee.

'Haynes,' they said, almost in unison.

'You know this morning, when we were following him,' said Gethin, 'thinking he was going to lead us to Amelia?'

'He was heading for Gartree, wasn't he?'

'Be easy to check, but I'll bet that's right. He's seen Izma and he's put the frighteners on.'

'You think he killed Hannah then?'

'Who? Haynes?'

'Yeah.'

'Why would he do that? Maybe he just has the evidence that Izma really did it and wants us to stop stirring the hornet's nest and disturbing their drug dealing operations. You think that might be it?'

Neither of them could answer that so they lapsed into silence as Gethin navigated his way round the outskirts of Barry and down the lane to the Judge's place.

They parked and gave Bex and the Judge the briefest of updates, before heading down the path till they came to a wall that stopped anyone driving any further. It wasn't a high wall, just four feet or so, and there was a gate to allow walkers access, but it was the ideal place to hide while keeping watch on the car park. It was fully dark now too, so they were unlikely to be spotted by anyone who didn't know exactly where to look.

It was a Friday evening so there was a steady trickle of cars coming down the approach road to the pub, disgorging passengers bent on nothing more sinister than ordering a pint of lager, a glass of Pinot Grigio and two plates of Hunter's Chicken.

They'd been there for fifteen minutes when a Mercedes came into view and, sure enough, once it entered the well-lit surrounds of the car park they could see the man himself at the wheel.

They waited while Shaun emerged from the car and started peering around. He looked every bit as nervous as he'd sounded on the phone. Though that didn't necessarily mean he was telling the truth. He could be on edge because he had Haynes hiding in the back seat of the car. The first thing they needed to do was to prise him out of the car park and see if he had any backup.

'Shaun!' Gethin called out from behind the wall.

Shaun looked round wildly, to see where the voice was coming from.

'Walk towards me, that's away from the pub. You'll see a gate ahead of you, walk through it and carry on along the path.'

Shaun followed the instructions as best he could, stumbling a little as his eyes sought to adjust to the darkness beyond the car park. Finally, he found the gate and started to walk along the path. Gethin, meanwhile, had his eyes trained on the Merc, waiting for Haynes to unfold from the back seat like some sort of ninja assassin.

Thankfully, there was no sign of movement. Neither were there any further cars coming down the approach road. It looked as if Shaun really was on his own, and every bit as scared as he had sounded on the phone. Gethin nodded to Lee and they came out from their hiding place behind the wall and started walking quietly along the path behind Shaun.

'Hey,' shouted Gethin, after they'd gone another twenty yards or so.

Shaun turned to face them, looking utterly terrified, like a condemned man trying to make out the faces of the firing squad.

'Calm down,' said Lee. 'It's only us.'

'Fuck,' said Shaun. 'You again.'

'Yep, and I'm still the one with the gun, so behave.'

'Yeah, yeah, don't worry.' Shaun looked defeated and exhausted. He sat down on the low wall that ran alongside the lane. 'We've all got the same problem now – Malcolm bloody Haynes.'

'So you said on the phone.' Gethin kept his distance from Shaun as he talked. 'You mind explaining what on earth is going on?'

'It's all about the money, like I told you.'

'What money?'

'Izma's money. All sitting there in a safe deposit box, waiting for big bad Malcolm Haynes to come and steal it. Just as soon as he has the code.'

'And where's he going to find this code?'

'From me. I'm the only one who knows it.'

'Okay,' said Gethin, slowly. 'You're telling me that Izma has a safe deposit box somewhere – with a lot of money in it – and you know the code to get in and open it up?'

'Yeah, that's what I just told you, man. Come on, let's leave. He might show up at any time.'

'Don't reckon so.' Gethin waved at the darkness all around them. 'He wasn't following you, we checked on that. So, if you don't mind humouring us a bit, can you explain how Izma has a safe deposit box full of money?'

Shaun slumped down into himself. 'It's a long fucking story, bruv, but if you insist. For one thing, I don't know if you know this, but it's not his real name.'

'No,' said Lee. 'He's Danny Bliss.'

'How the fuck did you know that?' said Shaun, then thought about it. 'Well, you should be able to figure out the rest of it. You know who Danny Bliss's dad was, right?'

'Some sort of gangster.'

'Major sort of gangster. Made fucking millions.'

'And that's what's in the safe deposit box?'

'Yeah, some of it anyway. About three million quids' worth right now.'

'Fucking hell,' said Gethin. 'No wonder Haynes is interested. How come he waited until now to make his move?'

'He didn't know about the money. He just thought Ty and me were regular drug dealers. I'm not sure how he found out. Something changed in the last couple of days. It's all been going to hell. Probably something to do with that guy with the hotel, Dante Green. He knew Ty from before, but I didn't realise he knew Mal as well. He must have said something that helped Mal join the dots between Ty and Danny Bliss and a whole lot of money in a safe deposit box. When you mentioned Dante this afternoon, that's when I started to realise what was going on, why Mal was starting to act so weird. And, thank God, I escaped just in time.'

'What were you doing hiding out there anyway?'

'I don't know, I panicked. Amelia Laverne came round asking questions about Izma's childhood and I knew she'd figure out soon enough that he wasn't who he said he was and then everything would start to fall apart. So I just needed to go somewhere while I worked out what to do. And that's when I made the same mistake I made before – I asked Mal to help out. He told me to take her to this place in the country and wait for him there. So that's what I did. I was just sitting there, waiting for him to come back. I had no idea it was at the back of Dante's hotel. And then, after what you told me, I realised if he found me there all he was gonna do was waste Amelia and torture me until I told him where the money was and what the codes were.'

'One thing I don't understand,' Lee chipped in. 'All that money sitting there, why didn't you just take it?'

Shaun looked at her as though she was mad. 'Cos it's Izma's. I would never steal from him. He was generous to me. I was just keeping it all safe till he was out.'

Lee stared at him, looking less than trusting. 'For real?'

'Yeah, for real.' Shaun was becoming increasingly jittery. 'Look – can we just go somewhere safe? Then I'll tell you anything else you want, all right?'

Gethin looked over at Lee: 'He has a point.' He waved his arm towards the car park. 'There's cars coming in all the time.'

'Fine,' said Lee. 'Let's go inside.'

They walked up the lane in silence; Gethin leading the way, Shaun next and Lee bringing up the rear, making it very clear that she had one hand on the gun in her shoulder bag.

Gethin pressed on the intercom when they arrived at the Judge's gate. His father didn't say anything, just buzzed the gate open. Gethin led the way through the undergrowth, thinking it really was time the gardener came round, and opened the front door. There was no one to be seen in the front room, which was odd. Gethin ushered the others inside and closed the door.

At which point, Mal Haynes stepped out of the kitchen, a gun held casually in his left hand.

Twenty-Five

HAYNES SWUNG THE GUN UP as Gethin started to turn, hoping he might somehow be able to rewind time and move back out of the door. Seemingly without bothering to aim, he fired. There was a loud blast that sounded more like a bomb than a gun and Gethin fell to the floor, wondering if he'd been hit without knowing it.

'That's to let you know I'm not fucking around here,' said Haynes. 'Anyone tries anything at all, you'll have one right in the stomach. Where it fucking hurts. Now stand up, you twat.'

Gethin staggered back to his feet.

'Right, we have some new house rules here. Number one, Uncle Mal keeps all the phones. Very slowly dig them out of wherever you keep them and slide them over to me.'

Gethin and Shaun did as they were told. As they did so, Gethin looked at Lee out of the corner of his eye. He knew she had the gun in her shoulder bag as well as the phone. Which was she going to go for?

Unfortunately, Haynes seemed to have identified Lee as the most likely danger.

'And you,' pointing the gun straight at Lee. 'Anything comes out of there that isn't a phone, you're fucking dead, so no funny business. You're the one I need to worry about. Isn't that right, Shaun? Bit too much of a handful for you, wasn't she?'

'Cunt,' said Shaun, under his breath.

Lee sighed and slid her phone over to Haynes.

'Thanks, darling. Now leave your bag on the floor and you can all raise your hands in the air, unless you want me to start shooting them off you.'

They did as they were told. Haynes picked up the phones one-handed and dropped them into his bag. There was nothing but survival on Gethin's mind. He just wanted Shaun to give up the code and Haynes to leave without killing them all. Surely he wouldn't do that? You can't just leave a load of dead bodies behind you, not in Britain, especially if one of them is a judge. Christ, the Judge, where was he? Surely Haynes hadn't...

Haynes answered that question almost immediately. 'Hey,' he shouted. 'You there in the kitchen – the old cunt and the fat bird – come in here. Just pick up your chairs and walk.'

There was a scraping noise from the kitchen. Gethin craned his neck round to see what was going on. First Bex, then his father appeared. They'd both been tied to kitchen chairs. Just tied around the waist so the legs and arms were free. Trying to walk while tied to a chair obviously wasn't easy and they were both bent over like tortoises under their shells. Gethin saw his father stagger and almost fall as he made his way into the living room.

Without thinking about it, Gethin realised he had started praying under his breath. Praying to escape from there alive and to have the chance to gain his revenge on Haynes for humiliating him and his father alike.

'Right, stop there,' said Haynes, once Bex and the Judge were in the centre of the room. 'And stick your hands in the air and all. Apologies for the inconvenience. None of this is how I like to do business, but this wanker here decided to run out on me.'

He turned his gun towards Shaun for emphasis and fired again. The report was deafening. Bex screamed and Shaun dropped to the floor, his face whiter than you would have thought it possible.

'So, Shaun boy, you can change your pants later. First up, you can give me a little bit of info.'

Shaun nodded furiously. 'Of course.'

'All right, that's my boy. First question – where is the safe deposit box? Deal or no deal time.'

'London,' said Shaun. 'St – St John's Wood. On the High Street, just next to the Caffè Nero.'

'Good boy. Now how's about the code?'

'It's a long number.'

'Hope you have a good memory. You make any slip-ups, I'm not going to be pleased.'

'I don't just know it like that. I have it in my phone.'

'Okay.' Haynes started rummaging around in his bag with his free hand. He pulled out Shaun's iPhone at the second attempt. He slid it towards him. 'Pick it up. Nice, slow moves, please. Then, open it up to wherever you've put the number.'

Shaun did as he was told, his hand shaking as he manipulated the touchscreen. 'Got it.'

'Slide it gently across the floor to me and put your hands back up in the air.'

Haynes picked up the phone, his gun pointing towards Gethin, Shaun and Lee the whole time. He looked at the phone and clicked on something on the screen. At which point his expression went from mocking to livid.

'Says here this document was edited today. Have you changed the code, you fucking scrote? You think I'm messing about? You think I'm fucking playacting? Well, I'll show you how I play.'

Moving very fast, Haynes stepped to his left and, with one hand, dragged the Judge towards him, chair and all.

'You may be wondering how come I knew you'd be here. Simple answer is because you're a bunch of fucking amateurs. Shaun boy should have realised when I gave him a nice new iPhone it was so I could track him. Soon as I saw he was over the Severn Bridge I had the idea where he was going. The old git here should realise that, if you go asking your old mates in the Bristol police force all about me, I might hear about it. I'm still very good friends with the chaps on the force – the chaps in the Lodge all the more so, if you get my drift. They saw fit to tell me that someone was asking. And when I said I wanted a little word, they were only too happy to give me your address. No one likes a judge, not really.'

Haynes paused for a moment, like a weightlifter preparing to go for a particularly heavy barbell.

'Bet you're in the Lodge and all, aren't you, old cunt? Let's see if you know the handshake.'

Grabbing the Judge's right hand, he twisted it with awful force. There was a clearly audible crack as the Judge's wrist broke, followed by a high unnatural scream. Both Gethin and Lee started to move towards the ex-copper, but he had his gun up immediately, pointing straight at them.

'Back off, both of you. I'll shoot you both in the kneecaps and you can lie there and watch me break your dad's fucking neck. Always hated judges. Bunch of supercilious cunts.'

Gethin stepped back, hating himself as he did so.

'Fuck!' Shaun now: 'You didn't have to do that, Mal. I was going to tell you anyway. I changed the last number from a 6 to a 7 in case someone who wasn't supposed to took hold of my phone. I just forgot I'd done it for a moment.'

'Uh huh,' said Haynes, 'you just forgot. Well, in case you

remember anything else you unfortunately forgot, you're coming with me all the way up to London. And if there are any little errors, well, you'd better pray there aren't. Now...' he held the phone up in his right hand, '... the last number should be a six, yeah?'

'Yeah,' said Shaun. As Haynes' eyes dipped down to the phone, the Judge let out another awful scream, further distracting everyone, and Shaun seized the moment to make his move. He seemed to actually throw himself towards the door. Haynes had his gun up and fired off a shot but either he missed or he didn't want to risk killing Shaun before he'd checked that the code worked. A second later, Shaun was out of the door and running for his life. Haynes didn't hesitate, just charged out of the door after him.

Gethin looked round frantically, his mind whirring.

'Lee,' he said. 'You stay here. Lock the doors. And give me your gun.'

Hesitating briefly, she dug into her shoulder bag and handed over the gun. 'Go on, Geth. And if you get a chance, you kill the cunt.'

Gethin ran down the path and through the gate, his scarred feet complaining bitterly, before pulling up short. There was no sign of either Haynes or Shaun. He had two options: turn to the left and run up the hill, and ultimately to the main road, or turn right, back down towards the pub. Uphill was probably the better option for Shaun, but Gethin suspected that instinct would have suggested the downhill route. A creature in flight seeks the fastest option, so downhill always trumps up.

Gethin started jogging along the path, moving as fast as he could without making too much noise. He was shaking with a murderous rage unlike anything he could remember, hearing the sound of his father's howl echoing in his brain.

The gate at the bottom of the path was swinging open, which suggested he was on the right track. Through the gate and there were again two options: turn right towards the pub, and surely safety, or left down on to the beach and ultimately towards the island. He heard a shout, tried to figure out where it was coming from. The beach, definitely the beach. Why on earth had Shaun headed that way? Probably he'd had no choice, with Haynes coming right up behind him.

Gethin made his way down on to the beach, the gun out in front of him. It gave him a welcome sense of security but meant that he had to pick his way carefully over the rocks to avoid losing his balance.

Another shout, much closer. There was very little light to work with, just a slight glow from the pub car park, but almost nothing from the moon, hidden behind thick cloud. All the light was behind him, so he and the two men he was chasing were all heading into the darkness. He was definitely closing, though. He could hear scuttling and cursing and then a heavy impact and a shout.

Coming round an outcrop of rock, he pulled up short. They were no more than ten yards ahead of him: two shadows, one standing over the other. The upright shadow was kicking the prone one.

'Get up, you prick, you're coming with me.'

He wasn't surprised that the hunter had vanquished his prey. Now, though, the odds were in his favour. There was no sign of a gun in Haynes' hand, and no sign either that he had heard Gethin's approach.

He inched closer, wrestling with the temptation to pull the trigger immediately, to cut Haynes down without warning. The gun – a Glock 9 mm according to Lee – didn't have any safety catch as such, just a weird little sort of double trigger.

Apparently, that meant you had to squeeze quite hard to make it fire. One squeeze and no more Mal Haynes. He couldn't do it, though. Not just like that. Besides, however much it felt like the right thing, it was still probably murder in a court of law. All this whirled through his mind in an instant.

Stepping forward, struggling to find the right words, he ended up calling out a strangled 'Oi!'

Haynes looked round. Probably he had a better view of Gethin than vice versa as Gethin had the light behind him. 'Well, fuck me, it's the seventh cavalry.' He stopped kicking Shaun and studied Gethin carefully. 'You pointing that thing at me?'

'Yeah,' said Gethin, trying to keep his voice from shaking, 'and if you don't step away from Shaun right now and put your hands in the air, I'll put one in your kneecap.'

'Done a lot of shooting, have we? Where d'you get the gun from, Toys "R" Us? Oh, wait a minute, I bet I know who it came from.' He swung his boot into Shaun's side one more time. Gethin tried to ignore it and kept the gun trained on Haynes who didn't look half as scared as he was meant to.

'Had it from this twat, didn't you? Well, not you, your friend the half-caste dyke. The thing is, son, I have a dilemma here. I know that when I gave this twat the gun, I didn't put any bullets in it. All he needed it for was to intimidate a film star and I didn't want him blowing his foot off in the process. So, the question is, do I reckon you're smart enough to have loaded it? Or do I reckon you're a clueless twat who's way out of his depth?'

Haynes was coming towards Gethin now, daring him to shoot. Gethin aimed the gun towards Haynes' legs, wondering if he was being double bluffed, then pulled the trigger. Nothing. Just a pathetic click.

'Shit,' he threw it as hard as he could, straight at Haynes' head. Haynes ducked but took a glancing blow, which in turn caused him to slip over with a speed that suggested he must have skidded on seaweed.

Gethin blundered forward, powered by blind rage and the overwhelming desire to kick in Haynes' smug head. But, before he could move close enough, he saw Haynes pull his own gun out of his pocket and fire blindly upwards.

Now, there was no option but to run away as fast as possible. He scrambled across the rocks with reckless speed, waiting for a bullet to strike him in the back, but nothing happened, just swearing from Haynes, who sounded as though he'd slipped over again, and then he was suddenly aware of Shaun running hard just a few yards to his right.

Finally, Gethin's feet hit a truer surface which felt like a concrete path. It had to be the causeway that linked the island to the shore. He could follow it to left or right. Left to the island or right to the pub and the possibility of escape. It wasn't exactly a choice. Gethin turned to the right and sensed, rather than saw, Shaun follow suit behind him. Picking up pace, he was another twenty yards or so closer to safety when he saw a shape moving up ahead.

Haynes had outmanoeuvred them and was soon going to reach the causeway closer to the shoreline. He'd have all the time in the world to pick them off as they approached. Thank God, at least, he'd spotted him. Gethin's only advantage now was that he was in the dark, relative to Haynes. Stopping to think, crouching low, he heard Shaun approach and urgently waved to him to duck down as well.

'What's happening?' whispered Shaun.

'It's Haynes. Up ahead. We have to go the other way.'

'Where's that to?'

'The island. Follow me. Quiet as you can.'

Keeping to a crouch, Gethin turned round and led the way, attempting desperately not to disturb any loose stones, and stopping every few seconds to try to hear whether Haynes was on the move. He couldn't hear anything definite, but it was hard to make out much over the sound of the tide water which was starting to flood the causeway. The closer they came to the island, the worse it became. A big wave soaked him up to the knees and even once it had receded, the water remained above ankle height. Shaun stumbled and cursed, the surface ever more treacherous beneath their feet. Haynes must've heard the noise as, a second later, there was the sound of a gunshot. Gethin had no way of telling whether it had gone anywhere near them but, clearly, there was no use in trying to be quiet any more. It was a matter of outrunning the incoming tide and making it to the island which should, if Gethin remembered rightly from childhood visits, offer a range of hiding places.

'Come on,' he said to Shaun. 'We have to run for it.'

That was easier said than done. The speed of the tide was extraordinary. No wonder people got stranded. In no time, they were wading up to their thighs in the water.

'I can't swim,' hissed Shaun, as another big wave brought the water up to waist level.

'Don't worry,' said Gethin, 'it isn't that deep.' Not that he was sure, but what else could he say?

They made it through what felt like the lowest point of the causeway shortly afterwards. Each step seemed to raise them just a little further out of the water and they could see the shape of the island looming ahead. Another shot came from behind but it didn't hit either of them and Haynes must've accepted that he was wasting his time and bullets as there were no more after that. Another fifty yards or so wading and they were on the island. Scrambling over the rocks, they blundered on to a path that led into an area of long reeds. Gethin swerved off the path, beating his way through the vegetation, until he came to a slight clearing and collapsed to the ground. He heard Shaun do likewise. They were soaked and freezing but alive. Safe for the moment on the island, while Haynes was stranded on the shore.

'He's going to kill me.'

'No, he's not.' Gethin did his best to sound reassuring. 'All we have to do is wait here until morning. No way is he going to shoot you in the light of day with a load of people watching.'

'You don't know him,' said Shaun. 'I do. Wish I'd never set eyes on the cunt.'

Gethin was acutely aware of how cold and uncomfortable he was. He tried to figure out whether it would be better to take his soaking trousers off or keep them on in the hope that his body heat would dry them off. Thankfully, his top half was okay. He had a North Face anorak on that Cat had bought him years ago. The thought of Cat almost made him cry. What he'd give now for a nice boring family evening, safe in their living room, in the warmth of their love. Their love now gone, or at least suspended. He tried jogging on the spot to warm up a little. Shaun quickly followed suit.

'I want to tell you what's happened,' said Shaun. 'All of it. Just so someone knows. It started about fifteen years ago. I was on holiday in Cyprus, Ayia Napa, you know, with a bunch of guys from home. It was really kicking off in Ayia Napa that summer man, dances on the beach. We had a fridge full of champagne back at the apartment and these massive water guns we used to soak all the girls on the beach. Everyone going boo! Remember that tune 'Booo!' with Ms Dynamite?'

'Not really.'

'Well, it was a tune, let me tell you. Oh fuck, man, I wish I was back there. Wish I'd never met him.'

'Who? Haynes?'

'No, no, Danny. Listen, we were all at Ayia Napa, like I said, and one day we're on the beach there and this guy showed up and began talking to Mikey. Mikey had met him in some club in London, I think. He looked sort of familiar and he fitted in with the rest of us, you know? White guy but quite dark complexion – you know his mum was some kind of Arab Jew? He looked like he might be a local Turkish guy or something. Not that you saw many of the locals out clubbing, as we had totally taken over the place. It was like the whole of UK garage had gone to Cyprus. Anyway, he seemed cool and we're all having a laugh and shit and then we were going back to the apartment and he asked if it was okay if he came too. He told us this story about how he'd been robbed and all he had was the bathers he was stood up in. I would have told him to fuck off but Mikey's a soft touch and anyway he told me later on that he reckoned the guy was absolutely loaded, or at least his old man was, so I was like what the fuck, if he wants to hang with us then no worries.

'So, that's how it went the next few days. This guy, Danny, was just hanging with us. He had his wallet in his trunks so he had a bit of cash and that. And then we were all heading back and Danny was really stressed about what he was going to do. He said he couldn't go to the police or the embassy or whatever. He didn't say why. I suppose we all assumed he was into something dodgy.

'And then this other guy, Tyrell, decided he was going to stay on for a while. He'd been offered a job in one of the clubs on the door, plus he had about five different women on the go. He was absolutely smashing it out there and Danny asked him if he could use his passport. He said he'd give him his watch – which was this Rolex Submariner worth about five grand – and Tyrell agrees to wait a week or two and say he's lost his passport. You could work that back then, because it wasn't all computerised when you went through immigration. You just waved your passport and that was that. So, that's what happened. Tyrell was mixed race but pretty light and Danny had a totally dark tan and, especially when he was with the rest of us, all black or mixed you know, well you just sort of assumed that he was too. I mean, I bet he was bricking it when we came through immigration, but it was like three in the morning and the guy hardly even looked at us, a bunch of British party boys coming back from Ayia Napa.'

'So that's how it started?'

'Yeah, well, when we all like split up at the airport, I didn't expect to see the guy again. But a few weeks later, there he was in Bristol in this bar called Po Na Na. Turned out he was renting a flat in Bristol and he was still calling himself Tyrell and, anyway, the point is we got to be close, you know, and eventually he told me the whole story. What happened to his dad and all and how he didn't dare go back to his own name. He had to keep pretending to be dead or the guys who killed his dad would come after him too.

'And I just, well, I really liked the geezer. He was the smartest guy I'd ever met and, after a bit, he asked if I wanted to go into business with him, putting on club nights and stuff and so that's what we did. I think he mostly wanted me round so I could be the face of it and he could just be in the background, like. And that's how it worked for a while. We were mates and I was working for him. And after a bit he bought the house.'

'The club nights must've done well.'

'No, he had the money in the safe deposit box. I mean I didn't know where the money came from at first, but he obviously had a lot as we didn't make anything much out of the clubs, lost money probably. That's sort of where the trouble started.'

'How do you mean?'

'Well, people started sniffing around. They could figure out we weren't making much money from the club nights but he was buying a house and all that and always had plenty of cash to flash around. So, people put two and two together and made 16. Everyone figured he was this London drug dealer. The fact that no one ever saw us dealing just made them think we must be dealing in serious weight. So, I started having people coming up to me, brers I've known around the place, asking if I could cut them in on it. And I had to say no, so they all think I'm stoosh or whatever, never mind. And that's all okay until Mal Haynes shows up.'

'How'd that happen?'

'Mal had like a protection thing going on. You wanted to deal drugs in the clubs, you had to pay him a fee. I would have told him to fuck off, because at the end of the day we weren't dealing, but Danny, he reckoned it was best if we played along, otherwise Haynes might start digging into where the money really came from. So I had to go over his office every week, pay him a couple of ton, and that's where it started. I mean, he was all friendly and that about it, but it was like having the devil for your mate.

'The thing is, Danny started becoming a bit twitchy. One time we were out in town, at Creation I think it was, and he saw some north London faces there or thought he did. So, he didn't want to go there anymore and he started talking about a gun. And like an idiot, I have a word with Uncle Mal, and sure enough he's like no problem, what do you want? So, we bought a gun off him and then it all went to hell.'

There was a catch in Shaun's voice, as if he was about to start crying. Gethin didn't say anything, just let him ride it out. He took the chance to stand up and stretch his legs, see if there was any sign of anything. But no, just darkness and the sounds of the sea and a few lights in the far distance. He tried to make some rough calculations about the tide. It must be nearly all the way in by now, surely? Meanwhile his legs in their wet trousers felt like blocks of ice. He hunkered down again and Shaun carried on with his story or confession or whatever it was.

'One night, Danny came back to the house and he was all excited and a bit scared. He said he was out in that place Zenon and this girl walked in who he knew from back home, his old girlfriend, and she recognised him straightaway. He'd been freaked out, he told me, cause she saw straight through him. I told him just to keep out of Zenon for a bit. But he said he really wanted to see her again. He still had a lot of feeling for her.'

'Did she know he was meant to be dead?'

'Nah, I asked him that and he said she didn't have anything to do with her family anymore, so she hadn't heard about it.'

'Lucky.'

'Yeah, well luck didn't exactly hold out did it? Anyway, it started totally freaking him out, seeing her again. He couldn't handle it, being two different people. He'd settled into being Tyrell, you know, and suddenly he was Danny again. And I knew it was only a matter of time before she found out about his parents and everything and then it would all go to shit. So, I was trying to tell him to back off her, but he just wouldn't listen so...'

'So...'

'So, I went up to where she worked, the bike place, but that didn't do any good, probably made her keener than ever and I didn't know what to do so I followed them, that night. I thought if I had a chance to talk to her on her own late at night I could frighten her off, you know...'

'Oh,' said Gethin. So that was what had happened. Shaun had killed Hannah Gold, killed her to keep Danny and his money close. He wasn't sure whether it was the man, or the money that was at the heart of it. Something in the way Shaun talked about Danny suggested a whole raft of unacknowledged feelings.

'I didn't kill her, man, if that's what you're thinking.' Shaun paused, his head bowed, 'But it was my fault.'

'So, what happened?'

'Okay, I've never told anyone this, right, and I know how it sounds. I followed Danny and the girl, Hannah. I was waiting outside that boat bar place and I was just about to give it up and leave them to it when out they came and started walking along the road and up to the Downs. They kept stopping for a snog and I kept coming too close but they didn't notice, wouldn't have noticed anything really. And then they reached the top of that path and went off in the woods to do, whatever, you know? And I'm just sitting there on a bench feeling like a prize wanker, but I was sort of determined to talk to her if I had a chance. Just, like I say, to frighten her off. I had a bit of a story planned. I was going to tell her that Danny was a major drug dealer and if she was involved with him she'd have the police all over her and stood a good chance of being shot. I thought that would make her back off, a nice middle-class student type like that.

'I was nearly ready to give up again when they came out of the bushes and I could tell things hadn't gone too great, because instead of being all lovey-dovey, they were sort of tense and arguing. I couldn't hear what they were saying, obviously some kind of a row, and Danny walked off towards Clifton village and the girl headed back towards the path down the hill. And I thought that was my chance.

'So, I waited for her to go past me. Doesn't notice me at all. It's not like she knew me anyway, but she just didn't register a guy on a bench, just went straight down the path. So, I stood up and followed her, and once we were out of sight of the Downs, I started speeding up to catch up with her and she – well, she heard me coming and she just freaked out and started running down the path and then there's this bit with the steps and... and she just fucking fell down them and I ran down after her and she was just lying there like a bloody, broken doll and I was sure she was dead and I didn't know what to do. If I'd had any sense, I'd have just ran out of there, but I didn't. I was convinced I'd be caught and blamed for it, so I sort of dragged her into the bushes in case anyone came down the path and then I made the really big mistake.'

'What was that?'

'I called Mal Haynes. I thought he'd know what to do, being a copper. I was just standing there, all shaking and shit.'

Gethin tried to picture it – Shaun standing over Hannah's body like a big scared kid. It wasn't hard. He was the same now.

'Turned out he wasn't far away. He was there in about fifteen minutes. I showed him Hannah's body and he asked me what was going on and I told him that this was the girl Danny had been seeing and she'd been threatening to go to the cops with what she knew. And I... oh God, this is bad, man... I told him that she knew his name, Haynes' name, she was going to tell everything. I only said it all to try and make him help. I had no idea what would happen. Honestly.'

'What do you mean? What more was there to happen?'

'Oh, God.' Shaun let out what you could only call a moan. 'Oh God, what happened was she started to come to, Hannah, she wasn't dead after all. And he just walked over to her, picked her up and into a kind of headlock with one arm, so her head was trapped under his right arm and he just jerked her upwards with one arm and bent the other arm back hard and he broke her neck. You could hear it fucking break, man. It's the worst thing I've ever heard. You can't imagine and I'm so fucking sorry, like I say, I've never told anyone this...'

Shaun was melting down in front of him. What a vision to have playing through your mind, what a sound to hear in your dreams.

'So, what happened next?'

'Mal made me help him dump her body in the river. He knew where all the CCTV cameras were and stuff, so we wouldn't be seen. The only problem was the body was found so quickly and you could tell that she'd been murdered. Mal's idea was that the body would be mashed up in the water by the time they found it, but no one would know for sure how she died. And it would be put down as a suicide. But, instead, it all went to shit.'

'How do you mean?'

'It was the DNA wasn't it? They had the match on the semen. They had Danny's DNA on file because they'd done him a few months before. Pulled him because he was in a nice car, driving while black. Cunts. So they busted him and, of course, he had the fucking gun, the gun Mal had sold him and, well, you know the rest.'

'Did Danny know who was really responsible?'

'Sort of. I told him Haynes killed her. He doesn't know exactly what I did. I told him Haynes had been following him, that he'd heard about Hannah, decided she was a threat to him and killed her. Took myself out of it. Not proud of that.'

'No, can't imagine you are.' Gethin thought about it. Poor fucking Danny. He must have realised he was completely bloody trapped. If he'd blamed Haynes that would have been a hell of a risk in itself, and he'd have had to explain who he really was. If he did that he'd alert whoever these guys were who'd killed his parents that he was still alive. Christ, prison must have been the least worst option. It explained a lot, all of it really, the way he was in prison, not really wanting to say anything, not really trying to leave.

'Fuck,' said Gethin eventually. 'What a fucking mess.'

They crouched there in the long grass, neither saying anything, both frozen and scared and tired. Gethin wondered how long it could be until the tide finally started dropping back down. Should they try and hide on the island until morning and hope that there would be people around to put off Haynes? Or, if it was still dark, should they try and sneak past Haynes and make it to safety? Neither option sounded all that appealing. It was cold now and becoming colder.

And then Gethin heard a noise, a noise that sounded very much like someone pulling a small boat on to the foreshore.

Twenty-Six

G<small>ETHIN TAPPED</small> S<small>HAUN ON THE</small> shoulder, whispered, 'You hear that?'

'Fuck,' said Shaun. And repeated it over and over under his breath.

'Just stay still. It's pitch dark. He's never going to find us unless he falls over us. Just stay quiet.'

This was easier said than done. Now he was listening out for Haynes, Gethin realised there were all kinds of noises on the island. Probably just little nocturnal creatures running around, he told himself, nice nocturnal creatures, voles or something, not rats. And the wind that had hardly registered as a sound now seemed deafening as he strained to hear Haynes approaching. He was pretty sure he had heard a boat landing and who else could it be but Haynes? Still, it was blessedly dark. All he had to do was follow his own advice and stay quiet and hope to hell that Shaun, who appeared to be rocking back and forth, could do the same. But, really, no way would Haynes find them in the dark. Not unless he had a torch.

Of course, Haynes would have a torch. Anyone with a phone had a torch these days. The moment the thought came into his head Gethin realised it was inevitable. He wasn't even surprised when he saw its beam wandering about, somewhere over near the foreshore. Nowhere near where they were hiding yet, but how long would it be? Did they just flatten themselves to the ground and pray, or was that to be caught in a trap? Should they move quickly to wherever the light wasn't? Could they manoeuvre around so Haynes was on the wrong side of the island and then, maybe, they could swim for it? Perhaps that was the best plan. He heard a noise, sounded like a sneeze. Then came a whole series of similar noises. Somewhere on the island, Mal Haynes was having a sneezing fit. Gethin didn't feel especially sympathetic.

Next to him, Shaun sounded as if he was hyperventilating. Gethin did his best to tune him out and just raised up a little higher from his crouch position to see which way Haynes' torch was heading. Amazingly enough, he did seem to be off in the opposite direction. It looked as if he was working his way round the island anticlockwise. If he'd gone the other way, he would have been close to them in no time, but as it was they had a distinct chance. Gethin willed himself to stay calm as the torch's beam moved further and further away and finally disappeared around the back of the island's central hill. Haynes had already shone the light up on to the hill a few times, but as it was almost completely bare and devoid of hiding places, he'd clearly and correctly figured they'd be hiding out somewhere lower down.

Finally, the beam completely vanished from sight.

'Come on,' he said to Shaun. 'Here's our chance – we need to get back to the mainland.'

'I can't swim, bruv, I told you before. Look, you get away from here, you tell Denise I love her right. And... and Connor. Can't do it, bruv, can't fucking swim, can't do it, bruv, can't fucking swim,' his voice steadily louder and louder.

'Shut up,' hissed Gethin, gripping Shaun hard around the upper arm, 'he'll hear you. It's not far, really. You don't need to swim, we just have to wade through it.'

Was that true? Gethin devoutly hoped so but he had no way of knowing for sure. Maybe it was no more than waist high, but he certainly couldn't bank on it. Gethin was a decent swimmer and reasoned he ought to be able to make it. Shaun, though, was another matter.

He was shaking uncontrollably now, in the grip of some total meltdown. There was no way he was going to make it through the water to the mainland. Gethin was on the edge of panic himself when he spotted the obvious solution. 'We don't need to swim,' he said, 'we're going to take the fucker's boat.'

It was hard to be sure exactly where Haynes had landed. Gethin led the way towards the foreshore, crouched but trying to keep up a decent pace. Once they'd made it out of the long grass, it was easier to get a sense of their surroundings. He couldn't actually see the boat yet, but he figured that, as long as they just followed the foreshore round to the east, they were bound to find. It. Both of them stumbled repeatedly in their eagerness to reach it before Haynes came back. Gethin heard Shaun curse behind him as he smashed his shin into some obstruction or other.

And then, there it was, the unmistakable outline of a boat lying on the sand just twenty yards or so away from them. Presumably, Haynes would have left the oars inside – it would have made no sense to take them with him. He held his hand up for Shaun to stop moving and looked around, checking for any sign of Haynes' torch. Nothing. He had to be all the way round the far side of the island.

'C'mon,' he said and led the way across the remaining yards of sand and rock pools until they were no more than ten yards from the boat and its promise of safety.

That was when a figure sat up in the boat and pointed a torch beam at them.

'What kept you lads?' he said. 'Uncle Mal was dozing off here.'

Did he have a gun in his other hand? Gethin couldn't be sure but it was a pretty safe bet. Instinctively, he dropped to the ground while Shaun just seemed paralysed, didn't move an inch. Gethin waited for a shot to ring out but there was nothing. Instead, the light just switched back and forth from Gethin to Shaun. Hope bobbed up once more in Gethin's brain. Maybe Haynes wasn't there to kill them, maybe he just wanted to cut some sort of deal.

Then came the gunshot. It missed, as far as Gethin could tell. Presumably it was just a warning shot, as it was hard to believe he could have missed from such close range. Gethin did the only thing he could think of which was to grab a handful of sand and fling it towards Haynes. Amazingly enough it had some effect. Haynes made a sort of grunt and the torch beam veered around wildly. Shaun seized his chance: yelling something incomprehensible, he just sprinted towards the water and launched himself in.

Another gunshot. Gethin could see no alternative but to follow Shaun into the water but knew immediately that it was hopeless, the water was freezing and the current far too strong. He stood there paralysed, his gambling instincts failing him under extreme stress. The names Scylla and Charybdis came into his mind from some half-forgotten Greek myth: Odysseus trying to sail between two deadly perils without falling victim to either.

There was another scream from Shaun and then Haynes was striding towards them, shining his torch. He wasn't focusing on Gethin, who was a standing target, but at Shaun, who was being carried away by the water. Gethin stood there in silence, his own plight forgotten for a moment, as he saw Shaun's head go under, bob up, go under again. And then nothing, no more Shaun. Without thinking he crossed himself and turned to face Mal Haynes, wondering if right there his life would be over too.

'You,' said Haynes from the shore, pointing the gun at Gethin, 'you stay right there while I decide what to do with you.'

Gethin's brain was working overtime to try and find an escape route. Oh, for a gun with bullets or even Lee's fabulous torch.

'I'm thinking maybe you got a result, mate,' said Haynes.

Gethin grunted, wondering what on earth Haynes was talking about.

'You don't follow, do you? Don't worry, I'll explain it for you, nice and simple. Our dear deceased mate Shaun, the one communing with the fishes right now. Well, looks to me like he just confessed to you that he killed that Jewish bird, then he couldn't stand the guilt anymore, so he drowned himself. Justice is served. You're a hero. Your mate, the Malcom X wannabe, leaves prison, and yours truly nips up to the Smoke, has a little look in his safe deposit box and if there's half what I think is in there, I'll be putting my feet up on a beach until the twelfth of never. Everyone's a coconut.'

Gethin struggled to his feet, all the while trying to figure out the angles. Could Haynes really just walk away like this? Maybe he could. His summary of the situation was accurate enough. Poor bastard Shaun had made it easy for everyone. All Gethin needed to do was ignore the fact that Mal Haynes had driven Shaun to his death and murdered Hannah Gold. That was all.

'Oh,' said Haynes, shining his torch in Gethin's face and obviously seeing the doubt there. 'You got scruples, have you? Genuine believer in truth and justice? At your age too.

Must have led a sheltered life. Now, let me guess. Did the dear departed tell you some fairy story where it was me who killed the Jew girl? Well, if it makes you feel better, I can tell you that he was lying. He just blamed me cause he couldn't live with what he'd done. Broke that girl's neck. You ask me, I think he was jealous, wanted your boy all to himself. All I did was come and help him clean up the mess.'

'Really?' said Gethin, aware that he was sounding horribly eager to believe, to have an honourable way out of this nightmare, knowing that justice was, in some cockeyed way, being done.

'Sure,' said Haynes, his voice greasy with triumph. He let the gun drop a little. It was now pointing at the foreshore between them. But then he shook his head. 'Nah, what am I talking about? No fucking way I can let you go telling tales.'

Haynes raised the gun and Gethin threw himself desperately to one side. A shot boomed out but evidently missed as Gethin sensed neither pain nor imminent oblivion. And then, in the next breath, something changed. Haynes started making a series of odd 'uh, uh' noises and his arm swung upwards just as he was about to fire again, so the next shot went way over Gethin's head. At first, he couldn't understand what was happening but Haynes made a noise that sounded like another gunshot and Gethin realised he'd been overcome by a sneeze. At any other time it might have been funny, but right at that moment it was a lifeline.

Gethin took his chance: he splashed out of the sea and away from the torch beam which was now flailing around wildly. Haynes fired again but he was aiming blind now as his body convulsed in a whole series of wild, racking sneezes. Within seconds, Gethin was in darkness and could feel solid ground beneath his scarred and aching feet. He ducked low and ran, zigzagging as he went, the sounds of Haynes' sneezes and erratic shooting disappearing into the wind behind him.

After what seemed like forever, Gethin made it into the relative safety of the long grass. He threw himself to the ground, soaked and shivering uncontrollably, but too wired from adrenaline to really feel the cold. Two minutes of quiet later, he raised his head a little and looked back in the direction of the foreshore. He could see Haynes' torch beam moving about more steadily now and ducked back down again, just in case.

When he looked again, there was no sign of the torch. Had Haynes given up and rowed back to shore? Gethin hoped so but he was wary of falling into another of his traps. Maybe Haynes was just sitting there in the darkness, waiting. Gethin lay back down, the cold really starting to bite now and tried to calm himself by running through his repertoire of memory exercises. Until finally, he could stand it no longer. He had to escape the island and find some warm clothes – otherwise hypothermia surely awaited.

Very slowly, he made his way to the edge of the long grass, his eyes adjusting better to the darkness, and peered towards the spot where Haynes had moored his boat. It had gone. Death by shooting had been avoided, at least for the time being. Death by cold was the next enemy to be dealt with.

* * *

In the end, it was nearly two dreadful hours later when Gethin finally made it back to his father's house. It had seemed to take forever for the tide to recede sufficiently for him to wade through it to the causeway. He'd fallen

over once, had come awfully close to being swept away like
Shaun, but had just about managed to regain his footing.
As he rang on the intercom, though, he was soaking and
shivering and utterly defeated.

'Are you on your own?' said a voice. Bex.

'Yeah.'

'Okay.' Bex buzzed him in. The front door was already
open by the time he made it to the end of the path and he
more or less toppled over into the arms of Bex.

'Christ, Geth, you mind letting go of me?' she said after
a few seconds. 'You're bloody soaking. Sit down.'

Gethin let go and looked around the room. Lee came up
and hugged him quickly, her face drawn and serious. And
there was his father, seated on a sofa with his arm in a sling.

Once he'd changed into some dry clothes, he told them
the essentials. Shaun had drowned, Haynes was off to
collect his winnings.

'Fucking bastard,' said Bex.

'You have a phone?' asked Lee.

'No,' said Gethin, 'so none of you...'

'Haynes took the lot and the landline. I was...'

'Lee wanted to go out and find a phone,' said Bex 'but
me and Tone outvoted her. We were safe here. I found some
painkillers for your dad.'

'He's gone now, then, Malcolm Haynes?' This was the
Judge's voice. He'd looked half asleep when Gethin came
in. Now he was sitting straight in his seat, his face intense.

'Yes, he's heading straight to London, I think.'

'Good,' said the Judge, 'let's go and find a telephone. I
realise you think I should have called the police before, but
you'll see why. I'm afraid I am reverting to the teachings of
the Old Testament.'

He was a tough old bird, the Judge, Gethin had to give

him that. His wrist must've been hurting like a bastard. But he wasn't letting on. Instead, he stood by the door looking impatient, while Bex ran around gathering up her belongings. As for what he'd meant about the Old Testament teachings, Gethin wasn't sure. An eye for an eye, perhaps?

Gethin looked at the clock. Unbelievably, it was still only two am. This must surely have been the longest day and night of his life. Finally, they were out of the house, Lee shining a flashlight ahead. They were all jumpy, apart from the Judge who simply looked resolute. Was he already preparing a case against Malcolm Haynes in his mind, Gethin wondered?

The Judge directed them back down the hill. Just before they got to the pub, there was a house on the right.

'I know these people slightly,' said the Judge, 'they'll do.'

The door opened and there was a florid looking man in a striped dressing gown, blinking at them.

'Awfully sorry, Richard,' said the Judge, 'but I'm afraid there's been a break-in at my house and I very much need to make a couple of phone calls to report it.'

'Oh,' said the florid chap, Richard. 'I'm so sorry. Of course you can, there's a phone in there,' he waved towards a kitchen diner.

While Lee stood talking to him, the others headed to the phone.

'God forgive me for what I'm going to do now,' the Judge said, picking up the receiver.

'Calling the police?' said Bex.

'No,' said the Judge.

Very gingerly, he used his good hand to dig out a small notebook from his jacket pocket. He passed it to Gethin.

'Do you mind looking through this and finding the home number for Terence Donoghue?'

Gethin took the notebook and leafed through the pages of indexed phone numbers until he found the lawyer, Terence Donoghue.

'Tony Grey here,' the Judge said and waited for the reply. 'Yes, apologies for the lateness of the hour but I understood that your client, the one you mentioned to me at lunch the other day, was extremely eager to receive certain information relating to a man called Danny Bliss.'

He waited again 'Oh yes, exactly so. What your client will wish to know is that the property they wish to locate is to be found at Capital Securities on the St John's Wood Road. And a man called Malcom Haynes – approximately fifty years old, six foot tall, grey hair, clean shaven, looks like a policeman – will be arriving there this morning, probably at opening time. He is in possession of the relevant information and is likely to be leaving with the property in question. It occurs to me that your client might want to discuss the ownership issue with him in person. Do I need to repeat any of that?'

Another pause. 'No, I thought not. And Terence, it goes without saying this phone call did not take place and, if you're in the habit of recording your phone calls, kindly delete this one immediately... yes indeed, for both our sakes.'

The Judge put the phone down and, as he did so, he crumpled to the floor. Bex and Gethin rushed to help him into a chair and waited while he gathered himself.

'If you don't mind,' he said, 'I would be very grateful if you could call an ambulance and the police now, preferably in that order.'

Twenty-Seven

IT WAS NEARLY SEVEN IN the morning and the dawn was making its presence known when Gethin finally made it back to Gwaelod-Y-Garth. The ambulance had indeed come first, but the police hadn't been far behind. The paramedics had insisted on taking the Judge up to the hospital in Llandough right away, so Gethin had been left to try and explain to the cops what on earth had happened. There had been two – both regular PCs he thought, but he couldn't recall for sure. He couldn't remember their names either, just how absurdly young they were. One was a blonde who may have been called Lisa or Lucy, the other was a regulation Valleys boy, who, in Gethin's overtired memory, appeared to have been wearing a rugby shirt but surely couldn't actually have been.

Exhausted as he was, he'd kept things to a simplified version. The way he told it, the Last Resort Legals team and the Judge had been caught up in a feud between Mal Haynes and Shaun over money. He described Shaun escaping from the Judge's house and Haynes chasing after him, and more or less left it there. Just in case he was on CCTV somewhere himself, he said he'd run after them and had ended up stranded on the island for a while but hadn't seen what had happened to either Haynes or Shaun.

The blonde and the Valleys boy were mostly interested in the crime that had very visibly been committed – the assault on the Judge. Gethin, Lee and Bex all gave statements describing what had happened. The cops weren't best pleased to learn that it was one of their own who was apparently responsible – but at least he was retired and not local.

The blonde asked Gethin if he had any idea where Haynes might have been heading, where this safe deposit box might be located. Gethin had shaken his head and told her he had no idea – 'somewhere in Bristol probably'. He gave a vague description of Haynes' car but not the number. If the Judge wanted vengeance, Gethin wasn't going to stand in the way of it.

The tiredness had really hit him on the drive home. His eyes actually closed for a second, and he'd had to react quickly to stop the car from swerving off the road. The shock of that provided just enough adrenaline to keep him going for the final mile or so but, as he opened the front door to his home, he wanted nothing more than to find the nearest bed and crash out for a very long time.

No such luck. The second he opened the door, there was a cry of 'Daddy!' from upstairs and the sound of his daughter coming down the stairs. Another few seconds and there she was in her pyjamas running towards him.

Gethin didn't say anything, just held on to her tight, then managed to croak the one word, 'Coffee'.

Hattie let go of him then. 'Come on up, I think mum's made some already.'

She led the way upstairs to the kitchen diner. Cat was seated there with a coffee in front of her. Next to her was Amelia Laverne. Gethin shook his bleary head. He'd almost forgotten about Amelia. And now he was hit with an awful sinking dread. He was going to have to give her terrible news.

'Oh my God,' said Cat, as he came fully into view. She

was up and hugging him to her before pulling back as if she'd only just remembered that they were no longer as they were, that the protocols granting free access to each other's bodies were, at the very least, on hold. 'What happened? And what on earth are you wearing?'

Gethin looked down at himself, and realised he was dressed in the most peculiar collection of his dad's clothing. Trousers that he could only imagine were used for playing golf, a T-shirt that he suspected had been a present from Hattie to her grandad with a picture of the Eiffel Tower on it, and was almost certainly now being worn for the first time ever, and a cardigan that was at least as warm as it was ugly. He was too tired to explain; just repeated his one word mantra, 'Coffee'.

'Sure,' said Cat, 'of course,' and she busied herself with the AeroPress machine. Subsiding into a chair, Gethin shook his head hard to try and gain some semblance of focus and became aware of Amelia, staring at him intently.

'Where is he?' she asked, once Gethin had settled himself. 'Where is my son?'

Gethin played for time, waited for Cat to bring him the coffee, his brain whirring. What could he tell her?

'I'm sorry,' he said eventually. 'He's drowned.'

Amelia just stared at him. What on earth could be going through her head? The son she had only met for the first time the day before had been taken from her already.

'Was it an accident?' she asked.

'I don't know. He couldn't swim.'

'Ah no, no, no, no, no!' Amelia looked like she'd been punched in the gut. 'Don't tell me that, I would have taught my baby to swim.'

'It wouldn't have helped,' Gethin finally had control of the words coming out of his mouth as the coffee hit, to make what had happened just a little less unbearable for the sobbing, desperate woman across the kitchen table. 'The tide was too strong. And Haynes would have killed him anyway.'

'Haynes?' asked Cat.

'This copper, the bastard behind all of this.'

Gethin was about to say something more but paused. Could he, in all conscience, say it? Could he tell Amelia that it was Haynes who had killed Hannah Gold and not Shaun, not her son? He thought about Shaun – so tough on the outside and yet so weak, such a lost boy on the inside, another fatherless, motherless boy with the brittlest, most fragile of shells. Could he see Shaun actually killing someone? He could imagine him lashing out in rage, perhaps. But to break Hannah's neck with the cruel efficiency that her murderer had? He couldn't imagine that. Could he imagine Haynes doing it? In a heartbeat.

'It was Mal Haynes who killed Hannah Gold. And Shaun was the only witness.'

Amelia didn't seem to register it. She looked utterly destroyed and was mumbling, over and over, the words 'he couldn't swim'. Cat moved her chair alongside and took Amelia in her arms. 'It's all right,' she said, 'it's all right.' Saying those words with that particular intonation we use when things really are not, in any way, all right. They worked their magic, those words, and slowly Amelia stopped the mantra and just burrowed her head deeper into Cat's breast.

It was Hattie who spoke first. Gethin had hardly realised she was still there. She'd been hanging in the doorway, caught between the blissful ignorance of childhood and her burgeoning, horrified fascination with the adult world.

'Does that mean Izma M is innocent?'

'Yeah,' said Gethin, wondering at the fact that this

question, that had seemed all important just a few days ago, was now just a side issue. 'Hopefully, we can prove that now.'

'Oh Dad, that's fantastic. You can come home now the job's finished.'

'Ah…' He was about to say that the job wasn't quite finished yet, that there was a whole aftermath to mop up, but he could hear the yearning in his daughter's voice, wanted someone at least to have good news on this day of reckoning. He looked over at Cat, still cradling Amelia, and their eyes met. Cat mouthed a word that might have been 'please'. He thought of her fucking Nils Hofberg and waited for the anger and jealousy to hit, but found there was nothing there, the brutality of the last twenty-four hours had trumped all of that. So she'd fucked Nils? So he'd nearly fucked Amelia? Had Amelia told Cat that? He wouldn't be surprised. Was any of it worth making their daughter unhappy? Right now, he didn't think so. In time, maybe that would change. There were wounds there, between Cat and him, but, right now, he was ready to wave the white flag.

'Yes love, here I am. I'm back.'

* * *

Gethin arrived at the Judge's house at 4 o'clock on the following afternoon. Most of the intervening time had been spent sleeping. He had been woken up at various times during the day: by the police coming to ask more questions, by Hattie on her return from school and by a phone call from Bex. Hattie brought him a plate of spaghetti sometime in the evening and he'd hardly finished eating before he was asleep again.

He had barely seen Cat. She hadn't come to share the

bed. He wasn't sure where she slept that night. Probably on the living room couch, as Amelia Laverne was still in the spare room.

By the time he surfaced the following morning, Sunday morning, Cat and Hattie were round at their neighbours and Amelia presumably still holed up in her room. Around lunchtime, the police had called back again. And this time they'd had some news. It was this news that he had come to discuss with his father.

Lee opened the door. She had picked up the Judge from the hospital that morning.

'Well, Geth, you look a fuck of a lot better than last time I saw you.' She ushered him inside.

The Judge was sitting at a table, his arm still in its sling, some playing cards in front of him. It looked like he'd been playing Patience. Gethin felt a momentary twinge, the lure of the green baize table, but shrugged it off.

He looked his father over. The Judge's arm was in a cast, but his colour wasn't too bad.

'How are you feeling?'

'Surprisingly reasonable. I think they may have given me the top of the range painkillers.'

'Glad to hear it. Have the police been in touch?'

'No,' said the Judge. 'Not since early this morning.'

'Well, it looks like there might have been a development. Why don't we sit out on the deck? I'll bring my laptop up and we can see if it's made the news yet. You want to come up, Lee?'

Lee made a face. 'Tell you what, Geth, if you're here for a while I have a few things I need to sort out. Be back in a couple of hours, Tone.'

Gethin still couldn't quite adjust to hearing his father addressed as Tone. The Judge didn't seem to mind, though.

Father and son waited for Lee to go and headed up to the deck. They sat next to each other at the table and Gethin fired up the laptop. He headed to the *Guardian* website and there it was on the front page – breaking news. 'Ex-policeman found burnt to death in car.'

He clicked on the link and together they read the report. A man believed to be former police officer Malcolm Haynes had been discovered burnt to death in a car somewhere in Epping Forest. The piece refused to confirm or deny rumours of a gangland connection. Thankfully, there were no pictures.

He turned to look at the Judge. He had his eyes closed but his lips were moving. If he didn't know better, Gethin might've thought he was praying.

Gethin looked out at the view over the Channel. There was still bright sunshine on the water but, further away, he could see thunder clouds over Exmoor. You could see the rain falling in a misty grey circle. Soon, it would be with them too.

Epilogue

TWO WEEKS LATER, GETHIN DROVE up to Gartree. The Indian summer felt like a distant memory. It was grey and cold and, all the way along the motorway, the rain had kept on at an infuriatingly intermittent drizzle, forcing him to continually turn his windscreen wipers on and off.

By the time he'd been through the prison formalities, he was tired and grumpy and not much looking forward to renewing his acquaintance with Izma M aka Ismail Mohammed aka Tyrell Hanson aka Danny Bliss.

His irritation dissipated a little when Izma came into the visiting room. Gone was the cocky, bantering fellow of previous visits. Pale and exhausted, he said a quick hello and had a good look around for potential eavesdroppers before sitting down. Gethin passed him a cup of tea.

'I've been praying for him, you know?' were the first words Izma said. 'Shaun, I feel like I've lost my right arm. Tell me he didn't suffer too much.'

'No,' said Gethin, 'I don't think he did.' He hoped that was true.

'I'm sorry, man,'

'What for?'

'Everything. None of this would have happened without me.'

Gethin didn't disagree, just nodded. 'If you say so. Now, why did you ask me to come here? Do you want me to start your appeal?'

314

'That's exactly what I don't want,' said Izma. 'Why I asked you to come was because, well, I just want to beg you to keep it quiet. My real name, all of that. No appeal, no nothing. I'll just sit here and finish doing my time, should only be another couple of years now. I just don't want all this shit to come out; my story, if you like.'

'Why is that?' said Gethin.

'Two reasons. One selfish, one not so much.'

'Uh huh?'

'Yeah, reason one is I don't want Vince's mob knowing my real identity. Otherwise, they'll be waiting for me the second I step outside.'

'Fair enough,' said Gethin, feeling an inner shudder as he thought back to Mal Haynes' fate. Whatever awfulness Izma's deceit had set in motion, he certainly didn't deserve that. 'And the second thing?'

'I don't want anyone knowing Izma M isn't exactly who he's meant to be. Not for me, boss, for the book. That's the one pure good thing I've done with my life and I don't want it wasted. It actually helps people, you know?'

Gethin had thought about this; the ethics of what Izma had done. Did it matter that he was a fraud, if his book had helped people find a path in life? Did it matter that it was all a lie, that Izma M was a middle-class Jewish kid who'd gone to private schools and not a mixed-race street kid from Bristol? Gethin wasn't sure exactly why, but he felt like it did matter.

'But it's not true,' he said to Izma. 'The bottom line is you're selling people a pack of lies and asking them to follow you. When you aren't even who you say you are.'

Izma lowered his head and nodded as Gethin spoke. When he looked up his face was full of anguish: 'But it's true, all of it.'

'How do you mean?'

'Like I say it's all true, it's just not one person's truth. The first half, the growing up part, it's Shaun's story. Me and him...' his voice faltered here, '... he was the brother I never had and I was his and we told each other everything, all this shit we'd never told anyone else. All the shit about his childhood, never knowing who his mum was, hardly knowing his dad, all of that. And the second part, the prison stuff, that's my reality since I've been in this place. All the political stuff, all the spiritual stuff, that's my journey. When I came in here I was a mess. Hannah was dead and I blamed myself for it. I felt like I was a fucking bad seed from the poison tree. I'd always hated my dad, the way he was. I mean, I didn't know about all the criminal stuff, but even the legitimate stuff he did I despised, and I thought I was better than that. And then Hannah – this lovely, smart girl she ends up dead because she knew me. I was in bits and looking for some meaning and I found it in Sufi, man.'

Izma stared down at the table. Gethin could see he was focusing hard, determined to make his case.

'I know it sounds ironic, a Jewish boy from North London becoming a Muslim, but it ain't. It's all part of the big picture. We're all people of the book, you know, and out there in the world – in Bristol the same as in Syria or Palestine – a lot of wrong is being done, people disrespecting each other because of what they believe. I wanted to do something to change that...' He paused. 'To do some good for once in my fucked-up life. And that's what this book is. So I'm begging you not to trash it. People love that book because it's true. Why should it matter that it's not just one kind of true? Does it matter who writes a book? Isn't the important thing what's in it?'

'Not if people expect it to come from your own experience,' said Gethin.

'So where does that leave you? Do you think Billie Holiday wrote 'Strange Fruit'?'

'I suppose you're going to tell me she didn't?'

'Right; it was some New York Jewish guy. But no one's saying it isn't authentic, are they? Do you think *The Wire* was written by street dealers? Course it wasn't. It was a bunch of white liberals sticking their politics in the mouths of black actors. People only see the actors – not the writers – so no one minds. My shit is realer than that. I am actually in prison, you know?'

'Can't argue with that.'

'Exactly. If you just leave me be, it will still be out there for people to learn from. And this is not just for me, either. It's for Shaun. That's his story there, his truth, but he couldn't tell it himself. He didn't have the education or the chances I had – same goes for practically all the people in here. Black people in Britain, right, if they want to go into sports or music, no problem. Or selling drugs – someone has to do that, keep the rich kids in their lines of charlie. And that's how it all goes to shit. Black boys – they reach fourteen and all of a sudden they can see their friends making money, having status and girls from drugs or rapping or boxing or whatever – and they're lost – they can't read a book or understand a contract. Like as not, sooner or later it all goes to shit and they end up in here. And then they're vulnerable to anything – to the Islamic terrorist shit or the Christian evangelism shit or the self-help bollocks. So what I'm saying, what my book is saying, is that you got to have more self-respect than that, and you've got to work harder than that. You have to be educated, properly educated. That's why I told Shaun's story like it was my own. You understand where I'm coming from?'

Gethin thought about it some more. He did understand

what Izma was saying. And he supposed he probably agreed with it but he still wrestled with the whole 'can two wrongs make a right?' thing. Could you help people with lies? Before he could formulate his thoughts into words, Izma carried on talking, his voice quieter than ever.

'He loved it, you know, Shaun did. The way I told his story. So, even if you don't want to do it for me, can you do it for Shaun? I know you were with him when he passed...'

Gethin sat back in his chair, overwhelmed by the memory of Shaun going down for the last time. Of course, it was his story in the Izma book, of course. That's where all the confusion had come from – why Amelia had thought Izma was her son. She recognised the details of Shaun's early life, the mother who gave him away. Christ, what a tangled web we weave.

He thought about Amelia. She was doing better now. What had changed things for her was the realisation that she had lost her son but gained a grandson. She was renting a house in Bristol, round the corner from Shaun's place, and by some miracle she was getting along with Denise, so there was at least that one shaft of light in the darkness of the past weeks. And, God bless her, she'd already paid Last Resort a generous bonus despite the fact that Izma was still right there in prison.

'One thing,' he said. 'Will you let Amelia come and see you? Will you tell her about Shaun?'

Izma nodded his assent, obviously too choked up to speak.

Gethin stared at him, all hunched up and half hidden behind his hair and his beard and his guilt. He looked, Gethin thought, like a true penitent, doing his time for crimes only he knew he'd committed. And he was trying to do some good, even if it was too little and too late for

Hannah Gold. He was doing his best to make reparations and Gethin knew a little about that himself.

'Okay, then,' he said and stood up and stretched his hand out.

'Goodbye,' he said. 'Goodbye, Izma.'

Acknowledgments

I'd like to thank my pub quiz team – Paul, Rob, Patrick, Julie, Euros, Katell, Andrew and Gruff – for support, laughs and casino visits; Des for reading an early draft; also Cathi, Pete, Tessa for their advice and support; my yacht-rocking agent Matthew Hamilton for suggesting it might be time I tried writing a crime novel. Many thanks to Ion Mills, Claire Quinlivan, Claire Watts and everyone else at No Exit. Thanks to Steven Mair for copy-editing and Jayne Lewis for proof-reading. And mostly I'd like to thank Anna Davis for everything.